In Bed with Her Ex

LUCY GORDON
MARION LENNOX
NINA HARRINGTON

Published in Great Britain 2015
by Mills & Boon, an imprint of Harlequin (UK) Limited,
Eton House, 18-24 Paradise Road, Richmond, Surrey, TW9 1SR

ISBN: 978-0-263-25222-4
eBook ISBN: 978-1-474-00401-5

05-0715

Harlequin (UK) Limited's policy is to use papers that are natural, renewable and recyclable products and made from wood grown in sustainable forests. The logging and manufacturing processes conform to the legal environmental regulations of the country of origin.

Printed and bound in Spain
by CPI, Barcelona

MISS PRIM AND THE BILLIONAIRE

BY
LUCY GORDON

Lucy Gordon cut her writing teeth on magazine journalism, interviewing many of the world's most interesting men, including Warren Beatty, Charlton Heston and Sir Roger Moore. She also camped out with lions in Africa and had many other unusual experiences which have often provided the background for her books. Several years ago, while staying Venice, she met a Venetian who proposed in two days. They have been married ever since. Naturally, this has affected her writing, where romantic Italian men tend to feature strongly. Two of her books have won the Romance Writers of America RITA® award. You can visit her website at www.lucy-gordon.com.

PROLOGUE

AS THE soft light of dawn crept into the room the young man looked down on the girl, asleep beside him, her long blonde hair cascading across the pillow, her face soft and sweet. He kissed her lips gently and she stirred, murmuring, 'Marcel.'

'Shh,' he said. 'I just want to tell you—'

'Mmm?'

'—lots of things. Some of them I can't say when you're awake. When I look at you I'm struck dumb. I can't even find the words to tell you how lovely you are—but then, you already know that.'

He drew the sheet back to reveal her glorious form, both slender and voluptuous.

'There are plenty of people to praise your beauty, those photographers, and so many other men who'd take you from me if they could. But you don't let them. Bless you, my darling, my sweet Cassie.'

Without opening her eyes, she gave a sleepy smile that made Marcel's heart turn over. He was in his early twenties with a face that was still boyish, and as gentle as her own. His naked body was lean, almost too much so. Time would fill out his shape and bring maturity to his features, but perhaps he would never be better than he was now, his dark eyes full of adoration as he gazed down at her.

'Can you hear me? I have something to tell you. You may

be cross with me for concealing it, but you'll forgive me, I know you will. And then I'll ask—no, I'll *beg* you to become my wife. What we have now is wonderful, but I want more. I want to claim you in the sight of the world, to climb to the top of the highest tower and cry aloud that you belong to me. To *me!* Nobody else. We'll marry as soon as possible, won't we, my darling? And all the world will know that you're mine as completely as I am yours.

'That time will come soon, but first I have to explain what I've been hiding. The fact is that I—no, let me keep my secret a little longer. In truth I'm a coward. I'm so afraid that you'll be angry with me when you know that I deceived you, just a little, that I let you think—never mind. I'll tell you when the right moment comes.

'For this moment I just want to say that I love you, I belong to you, and nothing will ever part us. My darling, if you knew how I long to call you my wife. I pray that our wedding will happen soon.

'But sleep now, just a little longer. There'll be time later. We have all our lives to love each other.'

CHAPTER ONE

'THE trouble with weddings is that they bring out the idiot in people.'

The cynical remark made Marcel Falcon glance up, grinning with agreement. The man who'd come to sit beside him was a business associate with whom he was on cordial terms.

'Good to see you, Jeremy,' he said. 'I'll get the drinks. Waiter!'

They were at a table in the bar of the Gloriana Hotel, one of the most luxurious establishments in London, providing not only rooms but wedding facilities for those who could afford them. Marcel gave his order, signed for it to go onto his bill and turned back to his companion, saying, 'You're right about weddings. No good to anyone. I'd just as soon have avoided this one, but my brother, Darius, is the bride's ex-husband.'

Jeremy stared. 'And he's a guest at her wedding to another man? I've heard of sophisticated, but that takes the biscuit.'

'It's for the children, Frankie and Mark. They need to see their parents acting friendly despite the divorce.'

'And I'll bet your father had a hand in the decision.'

'There aren't many decisions my father doesn't have a hand in,' Marcel agreed wryly. 'He actually got them to delay the wedding until a certain date had passed, so that he could come to England without incurring a huge tax bill.'

Amos Falcon was so extravagantly wealthy that he'd had to flee to the tax haven of Monaco where he lived for most of the time, venturing back to England for only ninety days of the year.

'Frankie and Mark are his only grandchildren,' Marcel said, 'so he's determined to stay part of their lives.'

'Strange, that. A man with five sons and only one of them has carried on the line so far.'

'He says the same thing. He's always urging us to marry, preferably Freya.'

'Who's Freya?'

'His stepdaughter, the closest thing to a daughter that he has, and he's set on marrying her to one of us, and so binding her into the family.'

'Don't any of you get a say in your choice of wife?'

'Are you kidding? This is my father we're talking about. Since when did anyone ever get a say?' Marcel spoke cynically but with wry affection.

'Failing Freya,' he went on, 'then some other wife to continue the great Falcon dynasty. But except for Darius we've all disappointed him. Jackson seems to find wild animals more interesting than people, Leonid is a man we hardly ever see. He could have a dozen wives, but since he seldom leaves Russia we wouldn't know. And Travis doesn't dare marry. He'd lose all his fans.'

He spoke of his younger half-brother, born and raised in America, and a successful television actor with an army of adoring female followers.

'No man could be expected to risk his fortune just for marriage,' Jeremy agreed solemnly. 'That just leaves you, the amorous Frenchman.'

Marcel grimaced. 'Enough!' he said. 'If you knew how that stereotype bores me.'

'And yet you make use of it. The life in Paris, the endless

supply of women—all right, all right.' He broke off hastily, seeing Marcel's face. 'But since you have what most men would give their eye teeth for, the least you can do is enjoy it.'

The waiter arrived with their drinks. When he'd gone Jeremy raised his glass.

'Here's to being a bachelor. I'd give a lot to know how you've managed to stay single so long.'

'A sense of reality helps. You start off regarding all women as goddesses, but you soon see reason.'

'Ah! Let you down with a crash, did she?'

'I can't remember,' Marcel said coldly. 'She no longer exists.'

She never really did, said the voice in his head. *A figment of your imagination.*

'Well, I reckon you've got it right,' Jeremy said. 'All the women you want, whenever you want.'

'Stop talking nonsense.'

'I'm not. Look at those girls. They can't keep their eyes off you.'

It was true. Three young women were at the bar, buying drinks then glancing around, seeming to take stock of the men, form opinions about them, each pausing when they came to Marcel. One of them drew a long breath, one put her head on one side, and the third gave an inviting smile.

You couldn't blame them, Jeremy reckoned, Marcel was in his thirties, tall, dark-haired and well built but without a spare ounce on him anywhere. His face was handsome enough to make the girls swoon and the men want to commit murder.

But it was more than looks. Marcel had a charm that was delightful or deadly, depending on your point of view. Those who'd encountered only that charisma found it hard to believe in the ruthlessness with which he'd stormed the heights of wealth and success—until they encountered that ruthlessness for themselves. And were floored by it.

But the willing females at the bar knew nothing of this. They saw Marcel's looks, the seemingly roguish gleam in his eyes, and they responded. Soon, Jeremy guessed, at least one of them would find an excuse to approach him. Or perhaps all three.

'Have you made your choice?' he asked caustically.

'I don't like to rush it.'

'Ah yes, of course. And there are some more just coming in. Hey, isn't that Darius?'

The door of the bar led into the hotel lobby, where they could just see Marcel's half-brother, Darius Falcon, pressing the button at the elevator. A young woman stood beside him, talking eagerly.

'Who's she?' Jeremy asked.

'I don't know,' Marcel replied. 'I think she comes from the island he's just acquired. A man who owed him money used it to pay the debt, and he's living there at the moment while he decides what to do. He told me he'd be bringing someone, but he didn't say a lot about her.'

By now Darius and his companion had stepped into the elevator and the doors had closed.

'I must go up and greet them,' Marcel said, draining his glass. 'See you later.'

It was an excuse. Before visiting Darius he meant to call on their father, who'd arrived an hour ago. But instead of heading straight for the main suite, he strolled about, inspecting his surroundings with the eye of a professional. The Gloriana might be among the top hotels in London but it couldn't compete with La Couronne, the hotel he owned in Paris.

He'd named it La Couronne, the crown, to let the world know that it was the queen of hotels, and his own pride and joy. He had personally overseen every detail of an establishment that offered conference facilities as well as luxurious accommodation, discretion as well as flamboyance. Anybody who was anybody had stayed there: top level businessmen, politicians, film stars. It was a place of fashion and influence. But most of all money.

Money was the centre of his life. And from that centre it stretched out its tentacles to every distant detail. He'd started his business with loans guaranteed by his father, who also added money of his own, to be repaid in due course. Marcel had returned every penny.

At the back of the hotel he found a huge room that would be used for the wedding next day. It was a grandiose place, decorated to imitate a church, although the ceremony would be a civil one. Flowers were being piled everywhere, suggesting a romantic dream.

'We'll marry as soon as possible, won't we, my darling? And all the world will know that you're mine as completely as I am yours.'

The voice that echoed in his head made him stiffen and take an involuntary step back, as though seeking escape.

But the voice was his own and there was nowhere to flee.

'If you knew how I long to call you my wife.'

Had he really said that? Had he actually been that stupid? Young, naïve, believing what he longed to believe about the girl he adored, until his delusions were stripped away in pain and misery.

But that was long past. Now he was a different man. If only the voice would stop tormenting him.

He left the wedding venue quickly and almost at once bumped into his father. They had last met several weeks ago when Amos had suffered heart trouble, causing his sons to hurry to his bedside in Monaco. Now, to Marcel's relief, the old man seemed strong again. His face had aged with the strain of his illness, but he was both vigorous and alert.

'Good to see you better,' he said, embracing his father unselfconsciously.

'Nothing wrong with me,' Amos declared robustly. 'Just a lot of fuss. But I was glad to have you all there for a while. Now you must come up and visit Janine and Freya. They're looking forward to seeing you again.'

Amos's private life might politely be described as colourful. Marcel's mother had been his second wife. Janine was his third. Freya, her daughter by a previous husband, was also part of the family. Amos, a man with five sons and no daughters, had particularly welcomed her as a plan formed in his mind.

'Let's go up slowly,' he suggested now. 'We can take a look at the place and get some ideas. It's not a bad hotel but you could do better.'

'I've been thinking of expanding,' Marcel mused. 'A change of scene might be interesting.'

'Then London's the place to look. Property prices have plunged and you could pick up a bargain. I've got some good banking contacts who'll help, and I can loan you some money myself, if needed.'

'Thanks. I might take you up on that.'

They toured the hotel, each making notes.

'The one thing this place has got that La Couronne hasn't is the wedding facility,' Amos observed. 'You might try that. Money to be made.'

'I doubt if it would increase my profit,' Marcel said coolly. There were many reasons why weddings didn't appeal to him, but none that he was prepared to discuss.

They finished on the eighth floor where there was a bar with magnificent views of London. Sitting by the window, Amos indicated a tall building in the distance.

'See that? Headquarters of Daneworth Estates.'

'I've heard of them,' Marcel mused. 'Things not going too well, I gather.'

'That's right. They're having to sell assets.'

Amos's tone held a significance that made Marcel ask, 'Any asset in particular?'

'The Alton Hotel. It was bought with the idea of development but the money ran out and it's ripe for takeover at a knock-down price.'

He quoted a figure and Marcel's eyebrows rose. 'As little as that?'

'It's possible, if someone with a certain amount of influence twisted the screw on Daneworth so that the sale became more urgent.'

'You don't happen to know anyone with that kind of influence?' Marcel asked satirically.

'I might. How long will you be in England?'

'Long enough to look around.'

'Excellent.' Amos made a noise that sounded like 'Hrmph!' adding, 'It's good to know I have one son I can be proud of.'

'Are you still mad at Darius because he gave his wife too generous a deal over the divorce? I thought you liked Mary. You've come to her wedding.'

'I won't quarrel with the mother of my only grandchildren. But sense is sense, and he hasn't shown any. Do you know anything about the girl he's bringing with him today?'

'I saw them arrive. She looks attractive and pleasant. I'm going to visit them in a minute.'

'While you're there take a good look at her. See if Darius is falling into her trap.'

'Thus spoiling your scheme to marry him to Freya?' Marcel said ironically.

'I'd like to have Freya as my daughter-in-law, I make no secret of it. And if Darius won't come up to the mark—'

'Forget it,' Marcel interrupted him.

'Why should I? It's time you were putting down roots.'

'There are plenty of others to do that.'

Amos snorted. 'Five sons! Five! You'd think more than one of you would have settled down by now.'

But Amos himself was hardly an advertisement for domesticity, Marcel thought cynically. Of the five sons, only two had been born to the woman he'd been married to at the time. His own mother hadn't married Amos until several years after his birth. Travis and Leonid were bastards and proud of it. But he didn't want to quarrel with his father, so he merely shrugged and rose to go.

'Tell Janine and Freya I'll be up as soon as I've been to see Darius,' he said.

As he approached his brother's room he was barely conscious of adjusting his mask. He donned it so often that it was second nature by now, even with a brother with whom he was on cordial terms. When he arrived his charming smile was firmly in place.

The door was already open, giving him a clear view of a pretty young woman, done up in a glamorous style, and Darius regarding her with admiration, his hands on her shoulders.

'Am I interrupting anything?' he asked.

'Marcel!' Darius advanced to thump his brother with delight, after which he turned and introduced his companion as Harriet.

'You've been keeping this lady a big secret,' Marcel said, regarding her with admiration. 'And I understand why. If she were mine I would also hide her away from the world.'

His father was in for a shock, he reckoned. Harriet was definitely a threat to his plans for Darius's next wife.

He chatted with her for a few moments, flirting, but not beyond brotherly limits.

'So Darius has warned you about the family,' he said at last, 'and you know we're a load of oddities.'

'I'll bet you're no odder than me,' she teased.

'I'll take you up on that. Promise me a dance tonight.'

'She declines,' Darius said firmly.

Marcel chuckled and murmured in Harriet's ear, 'We'll meet again later.'

After a little more sparring, he blew her a kiss and departed, heading for his father's suite. He greeted his stepmother cordially but he couldn't help looking over her shoulder at the window, through which he could see the building Amos had pointed out to him.

Daneworth Estates. Assets ripe for an offer. Interesting.

In an office on the tenth floor of a bleakly efficient building overlooking the River Thames, Mr Smith, the manager of Daneworth Estates, examined some papers and groaned before raising his voice to call, 'Mrs Henshaw, can you bring the other files in, please?'

He turned back to his client, a middle-aged man, saying, 'She'll have all the details. Don't worry.'

He glanced up as a young woman appeared in the doorway and advanced with the files.

'I've made notes,' she said. 'I think you'll find I've covered everything.'

'I'm sure you have,' he replied.

The client regarded her with distaste. She was exactly the kind of woman he most disliked, the kind who could have looked better if she'd bothered to make the best of herself. She had the advantage of being tall and slim, with fair hair and regular features. But she scraped her hair back, dressed severely, and concealed her face behind a pair of large steel-rimmed spectacles.

'It's nearly six o'clock,' she said.

Mr Smith nodded. 'Yes, you can go.'

She gave the client a faint nod and left the office.

He shivered. 'She terrifies me,' he admitted.

'Me too, sometimes,' Mr Smith agreed. 'But if there's one person whose efficiency I can rely on it's Mrs Henshaw.'

'It always sounds odd to me the way you call her "Mrs". Why not just Jane?'

'She prefers it. Familiarity is something she discourages.'

'But you're her boss.'

'Sometimes I wonder which of us is the boss. I hesitate between valuing her skills and wanting to get rid of her.'

'She reminds me of a robot.'

'She certainly doesn't have any "come hither" about her,' the manager agreed. 'You'd never think she'd once been a fashion model.'

'Get away!'

'Really. She was called "Cassie" and for a couple of years she was headed for the very top. Then it all ended. I'm not sure why.'

'She could still look good if she tried,' the client observed. 'Why scrape her hair back against her skull like a prison wardress? And when did you last see a woman who didn't bother with make-up?'

'Can't think! Now, back to business. How do I avoid going bankrupt and taking your firm down with me?'

'Can't think!' the client echoed gloomily.

Neither of them gave a further thought to Mrs Henshaw on the far side of the door. She heard their disparaging comments and shrugged.

'Blimey!' said the other young woman in the room. 'How do you stand them being so rude about you?'

Her name was Bertha. She was nineteen, naïve, friendly and a reasonably good secretary.

'I ignore it,' Mrs Henshaw said firmly.

'But who was that Cassie they keep on about? The gorgeous model.'

'No idea. She was nothing to do with me, I know that.'

'But they said it was you.'

'They were wrong.' Mrs Henshaw turned to look at Bertha with a face that was blank and lifeless. 'Frankly,' she said, 'Cassie never really existed. Now hurry off home.'

The last words had an edge of desperation. She urgently needed to be alone to think about everything that was happening. She knew the company was in dire straits, and it would soon be time to move on.

But to what? Her life seemed to stretch before her, blank, empty. Just as it had done for the last ten years.

The days when she could afford a car were over, and she took a bus to the small block of apartments where she lived in a few rooms one floor up. Here everything was neat, restrained, unrevealing. A nun might have lived in this place.

Tonight was no different from any other night, she assured herself. The name Cassie, suddenly screaming out of the darkness, had thrown the world into chaos, but she'd recovered fast. Cassie was another life, another universe. Cassie's heart had been broken. Mrs Henshaw had no heart to break.

She stayed up late studying papers, understanding secrets about the firm that were supposed to be hidden. Soon there would have to be decisions but now she was too weary in her soul to think about them.

She was asleep as soon as her head hit the pillow, but it wasn't a peaceful sleep. The dreams she'd dreaded were waiting to pounce. There was Cassie, gloriously naked, madly in love, throwing herself into the arms of the handsome boy who'd worshipped her. There were his eyes, gazing at her with adoration, but then with hate.

'I loved you—I trusted you—now I can't bear the sight of you!'

In sleep she reached out her hands to him, crying, 'Marcel, you don't understand—please—please—'

'Get out of my sight! *Whore!*'

She screamed and awoke to find herself thrashing around in bed, throwing her head from side to side.

'No,' she cried. 'It isn't true. *No, no, no!*'

Then she was sitting up, staring into the darkness, heaving violently.

'Leave me alone,' she begged. 'Leave me alone.'

Wearily she got out of bed and stumbled into the bathroom. A shambling wreck of a woman looked back at her from the mirror. Now the severe barriers of the day were gone, leaving no trace of the steely 'prison wardress'. The tense stillness of her face was replaced by violent emotion that threatened to overwhelm and destroy her. Her hair, no longer scraped back, flowed over her shoulders, giving her a cruel resemblance to Cassie, the beautiful girl who had lived long ago. That girl had vanished into the mists, but suddenly her likeness taunted Mrs Henshaw from the mirror. Tears streamed from her eyes and she covered them with her hands, seeking oblivion.

'No,' she wept. 'No!'

But it was too late to say no. Years too late.

CHAPTER TWO

'I JUST hope I don't regret this,' Mr Smith said heavily. 'The Alton Hotel is worth twice what he's offering, but it's still the best offer we've had.'

Mrs Henshaw was frowning as she studied the figures. 'Surely you can drive him up a little?'

'I tried to but he just said "Take it or leave it." So I took it. We have to sell off properties fast, before we go under.'

'Is that your way of telling me to find another job?'

'Yes, but I may be able to help you. I've told him you'll meet him to discuss details. Marcel needs an assistant with local knowledge, so I'm sure you can impress him. Why are you looking like that?'

'Nothing—nothing—what did you say his name was?'

'Marcel Falcon. He's one of Amos Falcon's sons.'

She relaxed, telling herself to be sensible. The Marcel she had known had been Marcel Degrande, and obviously no connection with this man. It was absurd to be still reacting to the name after so long.

'Play your cards right and you'll come out on top,' Mr Smith advised.

'When do I go?'

'Right now. He's staying at the Gloriana Hotel, and he's expecting you there in half an hour.'

'Half a—? *What?* But that doesn't give me time to research the background or the man—'

'You'll have to play it by ear. And these papers—' he thrust some at her '—will give you the details of his offer. Yes, I know we don't usually do it like this, but things are moving fast and the sooner we get the money the better.'

She took a taxi and spent the journey memorising facts and figures, wishing she'd had time to do some online research. She'd heard of Amos Falcon, whose financial tentacles seemed to stretch halfway across the world, but it would have been useful to check his son out too.

Never mind, she thought. A heavy evening's work lay ahead of her, and she would tackle it with the meticulous efficiency that now ruled her whole life.

At last she entered the Gloriana and approached the reception desk. 'Please tell Mr Falcon that Mrs Jane Henshaw is here.'

'He's over there, madam.'

Turning, she saw the entrance door to the bar and just inside, a man sitting at a table. At that moment he turned his head, revealing just enough of his face to leave her stunned.

'No,' she whispered. 'No…no…'

The world went into chaos, thundering to a halt, yet still whirling mysteriously about her.

Marcel. Older, a little heavier, yet still the man whose love had been the glorious triumph of her life, and whose loss had brought her close to destruction. What malign chance had made their paths cross again?

She took a step back, then another, moving towards the door, desperate to escape before he saw her. She managed to get into the hotel garden where there was a small café, and sat down. She was shaking too violently to leave now. She must stay here for a while.

If only he hadn't seen her.

If only they had never seen each other in the beginning, never met, never loved, never hated, never shattered each other.

Who were those two youngsters who seemed to stand before her now? Naïve, innocent, ignorant, perhaps a little stupid, but only with the stupidity of children who knew they could conquer the world with their beauty, talent and enthusiasm.

Jane Agnes Cassandra Baines had always known she was destined to be a model.

'Nobody could be that beautiful and waste it,' her sister had said. 'Go for it, girl. And choose a better name. Jane will make people think of plain Jane.'

Rebecca was eight years her senior, and had been almost her mother since their parents died in their childhood. These days Rebecca's misfortunes meant that she was the one who needed caring for, and much of Jane's money went in helping her.

'Cassandra,' Rebecca had said back then. 'Mum loved that name because she said it meant "enticer of men". Dad was outraged. I can still remember them squabbling, him saying, "You can't call her that. It's not respectable." In the end Mum managed to squeeze it in as your third name.'

'Enticer of men,' she'd murmured in delight. 'Cassandra. Yes—I'm Cassandra.'

Her agent had partly agreed. 'Not Cassandra, Cassie,' he said. 'It's perfect. You're going to be a star.'

She'd climbed fast. Jane no longer existed. Cassie's picture was everywhere and so were her admirers. Wealthy men had laid their golden gifts at her feet, but she'd cared only for Marcel Degrande, a poor boy who lived in a shabby flat.

He'd been earning a pittance working for a grocery store, and they'd met when he'd delivered fruit to her door. One look at his smile, his teasing eyes, and she'd tossed aside two millionaires like unwanted rubbish. From then on there was only him.

For Marcel it had been the same. Generous, passionate, he had offered himself to her, heart and soul, with nothing held back.

'I can't believe this is happening,' he said. 'You could have them and their money, but me—you've seen how I live. I can't take you to posh restaurants or buy you expensive presents.'

'But you give me something no other man can give,' she assured him, laying her hand over his heart. 'Who cares about money? Money's boring.'

'Yes. Money is boring,' he said fervently. 'Who needs it?'

'Nobody.' She threw herself back on the bed and wriggled luxuriously. 'But there's something I do need, and I'm getting impatient.'

'Your wish is my command,' he said just before his mouth came down on hers, his hands explored her willing body, and they quickly became one.

Returning his love had been the greatest joy of her life, a joy that she knew instinctively could never be repeated. It had lasted a few months, then ended in cruelty.

Jake, a rich, powerful man with criminal connections, used to getting his own way, had made it plain that he wanted her. She'd told him he had no chance. He'd departed without a word, and she'd congratulated herself on having dealt with the situation.

Marcel had been away making a long-distance delivery. When he called she said nothing about Jake, not wanting to worry him. Time enough to tell him everything when he returned.

He never did return. On the evening she expected him the hours passed without a word. She tried to call, but his phone was dead. At last there was a knock on her door and there was Jake.

He thrust a photograph into her hands. It showed Marcel in bed, bloodied, bandaged and barely alive.

'He had an accident,' Jake said, smirking. 'A van knocked him over in the street.'

'Oh, heavens, I must go to him. Which hospital is he in?'

'You don't need to know that. You're not going to see him again. Are you getting the message yet? I could have him killed in a moment, and I will if you don't see sense. And don't even try to find the hospital and visit him because I'll know, and he'll pay the price.'

He pointed to the picture. 'A doctor who works there owes me a favour. She took this. I'm sure you don't want him to suffer any more…misfortunes.'

She was left with the knowledge that not only was Marcel badly hurt and she could never see him again, but that he would think she had deserted him. That thought nearly destroyed her.

She risked writing him a letter, telling everything, swearing her love, begging him not to hate her, and slipped it through the door of his dingy apartment. He would find it when he returned from the hospital.

For days she waited, certain that Marcel would contact her, however briefly. But he never did, and the deafening silence blotted out the world. His phone stayed dead. In desperation, she called his landlady, who confirmed that she'd seen him arrive home and collect mail from the carpet.

'Ask him to call me,' she begged.

'I can't. He's vanished, just packed his bags and left. I think he still has some family in France, so maybe he's gone there. Or maybe not. His mobile phone's dead and it's like he never existed.'

But it was the other way around, she thought in agony. Marcel had wiped *her* out as though she'd never existed. Obviously he didn't believe her explanation that she had done it for him. Or if he did believe, it made no difference. He hated her and he would not forgive.

Now his voice spoke in her memory.

'It's all or nothing with me, and with you it's all, my beloved Cassie. Everything, always.'

And she'd responded eagerly, *'Always, always—'*

But he'd warned her, all or nothing. And now it was nothing.

Sitting in the hotel garden, she tried to understand what she'd just learned. The 'poor boy' with barely a penny had actually been the son of a vastly wealthy man. But perhaps he hadn't known. He might have been illegitimate and only discovered his father later. She must try to believe that because otherwise their whole relationship had been based on a lie. The love and open-heartedness, so sweet between them, would have been an illusion.

She shivered.

It was time to flee before he found her. She couldn't bear to meet him and see his eyes as he discovered her now, her looks gone. How he would gloat at her downfall, how triumphant he would be in his revenge.

But as she neared the building she saw that it was already too late. The glass door into the garden was opening. Marcel was there, and with him the receptionist, saying, 'There's the lady, sir. I was sure I saw her come out here. Mrs Henshaw, here is Mr Falcon.'

'I'm sorry I kept you waiting,' Marcel said smoothly.

'No…it was my fault,' she stammered. 'I shouldn't have come outside—'

'I don't blame you at all. It's stifling in there, isn't it? Why don't we both sit out in the fresh air?'

He gestured towards the garden and she walked ahead, too dazed to do anything else.

He hadn't reacted.

He hadn't recognised her.

It might be the poor light. Twilight was settling, making everything fade into shadows, denying him a clear view of her face. That was a relief. It would give her time to take control of the situation.

But she was shaken with anguish as they reached a table and he pulled out a chair for her. He had loved her so much, and now he no longer recognised her.

'What can I get you to drink?' Marcel asked. 'Champagne?'

'Tonic water, please,' she said. 'I prefer to keep a clear head.'

'You're quite right. I'll have the same since obviously I'd better keep a clear head too. Waiter!'

A stranger might be fooled by this, she thought wryly, but the young Marcel had had an awesome ability to imbibe cheap wine while losing none of his faculties. After a night of particular indulgence she'd once challenged him to prove that he was 'up to it'. Whereupon he'd tossed her onto the bed, flung himself down beside her and proved it again and again, to the delight and hilarity of them both.

Hilarity? Yes. It had been a joy and a joke at the same time—exhausting each other, triumphing over each other, never knowing who was the winner, except that they both were.

'Cassie, my sweet beloved, why do you tease me?'

'To get you to do what I wanted, of course.'

'And did I do it to your satisfaction?'

'Let's try again and I'll let you know.'

'You clearly believe that business comes before pleasure,' he told her now in a voice that the years hadn't changed. He spoke English well, but with the barest hint of a French accent that had always enchanted her.

How many women, she wondered, had been enchanted by it since?

'Smith recommended you to me in the highest possible terms,' Marcel continued. 'He said nobody knew as much about my new property as you.'

'I hope I can live up to Mr Smith's praise,' she said primly.

'I'm sure you will.' His reply was courteous and mechanical.

'Do you mean to make the hotel similar to La Couronne?'

'I see you've been doing your homework. Excellent. There will be similarities. I aim to provide many facilities, like a conference centre.'

'I wonder if the building is big enough for that.'

'I agree. There will need to be expansion. I want the best firm of builders you can recommend.'

For a while he continued to talk about his plans, which were ambitious, and she made notes, not even raising her head when the waiter appeared with their tonic water.

Her hand, and one part of her brain, were working automatically. There was nothing in him to suggest recognition, no tension, no brightening of the eyes. His oblivion was so total that she even wondered if she was mistaken and he wasn't her Marcel after all. But when she stole a sideways glance she knew there had been no mistake. The shape of his head, the curve of his lips, the darkness of his eyes; all these she knew, even at a distance of years.

This was her Marcel.

Yet no longer hers.

And no longer really Marcel.

The same was true of her. Cassie was gone for ever and only Mrs Henshaw remained.

He moved and she hastened to bury herself in her work. When she dared to look up he had filled her glass. In her best businesslike voice she said, 'I happen to know that the owner of the building next door has been thinking of selling.'

'That would be useful for my expansion. Give me the details and I'll approach him. Do you have any more information?'

She scribbled some details and passed them to him.

'Excellent. I'm sure Smith told you that I need an assistant to work with me on this project. You'd do better than anyone.'

'That's very impulsive. Don't you need more time to think about it?'

'Not at all. The right decisions are very quickly made. And so they should be.'

For a moment she was fired with temptation. To take the job, be with him day after day, with him not knowing who she was. The prospect was so enticing as to be scary.

But she could not. She *must* not.

'It's impossible,' she said reluctantly.

'Why? Would your husband object? He doesn't mind you working for Smith.'

'I'm divorced.'

'So you're the mistress of your own destiny and can do as you choose.'

She almost laughed aloud. Once she'd imagined exactly the same, and been shown otherwise in the most brutal fashion.

'Nobody chooses their own destiny,' she said. 'We only think we do. Wise people remember that.'

He gave her a curious look. 'Are you wise, Mrs Henshaw?'

'Sooner or later we all become wise, don't we?'

'Some of us.'

As he said it he looked directly at her. She met his eyes, seeking recognition in them, but seeing only a blank. Or merely a weariness and disillusion that matched her own.

'Things are moving fast in the property world,' he said, 'as I'm sure you know. When I tell Smith that I've decided to employ you I'm sure he'll release you quickly.'

He'd decided, she noted. No suggestion that she had a decision to make.

'I need a little time to think,' she hedged.

'I'll pay you twice what you're getting now.'

'I could lie about the amount.'

'And I could check with him. I won't, though, I trust you. Don't worry, I'm a hard taskmaster. I'll get full value from you.'

'Now, look—'

'I won't take no for an answer. Fine, that's settled.'

'It is not,' she said, her temper rising. 'Please don't try to tell me what to do.'

'As your employer I shall expect to.'

'But you're not my employer.'

'I soon will be.'

He'd always liked his own way, she recalled, but he'd used charm. Now charm was gone, replaced by bullying. Perhaps she couldn't entirely blame him after the way he'd suffered. But still she knew she had to escape.

'Mr Falcon, I think it's time you understood—'

'Well, well, well. Who'd have thought it?'

The words, coming out of nowhere, startled them both. Approaching them was a large man with an air of pathological self-satisfaction.

'Oh, no,' she groaned. 'Not him.'

'You know this man?'

'He's Keith Lanley, part financial journalist, part muck-raker. He spends his days scurrying around trying to work out who's going to go bankrupt next.'

'What a thing to happen!' Lanley exclaimed, coming up to them. 'So the rumours are true, Jane. You're a sly character, getting out of Daneworth while the going's good. Aren't you going to introduce me to your friend? Of course I already know who he is. Everyone's ears pricked up when the Falcon family came to town.'

'I'm here for a wedding,' Marcel said coldly. 'So are the other members of my family.'

'Of course, of course. But no Falcon ever passed up the chance of making money, now, did he? And a lot depends on how you present it to the world. Suppose we three—'

But she'd had enough.

'Goodbye,' she said, rising to her feet.

'Now, wait—'

Lanley reached to grab her but she evaded him and fled deeper into the garden. Trying to follow her, Lanley found himself detained by Marcel, his face dark with rage.

'Leave her alone,' he said furiously.

'Hey, no need to get irate. I could do you a favour.'

'The only favour you could do me is to vanish off the face of the earth. Now, get out before I have you arrested.'

'I suppose you could, too,' Lanley said in a resigned voice. 'All right, I'll go—for now.' He began to go but turned. 'You couldn't just give me a quote about your father?'

'Get out!'

When the man had departed Marcel looked around. He was breathing hard, trying to force himself to be calm when all he wanted to do was roar to the heavens. Anguish possessed him, but more than anguish was rage—terrifying anger at her, at himself, at the cruel fate that had allowed this to happen.

Where was she? Vanished into thin air?

Again!

He began to run, hunting her here and there until at last he came across her leaning against a tree, her back to him. He touched her and her reaction was instant and violent.

'No, leave me alone. I won't talk to you.'

'It's not Lanley, I've sent him away.'

But she didn't seem to hear, fending him off madly until she lost her balance and fell, knocking her head against the tree. He tried to catch her but could only partly break her fall, steadying her as she slid to the ground.

'Your head,' he said hoarsely. *'Cassie.'*

People were approaching, calling out.

'She's collapsed,' he called back. 'She needs a doctor.'

Lifting her in his arms, he hurried the hundred yards back to the hotel. Word had gone ahead and the hotel doctor was waiting for them.

Her eyes were closed but she was aware of everything, especially Marcel's arms holding her firmly. Where their bodies touched she could feel his warmth, and just sense the soft thunder of his heart.

Cassie. He'd called her Cassie.

Hadn't he?

Her mind was swimming. Through the confusion she could hear his voice crying 'Cassie,' but had he said it or had she imagined it through the fog of her agitation? Had he known her all the time and concealed it? What would he do now?

She felt herself laid down and heard voices above her. She gave a soft gasp and opened her eyes.

'I think Mrs Henshaw's coming round,' the doctor said.

Marcel's face hovered over her.

'I'm all right, honestly,' she murmured. 'I just bumped my head against the tree and it made me dizzy for a moment.'

'Let's do a check,' the doctor said.

She barely heard. Her eyes were seeking Marcel's face, desperate to know what she could read in it.

But it was blank. There was nothing there.

For a moment she fought the truth, but then she forced herself to accept it. He hadn't recognised her, hadn't spoken her name. She'd simply imagined what she wanted to believe.

No!

A thousand voices screamed denial in her head. That wasn't what she wanted. She wouldn't think it or allow him to think it.

The doctor finished checking her, cleaned the graze and pronounced himself satisfied. 'But I'd recommend an early night,' he said. 'Are you staying here?'

'No.'

'Does anyone live at home with you?'

'No.'

'Pity. I'd rather you weren't alone tonight.'

'She won't be,' Marcel intervened. 'She'll stay in my suite, with a woman to watch out for her.'

'Oh, will I?' she said indignantly.

'Yes, Mrs Henshaw. You will. Please don't waste my time with further argument.'

He walked out, leaving her seething. *'Cheek!'*

'Be fair,' said the doctor. 'He obviously cares a lot about you.'

'Not at all. I've only just met him.'

In a few minutes it was clear that Marcel had gone to make arrangements. He returned with a wheelchair.

'I don't need that,' she said, aghast.

'Yes, you do. Take my hand.'

This was the moment to hurry away, put the whole disastrous evening behind her and forget that Marcel had ever existed. But he had firm hold of her, ushering her into the chair in a manner that brooked no refusal.

Since arguing was useless she sat in silence as he took her into the elevator and upstairs to his suite, where a pleasant-looking young woman was waiting.

'This is my sister Freya,' he said.

'I've brought you a nightdress,' Freya said.

'I'll leave you.' Marcel departed quickly.

'This is the bedroom and bathroom,' Freya told her. 'I'll

look in often to make sure you're all right. Let me help you undress.'

As they worked on it Freya asked, 'Whatever did Marcel do to you?'

'It wasn't his fault. I fell against a tree.'

'Well, he obviously feels responsible.'

'He has no need.'

'Perhaps he's just a very generous and responsible man. I'm still getting to know him.'

'I thought he said you were his sister.'

'His stepsister.' Freya laughed. 'He keeps calling me his sister so that he doesn't have to marry me.'

'What?'

'Amos wants me to marry one of his sons so that I'll really be part of the family. His first choice is Darius but Darius is no more keen than I am. So then Marcel is "next in the firing line" as he puts it. That "sister" business is his way of protecting himself.'

'How do you feel about that?'

Freya chuckled. 'I'm not weeping into my pillow. He's not my style at all. Too much like his father. Oh, it's rotten of me to say that when Amos has been so kind to me, but now I can still escape. The thought of being married to a man like that—' She gave a melodramatic shudder.

'Like what?'

'Money, money, money. That and always being one step ahead of his enemies.'

'Does Marcel have a lot of enemies?'

'I've no idea. I don't think he has many friends. There's a coldness in him that it's hard to get past. There now, you're ready for bed. Would you like me to stay?'

'No, thank you. You've been very kind.'

She was desperate to be alone. As soon as the door closed

she pulled the covers over her head and tried to sort out her confused mind.

Freya had spoken of his coldness, but the young man she'd known and loved had been incapable of coldness. Somehow, one had become the other.

This isn't happening. It can't be. I'll wake up and find it was a dream. At least, I hope so. Or do I hope so? Is that what I really want? Did he recognise me or not? Is he just pretending not to? What am I hoping for?

But thinking was too troubling, so at last she gave up and fell asleep.

CHAPTER THREE

SHE awoke suddenly in the dark. Listening intently, she could make out the sound of footsteps nearing her room. Marcel. She slid further down the bed, pulling the duvet over her, not sure that she wanted to see him.

The door opened, someone came in and stood looking down at her. Her heart was thundering as the moment of truth neared. Last night he'd seemed not to know her, but then she'd heard her name whispering past. Surely that had come from him and now everything was different. What would he say to her? What could she say to him?

She gasped as a hand touched her.

'It's only me,' said Freya. 'I'm sorry, did I wake you?'

'No, no, I…I'm all right.' She didn't know what she was saying. Everything was spinning in chaos.

Freya switched on the lamp and sat down on the bed, placing a cup on the sidetable.

'I'm going now, but I brought you a cup of tea first.'

'Thank you.'

'Jane—do you mind if I call you Jane? Or should it be Mrs Henshaw?'

'Oh, please, no.' She shuddered. 'I've had enough of Mrs Henshaw.'

'Jane, then?'

'Yes, Jane. Although I think I've had enough of Jane too.'

'Goodness, what does that mean?' Freya's friendliness was charming.

'Suddenly I seem to be a lot of different people and none of them is really me. Does that sound crazy?'

'Not in this family,' Freya said wryly. 'You have to be a bit crazy to get your head around the way they all live. Sometimes I worry for my mother. She's Amos's third wife and he wasn't faithful to either of the others.'

'Where does Marcel come in the picture?' Jane Henshaw asked, careful to drink her tea at once to hide her face.

'When Amos was married to Elaine, Darius's mother, he travelled abroad a lot, and while he was doing business in France he met Laura, set up home with her and they had Marcel.'

'While he was still married to Elaine?'

'While he was still actually living with her in England. He divided his time between London and Paris, and even had another son by his wife. That's Jackson. A couple of years later Elaine found out about his infidelity and left him. He brought Laura and Marcel over to England and married her as soon as his divorce was through.'

'So Marcel grew up in England?' Jane said slowly.

'I think he was about eleven when he moved here. Of course it didn't last. When he was fifteen Laura discovered that Amos had been "at it" again, and she returned to Paris, taking Marcel with her. He came back seven years later, but not to Amos. He resented the way his mother had been treated, and he even stopped using the name Falcon and went back to using Laura's name, Degrande.

'He had a rebellious streak and set up home with some other lads, living from day to day, doing any job they could get. He enjoyed it for a couple of years, then went back to France. Eventually he and Amos were reconciled, and he returned to England and became a Falcon again. Actually I think that was bound to happen. In his heart he was always a chip off the old block. Those two years being free and easy were fun, but it was never going to last.'

'They might have done. Perhaps something happened to send that side of him into hiding.'

'Kill it off for good, more like,' Freya said robustly. 'Marcel is Amos's son through and through—hard, implacable, money-minded. Will it pay? What will I get out of it, and how can I squeeze more? That's how his mind works.'

'You don't like him, do you?'

'He's all right, always pleasant to me, but Amos can forget about me marrying him. I'd sooner marry the devil.'

'I'm surprised he isn't married already. Rich men don't tend to be short of women.'

'Oh, he's never been short of women,' Freya agreed. 'Just not the kind he's likely to marry, if you see what I mean. They serve their purpose, he pays them off. I believe his 'leaving tips' are quite generous. But he doesn't fall in love.' She gave a brief laugh. 'Don't take me too seriously. I'm only warning you that he'll be tough to work for. After all, you're not likely to want to marry him, are you?'

'Not if I've got any sense,' she said lightly.

'Right, I must be going, but first I need to take some of Marcel's clothes from the wardrobe. He's sleeping out there on the sofa and he says don't worry, he won't trouble you.'

'He's very kind.'

'He can be. Not always. Now I'm off.'

'Goodbye. And thank you.'

Freya slipped out of the door.

Cassie lay in silence, trying to come to terms with the storm of feeling inside her. It had started when she'd glimpsed him tonight, but now it had a new aspect. The woman who now convulsively clenched and unclenched her hands was no longer lovelorn and yearning, but possessed by a bitter anger.

Marcel had known all the time that he was Amos Falcon's son. And he'd deceived her, pretending to be poor as a joke, because it boosted his pride to think she'd chosen him over rich men. It might have started as an innocent game, but the result had been catastrophic.

If I'd known you had a wealthy, powerful father, I wouldn't have given in to Jake. I'd have gone to Amos Falcon, seeking his protection for you. He could have punished Jake, scared him off, and we'd have been safe. We could have been together all these years, and we lost everything because you had to play silly games with the truth. You stupid...stupid...

She pounded the pillow as though trying to release all the fury in her heart, until at last she lay still, exhausted, shocked by the discovery that she could hate him, while the tears poured down her face.

Finally she slept again, and only then did the door open and a figure stand there in silence, watching the faint light that fell from the hallway onto the bed, just touching the blonde hair that streamed across the pillow.

He moved closer to the bed, where he could see her face, relaxed in sleep and more like the face he had once known. In the first moments of their meeting he'd denied the truth to himself, refusing to admit that the evil witch who'd wrecked his life could possibly have returned.

But a witch didn't die. She rose again to laugh over the destruction she had wrought. With every blank word and silent laugh, every look from her beautiful dead eyes, she taunted him.

A wise man would have refused to recognise her, but he'd never been wise where this woman was concerned. Fate had returned her to him, freeing him to make her suffer as he had suffered. And the man whose motto, learned from a powerful, ruthless father, was 'seize every chance, turn everything to your advantage' would not turn away from this opportunity until he'd made the most of it.

Suddenly the figure on the bed before him changed, becoming not her but himself, long ago, shattered with the pain of broken ribs, half blinded by his own blood, but even more by his own tears, longing every moment to see her approach and comfort him, finally realising that she would never do so.

That was when his heart had died. He'd been glad of it ever since. Life was easier without feelings. The women who could be bought were no trouble. They knew their place, did their duty, counted their reward and departed smiling. In time he might choose a wife by the same set of rules. Friends too tended to be business acquaintances. There were plenty of both men and women, there whenever he wanted them. His life was full.

His life was empty. His heart was empty. Safer that way.

He kept quite still for several long minutes, hardly daring to breathe, before closing the door and retreating, careful that she should never know he'd been there.

She awoke to the knowledge that everything had changed. As she'd told Freya, she seemed to have been several people in the last few hours, without knowing which one was really her. But now she knew.

Cassie.

Somewhere in the depths of sleep the decision had been made. She was Cassie, but a different Cassie, angry, defiant, possessed by only one thought.

Make him pay.

He'd treated her with contempt, concealing his true identity because that had been his idea of fun. He hadn't meant any harm, but his silly joke had resulted in years of pain and suffering for her. Perhaps also for him, but she was in no mood to sympathise.

Freya knocked and entered. 'Just came to say goodbye,' she said. 'Marcel is waiting for you to have breakfast with him.'

She dressed hurriedly, twisted her hair into its usual bun and followed Freya out into the main room. Marcel was standing by the window with another man of about seventy, who turned and regarded her with interest.

'Good morning, Mrs Henshaw,' Marcel said politely. 'I'm glad to see you looking well again. This is my father, Amos Falcon.'

'Glad to meet you,' the old man said, shaking her hand while giving her the searching look she guessed was automatic with him. 'Marcel always chooses the best, so I expect great things of you.'

'Father—' Marcel said quickly.

'He's told me that your expertise is unrivalled,' Amos went on. 'So is your local knowledge, which he'll need.'

Since Cassie had refused the job this might have been expected to annoy her, but things were different now. In the last few hours she'd moved to a level so different that it was like being a new person. So she merely smiled and shook Amos Falcon's hand, replying smoothly, 'I hope he finds that I live up to his expectations.'

A slight frisson in the air told her that she'd taken Marcel by surprise. Whatever he'd expected from her, it wasn't this.

'If you'd care to go and sit at the table,' he said, 'I'll be with you in a minute.'

A maid served her at the table in the large window bay. She drank her coffee absent-mindedly, her attention on Marcel, who was bidding farewell to his father and Freya.

Now she had a better view of him than the night before. The lanky boy had turned into a fine man, not only handsome but with an air of confidence, almost haughtiness, that was to be expected from a member of the great Falcon dynasty.

But then haughtiness fell away and he smiled at Freya, bidding her goodbye and taking her into a friendly hug. Cassie noticed that, despite her avowed disdain for him, Freya embraced him cheerfully, while Amos stood back and regarded them with the air of a man calculating the odds.

So it was true what Freya had said. If Amos couldn't marry her to his eldest son, then Marcel was next in line. Doubtless she would bring a substantial dowry for which he could find good use.

Then it was over, they were gone and he was turning back into the room, joining her at the table.

'I owe you my thanks,' he said, 'for not making a fool of me before my father. If you'd told him of your intention to refuse the job I offered I would have looked absurd. I'm grateful to you for your restraint.'

'I doubt it's in my power to make you look absurd,' she said lightly. 'I'm sure you're well armoured against anything I could dream up.'

'Now you're making fun of me. Very well, perhaps I've earned it.'

'You must admit you left yourself rather exposed by allowing your father to think I'd already agreed. Still, I dare say that's a useful method of—shall we say—proceeding without hindrance?'

'It's worked in the past,' he conceded. 'But you're right, it can leave me vulnerable if someone decides to be difficult.' He saw her lips twitching. 'Have I said something funny?'

'How would you define "difficult"? No, on second thoughts don't say. I think I can guess. Someone who dares to hold onto their own opinion instead of meekly obeying you.' She struck an attitude. 'I wonder how I knew that.'

'Possibly because you're much the same?' he suggested.

'Certainly not. I'm far more subtle. But I don't suppose you need to bother with subtlety.'

'Not often,' he agreed, 'although I flatter myself I can manage it when the occasion demands.'

'Well, there's no demand for it now. Plain speaking will suit us both better, so I'll say straight out that I've decided it would suit me to work for you, on certain conditions.'

'The conditions being?'

'Double the salary I'm earning now, as we discussed.'

'And how much is that?'

She gave him the figure. It was a high one, but he seemed untroubled.

'It's a deal. Shake.'

She took the hand he held out to her, bracing herself for the feel of his flesh against hers. Even so, it took all her control not to react to the warmth of his skin. So much had changed, but not this. After ten years it was still the hand that had touched her reverently, then skilfully and with fierce joy. The sensation was so intense that she almost cried out.

From him there was no reaction.

'I'm glad we're agreed on that,' he said calmly. 'Now you can go and give in your notice. Be back here as soon as possible. Before you leave, we'd better exchange information. Email, cellphones.'

She gave him her cellphone number, but he said, 'And the other one.'

'What other one?'

'You've given me the number you give to everyone. Now I want the one you give to only a privileged few.'

'And what about your "privileged" number?'

He wrote it down and handed it to her. 'Now yours.'

She shook her head. 'I don't have one.'

'Mrs Henshaw—'

'It's the truth. I only need one number.'

Now, she realised, he could guess at the emptiness of her life, with no need for a 'privileged' number because there was nobody to give it to. But all he said was, 'You might have told me that before I gave you mine.'

'Then you wouldn't have given it to me. But if you object, here—take it back.'

She held out the paper but he shook his head.

'No point. You could have memorised it by now. Very clever, Mrs Henshaw. I can see I shall have to be careful.'

'If you're having doubts you can always refuse to employ me.'

His eyes met hers and she drew a sharp breath, for there was a gleam in their depths that she hadn't seen before—not for many years. It teased and enticed, challenged, lured her on to danger.

'I'm not going to accept that offer,' he said softly.

She nodded, but before she could speak he added significantly, 'And you know I'm not.'

It could have been no more than courtesy but there was a new note in his voice, an odd note, that made her tense. She was at a crossroads. If she admitted that she did actually know what he meant, the road ahead was a wilderness of confusion.

Ignore the challenge, said the warning voice in her head. Escape while you can.

'How could I know that?' she murmured. 'I don't know you.'

'I think we both know—all that we need to know. The decision has been taken.'

She wanted to cry out. He seemed to be saying that he really had recognised her, that the two of them still lived in a world that excluded the rest of the universe and only they understood the language they spoke.

But no! She wouldn't let herself believe it. She *must not* believe it, lest she go crazy.

Crazier than she'd been for the last ten years? Or was she already beyond hope? She drew a deep breath.

But then, while she was still spinning, he returned to earth with devastating suddenness.

'Now that we've settled that, tell me how you got here last night,' he said.

His voice sounded normal again. They were back to practical matters.

'In a taxi,' she said.

'I'm glad. It's better if you don't drive for a while after what happened.'

'My head's fine. It was only a tiny bump. But I'll take a taxi to the office.'

'Good. I'll call you later. Now I must go. I have an appointment with the bank. We'll meet tomorrow.'

He was gone.

At the office Mr Smith greeted her news with pleasure. When she'd cleared her desk he took her for a final lunch. Over the wine he became expansive.

'It can be a good job as long as you know to be careful. Men like him resemble lions hovering for the kill. Just be sure you're not the prey. Remember that however well he seems to treat you now, all he cares about is making the best use of you. When your usefulness is over you'll be out on your ear. So get what you can out of him before he dumps you.'

'Perhaps he won't,' she said, trying to speak lightly.

'He always does. People serve their purpose, then they're out in the cold. He's known for it.'

'Perhaps there's a reason,' she said quietly. 'Maybe someone deserted him.'

'Don't make me laugh! Dump him? Nobody would dare.'

'Not now perhaps, but in the past, maybe when he was vulnerable—'

Mr Smith's response was a guffaw. 'Him? Vulnerable?

Never. Amos Falcon's son was born fully formed and the image of his father. Hard. Armoured. Unfeeling. Oh, it's not how he comes across at first. He's good with the French fantasy lover stuff. Or so I've heard from some lady friends who were taken in when they should have known better. But don't believe it. It's all on the outside. Inside—nothing!'

'Thanks for the lunch,' she said hurriedly. 'I must be going.'

'Yes, you belong to him now, don't you?'

'My *time* belongs to him,' she corrected. 'Only my time.'

She fled, desperate to get away from the picture he showed her of Marcel—a man damaged beyond hope. Hearing him condemned so glibly made her want to scream.

You don't know him, don't know what he suffered. I knew him when he was generous and loving, with a heart that overflowed, to me at least. He was young and defenceless then, whatever you think.

Only a few hours ago her anger had been directed at Marcel, but now she knew a surge of protective fury that made her want to stand between him and the world. What did any of them understand when nobody knew him as she did?

She checked that her cellphone was switched on and waited for his call. It didn't come. She tried not to feel disappointed, guessing that the bank would occupy him for a long time. And she had something else in mind, for which she would need time to herself.

When she reached home she locked the front door behind her. For the next few hours nothing and nobody must disturb her.

Switching on her computer, she went online and settled down to an evening of research.

She forced herself to be patient, first studying Amos Falcon, which was easy because there were a dozen sites devoted to him. An online encyclopaedia described his life and career—the rise from poverty, the enormous gains in power and money. There was less detail about his private life beyond the fact that he'd had three wives and five sons.

As well as Darius and Marcel there was Jackson Falcon, a minor celebrity in nature broadcasting. Finding his picture, she realised that she'd seen him in several television programmes. Even better known was Travis Falcon, a television actor in America, star of a series just beginning to be shown in England. The last son was Leonid, born and raised in Russia and still living there. About him the encyclopaedia had little information, not even a picture.

There were various business sites analysing Amos's importance in the financial world, and a few ill-natured ones written in a spirit of 'set the record straight'. He was too successful to be popular, and his enemies vented their feelings while being careful to stay just the right side of libel.

The information about Marcel told her little that she hadn't already learned from Freya, but there was much about La Couronne, his hotel in Paris. From here she went to the hotel's own site, then several sites that gave customers' opinions. Mrs Henshaw studied these closely, making detailed notes.

Then Cassie took over, calling up photographs of Marcel that went back several years. Few of them were close-ups. Most had been taken at a distance, as though he was a reluctant subject who could only be caught by chance.

But then she came across a picture that made her grow tense. The date showed that it had been taken nine years ago, yet the change in him was already there. Shocked, she realised that the sternness in his face, the heaviness in his attitude, had settled over him within a year of their separation. This was what misery had done to him.

She reached out and touched the screen as though trying to reach him, turn time back and restore him to the vibrant, loving boy he'd once been. But that could never happen. She snatched her hand back, reminding herself how much of the tragedy was his own fault for concealing the truth. She must cling to that thought or go mad.

She came offline. But, as if driven by some will of their own, her fingers lingered over the keys, bringing up another picture, kept in a secret file. There they were, Cassie and Marcel, locked in each other's embrace. She had many such shots, taken on a delayed release camera borrowed from a photographer friend.

'I want lots of pictures,' she'd told Marcel, 'then we'll always have them to remember this time when we were so happy.'

'I won't need help to remember you,' he'd told her fervently. 'You'll always live in my heart and my memory as you are now, my beautiful Cassie. When I'm old and grey you'll still be there with me, always—always—'

Gently he'd removed her clothes.

'This is my one chance to have a picture of you naked, because I couldn't bear to have any other photographer take them. Nobody else must ever see you like this—only me. Promise me.'

'I promise.'

'Swear it. Swear by Cupid and his bow.'

'I swear by Cupid, his bow and all his arrows.'

As she spoke she was undressing him until they were both naked, and he took her into his arms, turning her towards the clicking camera so that her magnificent breasts could be seen in all their glory.

'This is how I'll always see you,' he murmured. 'When we're old and grey, I'll show you these to remind you that in my heart this is what you really look like.'

'You'll have forgotten me by then,' she teased.

To her surprise, he'd made a sound of anger. 'Why do you say things like that? Don't you know that we must always be together because I will never let you go?'

'I don't want you to let me go.'

But he hardly seemed to hear her.

'Why can't you understand how serious I am? There is only you. There will only ever be you. I'll never let you go, Cassie. Even if there were miles between us I would still be there, holding onto you, refusing to let you forget me. You might try to escape but you won't be able to.'

What mysterious insight had made him utter those words, so strangely prophetic of what was to come? Miles and years had stretched between them, yet always he'd been there as he'd promised—or was it threatened?—always on the edge of her consciousness until the day he'd appeared again to reclaim her.

There it was again, the tormenting question. Had he recognised her, or had she only imagined that he'd called her Cassie?

And his remark that the decision had already been taken, had she not simply read too much into it? Was she hearing what she wanted to hear?

But there was more. Just before she'd left him that morning there had been another clue, if only she could remember what it was. She'd barely noticed at the time, but now she realised that his words had been significant. If only—

Frantically she wracked her memory. It was connected with the cellphone number—something he'd said—something—something—

'What?' she cried out. *'What was it?'*

She dropped her head, resting it on one hand while she slammed the other hand on the table again and again with increasing desperation.

* * *

A few miles away someone else was conjuring up pictures online. The one word, 'Cassie' brought her before him in a website that analysed the careers of models who were no longer around.

> *For two years she rode high and could have ridden higher still, but suddenly she gave up modelling and disappeared from sight. After that she was occasionally seen in luxurious surroundings, places where only rich men gather. And always she seemed weighed down with diamonds.*

Why hadn't he seen it happening? Her choice of himself over wealthy admirers had made him love her a million times more, but it had always been too good to be true. It was a game she'd played, until she'd succumbed to the lure of serious money. While he'd thought he was her true love, he'd been no more than her plaything.

He should have known when she'd failed to visit him in the hospital. He'd lain there in pain and anguish, certain that she would be here at any moment. Every time the door opened he'd tensed with longing, which was always crushed.

He'd clung to the fragile hope that she didn't know what had happened to him. If only he could reach her, all would be well. But her cellphone was switched off. When he'd called her apartment the phone rang and rang, but was never answered.

He'd known then, known with such certainty that he'd torn up the letter she'd sent him without even opening it. Who needed to read her miserable excuses?

He'd seen her just once more, the day he'd left for Paris. There she'd been at the airport with her new lover, as he went into the departure lounge.

'You!' he'd spat. 'The last person I ever want to see.'

She'd held out her arms, crying frantically, 'Marcel, you don't understand—please—please—'

'I loved you,' he raged. 'I trusted you—now I can't bear the sight of you!'

'Marcel—'

'Get out of my sight! *Whore!*'

He'd turned and ran from her. He remembered that afterwards with self-disgust. It was he who had run, not her.

But there would be no running now.

The time had come.

CHAPTER FOUR

WHEN she rose next morning her mind was firm and decided. Today she would start working for Marcel, getting close to the man he'd become, watching to see where the path led. And, wherever it led, she was ready to explore.

Now she was glad that his younger ghost haunted her. Far from trying to banish that spectre, she would enlist him on-side and make use of his insights to confront the present man.

She made coffee and toast and sat eating it by the window, looking down at the street, thinking of another time, another window where she'd watched for a grocery delivery. Cassie had been riding high, with two great modelling jobs behind her and more in the offing. The world was wonderful.

And then the most wonderful thing of all had happened.

The grocery van had drawn up and the delivery man stepped out. That was her first view of Marcel's tall, vigorous body. Being only one floor up, she could appreciate every detail. When he'd glanced up she'd seen not only his good looks but the cheeky devil lurking in his eyes. That had been what really won her heart.

It was the same with him. She knew that by the way he came to a sudden halt, as though something had seized him, smiling at her with pleasure and an air of discovery. The words, *That's it! This is the one!* had sung in the air between them.

A week later, lying in each other's arms, he'd said, 'I knew then that I was going to love you.'

'I knew I'd love you too,' she'd assured him joyfully.

'Really? Me, the grocer's delivery lad? With all the men you could have?'

'If I can have them I can also reject them,' she'd pointed out. 'I choose the man I want. *I* choose.' With mock sternness she'd added, 'Don't forget that.'

'No, ma'am. Whatever you say, ma'am.'

He'd given her a comical salute and they'd dissolved into laughter, snuggling down deeper into the bed, and then not laughing at all.

How handsome he'd been that first day, getting out of the van and approaching her. How young, untouched by life!

'Good morning!'

She jumped, startled by the voice that came from below. A car had stopped and a man was calling up to her, pulling her back to the present, where she didn't want to be.

'I'm sorry…who…?'

'I said good morning,' Marcel repeated.

'Oh—it's you!'

'Who were you expecting?'

'Nobody. I thought you'd call me.'

'May I come up?'

'Of course.' She tossed down the keys.

She hadn't dressed and was suddenly conscious of the thin nightie. By the time he arrived she'd pulled on a house coat. It was unflattering, but it zipped up to the neck and at least he wouldn't think she was trying to be seductive. Anything but that.

When she emerged from the bedroom he was already there.

'I'm sorry to arrive so early, but I'm eager to get a close inspection of my new property.'

'Meaning me?' she asked, her head on one side and a satirical smile on her lips.

'A shrewd businesswoman like you should appreciate the description. So I came to collect you, which was perhaps a little thoughtless of me. Finish your breakfast.'

She fetched a cup and poured him a coffee. 'Let's talk. I can eat and work at the same time.'

'I see I've hired the right person. The hotel needs development, the sooner the better.'

'You spoke of making it like La Couronne, and there are several avenues that it would be profitable to explore. The success of your Paris hotel may be because of all the—' She launched into a list gleaned from her investigation of the hotel's website, adding, 'You could probably do some of these things more easily without the problems that arose in—' Here she made use of knowledge found on a business site that spilled the beans about some interesting battles.

'That man who caused you all the trouble didn't really give up, did he?' she asked. 'I gather he's still complaining about—'

Marcel listened to her with raised eyebrows. She could tell that he was impressed. Good. That was how she wanted him. She was taking charge.

'People who come to the London hotel should sense the connection with Paris,' she added. 'It'll be useful when you're ready to expand further.'

'That's looking rather far ahead.'

'But it's what you need to do. Eventually your hotels will be all over Europe, with your trademark. This one could be The Crown Hotel, and the one you'll open in Italy can be La Corona. Spain as well. Then it'll be Die Krone in Germany, De Kroon in Holland. Czech and Slovak will probably have to wait a while—'

'You don't say!' he exclaimed with a grin of wry appreciation.

'But when their time comes it'll be Koruna.'

'You've got this all worked out. And I thought *I* was organised.'

'I like to be prepared. Aren't I supposed to be?'

'Yes, indeed.' He added wryly, 'But how often are people what they're supposed to be?'

'People, rarely. But places can be exactly as planned, if you tackle the problem properly'

'Quite right.' He raised his coffee cup in her direction. 'And with your help that's what will happen.'

She clinked her cup against his. 'Now I must dash and get ready.'

When she'd gone Marcel looked around the apartment, surprised to find it so small and plain. Her fortunes might have dived over the years but a woman in her present position surely didn't need to live among second-hand furniture and walls that looked as though they needed repapering.

From the bathroom he could hear the sound of the shower, which made it awkward that the phone should ring at that moment. Since there was no way he could interrupt her now, he lifted the receiver.

'Is Jane there?' came a man's voice.

'She's occupied right now. Can I say who called?'

'Tell her it's Dave, and I need to talk to her quickly.'

The line went dead.

He replaced the receiver, frowning.

She emerged a few minutes later, fully dressed and with her hair swept back.

'Dave wants you to call him,' Marcel told her. 'It sounded urgent.'

She had seized the receiver before he even finished speaking, leaving him wondering even more curiously about Dave and the hold he evidently had over her.

He tried not to eavesdrop, or so he told himself, but certain phrases couldn't be shut out.

'Dave, it's all right, I'll take care of it. I can't talk now. I'll call you back later.' She hung up.

Marcel didn't speak. He wondered if he was being fanciful in imagining that she had ended the conversation quickly because he was there.

His mind went back years, to their time together. When had she ever spoken to himself in that placating tone? Never.

So what did this man have to make her subservient? Vast wealth?

No, she didn't live like a women with a rich admirer.

Good looks? Other attractions? Could his personal 'skills' make her cry out for more?

'Perhaps it's time we were going,' he said heavily.

She turned to him and her expression was as efficiently cheerful as a mask.

'Tell me something first,' she said briskly. 'Are they expecting you at the Alton?'

'No, I think I'll see more if I take them by surprise.'

'You'll see more if you take a room incognito. But I expect they'd recognise you, so it probably wouldn't work.'

'I doubt if anyone would know me. Are you serious?'

'You said you wanted to take them by surprise. There's no better way than this.'

'I suppose not,' he said slowly. 'I wonder—'

'Leave it to me.' She went to the phone and dialled the Alton's number.

'Hello, do you have a room free today? You do? Excellent. What kind of price? All prices? Really. Run them past me, single rooms and suites.'

As they were given to her, she recited them aloud, watching Marcel's expression of wry understanding. The Alton wasn't doing fantastic business.

'I'll take the best available suite,' he said quietly.

'What name?'

'My real name. I won't have anyone saying I deceived them.'

'Mr Marcel Falcon,' she said into the phone. 'He'll be there today.' She hung up.

He gave her a glance of grim appreciation. 'You're a wicked woman, Mrs Henshaw—I'm glad to say.'

'It has its uses,' she observed lightly.

'So I'll return to the Gloriana to check out. You'd better come with me, then we'll go on to the Alton. I'll wait for you downstairs.'

Once down in the street he glanced up at her window but there was no sign of her. He knew exactly what she was doing—calling Dave now that they could talk privately.

Whoever Dave was!

In this he was wrong. Cassie didn't return Dave's call immediately because there was no need. She knew what he wanted. Instead she went online, gave some instructions, shut the computer down and sent him a text saying, *All taken care of.*

Then she pushed Dave aside. Only Marcel occupied her thoughts now.

Against all reason, she was certain that he recognised her, but only against his will. And he refused to admit it to her.

But he could never deny it to himself. Instinct told her that. Try as he might, Marcel was fighting with Marcel, and it would be a losing battle on both sides.

That told her all she needed to know.

'Right,' she said to Mrs Henshaw in the mirror. 'Let's see if we can give him a run for his money.' She smiled. 'And maybe—just maybe—he'll give me a run for mine. That could be—interesting.'

She could almost have sworn Mrs Henshaw nodded.

The Alton Hotel had a disconsolate air.

'It used to be the London home of a duke,' she observed as they drew up in the car park, 'which is why it was built on such grand lines, but he had to sell it off, and the developers who bought it couldn't afford to complete their plans.'

Checking in went without a hitch. Nobody recognised Marcel and they were able to proceed upstairs to a luxurious suite of four rooms, one of which was dominated by a huge double bed.

Cassie ignored it and went to look out of the window, saying eagerly, 'Just the view I was hoping for. Look at that building next door. It's the one you need to buy to expand this place.'

'Let me see.' He came to stand beside her. 'Yes, it's ideal. I can connect the two and this side will be—'

He talked for a few more minutes but she barely heard him. Her whole body seemed to be hypnotised by the sensation of standing close to him so that the air between them seemed to sing. His extra height loomed over her in a way she'd once loved, and when he casually laid a hand on her shoulder she had to fight not to jump.

'Why don't we go and take a look?' she said.

'I can see all I want from here. I'm going to tear it down, and that's it.'

'I can put you in touch with three excellent building contractors—'

'Can't we just hire the best?'

'With three you can play them off against each other,' she pointed out.

'Splendid. I see you believe in reading your employer's mind and following his instructions exactly.'

'What else am I here for?'

'Then here's another instruction for you. I'll have no grim and forbidding ladies working for me.'

'Are you firing me?' she asked lightly.

'No, I'm telling you to make yourself less severe.'

'Flaunt myself, you mean?' she demanded in a voice that managed to sound shocked. 'Mr Falcon, I hope I've misunderstood you.'

'Only because you're determined to,' he replied with a smile that nearly destroyed her composure. 'I'm going to need you with me a lot of the time—'

'And you think I'm so ugly I'll frighten the horses?' she managed to say lightly.

'You're not ugly. But for some reason you're determined to pretend you are. Now that *is* frightening.'

'Why would any woman want to pretend that?' she murmured.

'A good question. We might talk about it later. Ah, I hear someone at the door. It must be the waiter with my order.'

He moved away and she clutched the windowsill to stop herself swaying. She was trembling from the feel of his hand on her shoulder, and also from the sensation that he too had been trembling.

It took several hours to walk slowly through the building, making notes, trying to be inconspicuous. They ended up back in his suite, thankfully drinking coffee.

'I'll just check my mail,' he said, opening his laptop, which he'd already connected to the hotel's Internet.

He didn't take long, sending a few messages and making a gesture of dismissal.

'Time to think of having some dinner,' he said. 'There's a place upstairs—'

Her phone rang. Marcel watched her face as she answered, saw her expression drop and heard her sigh.

'Dave, I've done my best—'

Dave, he thought. A man with some kind of hold over her, perhaps a man who'd once inspired her love and for whom she still felt some sympathy. Or was he blackmailing her?

'All right, all right,' she was saying. 'I'll send some more. Bye for now.' She turned to Marcel. 'Can I use your computer?'

'Be my guest.'

She was online in a moment, accessing her bank account. Marcel had the impression that she'd forgotten his existence. Totally absorbed, she was trying to transfer a large amount out of her account, into another one. But only trying. The bank refused, saying it would take her over her limit.

'Oh, no!' she said frantically.

'Look, I don't want to pry, but if this man is extorting money from you, then you need help,' Marcel told her.

She looked up as if wondering why he was there.

'Extorting—?'

'Why are you giving him money? Especially money that you clearly can't afford.'

'Dave's married to my sister Laura. They have a lot of financial problems, and I try to help them out.'

'He's...your brother-in-law?' he echoed, astounded.

'Yes, why do you sound so disbelieving?'

He couldn't have told her. It would take time to come to terms with the thoughts whirling chaotically in his head. All he knew was that somewhere the sun had come out.

'He didn't sound like a brother-in-law,' he said lamely.

'I know. He sounds like a needy child because that's what he is,' she said grimly. 'Also they have a little girl who needs a lot of care, so Laura can't take a job. Now, if you'd just give me a moment—'

'Well, I won't. Move over.'

She was forced to yield and let him get to the computer, where he accessed his own bank account in Paris, ordering them to transfer a sum of money to her.

'You'll have to fill in the details of your account,' he said.

She did so, too bewildered to argue, and in a moment it was done.

'Now, you just give the money to Dave and it's finished,' Marcel said.

'Actually, I give it to Laura. That way the bills get paid. He'd just be off down the pub.'

The contempt in her voice was plain. With more relief than he cared to admit, Marcel realised that Dave didn't have the place in her life that he'd suspected.

Dreaded?

'Thank you,' she said as she completed the transaction. 'I don't know how to—'

'Let's be clear. I've come to your aid for entirely selfish reasons. I want your whole attention and I won't get it if you're worried about money.'

'But you gave me so much.'

'Three months' wages in advance. Now you'll have to work for me whether you want to or not.'

'I've already said I will.'

'Yes, but you might have changed your mind.' His lips twisted. 'It's my opinion that women are notoriously unreliable about sticking to their word. So I've taken you prisoner. I'm sorry if you object.'

'I don't. I'm grateful. Laura needs all the help she can get.'

'By help you mean cash. Is that why you live in that shabby little dump?'

'What would you expect? Should I be revelling in the lap of luxury?'

It took him a moment to reply and she had the satisfying feeling that she'd caught him off-guard.

'I wouldn't know, would I?' he asked at last.

'No,' she said quietly. 'How could you?'

'I think we both need a good stiff drink and a large meal,' he said. 'The best restaurant seems to be the one on the roof, and so let's head up there.'

The restaurant had two halves, one with a glass roof, one with no roof at all. As the weather was clement they settled here with a magnificent view over London. In the distance the setting sun blazed crimson as it drifted slowly down the sky.

'It's like watching a fire that you don't have to be afraid of,' she said in wonder.

'Is there such a thing as a fire you need not fear?' he asked.

He spoke lightly, even casually, but she thought she sensed tension beneath the tone.

Only because you're listening for it, said her inner voice sternly. *Be careful of getting paranoid.*

'What did you say?' Marcel asked.

'Nothing, I—'

'It sounded like, "Sometimes paranoid is best."'

'Nonsense.' She laughed edgily. 'I didn't say anything.'

'I thought you did. Ah, here's the waiter. Time for a celebratory supper.'

He ordered the best of everything, including champagne and caviar, seeking her opinion, deferring to her as if she were a queen.

Until your usefulness is ended, Smith reminded her in her mind.

Get lost! she told him.

'What's so amusing?' Marcel asked, looking at her curiously. 'You suddenly started to smile in a very mysterious way. Share the joke.'

'I can't.'

'Ah, a private joke. They're often the most interesting.'

'Only while they stay private.'

'I see. All right, I'll back off—for the moment.'

Suddenly she came to a resolution. Clenching her hands beneath the table where he couldn't see, she said, 'There's something I meant to ask you,' she said.

'Go on.'

'When I fell against the tree, I thought I heard you call me Cassie. Who is she?'

He didn't reply at once, only looked at her strangely, as though trying to make up his mind. With sudden devastating insight she saw herself through his eyes—the severe clothes, the flattened hair, the steel-rimmed spectacles. She could even hear his thoughts. *How could I ever have thought this was her?*

'Just a girl I once knew,' he said at last.

'And you confused me with her? Am I like her?'

'Not at all,' he said instantly. 'The way she looked, the way she dressed—she gave herself to the world, at least—'

'Yes?' she urged when he didn't go on.

'Nothing.'

'She gave herself to the world, meaning I don't?'

'I think you prefer to withdraw and hide deep inside yourself.'

She laughed. 'That's one way of putting it. You said I looked grim and forbidding, and recently someone said I looked like a prison wardress.'

'To your face?'

'No, he didn't realise that I could hear.'

'You sound remarkably cheerful about it. Most women would be hurt or offended.'

'I'm not most women.'

'Indeed you're not. I'm beginning to understand that.'

'In my job it's an advantage if people think I'm dreary. They ignore me and overlook me, which is useful. You learn a lot when people have forgotten you're there.'

'But you're not at work every hour. What about the rest of the time?'

She gave a carefully calculated shrug. 'What rest of the time? Life is work, making a profit, turning everything to your advantage. What else?'

'You say that but you don't live by it, otherwise you wouldn't let your family bleed you dry.'

She shrugged. 'Their needs just mean that I have to make twice as much profit, be twice as determined to manage life my way. Eventually I'll make so much money that I can afford to help them *and* become a financial tyrant.'

'It has to be a tyrant, does it?'

'They seem to be the kind that flourish best.'

'Some people think there are other things that matter.' He was watching her.

'Some people are losers,' she observed.

'They certainly are,' he said slowly. 'No doubt about that. But not us. That's true, isn't it?'

'That's definitely true.'

The champagne arrived. Marcel filled both glasses and raised his. 'I think we should toast ourselves. To us and what we're going to achieve.' They clinked.

'I'm looking forward to the moment when you see La Couronne.'

'Am I going to?'

'Yes, I think we should head there as soon as possible. My lawyer here can deal with the formalities. When you've seen what there is in Paris you'll be better placed to take charge in London.'

'I must warn you that my French is very poor.'

'Really? I thought such an efficient lady must be an expert.'

'I know a few words—very limited—'

Mon seul amour, je t'aime pour toujours—

Words of passionate adoration that she had learned from him, and repeated with all her heart. To please him, as a surprise, she'd started to learn the language properly, but their parting had come before she could tell him.

'Don't worry,' he said now. 'There are so many English tourists in Paris that I insist that all my employees speak the language.'

'How long will I need to be in Paris?'

'Several weeks at least. Is that a problem?'

'No, but I shall need to sort out my affairs here. Perhaps I can take tomorrow off to make my arrangements.'

'Very well. Do you have other relatives? I assume you have no children since your sister and her family take so much from you. But what about Mr Henshaw? Does he have no claims?'

'None,' she said shortly. She held out her glass. 'Can I have another champagne?'

When Marcel had filled her glass she rose and went to the edge of the roof, leaning on the wall and looking down at London, where the lights had come on, glimmering in the darkness.

Mr Henshaw had never existed, although there had been a husband, one who still haunted her nightmares. She tried never to think of him and mostly succeeded, with that inner control that had become her most notable characteristic. But now events had brought him back so that he seemed to be there, infusing the air about her with fear and horror.

And there was no escape.

CHAPTER FIVE

LIFE with Jake had been a nightmare. He'd set his heart on marrying her and pestered her morning, noon and night. She'd refused, clinging to the hope that Marcel would come looking for her. Even after the agony of their last meeting she thought it might happen. He would suffer, lying in the darkness for long, sleepless nights, and during those nights the memories would come back to him. He would relive the joy of their youthful love, and at last he would realise that such love could never end in the way that theirs had seemed to. Then he would search for her, rescue her, and they would be together again.

But it hadn't happened. Days had become weeks, weeks passed into months and the silence stretched ahead endlessly. At last she'd faced the truth. Marcel hated her. For him she no longer existed. There would be no reunion, no hope of future happiness.

In this state of despair all energy had seemed to leave her. She no longer had the vigour to fight, and when Jake had marched in one day, seized her hand and slid a magnificent engagement ring onto it, she simply stared and left it there.

After that he was shrewd enough to move fast, arranging the wedding for the soonest possible date and never letting her out of his sight. In only one matter did she find the strength to oppose him, declaring that she would not be married in church. It must be a civil ceremony only. She refused to insult any religious establishment with this mockery of a wedding. Jake didn't care. As long as he claimed her it didn't matter how.

The ring he gave her was a spectacular creation of diamonds and sapphires, clearly designed to be a trophy. It was Jake's proof that he owned her.

The three years of her marriage were strange and haunted. He swore a thousand times that he was madly in love with her, and she came to believe that, in his own way, he was. He was cruel and egotistical, grasping whatever he wanted and careless of whom he hurt. But, like many selfish brutes, he had a sentimental streak. Cassie had a hold on his heart that nobody else could claim, and he took this as proof of his own humanity.

It gave her a kind of power, and she discovered that power could be enjoyable, especially when it was all you had. Jake's eagerness to please her was ironic, but she could use it to make him give money to charity. She supported two particular charities, one for children, one for animals, and for them she extracted as much as she could from Jake.

Afterwards he expected to be repaid. 'Now you'll be nice to me, won't you?' he'd say, and she would yield to the night that followed, trying not to show her revulsion. What Jake called 'love-making' was so horribly different to what she had known with Marcel that it came from another universe, one where she had to endure being slobbered over and violated.

At first she tried to pretend that she was back in the arms of her true love, but the contrast was so cruel that she gave it up in sheer self-defence. Otherwise she would have genuinely gone mad.

It was almost a relief to become pregnant, and have an excuse to banish Jake from her bed. Slightly to her surprise he accepted her decision without argument. At the thought of producing the next generation his sentimental streak was asserting itself again, and he withdrew to protect her.

And now she could at least feel that life held out some hope for her. She would have a child to love, a purpose in life.

But after five months she miscarried. No doctor could tell her why. There had been no accident, no trauma. It had simply happened, leaving her staring into a blank future.

Hope came from an unexpected source. By chance she discovered that Jake had been playing around.

'It's not my fault,' he defended himself. 'It's months since we could…well, it'll be different now.'

'Yes, it's going to be different,' she agreed. 'I'm divorcing you.'

His howls of protest left her unmoved, and so did his threats.

'If you want to destroy me, Jake, go ahead. What do you think is left to destroy? Do your worst. I don't care.'

Perhaps it was the thought of how many of his disreputable secrets she'd learned that warned him to be cautious. But something made him cave in. Before he could change his mind she hurled back at him every expensive gift he'd ever given her, including the engagement ring. Then she moved out the same day.

He made one last attempt to persuade her to remain his wife. When that failed he tried to get her to accept a financial settlement.

She agreed to very little for the sake of her family, but took nothing for herself. 'If I live off your money you'll still think you control me,' she told him. 'And I want to forget that you ever existed.'

He paled. 'You're breaking my heart,' he choked.

And he meant it, she thought afterwards. Oddly enough, this unpleasant man had a heart to break, where she was concerned. But it left her untouched. She no longer feared him. All she felt was a heady sensation of power at having brought him down.

She rejected his name, calling herself Henshaw because it had been her mother's maiden name, and using the 'Mrs' because she thought it made her sound older and more serious.

Refusing to live off Jake's money satisfied her but left her penniless. There was no chance of returning to modelling, even if she'd wanted to. Most people would still have called her beautiful, but she felt her magic 'something' had vanished for ever. She'd taken any menial job she could get, using her free time to go to evening classes, studying business to the point of exhaustion. She'd emerged triumphant, going to work in a bank and climbing fast. She had never looked back.

Now she was near the top of the tree, trying to believe it had all been worth it.

But as she looked back at Marcel, sitting quietly, watching her, she was filled with such a rush of hostility that she could have struck him down and enjoyed doing it.

You could have saved me, she thought. *If I'd known who you really were I'd have appealed to your father, and everything could have been different. Oh, why weren't you honest with me? You could have saved me from Jake, from that terrible marriage, losing my child. You could have stopped me turning into a heartless robot, but when it happened I had nowhere to turn. Damn you!*

'What's the matter?' Marcel asked, rising and coming beside her. 'You look upset.'

'Not at all,' she said brightly. 'I was just enjoying the view and the fresh air.'

'Come away from the ledge.' He led her firmly back to the table and stood over her until she was seated.

'Go on telling me about your life,' he said. 'What happened to your husband? Did you walk out on him?'

Like I did with you, you mean? she thought ironically. *That's what you're thinking right now, although you won't come out and say so.*

'Yes, I left him,' she said. 'But only because he was sleeping with someone else.'

Let's see what you make of that! If you want revenge I've just given it to you. But is that what you want? If only I knew.

'I hope he made some financial provision for you,' Marcel said politely.

'I wouldn't let him. It would have given him a hold on me, and no man has that. Ever.'

'When you finish with a man you really finish with him,' he murmured.

'It's the only way.' She gave a sharp, defiant laugh. 'When I've finished with him, he no longer exists.'

'No looking back?'

'Looking back is scary,' she whispered. 'It fills you with hate and makes you want to do things that you know you shouldn't, so then the person you hate is yourself.'

She didn't look at him as she said it. She didn't dare. And his reply was so soft that another person might have missed it. But she was alive to everything about him, and she heard the quiet words with their ominous warning.

'That's very true.'

She glanced at him just in time to meet his eyes, but not in time to read their expression before he looked away. She waited, hoping that he would turn back to her and they might even find a way to talk. But his eyes were fixed on the distance and the silence between them was as deafening as a roar.

All around them the lights were sparkling, arranged in arches by the walls, with dainty lamps near the tables.

The atmosphere on the roof had changed, grown softer, sentimental. This was a place for romantic trysts, with lovers' eyes meeting over the rims of wine glasses. Here there should be smiles of heartfelt understanding, unspoken promises of love. It was a world apart and anyone who did not belong in that world had no right to be here.

I don't belong, she thought wearily. *I did once. Not any more.*

Nearby was a couple sitting close together. The man was middle-aged and heavy. The girl was about twenty, gorgeous and flaunting it. She might have been the young Cassie.

'I guess there's no point in me trying to talk to him tonight,' said a male voice nearby. 'Sorry,' he added hastily, as Marcel and Cassie turned to look at him. 'It's just that I'd planned to talk business with that fellow.'

Marcel grinned. 'No chance now.'

'We should never have agreed to meet here. Too many good-time girls as a distraction. I gather this place is known for it. Everywhere you look there's a lush female trying to seduce a man into parting from his money.' He seemed to become aware of Cassie and hastily added, 'Forgive me. Not you, of course!'

'Of course,' she said.

'I mean you're obviously a very…sensible…businesslike woman, and I didn't mean to insult you.'

She regarded him with ironic humour. 'You mean it's quite impossible that I could ever lead a man down dark and dangerous paths? Some women would be more insulted by that than the other.'

'Look I…put my foot in it. I apologise.'

He retreated in a flurry of embarrassment.

'Well, you certainly made him sorry,' Marcel declared.

She managed to laugh. 'I did, didn't I? His face!'

The man had gone to join the couple at the other table,

talking wildly and making gestures, clearly explaining something to them. He glanced up, saw Cassie looking at him and gave her an embarrassed grin.

'He's terrified of me,' she murmured to Marcel.

'And you don't mind?'

'Why should I mind? I don't want to lead him down "dark and dangerous paths". Hey, the girl's looking at me now. I wonder if she's taking warning.'

'That your gaze might turn her to stone?' Marcel hazarded hilariously.

'No, that a woman can start out like her and end like me. Not that she'd believe it.'

She had a dizzying sensation of going too far. Surely now Marcel must be remembering the dark and dangerous paths down which they'd travelled together, and reading the truth in her eyes. But the time was not right. If things had been different she could have told him everything now, but that was impossible until he could bring himself to admit that he knew who she was.

And that day might never come.

Suddenly she doubted that she had the strength for this. She wanted to cry aloud and flee him. She even moved to rise from her seat, but his hand detained her.

'Are you all right? You look troubled.'

His voice was gentle, his eyes warm and concerned. It was as though another man had taken him over, or perhaps lured him back to the past, and it was her undoing.

'Look, I must go. It's late and I'm tired—'

'Of course. I'll take you home.'

'No!' The word was almost violent. 'No, there's no need for that. I'll be all right.'

'I'll tell Hotel Reception to send a car to the front for you. Then you'll be free of me.'

'It's not that—' she began wildly.

'Yes, it is,' he said. 'It's like that for both of us.' His voice grew softer, more intense. 'We both need some time to get our heads together.' His eyes met hers. 'Don't we?'

She nodded dumbly.

He escorted her out of the hotel and to the waiting car, assisted her into a seat at the rear, then stood with the door still open, leaning in slightly, holding onto her hand.

'It's all right about going to Paris, isn't it?' he asked.

'Of course.'

'Then be ready to travel tomorrow.'

'Tomorrow? But you said I could have the day off to sort out—'

'I've changed my mind. There's no time. You'll have to do it long-distance when you get there. I'll collect you at nine tomorrow morning.' His hand tightened on hers. 'You will be there, won't you?'

'Of course.'

'You won't vanish?'

'No.'

'Promise me.' His voice was almost harsh in its intensity.

'I promise,' she said.

His eyes held hers and for a moment she thought he would refuse to let go of her hand. But then he released her suddenly, slammed the door and stepped back. Her last view of him was standing there, completely still, his eyes fixed on the retreating car like a man clinging on to a vanishing hope.

He watched her until she was out of sight, then took out his phone and dialled a number given to him by his father. It was a private security firm. In a hard voice he gave her address.

'These are your instructions. You park outside and watch. If she comes out with a suitcase and gets into a taxi you call me. Then follow her. And don't let her out of your sight for a moment.'

* * *

In her time with Jake, Cassie had grown used to his ways of flaunting his wealth and what he fondly believed to be his status. He would book the most expensive seats on planes, then arrive at the last minute with the maximum of fuss.

Marcel, in contrast, reached the airport early, got through the formalities with courtesy and was driven quietly to the private jet that was waiting for him.

'My father's,' he explained.

The plane was pure luxury. It could seat eight people in soft, comfortable seats, and had its own galley from which food and drink was served to the two of them by a steward who existed solely for their comfort.

As they began to move down the runway he said, 'The weather's fine so it should be a smooth flight. Nothing to worry about.'

So he remembered that she was afraid of flying, she thought. After one modelling job she'd returned home still shaken and distraught from a bumpy flight. How bright his eyes had been, how full of expectancy for the night of passion to come. And how quickly he'd forgotten all thoughts of his own pleasure to take her trembling body in his arms and soothe her tenderly. There had been no sex that night, and in the morning she had loved him more than ever for his generosity.

'Have you ever been to Paris?' he asked now.

'No, but I've always wanted to. I'm looking forward to exploring it.'

'You won't have time for that. You'll live in the hotel, and have a desk in my office. Everything will be provided to help with your work and you'll be "confined to barracks", forbidden to leave.'

For a moment she almost thought he meant it, but just in time she saw the gleam of wicked humour in his eyes.

'Yeah, right!' she said cynically.

'You don't believe me? Wait until you see the locks on the doors.'

'Nonsense!'

'That's no way to talk to your employer.'

'If you were any other employer I wouldn't, but we both know that I'm not just here to study the facts of La Couronne. I'm here to absorb the atmosphere, and that means the atmosphere of the city as well.'

'Very subtle,' he said appreciatively. 'So you'll arrange the job to suit yourself.'

'It's what I'm good at,' she said impishly. 'Being in control.'

He grinned. She smiled back, happy in this brief moment of warmth and ease between them. But then a scream burst from her as the plane jerked and plunged a few feet.

'Sorry,' came the pilot's voice. 'Air pocket. It's going to be a little turbulent.'

'Don't worry.' Marcel took both her hands in his. 'It'll be over soon. There's no danger.'

'I know it's not dangerous,' she said huskily. 'It's just… being shaken…'

'Just hold onto me.' His hands tightened.

She did so, closing her eyes and shaking her head. It was foolish to be scared but she couldn't help it. As the plane shuddered she whispered, 'No, no, no—'

'Look at me,' Marcel commanded. 'Open your eyes.'

She did so, and the world vanished. His gaze held hers as firmly as if he had her in chains. And they were the most dangerous chains of all because she had no wish to break them.

'It's all right,' he said. 'It's finishing now.'

He was right. The plane's juddering was fading, then ceasing altogether. But that wasn't why the sense of peace and safety was stealing over her. She held him tightly because while he was there nothing could go wrong.

'I'm sorry,' she said in a shaking voice. 'It's stupid to be scared—'

'We all have our nightmares. They don't have to make sense.'

She managed an edgy laugh. 'So much for being in control.'

'We'd all like to be in control,' he said quietly. 'And we all spend our lives discovering how wrong we are.'

'No,' she said defensively. 'I don't believe it has to be like that.'

'I only wish you were right.'

He looked down at their hands, still clasped, and gently released her. She had to suppress the impulse to hold on, refusing to let him go. But she must not give in. She was strong. She was in control. She'd just said so.

At the airport a limousine was waiting to convey them into the heart of Paris. She watched in delight as the landmarks glided past, and they came to a halt in the Champs Elysées in the glamorous heart of the city.

La Couronne towered above her, grandiose and beautiful. Stewards hurried forward to greet their employer and regard herself with curiosity. One of them seized Cassie's bags and invited her to follow him.

'I'll join you later,' Marcel said.

Her accommodation was high up, a luxurious suite where a maid was waiting for her. She'd been wondering what to expect, but the reality took her breath away.

'My name is Tina,' said the maid. 'I am here to serve you. I will start unpacking.'

'Thank you. I'll go and freshen up.'

She went into the bathroom and regarded herself critically in the mirror. Marcel had told her to soften her appearance, but so far she hadn't done so. On the journey he'd glanced at her appearance but made no comment. Now she loosened her hair, letting it fall about her face, not in waves as he'd once known it, but long and straight.

I'm not really Cassie any more, she thought. *I've been fooling myself.*

Sighing in frustration, she left the bathroom and immediately halted at the sight that met her eyes.

'Tina let me in,' Marcel said. 'I came to see how you were settling. If you're ready I'll show you around.'

'Fine, I'm almost finished. I'll just—' She raised a hand to her hair, but he stopped her.

'Leave it.'

'But it's all over the place. I can't go around looking as though I'd been pulled through a hedge backwards.'

'True, but it won't take much to make you a little neater. Just brush it back here—and here—'

As he spoke he was flicking his fingers against her blonde locks, sending them spinning back over her shoulders, then smoothing them away. She tried not to be conscious of his fingertips softly brushing her face, but some things could never be driven away. The touch of a lover's hand, the feel of his breath whispering against her face in agitated waves.

But he's no longer my lover. Remember that.

Firmly she pushed feelings aside. She couldn't afford them.

'Let's go,' she said. 'I really want to see the hotel.'

'I suppose you've read enough to know the background,' he said, showing her outside.

'I know it was once the home of the Marquis de Montpelier, a friend of royalty, who could have anything he wanted, including three wives, five mistresses and more children than he could count.'

'Until the Revolution began, and they all went to the guillotine,' Marcel supplied. 'If you look out of this window you can almost see the place where they died.'

There in the distance she could just make out the Place de la Concorde, where the guillotine had once stood.

'I wonder how often they looked at that view, never dreaming of what would happen to them in the end,' she murmured.

Now, she thought, their palace was the centre of a business empire, and the man who controlled it was safely armoured against all life could do to him.

'Some of the building still looks as it did then,' Marcel told her. 'I keep it that way for the historical interest. Plus I have a friend who claims to have second sight and swears she can see the ghosts of the Montpelier family, carrying their heads under their arms.'

'And you make the most of it,' she said, amused.

'Let's say the rooms on that corridor are always the first to be hired.'

'Do you live on that corridor?'

He grinned. 'No, I don't like to be disturbed by howling spectres.'

As they went over the building she recorded her impressions into a small microphone while Marcel listened, impressed.

'Now let's go to my apartment,' he said, 'unless you're tired.'

'No, let's keep working.'

She was eager to see where he lived and learn what it could tell her about his present personality. But when they arrived she was disappointed. Only the room he used as an office was accessible. The rest was kept hidden behind closed doors.

'I'll be back in a moment,' he said. 'Access anything you want on the computer.'

He went out into the corridor, and she began to familiarise herself with his computer, which was state-of-the-art. She had expected no less. There was a mountain of information for her to take in and she went quickly from one item to the next. A casual onlooker would think she couldn't possibly be absorbing information with such brief glances, but that would be a mistake. She had a photographic memory, which in the old days she'd hidden because it clashed with her sexy image. Marcel had been one of the few people to discover that beneath the ditzy surface was a mind like a machine.

That was it!

She gasped as she realised that she had the answer to the question that had teased her. When she and Marcel had exchanged phone details yesterday, she'd offered to return his and he'd said, 'You could have memorised it by now.'

She'd barely glanced at the scrap of paper, yet he'd known that would be enough for her because he knew something about her that no stranger could have known.

'A great brain', he'd called her, laughing as he clasped her in his arms.

'How do I dare to make love to a woman with such a great brain? A mighty brain! A genius! Some men might find that intimidating.'

'But not you, hmm?'

'No, because she has other virtues. Come here!'

Now, sitting in Marcel's office, she began to shake with the violence of the emotion possessing her. She'd guessed that he recognised her, but now she was sure. He had brought her here, to the heart of his own world. Couldn't she dare to hope that they might open their arms to each other and put right the wrongs of the past?

She'd thought she wanted vengeance, but that was being crowded out by other sensations beyond her control.

Now was the moment, and she would seize it with eager hands. If only he would return quickly.

She heard footsteps in the corridor. He was coming. In just a few moments everything would be transformed. The old attraction was beginning to rise up inside her, and surely it was the same with him. There might even be happiness again.

But the next instant the dream died, smashed to smithereens by something she knew she should have anticipated, but had carelessly overlooked.

Which meant there was no one to blame but herself.

CHAPTER SIX

FROM outside came an urgent tapping on the door and a woman's voice in a high-pitched scream of excitement.

'Marcel, mon chéri—ouvrez le porte et me prendre dans tes bras. Oh, combien je suis heureux que mon véritable amour est de retour.'

Her limited French was just up to translating this.

'Marcel, my darling—open the door and take me in your arms. Oh, how happy I am that my true love has returned.'

So that was that. Another stupid fantasy destroyed.

Don't be so naïve again!

Bringing herself under control, she opened the door and backed away just in time to avoid being lovingly throttled by a girl who was young, sexy, beautiful, vibrant with life.

And she'd called Marcel 'my true love'.

The newcomer began to babble again in French, then switched abruptly to English.

'I'm sorry—you must be Mrs Henshaw—and English, yes?'

'Yes.'

'Marcel has told us all about you.'

'Us?'

'My papa is Raul Lenoir, Marcel's lawyer. He has spoken much of Mrs Henshaw, his new assistant who will handle important business for him in London. I am so pleased to meet you.'

Cassie took the hand she held out, murmuring untruthfully, 'And I am pleased to meet you.'

'My name is Brigitte Lenoir. Where is Marcel? I have missed him so much.'

'He went out a moment ago, but he'll be back soon.'

'Oh I can't wait. I have so much to tell him.'

'I think that's him now.'

The door opened and Marcel appeared, his face brightening as he saw his visitor. They next moment they were in each other's arms. Brigitte covered his face with kisses and he laughed, returning the compliment again and again.

'Brigitte, *ma chérie, mon amante*—'

Cassie returned to the computer, trying not to hear the sounds coming from behind her.

'Brigitte, I want you to meet Mrs Henshaw,' Marcel said at last, freeing himself from her clasp.

'But we have already met, and I am so impressed,' Brigitte declared.

'So you should be,' Marcel said. 'She's a great brain and we're all afraid of her.'

'Papa will be most interested to meet her. You must both come to dinner with us tonight.'

Cassie flinched. 'I'm not sure—'

'Oh, but you must,' Brigitte assured her.

Both her mind and heart rebelled at the thought of spending an evening with these two, watching them all over each other.

'I have a lot of work to do—'

Brigitte began to mutter in French. Without understanding every word, Cassie gathered that she was telling Marcel that he must persuade her. Another woman was vital and Mrs Henshaw would be useful.

'She's just what we need. She can keep Henri talking without—you know—'

The meaning of 'you know' was all too clear. Whoever Henri was, her duty was to keep him talking without attracting him in a way that might be 'inconvenient'. In other words, a plain woman. Like Mrs Henshaw.

'I applaud your desire to work,' Marcel told her, 'but joining us for dinner tonight will be part of that work. We'll dine in the hotel's most splendid restaurant, and you can give me your opinion of it later. Now, I suggest you return to your suite and prepare for tonight.'

Leaving him free to succumb to Brigitte's charms, she thought. As she walked away down the corridor she could hear shrieks of laughter which abruptly faded into murmurs. She increased her speed.

In her rooms she found Tina just finishing, and complimented her on the job.

'It looks so comfortable in here. If only I could just put my feet up, but I've got to attend a formal dinner tonight, with the lawyer and somebody called Henri. Why? What's up?' Tina had smothered a laugh.

'Forgive me, *madame,* but if Henri Lenoir is there it will not be formal.'

'You know him?'

'He is the son of the lawyer and Mademoiselle Brigitte's brother. But apart from that—' Tina hesitated before going on, 'Every girl knows him. He is a very naughty man. The rumour says that his wife has thrown him out for the third time.'

'Because of—?'

'Because he's naughty with many ladies. They say he's returned to his father's home, and the family is watching over him to make sure that…well…'

'That he isn't naughty again. I see.'

'If he behaves she may take him back.'

And evidently Brigitte saw no danger of her brother misbehaving with Mrs Henshaw. It was practically an insult.

When Tina had gone she threw herself onto the bed, reliving the scene she had just endured. Something had happened that hurt more than anything else so far.

A great brain!

That was what Marcel had called her to Brigitte, but using the words so differently from the way he had once spoken them to herself that now the tears welled up and she rolled over, burying her face in the pillow. Suddenly there was only despair, with nothing to hope for, and she yielded to the darkness, weeping until she was too drained to weep any more.

As she recovered she realised that Marcel hadn't given her details about when, where and how to present herself tonight. Quickly she called his cellphone, but it had been switched off. She tried his hotel phone but it stayed unanswered.

Whatever he was doing left him with no attention for anything else.

She stared up at the ceiling, aware that she had reached a crossroads. Since Marcel had reappeared in her life she'd been cautious to the point of dithering.

'Not any more,' she vowed. 'Time for a final decision, and I'm making it.'

When Brigitte had finally departed Marcel paced the floor restlessly.

Today he'd shocked himself by doing things he'd never intended, and not doing things he'd vowed were essential.

He'd brought Cassie here to redress the past, although the meaning of that was still vague in his mind. To let her see the riches she'd thrown away, show her the life she could have had instead of the bleak impoverished existence she had now—yes, definitely.

Revenge? Possibly.

But during the flight there had been an unexpected change. At the first sign that she might be vulnerable he'd known a passionate desire to protect her. It was what he'd felt long ago and she'd thrown it back in his face, yet it had leapt out of the darkness at him, like an animal waiting to pounce. And, weakling that he was, he'd yielded to it.

No more weakness. Bringing her here had been a risk, but he wouldn't back down now. One day soon he would confront her with all the memories she seemed determined to avoid. Then she would answer for what she had done to him.

But that must wait until he was ready.

In one sense at least Cassie and Mrs Henshaw were the same person. When a decision was taken there were no second thoughts, no weakening, only a determined follow-through to the end.

This particular decision took her downstairs on winged feet, heading for the fashion shop at the back of the hotel. After studying several glamorous gowns she rejected them all in favour of a pair of tight black satin trousers. Only a woman with her very slender figure could have worn such a garment, but that suited her just fine. To go with them she bought a black silk top with a plunging neckline and bare arms.

It was outrageous, and for a brief moment she hesitated. But then she recalled Brigitte's face that afternoon, not in the least troubled by the sight of her.

'So you're not afraid of Mrs Henshaw,' she addressed the vision. 'Let's see if Cassie can scare you.' She gave a brief laugh. 'Perhaps she ought to. She's beginning to scare me.'

At the beauty salon she described how she wanted to look, aware of the stares of the assistants, incredulous that this plain Jane could indulge such fantasies. But they smiled and got to work, and when they'd finished her curled hair was tumbling over her shoulders, partly—but only partly—hiding her daring décolletage.

Back in her room she inspected the satin trousers, wondering if she was being wise. She had a dress that would do. It was adequate rather than outstanding, but that might just be better than outrageous.

She tried on the dress, then removed it and donned the trousers, fighting temptation as she studied her magnificent appearance in the mirror.

'Oh, heck!' she sighed at last. 'I can't do it, can I? But one day I will do it. I must. I can't settle for being "adequate" for ever, but just for tonight maybe I should.'

There was a knock at the door.

'I'm coming,' she called without opening it. 'Just give me a moment.'

'No, now,' came Marcel's voice. 'I need to talk to you at once.'

She opened the door, pulling it back against her and retreating so that she was mostly concealed behind it. Even so, he could see the cascade of her glorious hair and it stopped him short.

She could have screamed with frustration. The stunned look on his face was the one she'd longed to see, but what maddening fate had made it happen just at this moment?

'Mrs…I don't…I wasn't expecting…' He was stammering, which would have filled her with delight at any other time.

'You said I should look less severe,' she told him loftily. 'Is this sufficiently "un-severe" for you?'

'I…that wasn't…yes…I suppose…'

The last time she'd seen him lost for words was nine years ago when her landlady had walked in when they were lying naked on the floor.

'I'm glad you approve,' she said now, still taking care to

conceal as much of herself as possible. 'Is the Lenoir family here yet?'

'Part of it. Madame Lenoir won't be coming, but there's—'

'Marcel, *ou êtes vous?*' Brigitte's voice came floating down the corridor.

'I'm here, *chérie*.'

She was speaking French in a low voice, clearly meaning not to be overheard. Even so, Cassie managed to make out enough to learn that the mysterious Henri was reluctant to attend the dinner, not wanting to be saddled with 'the English woman nobody else wanted'. He'd agreed only on condition that he could leave early. Marcel gave a sharp intake of breath, but could say no more because of sounds from further along the corridor. Two men were approaching, hailing them, receiving Marcel's greeting in return. Then they were in the room, full of polite bonhomie.

'We can't wait to meet the brilliant lady you've brought with you,' Monsieur Lenoir declared. 'Isn't that so, Henri?'

'I've been looking forward to this moment all day,' came a courteous if unconvincing voice. 'Where is she?'

'Here,' Cassie said, stepping out from behind the door.

With the first glance Cassie understood everything she'd heard about Henri. Good looking in a 'pretty boy' style, he had a self-indulgent manner and dark hair worn slightly too long for his age, which she guessed at about forty. Definitely a 'naughty man', fighting the years.

His behaviour confirmed it. He was wide-eyed at the vision that confronted him.

'Madame,' he murmured, 'I am more glad to meet you than I can say.' He advanced with his hands out. 'What an evening we are going to have!'

He would have thrown his arms around Cassie, but she stopped him by placing her hands in his. Nothing daunted, he kissed the back of each hand. Then he jerked her forward and in this way managed to embrace her. Turning her head against his shoulder, she had a searing vision of Marcel's face as he gained his first complete sight of her.

What she saw would stay with her for ever. For one blinding second he looked like a man struck over the heart—astonished, bewildered, aghast, shattered. But in the next instant it was all gone, and only a stone mask remained.

No matter. She'd seen all that she needed to see. He'd expected to find Mrs Henshaw, but Cassie's ghost had walked and nothing would ever be the same.

Now she was glad there hadn't been time to change into something more respectable. There was a time for restraint and a time for defiance. Mrs Henshaw would have been left floundering, but Cassie was the expert.

Monsieur Lenoir cleared his throat and came forward, sounding embarrassed. 'Madame Henshaw, allow me to introduce my son.'

'Well, I think he's already introduced himself,' Cassie said with a little giggle.

'But you haven't introduced *your*self,' Henri said.

Brigitte intervened. 'Mrs Henshaw is masterminding Marcel's purchase of the London hotel.'

'That's a bit of an exaggeration,' Cassie said hastily. 'I'm not exactly masterminding it.'

'But Marcel says that you are a great brain,' Brigitte reminded her.

'I'm no such thing,' she defended herself.

Henri gave an exaggerated sigh of relief. 'Thank goodness for that. Brainy women terrify me.'

'Then you've nothing to fear from me,' she cooed, giving him her best teasing smile.

'But you must be brainy or Marcel wouldn't have employed you,' Brigitte pointed out.

'That's true,' Cassie said as if suddenly realising. 'I must be brighter than I thought.'

Her eyes met Marcel's, seeing in them floundering confusion wrestling ineffectively with anger. She was beginning to enjoy herself.

'It's time were going,' Monsieur Lenoir declared, edging his son firmly out of the way and offering Cassie his arm. 'Madame Henshaw, may I have the pleasure of escorting you?'

'The pleasure is mine,' she replied.

But then Henri too stepped forward, offering his other arm so that she walked out of the door with a man on each side, leaving Marcel to follow with Brigitte.

They made a glamorous spectacle as they went along the corridor, the men in dinner jackets and bow ties, Brigitte in flowing evening gown, and Cassie in her luxurious black satin that left nothing to the imagination.

Perhaps that was why Marcel never so much as glanced at her as they went down in the elevator.

But as they stepped out and headed for the restaurant he raised his voice. 'Mrs Henshaw, there's a small matter of business we need to clear up before the evening starts. The rest of you go on and we'll join you.'

His hand on her arm was urgent, holding her back and drawing her around a corner, where there was nobody to see them.

'Just what do you think you're doing?' he muttered furiously.

'Being civil to the people who are important to you.'

'You know what I mean—the way you're dressed—'

'But you told me to.'

'I—?'

'Be less severe, you said. And only today you brushed my hair forward so that—'

'Never mind that,' he said hastily.

'I'm only doing what I thought you wanted. Oh, dear!' She gasped as if in shocked discovery. 'Didn't I go far enough? Should the neckline be lower?'

She took hold as though to pull it down but he seized her hands in his own. Instinctively her fingers tightened on his, drawing them against her skin, so that she felt him next to the swell of her breasts just before they vanished into the neckline.

He stood for a moment as though fighting to move but unable to find the strength. There was murder in his eyes.

'Damn you!' he said softly. *'Damn you, Cassie!'*

He wrenched his hands free and stormed off without waiting for her to reply. She clutched the wall, her chest rising and falling as conflicting emotions raced through her. The signals coming from him had been of violence and hostility but, far from fearing him, she was full of triumph.

He recognised her. He'd admitted it.

He'd blurted it out against his better judgement and they both knew it. Whatever the future held, thus far the battle was hers.

As she turned the corner she saw that he was still there, standing by the door through which they must go. He offered her his arm without meeting her eyes, and together they went on their way.

The others were waiting for them just inside the restaurant, agog with curiosity, but their polite smiles acted as masks and curiosity went unsatisfied. Monsieur Lenoir pulled out a chair, indicating for her to sit beside him, and Henri nimbly seized the place on her other side. For a moment she thought Marcel would say something, but Brigitte touched his cheek and he hastened to smile at her.

Cassie looked about her, fascinated. Chandeliers hung from the ceiling, golden ornaments hung from the walls. The glasses were of the finest crystal, just as the champagne being poured into them was also the finest.

She wasn't usually impressed by luxury, having seen much of it in earlier years, but there was an elegance about this place that appealed to her. She sipped the champagne appreciatively, then took a notebook from her bag and began to scribble.

'What are you doing?' Henri murmured in a tone that suggested conspiracy.

'Observing,' she said briskly. 'That's what I'm here for.'

'Surely not,' he murmured. 'You're here to have a wonderful time with a man who admires you more than any other woman in the world.'

'No, I'm here to do a job,' she said severely. 'Monsieur Falcon has employed me for my efficiency—'

'Ah, but efficiency at what?' His eyes, raking her shape left no doubt of his meaning.

'At business matters,' she informed him in her best 'prison-wardress' voice.

'But there's business and business,' he pointed out. 'It's not just facts and figures he wants from you, I'll bet.'

'Monsieur Lenoir!' she exclaimed.

'Henri, please. I already feel that we know each other well.'

'Henri, I'm shocked!'

'And I'll bet you don't shock easily. Do go on.'

'You cannot know me well if you think *that* of me.'

'Think what of you?' he asked with an innocence that would have fooled anyone not forewarned. 'I don't know what you mean.'

'I'm sure you do.'

'Well, perhaps. I can't imagine Marcel wasting you on business efficiency when you have so many other lavish talents. He's known as a man with an eye for the ladies.'

He inclined his head slightly to where Marcel was sitting. Cassie waited for him to glance across at her, disapproving of Henri's attention, but he didn't. He seemed engrossed by Brigitte, sitting beside him, his eyes fixed on her as though nothing else existed in the world. Suddenly he smiled into her eyes and Cassie had to check a gasp. Surely no man smiled at a woman like that unless he meant it with all his heart?

There was a welcome distraction in choosing the food, which was of the high standard she'd expected. While they ate Henri surprised her by talking sensibly. Her questions about Paris received knowledgeable answers and she was able to listen with such genuine interest that when Marcel spoke to her across the table she failed to hear him.

'I'm sorry…what…?' she stammered.

'I was merely recommending the wine,' he said. 'It's a rare vintage and a speciality of this hotel.'

'Of course, yes. Thank you.'

'Never mind him,' Henri said. 'Let me finish telling you—'

'You've had your turn,' Monsieur Lenoir objected. 'I may be an old man, but I'm not too old to appreciate a beautiful woman.' He gave a rich chuckle. Liking him, Cassie gave him her most gracious smile and they were soon deep in conversation. On the surface he was more civilised and restrained than his son, but his observations about Paris tended to linger on the shadowy romantic places. Clearly Henri wasn't her only admirer.

At last an orchestra struck up and dancers took to the floor. Monsieur Lenoir extended his hand and she followed him cheerfully.

He was a reasonably good dancer for his age and weight, but what he really wanted, as she soon discovered, was to flaunt his sexy young companion, enjoying envious gazes from other men. She laughed and indulged him, careful not to go too far, and they finally left the floor, laughing together in perfect accord.

Henri was waiting for them, looking theatrically forlorn.

'I'm all alone,' he mourned. 'You've got my father. Marcel and Brigitte look like they're set up for the night.'

'Yes, they do, don't they,' Cassie said, observing them from a distance, dancing with eyes only for each other.

'So when will it be my turn?' Henri wanted to know.

'Right now,' she said firmly. 'Do you mind my leaving you alone?' This was to Monsieur Lenoir.

'No, you two young things go and enjoy yourself. I'm puffed.'

Before she knew it she was spinning around the floor. Henri was a good dancer. So was she, she suddenly remembered. How long had it been since she'd had the chance to let go and really enjoy herself?

For a little while she gave herself up to the thrill of moving fast. Her mind seemed to be linked to Henri, so that when he waggled his hips she instinctively did the same, and heard cheers and applause from the rest of the floor. The world was spinning by in a series of visions. They came and went in her consciousness, but the one that was always there was Marcel, watching her with narrowed, furious eyes. No matter how often she turned, he always seemed to be directly in front of her. She blinked and he vanished. And yet he was still there, because he was always there.

As the dance ended there was a mini riot, with Henri indicating that he wanted to partner her again, and at least three other men prepared to challenge for the privilege. But they all backed off when they saw Marcel, with murder in his eyes, stretching out his hand to her.

'My dance, I think,' he said.

His voice was soft but dangerous, and tonight danger had an edge that she relished.

'I don't think so,' she said with a challenging glance at her other suitors. 'I think you have to wait your turn.'

It was a crazy thing to say but she couldn't have stopped

herself for anything in the world. Suddenly she felt herself yanked fiercely against him, his arm so tight about her that she was breathless.

'I wait for no man,' he said. Then, in a voice even softer and more menacing than before, he added, 'And no woman.'

'Then I guess I have no choice,' she said. 'Let's go.'

The music had slowed, enabling him to draw her onto the floor in a waltz, his body moving against hers. She tried not to feel the rising excitement. That was to be her weapon against him, not his against her. But the shocking truth was that he was equally armed and her defences were weak. Now her only hope of standing up to him was not to let him suspect her weakness.

She reckoned a suit of armour would have been useful: something made of steel to protect her from the awareness of his body so dangerously close to hers. Lacking it, she could only assume the nearest thing to a visor, a beaming, rigid smile that should have alarmed him.

'I don't think you should hold me so tightly,' she said.

'Don't try to fool me,' he murmured in soft rage. 'This is exactly what you meant to happen.'

'You do me an injustice. I was going to wear something more conventional but you arrived before I could change.'

'Oh, please, try to think of something better.'

'Why must you always judge me so harshly?'

'If you don't know the answer to that—*mon dieu,* you're enjoying this, aren't you?'

'That's not fair.'

'When is the truth fair? I know how your deceiving little mind works—'

'How can you be so sure you know about me—a woman you met only a few days ago?'

His face was livid and she thought for a moment he would

do something violent. But he only dropped his head so that his mouth was close to her ear. *'Ne me tourmente pas ou je vais vous faire désolé. Prenez garde pendant qu'il est encore temps....'*

She drew in her breath. He'd warned her against tormenting him, telling her to take heed while there was still time.

'Don't torment me,' he groaned again. 'I warn you—I warn you—'

'Why?' she challenged. 'Whatever will happen?'

'Wait and see.'

'Suppose I can't wait. Suppose I'm impatient. What will you do then?'

'Wait and see,' he repeated with slow, deliberate emphasis.

She smiled. 'I'll look forward to that.'

His hand had been drifting lower until it almost rested on the satin curve of her behind. Suddenly he snatched it back, as though in fear, though whether of her or himself perhaps, neither of them could have said.

'Witch!' he breathed.

She chuckled. 'Anything you say. After all, you're my employer. Your word is law. I exist only to obey.'

Now his eyes were those of a man driven beyond endurance, and she really thought he would explode. But it lasted only a moment, then his steely control was in place again.

'I'm glad you realise that,' he said. 'There are things I won't tolerate.'

'You must tell me what they are,' she challenged.

His gaze was fierce and desperate. What would he say? she wondered. Was this her moment?

But the music was drawing to a close. The moment was over.

'Later,' he growled.

'Later,' she agreed.

'But soon.'

'Yes. Soon.' Her eyes met his. 'Because we've waited long enough.'

CHAPTER SEVEN

POLITELY they walked each other off the floor, slowing suddenly as they came within sight of the table.

'Oh, no!' Marcel groaned.

Cassie didn't need to ask about the newcomer. A woman in her thirties, tense, angular and furious, sat next to Henri, hectoring him as only a wife would have done.

'You found another floozie fast enough. I've been watching you dance with her.' Her eyes fell on the blonde bombshell approaching the table on Marcel's arm, and an expression of contempt overtook her face. 'And here she is.' She rose and confronted Cassie.

'Got another one, have you? Finished with my Henri, think this one'll have more money? That's how your kind operate, isn't it? Find out what they're worth and move from one to the other.' She glared at Marcel. 'Don't fool yourself. When she meets a man with more cash you'll be history. Don't suppose you know what it's like to be dumped, do you? Well, you'll find out with her.'

The air was singing about Cassie's head. How would Marcel respond to these words that seemed to home in on his own experience with such deadly accuracy?

His reply amazed her.

'Good evening, Madame Lenoir. I am so glad you could join your husband.'

'Join him? I'm going to get rid of him for good. I saw him dancing with *her,* and what an exhibition that was! Now she can have him.'

'You are mistaken, *madame,*' Marcel said coolly. 'Mrs Henshaw danced with your husband only out of courtesy. She is with me tonight, and I would prefer it if you did not insult her.'

'Oh, would you? Well, I'd prefer it if—'

She got no further. Scenting danger, Henri started to draw her away, apologizing frantically. When they had gone there were sighs of relief. Monsieur Lenoir indicated for Cassie to sit beside him but she'd had as much as she could stand.

'Forgive me,' she said, 'but I'm rather tired. I just want to go to bed. I'll be at work first thing tomorrow morning. Goodnight.'

She was backing away hastily as she spoke, giving Marcel no chance to object. Not that he wanted to, she thought. He must be glad to be rid of her.

In her room she stripped off, showered and dressed for the night. Her pyjamas were 'Mrs Henshaw', plain linen, loose trousers, high buttons.

Stick to Mrs Henshaw in future, she thought. You could argue that Cassie hadn't been a success.

Or you could argue that she'd been so much of a success that it had put the cat among the pigeons.

She paced the floor, too agitated to sleep. Everything that had happened this evening had been unexpected. She'd coped with surprise after surprise, and the biggest surprise of all had been Marcel's defence of her.

But it hadn't been personal, she thought with a sigh. Only what conventional courtesy demanded. If only…

There came a sharp knock on her door.

'Who is it?' she called.

'Me.' It was Marcel. He tried the door, rattling it. 'Open the door.'

She did so. Instantly his hand appeared, preventing her closing it if she'd wanted to. But she didn't want to. This moment had been too long in coming, and now she was ready for it with all guns blazing.

He pushed in so fast that she had to back away. His eyes darted around the room.

'I'm alone,' she said ironically. 'Henri left tamely with his wife. He didn't come flying back to me, whatever you think.'

'You'll pardon me if I don't take your word for that.'

'No, I won't pardon you,' she said. 'I'm not a liar. There's nobody here but us.'

He ignored her. He was opening doors, looking into the bathroom, the wardrobe. Her temper rose sharply.

'Look at me,' she said, indicating her dull attire. 'Do you think any woman entertains a lover dressed in clothes like this?'

'That depends how long she means to wear them. When she knows he'll rip them off her as soon as possible—'

'Is that what Henri wanted?' she asked sarcastically. 'He didn't say.'

'He didn't need to. It's what he wanted and every man in the room wanted. That's the truth and we both know it.'

'Now, look—'

He turned on her in swift fury. 'Don't take me for a fool!'

'But you are a fool,' she raged. 'The biggest fool in creation. Hey, what do you think you're doing?'

'Locking the door so that we're not disturbed. Since the conversation is getting down to basics, I have things to say to you.'

'I think we both have things to say.'

He nodded. 'Yes, and they've waited too long, *Mrs Henshaw.*'

For a moment she didn't speak. Then she said quietly, 'Are you sure that's what you want to call me?'

'I don't want to call you anything. I'd rather not have to endure the sight of you. I thought you were safely out of my life, just a bitter, evil memory that I could kick aside. But now—' He checked himself and looked her up and down, breathing hard with the emotion that threatened to overwhelm him.

'It is you, isn't it?' he said at last.

It was the question he'd promised himself not to ask, because that would be a sign of yielding. But now he knew there had never been a choice.

'It is you,' he repeated.

'You've known that all along.'

'I thought so—sometimes I wasn't sure—it didn't seem possible that you could be—' He broke off, breathing harshly. 'I've tried not to believe it,' he said at last.

'So you didn't want it to be true?'

'Of course I didn't,' he said with soft violence. 'Why should I want to meet you again? I can still hardly comprehend—what evil design made you come after me?'

'Don't flatter yourself,' she cried angrily. 'I didn't seek you out. I went to see Marcel Falcon. Until I saw you I had no idea it was the man I'd known as Marcel Degrande. If I *had* known I'd never have gone to that meeting. When I recognised you I ran away as fast as I could.'

'But you turned back.'

'I didn't mean to. At first I ran into the garden, but to finally escape I had to come back through the hotel and I met you coming out. Don't you understand? *I* didn't want to see *you* again. There was just too much—'

Suddenly the words choked her, and she turned away with a helpless gesture.

'Yes,' he growled. 'Too much. We could never have met peacefully.' He took hold of her and twisted her around.

'Don't turn your back on me. You flaunted your charms tonight, and I endured it, but no more! Did it please you to taunt and jeer at me?'

'I wasn't—' She tried to free herself but he gripped her more tightly.

'Don't lie. You knew exactly what you were doing to me, wearing those—those—you know what I mean. What kind of twisted pleasure did it give you? Or don't I need to ask? You played your games, the way you've always done—'

'I never played games with you,' she said desperately.

'Oh, but you did. You just weren't so frank about it in those days. Sweet, loving little Cassie, wide-eyed and innocent, honestly in love. And I believed it. Until I discovered that you were heartless, incapable of honest love. That was a useful lesson. Once learned, never forgotten. That's the Cassie I knew. So tell me, who is Mrs Henshaw?'

'She's who I am now,' she cried. 'At least I thought so. I thought Cassie had died a long time ago.'

'But tonight she rose again, didn't she? Because some creatures never die. You showed me that nothing had changed, and stood back laughing at the result. I hope I didn't disappoint you.'

'Can that be true?' she challenged him. 'That nothing has changed?'

She heard his swift intake of breath, saw the wild look in his eyes and knew that she'd hit a nerve. He didn't reply. He couldn't. So she answered for him.

'Of course it isn't true, Marcel. It *can't* be true.'

'You said yourself that Cassie hadn't really died,' he reminded her coldly.

'But she's not the same Cassie. She's seen things she never thought to see, things she didn't want to see, but can't forget. She's trapped in her own memories. What about you?'

His terrible expression was her answer. It was the look of a man struggling to get free, knowing he was doomed to fail.

'I can cope with memories,' he said. 'But from some things there's no escape.'

'If you're accusing me of pursuing you, I've already explained—'

'I'm not. Not the way you mean.'

She had pursued him in dreams and fantasies, visions and nightmares. He'd tried to drive her off, crying out that he hated and despised her—that if they met again he would take revenge. But her ghost laughed at his rage, jeered that she was stronger than he, and haunted him so relentlessly that when she'd actually risen before his eyes it was as though he'd summoned her by the force of his will.

He knew he shouldn't tell her this. It would give her too much power, and her power was already alarming. But he couldn't stop himself saying, 'You were always there. A million times I tried to make you go, but you wouldn't. Now you're really here, and I'm no longer a callow boy to let you trick me and run.'

'Why must you think the worst of me?' she cried.

'Haven't I reason? Didn't you desert me when I was almost at death's door?'

'No, I didn't desert you,' she cried. 'I did it for you—'

'Surely you can think of something better than that,' he sneered.

'It's true. I had no choice.'

'You're lying and it's not even a clever lie. Anyone could see through it.'

'Listen to me—' she screamed.

'No, you listen to me. I hate you, Cassie, or Mrs Henshaw, whoever you are today. I shall hate you as long as I live. There's only one thing about you that I don't hate, and it's this.'

He pulled her hard against him and looked down into her face. She felt his hands move away from her shoulders to take her head, holding it in the right position so that she couldn't resist. She knew what he was about to do, but nothing could prepare her for the feel of his lips on hers after so long.

'Marcel,' she gasped.

'You've been trying to drive me insane all evening, and now you've done it. Are you pleased? Is this what you wanted?'

It was exactly what she wanted and only now did she admit the truth to herself. All her anger and defiance had been heading for this moment, trying to drive him to take her into his arms. Her body, her senses and, if she were honest, her heart, had been set on this, and if he'd resisted her it would have been an insult for which she would never have forgiven him. A sigh broke from her, and her warm breath against his mouth inflamed him more. He deepened the kiss with his tongue, seeking her response, sensing it, driven wild by it.

Her arms seemed to move of their own accord, gliding up around his neck, holding, drawing his head fiercely against hers, sending him a message with her lips and tongue.

But suddenly he drew back as though forcing himself with a great effort.

'Tell me to stop,' he growled. 'Tell me. Let me hear you say it.'

'How can I?' she said huskily. 'You never took orders from me.'

'You never needed to give me orders. I did what you wanted without you having to say it.'

'You were always so sure you knew what I wanted,' she murmured, looking up with teasing eyes that were as provocative as she meant them to be.

'You never complained.'

'Perhaps I was afraid of you.'

'You?' he echoed in a voice that was almost savage. 'Afraid of *me?*'

'Perhaps I'm afraid of you now. I'm in your power, aren't I?'

'Then tell me to stop,' he repeated with grim emphasis.

For answer she gave him a smile that tested his self control to the limit. She felt the tremor go through him, and smiled again.

'Tell me to stop!' he said desperately.

'Do *you* think you should stop?' she whispered.

'Damn you! *Damn you!*'

His hands were moving feverishly, finding the buttons of her pyjamas, wrenching them open, tossing the puritanical jacket aside. He touched her breasts with his fingers, then his lips, groaning softly so that his warm breath whispered over her skin, sending a frisson of delight through her.

She was aware of him moving towards the bedroom, taking her with him, but then all sensations merged until she felt the bed beneath her. He raised his head to gaze down at her and she instinctively began to work on his buttons, ripping them open even faster than he had ripped hers.

It was dark in this room and all they could see of each other was their eyes, fierce and gleaming with mutual desire. And then the moment came. After so many years they were one again, moving in a perfect physical harmony that defied their antagonism. The old memories were still alive, how to please each other, inflame each other, challenge, defy, infuriate each other. And then how to lie quietly in each other's arms, feeling the roar die away, leaving only fulfilment behind.

She could barely make out his features, but she sensed his confusion. For once in his life, Marcel was lost for words. She gave him a reassuring smile.

'Would you really have stopped if I'd asked you?' she murmured.

A long silence.

'Let's just say…I'm glad you didn't ask me,' he said at last, slowly.

She waited for him to say more. Whatever the past, they had suddenly discovered a new road that could lead back to each other. Surely now he would have words of tenderness for her?

Full of hope, she reached out, brushing her fingertips against his face.

But he drew back sharply, stared at her for a moment, then rose from the bed like a man fleeing the devil.

'No,' he said softly, then violently, *'no!'*

'Marcel—'

'No!' he repeated, then gave a sudden bitter laugh. 'Oh, *mon dieu!*' He laughed again, but there was no humour in it, only a grating edge.

'Look at me. How easily I…well done, Cassie. You won the first battle. I'll win the others but it's the first one that counts, isn't it? Did you hear me on the dance floor tonight, saying I waited for no woman? That has to be the biggest and stupidest piece of self deception of all time. All those years ago I waited for you—waited and waited, certain that you would come in the end because my Cassie loved me. Waited… waited…' He broke off with a shudder.

So the past couldn't be dealt with so easily, she thought. She must tell him everything, help him to understand that she'd had no choice but to save him from harm. But surely it would be easier now?

'Marcel, listen to me. I must tell you—'

But he couldn't hear her. He'd leapt up and was pacing about, talking frantically, lost in another world. Or perhaps trapped in a cage.

'Once I wouldn't have believed it possible to despise anyone as I've despised you. In those days I loved you more than my life, more than—' He stopped and a violent tremor went through him. 'Never mind that,' he said harshly.

'I guess you don't want to remember that we loved each other.'

'I said never mind,' he shouted. 'And don't talk about "each other". There was no love on your side, or you could never have done what you did.'

'You don't know what I did,' she cried.

'I know that I lay for days in the hospital, longing to see you. I was delirious, dreaming of you, certain that the next time I opened my eyes you'd be there. But you never were.

'I called your mobile phone but it was always switched off. The phone in your apartment was never answered. Tell me, Cassie, didn't you ever wonder why I vanished so suddenly? You never wanted to ask a single question?'

She stared. 'But I knew what had happened, that you'd had an accident and were in hospital. I told you that in my letter.'

'What letter?'

'I wrote, telling you everything, begging you to understand that it wasn't my fault. I put it through your door—I was sure you'd find it when you came home. Oh heavens! Do you mean—?'

'I never read any letter from you,' he said, and she was too distracted to notice how carefully he chose his words.

'Then you never knew that I was forced to leave you—I had no choice.'

He made a sound of impatience. 'Don't tell me things that a child couldn't believe. Of course there was a choice.'

'Not if I wanted you to live,' she cried. 'He said he'd kill you.'

'He? Who?'

'Jake Simpson.'

'Who the hell—?'

'I'd never heard of him either. He was a crook who knew how to keep his head down. People did what he wanted because they were scared of him. I wasn't scared at first. When he said he wanted me I told him to clear off. You were away at the time. I was going to tell you when you got home, but you had the accident. Only it wasn't an accident. Jake arranged it to warn me. He showed me a picture of you in hospital and said you'd die if I didn't drop you and turn to him. I couldn't even tell you what had happened because if I tried to visit you he'd know, and you'd have another "accident".

'I went with him because I had to. I didn't dare approach you, but I couldn't endure thinking of you believing that I'd played you false. In the end I wrote a letter and slipped it through your letter box. Obviously you never got it. Perhaps you'd already left by then. Oh, if only you could have read it. We'd still have been apart, but you'd have known that I didn't betray you, that I was forced to do what I did, and perhaps you wouldn't have hated me.'

She looked at him, standing quite still in the shadows.

'Or maybe you'd have hated me anyway. All these years—'

'Stop,' he said harshly. 'Don't say any more.'

'No, well, I guess there's no more to say. If I could turn back the clock I'd put that letter into your hands and make you read it and then perhaps I wouldn't have been such a monster in your heart—'

'I said stop!' he shouted.

She came to a sudden resolution. Reaching up from where she was sitting on the bed, she took his hand and urged him down until he was sitting beside her.

'You don't know whether to believe me or not, do you? Everything about us is different—except for one thing. Very well. If that's the only way I can make you listen to me, then that's the way I'll take.'

'Meaning?'

'You've implied that I'm a bad woman who'll use her physical charms to get her way with you. Well, maybe you're right. After all, I know now that I can do it, don't I?'

'What are you saying?'

'That I'll do what I have to. Maybe you know me better than I know myself. Perhaps I really am that unscrupulous. Maybe I'll enjoy it. Maybe we both will.'

As she spoke she was touching his face. She knew she was taking a huge risk, but there was no other way. At all costs she would soften him, drive the hostility from his eyes.

To her relief she could feel him softening, feel the hostile tension drain from him, replaced by a different kind of tension.

'Hold me,' she whispered.

He did so, reaching for her, drawing her down to stretch out on the bed, or letting her draw him down. Neither of them really knew.

Their first encounter had been entirely sexual. This one was on a different plane. No words were spoken, but none were needed. In each other's arms they seemed to find again the things that had been missing the first time—sweetness, warmth, the joy of the heart.

Afterwards they held each other with gentle hands.

'We'll get there,' she promised. 'We'll find a way, my darling, I promise we will.'

He didn't reply, and she suddenly became aware that his breathing was deep and steady. She turned her head, the better to see his face, and gave a tender smile as she saw him sunk in sleep.

It had always been this way, she remembered. He would love her with all the power and vigour of a great man, then fall asleep like a child.

'That's right, you sleep,' she murmured. 'Sleep and I'll take care of everything.'

Slowly her smile changed. Now it was one of triumph.

In the twilight world that came just before awakening she relived a dream. So many times she'd fallen asleep in his arms, knowing that he would still be there in the morning. Sometimes she'd opened her eyes to find him looking down at her adoringly. At other times he would be sunk in sleep, but always reaching for her, even if only with his fingertips. It was as though he could only relax with the assurance of her presence.

And me, she thought hazily, *knowing he would be there meant that life was good.*

She opened her eyes.

She was alone.

He was gone.

She sat up, looking around frantically, certain that there was some mistake. The room was empty. Hurrying out of bed, she searched all the rooms but there was no sign of him. Marcel had stolen away while she slept.

But he'd vowed to keep her a prisoner. The outer door would be locked.

It wasn't. It yielded at once and she found herself looking out into an empty corridor. Something about the silence was frightening.

She slammed the door and leaned back against it, refusing to believe that this could have happened. Last night they'd found each other again, not totally but enough for hope. They should have spent today talking, repairing the past. Instead he'd walked out.

But he might have fled through caution, she thought. Don't judge him until you've spoken to him.

She dressed carefully. Cassie or Mrs Henshaw today?

Finally she settled on a mixture, restrained clothing as befitted her job, but with her hair flowing freely. He would understand. A quick breakfast and she was ready to face whatever the challenge was.

The door to Marcel's apartment was opened by a middle-aged woman with a friendly face.

'*Bonjour.* I am Vera, Marcel's secretary. He has left me instructions to be of service to you.'

'Left you—? Isn't he here?'

'He had to leave suddenly. For what reason he did not say. I'm a little surprised because he has so much to do, and he didn't even tell me where he was going.'

So that was that. He was snubbing her, escaping to some place where she couldn't follow. Perhaps she should simply take the hint and leave, but that seemed too much like giving in without a fight. How he would triumph if he returned to find her gone. Grimly she settled down to work.

CHAPTER EIGHT

LAURA Degrande had settled contentedly in a small house in the suburbs of Paris. It wasn't a wealthy district, but she always said life was better without wealth. Her marriage to Amos Falcon had not been happy, and the only good thing to come from it was her son, Marcel. He would have kept her in luxury, but she refused, accepting an allowance that was comfortable, but no more, despite his indignant protests. It was the only blot on their otherwise affectionate relationship.

Her face lit up when he appeared at her door.

'My darling, how lovely to see you. I was thrilled to get your call this morning. What is it that's so urgent?'

Hugging her, Marcel said, 'I need to look through some old stuff that you stored for me.'

'Have you lost something?'

'You might say that. Are the bags where I left them?'

'Still in the attic.'

'See you later.'

He hurried up the stairs before she could answer, and shut himself away in the little room, where he began to pull open bags and boxes, tossing them aside when they didn't contain what he wanted. When Laura looked in he turned a haggard face towards her.

'There's something missing—a big grey envelope—I left it here—it's gone—'

'Oh, that. Yes, I found it but there was only rubbish inside, shreds of paper that you'd obviously torn up. I thought they should be thrown out.'

'What?' The sound that broke from him was a roar of anguish. His face was haggard, desperate. 'You threw it out?'

'No, calm down. I thought about it but then I remembered what you're like about not throwing things away. So I stored them safely—up here on this shelf. Yes, here's the envelope.'

He almost snatched it from her with a choking, 'Thank you!'

Laura left the room quickly, knowing that something desperately important had happened, and he needed to be alone to cope with it.

Marcel wrenched open the envelope and a load of small bits of paper cascaded onto the floor. Frantically he gathered them up, found a small table and began to piece them together. It was hard because his hands were shaking, and the paper had been torn into tiny shreds.

As he worked he could see himself again, on that night long ago, tearing, tearing, desperate with hate and misery.

He'd left the hospital as soon as he was strong enough, and gone straight to Cassie's home. The lights were out and he knew the worst as soon as he arrived, but he still banged on the door, crying her name, banging more desperately.

'You're wasting your time,' said a voice behind him. 'She's gone.'

Behind him stood a middle-aged man who Marcel knew vaguely. He was usually grumpy, but today he seemed pleased at the bad news he was imparting.

'Gone where?' Marcel demanded.

A shrug. 'How do I know? She packed up and left days ago. I saw her get into a posh car. Bloke who owned it must be a millionaire, so I reckon that's finished you. She saw sense at last.'

Seeing Marcel's face, he retreated hastily.

At first he refused to believe it, banging on the door again and screaming her name, until at last even he had to accept the truth. She'd gone without a backward glance.

He didn't remember the journey home, except that he sat drinking in the back of the taxi until he tumbled out onto the pavement and staggered into the building.

On the mat he found an envelope, with his name in Cassie's handwriting. The sight had been enough to make him explode with drunken rage and misery, tearing it, tearing, tearing, tearing—until only shreds were left.

He'd left England next morning. At the airport he'd had a brief glimpse of Cassie, dressed up to the nines, in the company of a man who clearly had money coming out of his ears. That sight answered all his questions. He'd screamed abuse, and fled.

In Paris he'd taken refuge in his mother's home, collapsing and letting her care for him. When he unpacked it was actually a surprise to discover that he'd brought Cassie's letter, although in shreds. He had no memory of putting it into his bag.

Now was the time to destroy it finally, but he hesitated. Better to keep it, and read it one day, years ahead. When he was an old man, ruling a financial empire, with an expensive wife and a gang of children, then he would read the whore's miserable excuses.

And laugh.

How he would laugh! He'd laugh as violently as he was weeping now.

When at last he could control his sobs he took the bits of paper to his room, stuffed them into an envelope and put it in a drawer by his bed. There it had stayed until he'd moved out. Then he'd hidden it away in the little attic, asking his mother to be sure never to touch his things.

As the years passed he'd sometimes thought of the day that would come when he could read her pathetic words and jeer at her memory. Now that day was here.

He worked feverishly, fixing the pieces together. But gradually his tension increased. Something was wrong. No, it was impossible. Be patient! It would come right.

But at last he could no longer delude himself. With every tiny wisp of paper scrutinised to no avail, with every last chance gone, he slammed his fist into the wall again and again.

When there was no word, and her calls went unanswered, Cassie came to a final reluctant decision. As she packed she chided herself for imagining that things could ever have been different. Her flesh was still warm from their encounters the night before, but she should never have fooled herself.

He was punishing her by abandoning her in the way he felt she'd abandoned him. The generous person he'd once been would never have taken such cruel, carefully thought out vengeance, but now he was a different man, one she didn't know.

She called the airport and booked herself onto the evening flight to London. There! It was done.

'You are leaving?' asked Vera, who'd been listening.

'Yes, I have to. Would you please give this to Marcel?' She handed over a sealed envelope. Inside was a small piece of paper, on which she'd written: *'It's better this way. I'm sure you agree. Cassie.'*

'Can't you wait just a little?' Vera begged.

'No, I've stayed too long already.'

Take-off was not for three hours but she felt an urgent need to get away at once. She took a taxi to the airport and sat, trying not to brood. She should never have come to this place, never dreamed that the terrible wrongs of the past could be put right. How triumphant he would feel, knowing his snub had driven her away! How glad he would be to be rid of her!

At last it was time to check in. She rose and joined the queue. She had almost reached the front when a yell rent the air.

'Cassie!'

Everyone looked up to see the man standing at the top of a flight of stairs, but he saw none of them. His eyes were fixed only on her as he hurled himself down at breakneck speed and ran to her so fast that he had to seize her in order to steady himself.

'What do you think you're doing?' he demanded frantically.

'I'm going home.'

'You're staying here.'

'Let go of me.'

'No!' He was holding her in an unbreakable grip. 'You can either agree to come back with me, or we can fight it out right here and now. Which?'

'You're impossible!'

'It took you ten years to discover that? I thought you were clever. Yes or no?'

'All right—yes.'

'Good. Is this yours?' He lifted her suitcase with one hand while still holding her wrist with the other. Plainly he was taking no chances.

In this awkward fashion they made it out of the building to where the car from La Couronne was waiting for them. While the chauffeur loaded the suitcase Marcel guided her into the back and drew the glass partition across, isolating them. As the car sped through the Paris traffic he kept hold of her hand.

'There's no need to grip me so tightly,' she said. 'I'm hardly going to jump out here.'

'I'm taking no chances. You could vanish at any time. You've done it twice, you won't do it to me again. You can count on that.'

'I went because you made it so obvious that you wanted to be rid of me.'

'Are you mad?' he demanded.

'I'm not the one who vanished into thin air. When a woman awakes to find the man gone in the morning that's a pretty clear message.'

'Tell me about vanishing into thin air,' he growled. 'You're the expert.'

'I left a note with Vera—'

'I didn't mean today.' The words came out as a cry of pain, and she cursed herself for stupidity.

'No, I guess not. I'm sorry. So when you left this morning, that was your way of paying me back?'

'I went because I had to, but…things happened. I never meant to stay away so long. When I got back and Vera told me you'd left for England I couldn't believe it. I tried to call you but you'd turned your phone off—*like last time.*'

She drew a sharp breath. Something in his voice, his eyes, revealed all his suffering as no mere words could have done.

'But why did you have to dash off?' she asked.

'To read the letter you wrote me ten years ago.'

'But you said you never got it.'

'No, I said I never read it. I was so blazing mad I tore it up without reading it.'

'Then how could you read it now?'

'Because I kept it,' he said savagely. 'Fool that I am, I kept it.'

She could hardly believe her ears. 'And you never—in all these years—?'

'No, I never read it. But neither did I throw it away. Today I went to my mother's home where it's been stored, meaning to fit it together. But it isn't all there. Some of the pieces are lost. I came straight back to find you, and you were gone. Vera heard you booking the flight so I had to act fast.'

'You only just got there in time,' she murmured.

'Well, actually—I have a friend who works in airport security. I called him. You wouldn't have been allowed to get on that plane.'

'*What?* You actually dared—?'

'I couldn't risk you getting away. It's too important.'

'And suppose I want to get away?'

He looked at her in silence. Words could never have said so clearly that what she wanted played no part in this. This was a man driven by demons that were too strong for him, and perhaps also for her.

'So you want me to explain the missing pieces?' she guessed.

'If you can remember them.'

'Oh, yes,' she murmured. 'I can remember everything.'

They had reached La Couronne. Marcel hurried her inside, his hand still on her arm. Several people tried to attract his attention, but he never saw them. Only one thing mattered now.

As soon as they were inside his apartment he locked the door. She almost told him there was no need, but then kept silent. Marcel was in the grip of an obsession and she, of all people, couldn't say it was irrational. She knew a burst of pity for him, standing on the edge of a dangerous pit. If he fell into its fearsome depths, wouldn't she be at least partly to blame?

He held out the letter, where she could see tiny scraps stuck onto a base sheet, but with gaping holes.

'Do you recognise this?' he demanded.

'Yes, of course.'

He thrust it into her hands and turned away. 'Read it to me.'

It felt weird to see the words over which she'd struggled so hard and wept so many tears. She began to read aloud.

'"*My darling, beloved Marcel, you will wonder why I didn't come to you when you were in pain and trouble, but I didn't dare. What happened wasn't an accident. It was done on purpose by a man who wants to claim me for himself. I refused him, and*—"' She stopped. 'There's a gap here.'

'What are the missing words?' he asked.

She closed her eyes, travelling back to the past. '"*He hurt you, to show me what would happen if I didn't give in,*"' she said slowly. She opened her eyes.

'Then the letter goes on, *"I couldn't risk coming to you in the hospital because he would have known and he might kill you. I'm delivering this through your door, because it's the only way I can think of that he won't find out. I hope and pray that it will be safe. I couldn't bear it if you believed I'd just walked away, or stopped loving you."* Then there's another gap.'

'Do you know what's missing?' When she didn't answer he turned and repeated harshly, 'Do you?'

'Yes. I said—'*"I will never stop loving you, until the very end of my days, but this is the last time I can ever say so."*' The signature is still there if you want to read it.

'I don't need to read it,' he said quietly, and recited, *'Your very own Cassie, yours forever, however long "forever" may last.'* I don't suppose you remember writing that.'

'Yes, I remember writing every word, even the ones that aren't here any more.'

'"*I will never stop loving you until the very end of my days,*"' he repeated. 'You're sure you wrote that?'

'Yes, I'm quite sure. But even if you doubt me, the rest of the letter is there. I told you what had happened and why I had to leave you. If only you'd read it then, you'd have known that I still loved you—oh, Marcel—all these years!'

'Don't,' he begged, shuddering. 'If I think of that I'll go mad.'

'I'm surprised we haven't both gone mad long before this. And it was all so unnecessary.'

'Yes, if I'd read this then—'

'No, I mean more than that. There's another reason the last ten years could have been avoided.' She broke off, heaving.

'What do you mean?' he demanded.

She raised fierce eyes to his face.

'I mean that you played your part in what happened to us. It could all have been so different if only you'd been honest with me. Why didn't you tell me who you were, who your father was? We need never have been driven apart.'

He stared. 'What difference—?'

Her temper was rising fast. 'If I'd known you were the son of Amos Falcon I'd have gone to him for help. He's a powerful man. When he heard what Jake had done he would have dealt with him, had him arrested, sent to jail. We'd have been safe.

'Everything since then could have been different. You'd have been spared all that suffering and disillusion. I'd have been spared that terrible time with Jake. So much misery because you had to play a silly game.'

He tore his hair. 'I was just...I didn't want you to know I came from a rich family.'

'Because you thought I'd be too interested in your money. Charming!'

'No, because you thought I was poor and you chose me over your rich admirers. That meant the world to me—'

'Yes, but there was a high price, and you weren't the only one who paid it. You spoke of hating me, but I could hate *you* for what you did to my life with your juvenile games. When I found out the truth recently I...I just couldn't...so much misery, and so needless—*aaaargh!*'

The last word was a scream that seemed to tear itself from her body without her meaning it. It was followed by another, and another, and now she couldn't stop screaming.

'Cassie!' he tried, reaching for her. *'Cassie!'*

'Get away from me,' she screamed. 'Don't touch me. *I hate you.*'

He wouldn't let her fight him off, drawing her closer until her face was against his shoulder, murmuring in her ear, 'That's right, hate me. I deserve it. Hate me, hate me.'

'Yes,' she wept.

'I'm a damned fool and you suffered for it. Call me every name you can think of. Hit me if you like.' He drew back so that she could see his face. 'It's no more than I deserve. Go on, I won't stop you.'

She couldn't speak, just shook her head while the tears ran down her cheeks. Then she was back in his arms, held against him, feeling him pick her up, kick open a door and lay her down on a soft bed.

But this was no love-making. Lying beside her, he held her gently, murmuring soothing words, stroking her hair. Her efforts to stop weeping were in vain, and he seemed to understand this because he murmured, 'Go on, cry it out. Don't try to hold back.'

'All those wasted years,' she choked.

'Years when we could have been together,' he agreed, 'loving each other, making each other happy, having children. All gone because I was a conceited oaf.'

'No, you weren't,' she managed to say. 'You were just young—'

'Young and stupid,' he supplied. 'Not thinking of anyone but myself, imagining I could play games without people being hurt—'

'Don't be so hard on yourself,' she said huskily.

'Why not? It's true. I did it. My silly pretence meant you

couldn't seek my father's help and, even after that, if I'd only read your letter I—*imbécile, stupide!*'

'Marcel,' she wept, 'Marcel—'

Distress choked her again, but now it was the same with him. She could feel his body heaving, his arms around her as hers were around him.

'I did it,' he sobbed. 'I did it. It's all my fault.'

'No…no…' She tightened her embrace, tenderly stroking his head as a mother might have done with a child.

'Ten years,' he gasped. 'Ten years! Where did they go? How can we get them back?'

'We can't,' she said. 'What's done can never be undone.'

'I don't believe that!'

'Marcel, you can't turn the clock back; it isn't possible. We can only go on from here.'

He didn't reply in words, but she felt his arms tighten, as though he feared that she might slip away again.

Go on where? said the voice in her head. *And what do you mean by 'we'? Who are you? Who is he now?*

She silenced the voice. She had no answer to those troublesome questions. Everything she'd suffered, the lessons learned in the last ten years, all the confusion and despair, were uniting to cry with a thousand voices that from this moment nothing would be simple, nothing easy, and it might all end in more heartbreak.

It was a relief to realise that he was relaxing into sleep in her arms, as though in her he found the only true comfort. She stroked him some more, murmuring soft words in his ear. 'Sleep, my darling. We'll find a way. I only wish I knew…I wish I knew…'

But then sleep came to her rescue too, and the words faded into nothing.

It was dark when she awoke and the illuminated clock by the bed told her they had dozed for barely an hour. Careful not to awaken Marcel, she eased away and sat on the side of the bed, dropping her head into her hands, feeling drained.

The concerns that had worried her before were even stronger now. Their tumultuous discoveries could bring great happiness, or great despair. They had found each other again, and perhaps the troubles of the past could be made right. But it was too soon to be sure, and she had a strange sensation of watching everything from a distance.

She walked over to the window, looking out on the dazzling view. Paris was a blaze of light against the darkness.

'Are you all right?' came his voice from behind her.

'Yes, I'm fine,' she said quickly.

He came up behind her and she felt his hands on her shoulders. 'Are you sure? You seem very troubled.'

How had he divined that merely from her back view? she wondered. How and where had he gained such insight?

'What are you thinking?' he asked softly.

'I don't know. My thoughts come and go so quickly I can't keep up with them.'

'Me too,' he agreed. 'We must have many long talks.'

'But not now,' she said. 'I feel as though I'm choking. I need to go out into the fresh air.'

'Fine, let's go for a walk.'

'No, I have to be alone.'

'Cassie—'

'It's all right, I won't vanish again. I'll return, I promise.'

'It's dark,' he persisted. 'Do you know how late it is?'

'I have to do this,' she said in a tense voice. 'Please, Marcel, don't try to stop me.'

He was silent and she sensed his struggle. But at last he sighed and stood back to let her pass.

Without even going to her own apartment, she hurried directly down to the entrance. The hotel was close to the River Seine, and by following the signs she was able to find the way to the water. Here she could stand looking down at the little ripples, glittering through the darkness, and listen to the sounds of the city. Late as it was, Paris was still alive. Far in the distance she could see the Eiffel Tower reaching up into the heavens.

She turned around slowly and that was when she saw the man, fifty yards away along the embankment, standing quite still, watching her. At first she thought he was a stalker, but then she recognised him. Marcel.

When she began to walk towards him he backed away. When she turned and moved off he followed.

'Marcel,' she called. 'What do you think you're doing?'

At last he drew close enough for her to see a slightly sheepish look on his face.

'I was just concerned for your safety,' he responded. 'I'll keep my distance, and leave you in peace. But I'll always be there if you need me.'

Her annoyance died and she managed a shaky laugh. 'My guardian angel, huh?'

'That has to be the first time anyone's mistaken me for an angel,' he said wryly.

'Why do I find that so easy to believe? All right, you can stay.'

Recently she had forgotten how much charm he had when he was set on getting his own way. Suddenly she was remembering.

He completed the effect by taking two small wine bottles from his pockets and handing her one. 'Let's sit down,' he said.

She did so and drank the wine thankfully.

'It's a lot to take in all at once, isn't it?' he said.

'Yes, I guess so.'

'These last few years must have been terrible for you. The

man who had me run down—was that the man I saw you with at the airport?'

'Yes, that was Jake. I'd spent the previous few days at his house, "entertaining him" as he put it.'

'You don't need to say any more,' Marcel said in a strained voice.

'No, I guess not.

'We were travelling to America that day. After he'd seen you he kept on and on at me, demanding to know if I'd been in touch with you. I swore I hadn't, and in the end he believed me because he said if you'd known the truth you wouldn't have called me "Whore".

'I didn't know what to believe. I thought perhaps you'd read my letter and were pretending, or maybe you hadn't been home yet and would get it later. But I told Jake that he must be right about that.' She gave a wry smile. 'It was always wise to tell Jake he was right. He'd already destroyed my cellphone so that nobody could get in touch with me.'

'So you were his prisoner?' he said, aghast. 'All that time you were suffering and I did nothing to help you.'

'How could you? I must admit that I did hope for a while, but in the end I realised you'd accepted our parting and that was the end. So I married him.'

'You married him?'

'Why not? I felt my life was over. I just went with the tide. When I found he'd been fooling around with other women it gave me the weapon I needed to divorce him. Suddenly I wasn't afraid of him any more. I accepted some money from him because I had people who needed it, but I didn't keep any for myself. I didn't want anything from him, even his name. I used Henshaw because it was my mother's maiden name.'

'What's happened to him since? Does he trouble you?'

'He's in jail at the moment, for several years, hopefully. I told you how I took business courses after that, and started on the life I live now.' She raised her wine bottle to the moon. 'Independence every time. Cheers!'

'Independence or isolation?' he asked.

She shrugged. 'Does it matter? Either way, it's better to rely on yourself.'

He sighed. 'I guess so.'

He was glad she couldn't see his face, lest his thoughts showed. He was remembering one night, a lifetime ago, when she'd endured a bad day at work and thrown herself into his arms.

'What would I do without you?' she'd sighed. 'That rotten photographer—goodness, but he's nasty! Never mind. I can put up with anything as long as I know I have you—'

'And you'll always have me,' he'd assured her.

Three weeks later, the disaster had separated them.

'Better rely on yourself,' he repeated, 'rather than on a fool who thought it was funny to conceal his real background, and plunged you both into tragedy.'

'Hey, I wasn't getting at you. Nobody knows what's just around the corner.' She laughed. 'After all, we never saw this coming, did we?'

'And you'd have run a mile if you'd known. I remember you saying so.' He waited for her answer. It didn't come. 'How long ago since your divorce?' he asked.

'About five years. Since then I've been Mrs Henshaw, bestriding the financial world. It suits me. Remember you used to joke about my having a great brain?'

'It wasn't entirely a joke. I think I was a bit jealous of the way you could read something once and remember it like it was set in stone.'

'There now, I told you I was made to be a businesswoman.'

'But that's not your only talent. Why didn't you go back to modelling? You're still beautiful.'

'Not really.'

'I say you are,' he said fiercely.

'I won't argue about it. But it takes more than beauty and I've lost something special. I know that. I knew it then. I'd look in the mirror and see that a light had gone out inside me. Besides,' she hurried on before he could protest, 'I wanted to try something new. It was my choice. Life moves on, we don't stay in the same place.

'Cassie was one person. Mrs Henshaw is another. I became quite pleased with her. She takes people by surprise. Some of them are even scared of her.'

'And you like people being scared of you?'

'Not all the time, but it has its uses. She's a bright lady is Mrs Henshaw. Lots of common sense.'

'Now you're scaring *me*.'

'Good.'

'So I've got to get used to Mrs Henshaw hanging around, when the one I want is Cassie?'

'I'm not sure that's a wise choice. Mrs Henshaw has to get that hotel set up. You need her expertise, her "great brain". Cassie wouldn't be up to the job.'

She managed to say it in a teasing tone, and he managed a smile in reply. But they both knew that she was conveying a subtle warning.

Go slowly. Don't rush it. A false step could mean disaster.

'I think we should go back now,' she said.

She rose and offered him her hand. He hesitated only a moment before nodding and taking it. In this way, with him following her lead, they strolled back to the hotel.

CHAPTER NINE

SHE slept alone that night. Marcel kissed her at the door, touched her face with his fingertips and hurried away. She smiled at his retreating figure, glad that he had the sensitivity not to try to overwhelm her with passion at this moment.

After everything that had happened, all the unexpected revelations, the business of deciding her appearance next morning was a minefield. In the end she selected clothes that were respectable rather than forbidding, and wore her hair drawn back, but not scraped tightly, so that it framed her face softly before vanishing over her shoulders.

When she entered the office he was deep in a phone call, his manner agitated. He waved for her to come in, then turned away. He was talking French but she managed to make out that he was about to go away. The idea didn't seem to please him, for he slammed down the phone and snapped, *'Imbécile! Idiot!'*

'Somebody let you down?' she asked.

'Yes, he's made a mess of a deal I trusted to him, and now I have to go and rescue it. It'll take a few days. Come here!' He hugged her fiercely. 'I don't want to leave you. You should come with me and—'

'No,' she said firmly. 'I'd be a distraction and you've got to keep your mind on business.'

'I'd planned such a day for us. I was going to take you over Paris—'

'Paris will still be here when you get back.' She added significantly, 'And so will I.'

His brow darkened. 'Your word of honour?'

'I told you, I have no reason to leave now.'

Reluctantly he departed, giving her one last anxious look from the door. She saw him go with regret, yet also with a faint twinge of relief. His possessiveness was like a reproach to her. She couldn't blame him for it, but she sensed that it could be a problem, one to which he was blind.

Knowing herself better than Marcel could, she sensed that Mrs Henshaw was more than just an outward change. Her businesslike appearance really did represent a certain reality inside. For the moment Cassie and Mrs Henshaw must live side by side, each one taking the spotlight according to need. But which one of them would finally emerge as her true self? Even she could not be certain about that.

She'd hinted as much to Marcel the previous evening, but she knew he didn't really understand. Or perhaps didn't want to understand. That was the thought that made her a little uneasy.

For the next few days she was Mrs Henshaw, deep in business and thoroughly enjoying herself. Vera introduced her to the chief members of the staff, who had clearly been instructed to cooperate with her. She went through the books and knew she was impressing them with her knowledge of finance.

Then there were the builders who had renovated and extended La Couronne, and who spoke to her at Marcel's command. The more she listened, the more she understood what he'd been trying to do, how well he'd succeeded, and what he wanted in London. Ideas began to flower inside her. She would have much to tell him when he returned on Thursday.

He called her several times a day on the hotel's landline. Wryly she realised that in this way he could check that she was there. Just once he called her cellphone, and that was when she was out shopping. He managed to sound cheerful but she sensed the underlying tension, especially when he said, 'Don't be long getting back to the hotel. There's a lot to do.'

'I'm on my way back now,' she assured him.

Vera greeted her in a flurry of nerves. 'He was very upset when he called and found you not here,' she said.

'Don't worry; he tried my cellphone and I answered at once.' She added reassuringly, 'So when he calls, you can tell him that I'm not slacking on the job.'

Not wanting to embarrass the secretary, whom she liked, she got straight back to work. A few minutes later Vera's phone rang and she shut the door to answer it discreetly.

Poor Marcel, Cassie thought. *I suppose I can't blame him for expecting me to vanish in a puff of smoke. He'll understand, in time.*

By now everyone knew who she was, and the power she possessed, and they would scurry to give her only the best. On Wednesday evening the cook and head waiter joined her at the table for a few minutes, urging her to try new dishes.

They were both attractive men, middle-aged but with appreciative eyes, and they enjoyed talking to her about Paris, which they insisted on calling 'the city of love'.

'You work too hard, *madame,*' the cook told her. 'You should be out there exploring this magical place, becoming imbued with its spirit. Then you would know what to do for the hotel in London.'

'I'm afraid London lacks Paris's air of romance,' she mourned, and they solemnly agreed with her.

Once, long ago, Marcel had whispered in the night, 'I will take you to Paris and show you my city. We will walk the streets together, and you will breathe in the atmosphere of love that is to be found nowhere else.'

'You sound like a guidebook,' she'd complained.

'Actually, I got it out of a guidebook,' he'd admitted sheepishly.

She began to laugh, and he'd joined her. They had clung together, rocking back and forth in bed until the laughter ended in passionate silence, the way everything seemed to end in those days.

He never did take me to Paris, she thought now, sadly. And it would have been so wonderful.

Suddenly he seemed to be there in front of her, laughing joyfully as he'd done in his carefree youth, before cares had fallen on him in a cruel deluge.

'Ah, Monsieur Falcon,' the waiter called. 'How nice to see you back.'

She blinked in disbelief. It wasn't a fantasy. He really was there, standing before her, as though he'd risen from her dreams.

'Good evening,' he said cheerfully. 'I needn't ask if you've missed me. Clearly you haven't.'

'I've been so well looked after that I've barely noticed you were gone,' she teased.

His employees greeted him respectfully before rising from the table and leaving them alone.

'Come with me,' he said, drawing her to her feet.

'But the chef has spent hours preparing—'

'I said come *on.*'

He was laughing but also totally serious, she realised, as she felt herself drawn across the floor and out of the restaurant.

'Where are we going?' she asked breathlessly.

'Wait and see. *Taxi!*'

When they were settled in the back seat she said, 'You weren't supposed to come back until tomorrow.'

'Sorry to disappoint you. Shall I go away again?'

'No, I think I can just about put up with you. Hey, what are you doing?'

'What do you think? Come here.'

'Mmmmmmm!'

Suddenly the boy she'd loved long ago was in her arms again, banishing the severe man he'd become. Eventually that might prove unrealistic, but right now she was too delighted to care about anything else.

Especially being realistic.

'Where are we going?' she asked when she could breathe again.

'Sightseeing. Look.'

Gazing out, she could see that they were driving along the River Seine, with the Eiffel Tower growing closer and closer, until at last they turned over a bridge, heading across the water, straight to the Tower. There they took the elevator up higher and higher, to a restaurant more than four hundred feet above the ground, where he led her to a table by the window.

From here it seemed as if all Paris was laid out for her delight, glittering lights against the darkness, stretching into infinity. She regarded it in awed silence.

'I think it's the most beautiful thing I've ever seen,' she whispered.

'We dreamed of coming here. Do you remember?'

'Oh, yes, I remember.'

She didn't speak for a while, but gazed out, transfixed by the beauty.

'I've always wanted to come to Paris. I kept hoping that the next modelling job would take me there, but I was always unlucky.'

'So now I can show it to you, as I promised.'

'And every girl in Paris will envy me the attention of Marcel Falcon, famous for his harem.'

'Nonsense!'

'It's not.' She chuckled. 'After we met that first night I researched you online, and discovered a lot of interesting things.'

'Don't believe everything you read,' he said wryly.

'Oh, but I'd like to believe it. It was so fascinating. I looked in a web encyclopedia and the entry under "Personal Life" went on for ever. I couldn't keep up. Josie and Leyla, Myra, Ginette and—now, who was the other one? Just let me think.'

'All right,' he growled, 'you've had your fun.'

'After what I read, I don't think you should lecture me about having fun. Tell me about that woman who—'

His scowl stopped her in her tracks. 'Have you finished?' he grunted.

'I've barely started.'

'What would you think of me if I'd had no social life?'

'That you were honest, virtuous, shining white—and the biggest bore in the world. Of course you've had women, lots of them. So you should.'

'Now you sound like my father.'

'I take it that's not a compliment. I only saw him for a moment that night in London, but I thought you seemed tense in his company. Do you dislike him?'

'Sometimes. Sometimes I admire him.'

'Not love him?'

'I don't think he's bothered whether anyone loves him or not. If he was he wouldn't alienate them as he does. All he really cares about is making people do what he wants.' Seeing her wry smile, he ground his teeth, 'OK, fine! Say it.'

'You have been known to want your own way,' she teased.

'And to go about getting it in a way that's—shall we say, cunning and determined?'

'If you mean cheating and bullying, why not say so?'

'I didn't want to insult you. Or would it be a compliment?'

'My father would certainly take it as a compliment. A chip off the old block, that's what he'd call me.'

'Were you at odds with him when you were living in London, that time?'

'I resented him, the person he was, the way he lived, the way he treated people. He seemed to think he could do exactly as he liked, and everyone would just have to put up with it. When I was a child I thought he and my mother were married. They seemed like a normal couple. He wasn't at home very much but I thought that was just because of his work. Then suddenly it all changed. It seemed he'd had a wife in England all the time. At last she'd found out about his other family and divorced him, taking Darius and Jackson.'

Cassie had heard some of this before, from Freya, but Marcel's own view of his colourful childhood had a new significance.

'So then my mother married him and we went to live in England. After a couple of years his first wife died and Darius and Jackson came to live with us.'

'That must have made for a tense situation.'

'It could have been, but Darius and I got on better than you might expect. We were both naturally rebellious and we used to team up against Amos, be co-conspirators, give each other alibis when necessary. I really missed the fun of being wicked together when it was all over.

'Of course the marriage didn't last. He got up to his old tricks and she was expected to put up with it because he was Amos Falcon, a man with enough money to do as he liked.'

'That would be enough to put you off money for life,' she mused.

'That's what I felt, disgust with him and everything he stood for. We found out about his other sons, Travis in America, and Leonid in Russia. I often saw my mother crying, and there were times when I did hate him. I might be his son but I wanted to be as different from him as possible.

'Mama and I came back to Paris and tried to forget him. But he wouldn't let us. He kept turning up on the doorstep. Once his property, always his property. Especially me. I was his son so I was bound to be like him. It was no use telling him that I didn't feel at all like him and didn't want to.'

He made a wry face. 'I guess he knew me better than I knew myself. I fooled around in London, pretending I wasn't connected with him, not using his name, but when the crash came I fled back to my mother in Paris. At first I told myself the future was open, all paths were open to me. I didn't have to take the one that led to Amos.

'But in the end I faced reality. There was only one road, and he stood at the end, waiting for me to admit the truth. I called him in Monte Carlo, where he was living for tax reasons. After that I took lessons in being Amos Falcon.' He assumed a flourishing air. 'I passed them with flying colours.'

'Or you think you did,' she said gently.

'What does that mean?'

'It means I don't think you're as like him as you believe.'

'Maybe. I'm not sure any more. I was certain in those days because I thought he and his way of life was all I had left in the world. Nothing mattered but money, so I went after it because it could fill all the gaping holes.'

'And did it?' she asked.

He shook his head. 'Nothing could. But I wouldn't face it. I told myself it was all your fault. Every bad thing that happened, every cruel disappointment was your fault. That was the only way I—' His hand tightened on his glass.

'Steady, you'll break it,' she said.

'If you only knew—'

'But I do. I had a bad time too, but I don't think I suffered as much as you did. I missed you and grieved for you, but I never had the pain of thinking you'd betrayed me.'

'Didn't you? After what I called you when I saw you at the airport? Didn't I betray you when I tore up that letter?'

'Marcel, stop it,' she said firmly. Taking his hands in hers, she went on, 'You mustn't obsess about that.'

'How can I help it? I could have made it right and I made a mess of everything. I could have spared us ten years of suffering. Why don't you blame me? Why don't you hate me?'

'Would that make you feel better?' she asked softly. 'Shall I beat you up and then say, "Fine, now we're even"?'

'It's what you ought to do.'

'Yes, but I never did do what I ought to do. You said so a hundred times. I never hated you, and if anything good comes out of this it will be that you won't hate me any more.'

'If anything good—? Can you doubt it?'

'I hope for a thousand good things, but we don't know what they are yet.'

'But surely we—?'

'We have to be patient. We're strangers to each other now.'

'You'll never be a stranger to me.'

'That's lovely, but it isn't true. It can't be. We know the people we used to be, but not the people we are now. We have to discover each other again before—'

'Before we can love each other? Don't you want us to?'

Before the intensity of his eyes she looked away. 'I don't know,' she admitted. 'It frightens me. I guess I'm just easily scared these days.' She clasped his hands again. 'I need a friend.'

'Friend,' he echoed, as though trying to believe what he'd heard.

'Someone who understands things that nobody else in the

world understands. Please, Marcel, be my friend. Be that first, and then maybe—if we're patient—and lucky—'

'You know what you're telling me, don't you? You can't love me and you don't want me to love you.'

'No!' she said fiercely. 'It isn't that. But I'm scared. Aren't you?'

'I wasn't before. I am now. I thought the other night—'

'The other night we found each other again, but only in one way. And—' she gave a reminiscent smile '—it was so lovely.'

'But not enough,' he said.

'Would it be enough for you, always? Won't there come a time when you're lying in my arms wondering if you can really trust me?'

He didn't answer, and she followed his thoughts. She'd hit a nerve, leaving him shocked and appalled at himself. He'd had as much as he could stand, she decided, and she must bring this to an end.

'I want to look at the view again,' she said, rising and going to the window. 'I've never seen such beauty.'

He made a suitable reply, and they left the dangerous subject behind. For the rest of the evening they kept carefully to indifferent subjects, presenting the appearance of a conventional couple, with no sign of the turbulence whirling inside them.

She knew that she must face the fact that there was a sad but crucial difference between them. With the truth finally revealed he'd become open to her, as though he was hers again. It was she who was holding back.

The feeling of detachment was painful. She longed to throw open her arms in welcome, vowing that everything was good again and all suffering would be forgotten. But the lessons of the past few years couldn't simply be unlearned. Most piercing of all was the fear of hurting him again.

Returning to the hotel, he saw her to her door but, to her relief, didn't try to come in. He'd read the signal she'd sent him and accepted it, however reluctantly. He would give her time, but his eyes told of his turmoil.

'I'll see you tomorrow, then,' he said. 'There are some figures we must go through. Goodnight.'

'Goodnight,' she whispered.

He touched her cheek, then departed quickly.

He had to be away several times in the next couple of weeks. When he returned they would dine together and talk, just as she'd hoped. On those evenings he kept his distance both physically and emotionally, making her wonder if he was following her lead or if he'd really decided against her. That thought filled her with irrational dismay.

You're mad, she told herself. *You don't know what you want.*

Which was true.

One afternoon, working together in his apartment, they had a bickering disagreement which threatened to turn into a quarrel. Afterwards she could never remember exactly what it had been about. Or if it had been about anything except the fact that a final separation might be looming.

'I should never have taken this job,' she sighed. 'Let's end it now. I'll go back to England and we need never see or think of each other again.'

'Do you imagine I'll allow that?'

'I don't think you could stop me leaving.'

'I could stop you any time I want to. You won't leave me, Cassie. I won't stand for it.'

'Don't,' she said harshly. 'That's the sort of thing Jake used to say. I can't bear it when you talk like him.'

He stared. 'Do I talk like him very often?'

'Sometimes. He regarded me as bought and paid for, and he made it plain.'

'And you think that's how I see you?'

'No, I—'

'Can't you understand that I still dread the thought of waking up to find you not there? I try to tell myself to be sensible but in that great echoing vacuum there's no sense, only horror. Every time you leave the room there's a voice in my head that says you won't come back. You fill my dreams but you also fill my nightmares.'

'Then perhaps you should let me go, and never think of me again.'

'And know that you'll never think of *me* again? That's the biggest nightmare of all. Sometimes I wish I had the strength to let you go, because then I might find peace. Not happiness, but peace. But I can't do it.'

She nodded. 'I know,' she said huskily. 'Me too.'

Now, she thought hopefully, they could talk and rediscover each other in yet another way. The road lay open before them.

But he seemed reluctant to take it, turning back to the computer screen.

Never mind, she thought. The chance would come again.

Next day Marcel announced that they needed to spend a few days in London.

'My purchase of the hotel isn't finalised yet and I'm getting impatient, so let's see if we can put some rockets under people. Vera, we'll need train tickets.'

'Train tickets?' his secretary echoed.

'That's what I said,' he called over his shoulder as he left the room.

'First time I've ever known him not take a plane,' Vera mused. 'I wonder why.'

Cassie thought she knew why and her heart was warmed by his concern for her, although when she tried to thank him he loftily brushed the matter aside as 'Pure convenience.'

'Of course,' she said, and kissed him.

This was the side of him she had loved, and for which she could feel the love creeping back. That might be dangerous while she was still unsure who this new man was, and how much of his old self still existed. But right now she was happy to take the risk.

Rather than leave it to Vera, she volunteered to book their hotel rooms.

'At the Crown Hotel,' she announced.

'Not The Crown yet,' Marcel pointed out. 'Until I sign the final papers it's still The Alton.'

'To them it's The Alton, to us it's The Crown,' she declared triumphantly. 'Everything's going to go right, and nothing will go wrong.'

'Yes,' he said with a smile that touched her heart. 'Nothing will go wrong. We won't let it.'

But he frowned when he saw the bookings she'd made.

'Separate rooms? Surely we could be together?'

'You're going to be the big boss. We need to preserve your dignity,' she said.

'If that means Mrs Henshaw in steel spectacles, forget it. I don't like that woman.'

'Then why did you hire her?'

'Because she didn't fool me. I want the real woman, the one she hides inside.'

'Unfortunately,' she murmured, 'it's Mrs Henshaw who's good with figures.'

He seemed struck by this. 'Ah, yes! Problem!'

Then someone came into the room and it could be passed off as a joke. But it lingered in her mind as a warning that troubles might lie ahead.

When they arrived in London Mrs Henshaw was at her most efficient, ironing out last minute problems, talking with bank managers and accountants. Marcel dominated the meetings, but whenever she spoke he listened intently, even admiringly. But afterwards he observed, to nobody in particular, 'I shall be glad when this is all over.'

There was an infuriating delay in the finance, owing to the bank demanding extra guarantees.

'Is this going to make it impossible?' she asked, seeing him gloomy.

'No, I can manage it, one way or another. I just don't want to have to ask my father's help. His fingers are in too many pies already.' He gave a slight shudder. 'Now come on, let's have some dinner.'

'Yes, let's see if I can cheer you up.'

'*You* can't,' he said, eyeing her 'Mrs Henshaw' appearance. 'But *she* could.'

'Mmm, I'll see if she's free tonight.'

'She'd better be.'

She wore her hair long, tumbling over her shoulders, and when they met for dinner in the restaurant he nodded approval.

'Will I pass?' she teased.

'You will, but we can't go on like this. It's like living with Jekyll and Hyde.'

'Really? So am I Dr Jekyll, middle-aged, scientific, brainy and kind? Or am I Mr Hyde, young and cruel?'

He sipped his wine for a moment before saying, 'Joking apart, it's more subtle than that. With Jekyll and Hyde you could always tell from the appearance. But with you I can't always tell. Whichever one you look like, the other one is always likely to pop out for a few moments, then dash back.'

'Yes, we exist side by side,' she agreed. 'Which may be confusing.'

'*May* be?'

'But why worry if ditzy Cassie sometimes has a great brain? There was a time when you knew that.'

'I know, I know. In those days—the great brain was just a part of you. I never dreamed it would take over your whole life in the form of Mrs Henshaw!'

'I know. But Mrs Henshaw was always there, lurking.'

'Yes, lurking, but now she's pounced. She's a bit alarming.'

'Maybe she wouldn't be if you knew her better,' she said, smiling.

This was the tone of the rest of the evening, light, easy, full of merriment and goodwill. She was happy, although still disturbed by a feeling that was half hope, half caution.

On the one hand there was the thoughtfulness that had made Marcel take the train for her sake. On the other hand was his reluctance to accept Mrs Henshaw as part of who she was. But that would sort itself out soon, she reassured herself.

In the meantime she was feeling exhausted. She'd worked through most of last night and all today, determined to stay on top of her duties. Now she would have given much to be able to sleep.

Hoping to liven herself up a little she took an extra glass of wine, and knew fairly soon that she'd made a mistake. If anything, she was woozier than before.

'I think I'll have an early night,' she said, and he rose at once, giving her his arm.

He followed her into her room and turned her towards him, looking down at her face with a questioning look. 'Are you all right?'

'Yes, just tired.'

'I'll say goodnight then.' He lifted her chin and laid his lips gently against hers.

Her head swam. The last time they had kissed there had been an edge of hostility, even violence, on her side as well as his. But now his touch was gentle, reminding her of happier times, and she responded with pleasure, although its edge was blunted by drowsiness.

'Cassie,' he murmured, 'Cassie…don't shut me out… please…'

'I don't…mean to…'

'Kiss me—I've waited for this so long and now…kiss me…'

She could feel the softness of the bed beneath her, his fingers opening her dress. Deep inside she sensed her own response, but waves of sleep washed over her brain.

Now, she thought, he would take what he pleased, knowing she was beyond resistance. She hadn't wanted it this way. Their next love-making should have been a union of hearts as well as bodies—not like this.

'Cassie—Cassie—*Cassie?*'

She opened her eyes, whispering, 'Marcel.'

His face was full of sudden suspicion. 'Are you entirely sober?'

'I…don't think so. I shouldn't have…oh. dear.'

His face tensed. He drew back and looked down at where her breasts were partially exposed, showing all the lushness that he'd always enjoyed. For a brief moment he let his fingertips linger on the swell, relishing the silky skin. His head drooped and she waited for the feel of his lips. But then he stiffened as though a bolt of lightning had gone through him. Next moment he'd practically hurled himself off the bed.

'Marcel—' she whispered.

He was breathing hard. 'Goodnight.'

He yanked at the duvet and threw it over her so that he could no longer see the glorious temptation, and moved towards the door.

'You're going?' she asked vaguely.

'Of course I'm going,' he answered. 'You really think I'm

going to—when you don't really know what you're doing? A fine opinion you have of me. Goodnight.'

'Marcel—'

The door slammed. There followed the noise of his footsteps running down the corridor, but she never heard them. She was already asleep.

CHAPTER TEN

NEXT morning he greeted her briskly. 'Just one more day and then we can be gone. There's some papers over there that need—' He couldn't meet her eyes.

It was almost funny, she thought. Last night he'd behaved like a perfect gentleman, refusing to take advantage of her vulnerability. It was practically worth a medal for chivalry. And he was secretly ashamed of it.

Which was a pity, because she couldn't tell him how proud she was of his generosity.

That evening they were invited to a business dinner, where networking would be a high priority.

'And I promise not to touch anything stronger than orange juice,' she said.

'And then—?'

'And then I'll be fully awake and alert, and I'll know exactly what I'm doing.'

She gave him a quick kiss and vanished, leaving him staring at her door in frustration, admiration and bemusement.

In her preparations, Cassie and Mrs Henshaw came together, the dress with a mysterious combination of severity and temptation, the hair drawn lightly back, but not scraped. She was a huge success. It was Marcel who had a lacklustre evening, unable to take his eyes off her and letting business opportunities slip by.

Later, as they approached his suite, she pulled her hair free, shaking it so that it flowed over her shoulders and forward down her breasts.

'You should be careful,' he murmured. 'A conceited man might interpret that as a hint.'

'Better a conceited man than a slow-witted one,' she said, slipping her arms around his neck. 'Just when will you get the message?'

'Right now,' he said, clasping her with one hand and pushing the door open with the other.

Twice since their meeting they had shared passion. The first time had been in anger, the second time the feeling had been gentler, but still tense.

But now they rediscovered many things they had both thought lost for ever. His touch brought her only delight, the look in his eyes raised her to the heights. He loved her slowly, prolonging every moment so that she could feel his tenderness.

And something else, perhaps. Love? Did she dare to hope?

When he finally abandoned control and yielded to her completely she held him close, hoping and praying for the miracle.

At last he whispered, 'Is everything all right?'

'Yes,' she said slowly. 'Very much all right.'

In the next few hours they loved, slept, and loved again. Now she was filled with deep joy, sensing the approaching moment when all would be made well.

Next day they returned to Paris and plunged back into work, both content to do so, knowing that better times were coming.

Soon, she promised herself, she would say the words that would make everything different between them. But first she would enjoy the pleasure that only he could give her. There would be plenty of time for talk.

He didn't even ask if he could come to her room. Now he knew he didn't need to ask. Nestled down in bed, they found themselves and each other again and again, before sleeping in utter contentment.

She awoke to find him watching her, and made a decision.

'Marcel—'

'Yes, Cassie?'

She took a deep breath. All hesitation gone. What better time could there ever be?

But before she could speak his cellphone shrilled.

He swore and grappled for it in his clothes. Cassie closed her eyes and groaned.

'Yes?' he answered. Then his face changed and he grew alert. 'Freya! What's the matter? You sound upset—all right, calm down. How can I help? What?—What's got into the old man now?—I don't believe it, even of him.'

At last he hung up and flung her a despairing glance.

'My father's up to his tricks again. He's on his way here. I think he's beginning to realise that he's not going to marry her off to Darius so he's turning his fire on me.'

Groaning, she covered her eyes with her hands. Of all the times for this to happen! Now she couldn't say what she'd meant to. For the moment the spell was broken.

'I need your help,' Marcel continued. 'So does Freya. If there's one thing she doesn't want it's to be stuck with me.'

Cassie forced herself to concentrate. 'Well, Freya was very kind to me, so I'll do all I can to save her from that terrible fate. Just tell me what to do.'

'When we take them to dinner we must act like a couple, just until he gets the message.'

'When are they going to arrive here?'

'Soon. Let's hurry.'

He was out of bed, throwing on his clothes. She sighed

and followed suit. The time would come, she promised herself. But she must be patient for a while.

Amos and Freya arrived two hours later. When Marcel had shown them to their rooms Amos said, 'I thought you'd still be in London working on that new place. But I dare say the admirable Mrs Henshaw is taking care of everything.'

'Admirable certainly,' Marcel agreed. 'In fact I've brought her here to study La Couronne so that she'll have a more precise idea of my wishes. She's looking forward to meeting you again when we all have dinner tonight.'

Amos made a displeased face. 'No need to invite her to dinner. I'm not in the mood for business.'

'But I'm in the mood to meet Mrs Henshaw again,' Freya said quickly. 'I liked her so much when we met in England.'

'She's eager to see you too,' Marcel assured her. 'Why don't you go up to the office and talk to her?'

The meeting between the two women was friendly and eager. Cassie had pleasant memories of Freya's kindly attention when she'd banged her head, but she'd been too confused to notice much about her. Now she saw an attractive young woman in her late twenties, slim and vigorous, with light brown hair that was almost auburn, green eyes and a cheeky smile. She ordered tea for them both and they settled down comfortably.

'I'm so glad you took the job with Marcel,' Freya said. 'He was so afraid that you wouldn't.'

'He thought I'd refuse it?'

'I don't know, but he seemed very worried about it. He must have heard a lot about your business skills.'

'Yes, I guess it must have been that,' Cassie murmured.

'He says you're having dinner with us. I'm so glad.'

Her fervent tone prompted Cassie to say cautiously, 'I gather Mr Falcon is trying to throw the two of you together.'

'Sort of. I don't think he's quite given up hope of Darius, but—'

'But he's keeping all his options open,' Cassie supplied. 'Just what you'd expect an entrepreneur to do.'

'Yes. Do you know what they're talking about now, why Amos originally came here? Bringing me was just an afterthought. He's helping Marcel raise extra funds for the London hotel. Somebody owes him money and there's a loophole in the contract by which Amos can get repaid earlier. So he's twisting the poor fellow's arm.'

'Not a nice man,' Cassie agreed.

'He's always thought Darius was that way inclined too. And Marcel is next in the money-making stakes. Honestly, who'd want to marry a man like that?'

'Nobody in their right mind,' Cassie agreed.

The phone rang. It was Marcel, wanting Vera, but the secretary had just left.

'I need some papers. Can you bring them to me? You'll find them—'

'No problem,' she said when he'd explained. 'I'll be right down with them.'

Approaching Amos's room, she could hear raised voices. One of them was Amos, but the loudest belonged to a young man who seemed almost hysterical.

'But it isn't fair. Can't you see that?'

'It's in the contract.' That was Amos.

'But you said it was just a fallback, and you'd never make use of it—'

'I said I probably wouldn't make use of it. It wasn't a guarantee.'

'You made it sound like one—as long as I kept up the repayments—'

'Which have sometimes been late.'

'They're up-to-date at this moment. Surely that's what counts?'

'*I* say what counts.' Amos's voice was as harsh as sandpaper, and Cassie stepped back from the door in revulsion.

The next moment she was glad of it for the door was yanked open by a man who came flying out. He turned to scream back, 'Be damned to you! I hope you rot in hell!'

Then he dashed off, forcing her to flatten herself against the wall. She stayed there, breathing out, trying to calm down. But before she was ready to enter the room she heard Marcel's voice.

'There was no need to go quite so far.'

'Don't give me that. I know just how far to go. I didn't get where I am by weakening. Nor should you.'

'I don't. I can be tough when I have to, but it's a new age. Subtlety can be better.'

'Only one thing matters,' came Amos's rasping voice. 'Does he have the cash or doesn't he?'

'According to him he doesn't. It might not be wise to press him too far.'

'Give me patience! Will nothing cure you of the habit of believing what people say?'

'It can actually be useful sometimes.'

'Not this time. Leave that man for me to deal with.'

Cassie backed away, wishing she could run far away from this horrible conversation that exhibited all the worst of Amos Falcon. She was glad that Marcel had had the decency to argue against him, although she wished he'd done so more strongly.

He'd advised his father to soften his stance, not out of kindness, but because subtlety offered a better chance of a profit. It was only a different road to the same money-filled destination.

Suddenly she was glad that she hadn't opened her heart to him that morning.

Amos Falcon was exactly as Cassie remembered him from their brief earlier meeting—in his seventies, heavily built with a harsh face and piercing eyes. He smiled a lot and his words were often cordial, but his eyes were cold.

He greeted her politely at dinner that evening and indicated a chair next to himself. Since the table was oblong, this effectively separated them from Marcel and Freya, sitting on the other side.

As so often these days, her appearance was a subtle combination of the two women who seemed to inhabit her. Amos regarded her with admiration.

'I'm going to enjoy talking to you this evening. Marcel, you entertain Freya. I want to get to know Mrs Henshaw.'

He proceeded to give Cassie all his attention, asking about her career, her abilities, the recent trip to England.

'Don't know why problems are cropping up now,' he growled. 'Those damned banks!'

'Well, I suppose they—' Cassie began.

She continued in this way for a while, talking generally without giving away any information about Marcel's dealings. Amos listened, nodding sometimes, and in this way the meal passed.

Over coffee things changed. Marcel joined in and the talk became all business. Amos mentioned the man who'd been there earlier, refusing to hand over money.

'He'll see sense,' he said. 'I'll make sure of that. He thinks he can defy me and get away with it. The best way—'

The two women met each other's eyes.

'You two don't need us for this kind of talk,' Freya said. 'Shall we—?'

'Yes, let's,' Cassie said, rising and following her. 'Goodnight, gentlemen.'

They said goodnight and returned at once to their discussion.

'They hardly noticed us go,' Freya said as they went up in the elevator, and Cassie nodded.

Upstairs in Cassie's rooms, Freya threw herself into an armchair with a sigh of relief. 'Oh, thank heavens!' she said. 'I'd had as much as I could stand.' She gave a laugh. 'Of course you probably find it interesting. Sorry, I forgot about that.'

'No, I was just as glad to get away,' Cassie said. 'I don't like it when it gets brutal.'

'Me too. I much prefer a good TV show and a handsome man. Hey, look at him!'

She'd flicked on the set, and suddenly the screen was filled with a staggeringly handsome young man.

'Know who that is?' she asked.

'Yes, it's Marcel's half-brother, Travis,' Cassie said. 'They started showing *The Man From Heaven* a few weeks ago, and I've been watching it because of Marcel. Who was his mother? Another of Amos's wives?'

'No, she was an American girl he met while he was over there on business.'

'So if he can't marry you to Darius or Marcel, Travis is the next in line?' Cassie asked, amused.

'Either him or Leonid, who lives in Russia, and who nobody seems to meet. Or Jackson, the naturalist. I'd have to be crazy to marry any of them, but especially Travis. His wife would never have a moment's peace he's so handsome. Mind you, it would be much the same with Marcel, who's also very handsome.'

'Is he?' Cassie asked indifferently.

'Well, some women think so. Is that tea? Thank you, I could do with it. Sometimes I think Amos insists on champagne all the time as a kind of status symbol, just to underline how far he's come from his days of poverty, when actually I'm dying for a cuppa.'

They sipped their tea in deep contentment.

'Why do you put up with it?' Cassie asked. 'Can't you escape him?'

'Yes, soon, hopefully. I'd like to go back to working as a nurse. The high life doesn't really suit me. I suppose I shouldn't complain. He's decent to my mother, and good to me. He wants me in the family.'

'I suppose that's nice of him.'

'Ye-es,' Freya said, unconvinced. 'It's only because he's never had a daughter and he sees a chance of "completing the set". A sharp businessman covers every angle.'

'That's true.'

'A few months ago Amos had a scare with his heart. He's too stubborn to admit that it might be serious so my mother asked me to come and stay with them for a while. This way he always has a nurse on hand, but he can pretend I'm just visiting.

'All his sons came to see him, just in case it was the last time. From things he said, I know he wanted to take a good look at them and decide which one was really his true heir. Whichever one he decides on will get an extra share of his fortune. And whichever one marries me will get an extra dose of money too, as a reward for "doing what Daddy wants".'

'Oh, heavens!' Cassie exclaimed in horror. 'How do you put up with it?'

'Because basically I'm free. I can walk out and get a job elsewhere any time I want. He got me on this trip by staging a dizzy spell at the last moment, so I came with him to keep my mother happy. But that's it! From now on I'm going to reclaim my life.'

A sense of mischief made Cassie say, 'Amos is a man very used to getting his own way. You might yet end up as his daughter-in-law.'

'I suppose anything's possible, however unlikely. But it won't be Darius because I think he's going to make it work with Harriet, the young woman he brought to the wedding in London. And it won't be Marcel. He wouldn't suit me at all.'

'You sound very sure,' Cassie said, not looking at her. 'Why is that?'

'He just sees things in black and white all the time. Where brains are concerned he's as sharp as they come. But emotionally I think he imagines things are more straightforward than they ever really are. Maybe that's because he doesn't seem to have much emotional life.'

'Doesn't he? Let me pour you some more tea.'

'I don't think so. Women galore but no real involvement. And if that's what satisfies him, he's not for me. And he won't marry for Amos's money because he doesn't need it. Sometimes I think he's just that little bit too much like Amos.'

'Or maybe he just likes to believe that things can work out simply and straightforwardly,' Cassie mused.

'True. Actually, I think a lot of men are like that—just not geared up to see how complicated life can be.'

'Yes,' Cassie said quietly. 'That's it.'

'Oh well, let them get on with it.'

Freya gave a theatrical shudder and glanced back at the screen where the drama series was still showing. Travis's face was still there.

'Why is this show called *The Man From Heaven?*' she queried.

'I think he's supposed to be at least partly an angel,' Cassie said.

'No guy as good-looking as that was ever an angel. But hey, don't you dare tell Amos I said that. I'd get no peace afterwards.'

Cassie chuckled and they continued the evening in perfect accord. She was beginning to feel that Freya was exactly the kind of person she would like to have as a close friend.

But she couldn't guess the astonishing way in which that would one day become true.

It was a couple of weeks later that she opened Marcel's door, stopped on the threshold, then prepared to back off, saying, 'I'm sorry, I didn't know you had someone here.'

'Come in, Mrs Henshaw,' Marcel called cheerfully. 'This is my brother, Darius.'

She'd recognised him from her research of the Falcon family, and knew part of his history. Eldest son of Amos Falcon and a skilled entrepreneur in his own right. Like many others, he'd been hit by the credit crunch and was now the owner of Herringdean, an island that a debtor had dumped on him by way of repayment.

'Darius has just invited me to his wedding,' Marcel explained now. 'He's finally persuaded Harriet to put up with him.'

'It wasn't easy.' Darius grinned. 'She's part of the lifeboat crew on Herringdean and she saved me from drowning in the first few days. Now I never feel safe if she's not around.' He thumped Marcel's shoulder. 'You've got to come. The other lads are all going to be there.'

'Yes, you have brothers all over the world,' Cassie said. 'I remember Freya telling me.'

'That's right, Jackson's going to get a few days off from interviewing animals. I had to twist his arm for that because he finds ferrets more interesting than people. Leonid's going to drop whatever he's doing in Russia and come on over, and the man from heaven has promised to put in an appearance.'

'Ah, yes, I've been watching that on television,' she said, smiling.

'So Travis will be there for the wedding, and so will Marcel. Come on Marcel, say you will.'

'Oh, no. I'm avoiding Amos at the moment. Now he can't marry you to Freya I'm in danger.'

'Dad probably won't be there. He's that mad at me for marrying Harriet that he's snubbing our wedding.'

'Yes and, knowing him, he'll drop in at the last minute,' Marcel observed.

'Coward,' Darius said amiably.

'No, I'll be there, but I want some protection. Mrs Henshaw must come with me and if Dad starts any funny business she'll deal with it.'

'That's the spirit,' Darius said. 'Mrs Henshaw, are you up to the job?'

'I think so,' she said cheerfully. 'If Mr Falcon tries to speak to Marcel I just tell him he must make an appointment through me first.'

'Hey, she's good.' Darius grinned. 'I'll leave you in safe hands. The wedding is next week. I know it's short notice but I can't risk Harriet changing her mind. Besides, she's got this dog—lovely fellow called Phantom. He did a lot to bring us together but he's very old and we want to marry while he's alive to see it.'

'It's not like you to be sentimental,' Marcel said.

'It's not like me to do a lot of things I'm doing these days. But Harriet…well… I don't know how to describe her…she's "the one"…no, that's not it. Well, yes, it is, but it's much more…at least…'

'You're stammering,' Marcel observed.

Darius gave an awkward laugh. 'I guess I am. It's the effect she has on me. She kept her distance for a while because she thought I only wanted to marry her for the sake of the children. I had to…persuade her otherwise.'

'Now you're blushing,' Marcel accused him. 'You, the man I've always admired because he could make everyone scramble to please him, you're scrambling to please Harriet.'

'Yes, I am,' Darius said with a touch of belligerence. 'I've finally got my priorities right, and she's what matters. I know you think I'm making a fool of myself, but I don't care what anyone else thinks. When you find the one, grab her, or you'll regret it all your life.'

'But that's assuming that you find the one in the first place,' Mrs Henshaw pointed out with a friendly smile.

'True. Marcel will probably never find her. Too busy playing the field. Never could commit himself. Probably never will now. Right, I must be off. Here's the details.' He gave her a sheet of paper. 'Get him there on time, see that he behaves.'

'That won't be easy,' she joked. 'But I'll do my best.'

When Darius had gone Marcel said, 'We need to go to London for a few more days to sort out some final details. Then we'll go on to Herringdean in time for the wedding.' He added significantly, 'I'm looking forward to that.'

In the atmosphere of a wedding anything might happen. Answers could be found, love might flower. His eyes told her that he was thinking the same thing.

He began to reach for her, but suddenly her cellphone rang. She answered it, then tensed, growing so still and silent that Marcel was alarmed.

'Don't hang up,' said a man's voice at the other end. 'You know who this is.'

Without replying, she ended the call.

'What's the matter?' Marcel asked, concerned. 'Why are you looking like that? Who was it?'

'Jake,' she said. 'I don't know how he got my number. He must be out of prison. How dare he contact me again!'

'Don't worry; I'll keep you safe,' he promised. 'I won't let him get to you again.'

She longed to believe him, but Jake could always get to her because he never really left her. That was the cruel truth that poisoned her life. Even now he must have been keeping tabs on her to have discovered her new phone number.

It rang again. She answered, saying sharply, 'I'm shutting this down—'

'I'm dying,' Jake said.

'What?'

'I've only got a few days left. I want to see you, Cassie—one last time.'

'No!'

'I'm not in prison any more. They let me out to die in hospital. You know the place—'

He gave her the name, while she clenched her free hand, whispering, 'No…no…no…'

'Please—I beg you—'

'No. Understand me, Jake, I don't care if you are dying. I don't want to see you again, ever.'

'Dying?' Marcel echoed.

'He wants me to go and see him.'

'Then tell him you'll go.'

'What?'

'I'll take you. You won't be alone.'

'Are you mad?'

'No, I want you to find closure, and this may be the only way you can do it. See him, Cassie. Tie up the ends. Then tell him from both of us to go to hell.'

She stared at him, mesmerised by something fierce and desperate in his voice. This mattered to Marcel. It was there in the tension of his body and the sharp edge of his voice.

'Tell him,' he said. 'Say you'll do it. Say it!'

'Marcel—'

'Say it!'

'Jake,' she said slowly, 'I'm on my way.'

CHAPTER ELEVEN

THIS time they took the plane to London. On the flight Marcel held her hand in his. She gave him a brief wan smile, but mostly she stared out of the window.

To see Jake again. To be forced back into his company. This was the stuff of nightmares, yet the road was taking her inexorably there and she had no chance of escape.

At last she turned to Marcel, trying to read his expression.

'Why are you doing this?' she murmured. 'It's not just for me, is it?'

'No,' he conceded. 'I need to see him myself. Can you understand that?'

'Yes, I suppose I can understand, but I'm afraid, Marcel.'

'Don't be. I'm here.'

The thought, *Not afraid of him—afraid of you*, winged its way through her mind and vanished into the distance. She didn't really know what she meant by it, and there was no way she could have told him, even if she had known.

She realised that Marcel was pursuing some goal of his own, and she was only part of it. He was like a man who'd travelled on an epic journey and who saw the end in sight.

'I heard you ask how he got your number,' he said. 'Do you think he's been keeping tabs on you?'

'He must have been. Even in prison he's had people on the outside taking his orders. When we were together he had a horrible obsession with me. All he saw was that I was his property. We'd go out to dinner and he'd flaunt me—that's the only word for it. And I'd have to smile and look proud, knowing that as soon as we got home he'd grab me and—'

'Don't!' Marcel said with soft violence. 'Don't.'

He threw himself back in his seat, his eyes closed.

'I'm sorry,' he said at last. 'I can't bear to hear it, but you had to live through it. You must despise me. I don't blame you.'

'We're past that,' she said gently. 'Neither of us knows what it was really like for the other. Let's take it carefully.'

He nodded and they held each other for a few moments.

'Talk to me,' he said at last. 'Tell me anything you like. I want to be part of your life, even that stage of it.'

She sighed. 'There was one moment when I hoped life might not be completely wretched. I was pregnant.'

'You've had a child?' he asked, startled.

'No, I miscarried. That was when Jake went sleeping around. I didn't mind. The less I saw of him, the better. And it gave me a way of divorcing him. He fought me but I had one big weapon.'

'Yes, you must have known a lot of his dark secrets by then.'

'I did, but that wasn't it. The real weapon was the fact that I didn't care about anything. He defeated people by scaring them, and when he knew I couldn't be scared he was left floundering.

'The last thing he said to me was, "You think you've got away from me, but you haven't really." And he was right. Once I'd escaped him all the feelings he'd killed began to come back, and I started caring again. He was always there in my nightmares, and I haven't been able to banish him.'

'But things are different now,' Marcel said firmly. 'We'll defeat him together.' Seeing the confused look in her eyes, he put his hands on either side of her face. 'We will. I promise you.'

'Will we?' she mused. 'Perhaps.'

'You don't believe me, do you? *Do you?*'

'I want to,' she said desperately. 'You don't know how much I want to believe that all the problems could be swept away so simply, but oh, my darling, it's more complicated than that, more worrying, more frightening.'

'But we're together now. How can we be frightened, either of us, while we have each other? We're going to defeat Jake, I promise you.'

She longed to believe him. She didn't have the words to tell him how confused and bewildering was the universe in which they lived now. He'd always seen things in simple black and white, she remembered. And sometimes he'd been right. If only he could be right now. But she was full of apprehension.

They were beginning the descent, and there was no chance to say more.

They had booked a hotel near Heathrow Airport, and after checking in they went straight to the hospital where Jake was living out his last few days.

They found him in a private ward. A guard was sitting by the bed, but he moved discreetly away.

Marcel had kept a firm, comforting grip on her hand, but then he released her and backed into the shadows.

She barely recognised Jake. Once a big, beefy man, he was now skeletally thin.

'Cassie?' he croaked. 'Is that you? I can't see you properly.'

'Yes, it's me.'

'Come closer.'

Reluctantly she leaned down and he reached up a hand to touch her cheek. With an effort she stopped herself from flinching and sat on the bed. He managed a ghastly travesty of a smile, croaking, 'You're still beautiful, still my Cassie.'

'I was never your Cassie,' she said at once.

'You were my wife.'

'Not in my heart. Never.'

'But you're here,' he gasped. 'I knew you'd come.'

'No,' she said quietly. 'Don't fool yourself, Jake. I'm sorry for you, but there's nothing between us. There never was.'

'Oh, you always played hard to get. That's what I loved about you. Yes, we belonged together. I always knew it.'

'And you deluded yourself,' she said, filled with disgust. 'You hurt the man I loved and I stayed with you to protect him. That's the only reason.'

'Him? Don't make me laugh. He was nobody. By now he's probably scraping a living sweeping the streets.'

This was Marcel's moment and he took it, moving out of the shadows to stand beside Cassie.

'You were wrong about that,' he said, 'as you have been wrong about everything.'

'Who the hell are you?' Jake demanded.

'You don't know me? No, I suppose you wouldn't. You got someone else to do your dirty work. They left me lying in a pool of blood in the street. But here I am and now I've seen all I needed to.'

Then Jake did something that astounded them both. He began to laugh.

'Fine talk,' he gasped. 'You think you've won, don't you? If you'd *won* back *then* you would have won. She was young and glorious, better than she'll ever be again in her life. Those were her best years, and they were mine, d'you hear? Mine. I had things you'll never know.'

'No, he had things *you* never knew,' Cassie said. 'He had my love, given freely. That's something you never had.'

Jake barely heard her. His hate-filled eyes were on Marcel.

'You didn't win,' he spat, 'and one day you'll realise that. Cassie died years ago. All you've got now is the shell. You think you have a future? What kind of future? No children. She can't have any.'

'Not with you, maybe,' Marcel said softly.

Jake turned to Cassie and he was suddenly shaken with a coughing fit. His hands gripped her arms with the last of his strength. She hated him but a feeling of pity made her clasp him back.

'You came to me,' he choked. 'You came…you couldn't stay away…'

'I came because he asked me to,' she said with a fierce glance at Marcel. 'Nothing else would have brought me here.'

'You're lying…I'm your husband…Cassie…my Cassie…mine…'

Gasps tore him, growing faster, noisier, until at last he fell back against the pillows.

'You were always mine,' he murmured as his eyes closed.

'No,' she breathed. 'Never, *never!*'

He could no longer hear her. His eyes, half open, stared unseeingly into a hidden distance. His rigid hands, clasping her arms, held her prisoner.

'No,' she wept. 'Please, no.'

In a flash Marcel was there, wrenching Jake's hands away, setting her free.

'Let's go,' he said.

In the taxi he held her shuddering body.

'Everything's all right,' he said. 'It's over now.'

But it wasn't over. And suddenly she doubted that everything would ever be all right.

Back in the hotel he came to her room and immediately called Room Service to order supper. While they waited he went to his own room, returning with his night clothes. When the food arrived he prepared to serve her.

'I'm not really hungry,' she sighed.

'I know, but you have to eat anyway. Don't argue.'

His tone was gentle but firm, and she let him take over. She felt drained and defeated. Where was the sense of triumph that should have filled her? Nothing. Only the troubling sense that Jake had mysteriously won again.

He helped her to undress, then he put her to bed and got in beside her, taking her into his arms, holding her as though in this way he could keep her safe. She snuggled against him, reaching out for that safety.

She fell into a contented sleep and awoke to find him touching her intimately. She responded, giving and seeking love, letting him take her into the dream.

'It's all right,' Marcel murmured. 'He's gone. Now it's just us.'

'Yes,' she said, trying to believe that this was really so.

But there was still a dark and worrying cloud hanging over her. She didn't look at it too closely. She didn't want to understand it.

But some kind of understanding was forced on her when she awoke in the early hours with a headache. Moving quietly not to wake Marcel, she slipped out of bed, and went to her bag, seeking a pill. Not finding what she wanted, she reached her fingers into a small pocket inside that normally she never used. What she found there almost made her heart stop.

Drawing the tiny object out into the light, she surveyed it with horror. It was the ring Jake had given her long ago, and which she'd flung back at him during the divorce.

She remembered how she'd sat by his bed that afternoon, leaning over him, the bag lying on the coverlet. He must have slipped the ring inside when his hand moved towards her. It had fallen into the pocket without her noticing.

With a horrified, sick feeling she realised that it was what he'd always meant to do. By returning it he'd reasserted his claim on her from beyond the grave.

'Cassie?' Marcel appeared, rubbing sleep from his eyes. 'Are you all right?'

'Yes, fine,' she said, closing the bag. 'I'm just coming back to bed.'

Briefly she thought of confiding in him and letting him deal with the matter. But she rejected the thought. Her head was invaded by confusion, and she wouldn't have known what to say.

In bed he took her back into his arms, comforting her with his warmth and strength. Seeking more, she ran her hands over him, taking reassurance from the feel of him. Suddenly she stopped.

'What is it?' he whispered.

She switched on the light and leaned back to survey his chest with the livid scar that ran across it. Slowly, almost fearfully, she touched it.

'That's what he did,' she murmured. 'Oh, God!' She laid her face against it.

'It's all right,' he said gently. 'It was bad at the time but they made me right again. I'm fine now. Don't grieve. It's over.'

'It's not over,' she wept. 'It'll never be over. You might have died.'

'I didn't die.'

But in another sense he had died, and so had she. The wounds had healed but the scars would be there for ever, and they both knew it. Through the barrier of time, from prison, from beyond the grave, Jake had put the shackles back on her.

Darius's wedding was drawing near. Back in Paris, Cassie booked them both into The Conway Hotel on Herringdean

Island. Freya called to say she would be there, but not Amos, which was a relief to them both.

'And my mother's coming,' Marcel said.

Since Laura Degrande also lived in Paris she would join them the night before their departure and travel with them. Cassie was curious to meet her, but also a little apprehensive, wondering what Marcel would have told her. Laura greeted her civilly but was not forthcoming. Sometimes Cassie would look up to find Marcel's mother watching her. Then Laura would smile, but not speak.

Between herself and Marcel, recent events were never mentioned. She shut him, and all to do with him, away in a compartment of her mind, which she bolted, barred, and threw away the key.

Marcel too never spoke of that time. He might have been waiting for a signal from her, which never came. With the wedding coming up they both assumed a cheerful demeanour. Nor was it entirely a pretence. She discovered that a locked compartment could work well, even if only intermittently.

Since it wasn't possible to take the train to Herringdean they travelled by helicopter and Cassie forgot her fear in the dazzling pleasure of skimming low over the Channel and seeing the island come into view.

'How beautiful,' she murmured.

'Yes, you really have to envy Darius,' Marcel agreed.

'Living in a place like this? I agree.'

'I meant more than that,' he murmured.

She turned her head and found him looking at her with a mysterious smile, but the helicopter was descending and there was no time to talk.

Darius was waiting as they landed, with a cheerful young woman by his side. Cassie took to Harriet at once.

Darius seemed on good terms with Laura, whom he hugged. After the introductions he said, 'I'll drive you to the hotel. When you've settled in, you come on to my place. We're having a big party.'

'Who else is here?' Marcel called.

'Jackson's arrived, and Travis. Travis is staying with me so that he can hide. He daren't go out in the street without girls shrieking, *"That's him!"* Jackson ribs him something terrible. They've started showing his series on Herringdean now, so there's no escape.'

'But not Amos,' Laura said. 'You assured me—'

'No, not Amos. Promise.'

They got through the hotel formalities as fast as possible, and were taken straight to Giant's Beacon, where Darius lived, which turned out to be a magnificent building overlooking the sea. They arrived to find Jackson and Travis standing outside, watching for them.

She recognised Travis at once as the actor she'd seen on screen. He greeted her with charm and practised friendliness, and she immediately understood why Freya was wary of him. Too charming. Too handsome.

She also recognised Jackson as a naturalist she'd seen onscreen. Not handsome in the Travis style, but good-looking in a 'kid brother' fashion. She liked him.

The house was decked out with flowers in the halls and one huge room filled with tables. Because this had to be saved for the wedding reception the next day, the family gathered outside that night and partied under lights hanging from the trees.

The Falcon family might be riven with divisions, but tonight they were forgotten and only the warmth could be felt. Cassie thought that Harry, as everyone called her, was exactly as a bride should be, full of happiness at her love but, more than that, the deep contentment of someone who knew, beyond all possible doubt, that she had come to the right place.

'When did you know for sure?' she asked when they were alone for a moment.

'It was him,' Harry said, pointing to a large dog who lay curled up on the sofa.

'Is that Phantom?' Cassie asked. 'Darius said he'd done a lot to bring you together, and you wanted him at the wedding.'

'That's right. We thought he was going to die one day, and I was called out on the lifeboat. I hated leaving him to die without me, but Darius stayed with him, talking to him, letting him know he was loved and wanted. And he didn't die. I still have my darling Phantom, and it's all because of Darius. I'd been wondering about him for a while, but that was the turning point, when it all became clear.'

Cassie nodded. 'If you were lucky enough to have a turning point everything would be easy,' she mused.

'Of course most people aren't that lucky,' Harry agreed. 'They have to just hope they've got it right. But I knew then that I mustn't let this wonderful man get away. When you find a man who understands you so perfectly you've got to hold onto him.'

'Yes,' Cassie murmured. 'If he understood you, and you understood him—everything would be simple.'

She reached down and stroked Phantom's head, wishing that she too could have a Phantom instead of the unruly ghosts who seemed bent on confusing her.

There was an excited murmur in the hall.

'That'll be Leonid,' Harry said. 'Darius went to collect him. He's the mystery man of the family, and I'm dying to meet him.'

From the first moment Leonid lived up to the tag 'mystery man'. He had black hair, dark blue eyes and an ultra-lean face.

'Haunted,' Cassie murmured. 'Or am I being too melodramatic?'

'I don't think so,' Harry murmured back.

Freya joined in. 'Where has he come from and where is he going?' she said. 'The rest of the world will never know.'

'Oh, that's really being a bit fanciful,' Harry protested.

'No,' said Freya. 'It isn't.'

The other two women exchanged glances that said, *Maybe he's the one she'll marry. This is going to be interesting.*

Watching Leonid make the rounds, Cassie had the impression that he knew none of his family well. She wondered how often he left Russia. He greeted her courteously, speaking in a deep voice with a distinctive accent. He was an attractive man, she thought, but very reserved, which some women might find intriguing.

Cassie suddenly realised that Laura was looking at her, then towards the trees with a question in her face. She nodded and rose, moving quietly away from the lights and under the trees, where she waited for Marcel's mother, who joined her a moment later.

'I have wanted to meet you for some time,' she said.

'Yes, I suppose Marcel has told you all about me. You must hate me.'

'I did once,' Laura agreed, 'many years ago. He came flying home from London, ran to me and shut himself away in his room. I used to stand outside the door and hear him sobbing. When he told me how his beautiful girlfriend had betrayed him when he was ill, then I hated you.

'I hated you even more as the years passed and I saw my generous, gentle son retreat into himself and turn into a terrible copy of his father. But a few weeks ago he came back home and found the letter. I saw his distress when he discovered pieces missing. It mattered so much to him. I wonder if you can understand how much it meant.

'When he was back in Paris he called me to say he'd spoken to you and all was now well. You had never betrayed him, and he could have known that if he hadn't torn up the letter. I've never heard him so happy. I thought soon he would tell me that you were reunited, but there has been nothing. And I came to ask you—to beg you—please don't break his heart again.'

'I don't want to, but—'

'But you're not sure you love him?'

'How can I be when I don't know who he is? We've both changed in ten years. I love—part of him, but the other part worries me. You said he'd become like his father. I need to know how much before I can make a decision.

'He's compared it to Jekyll and Hyde, and he's right. There are two people living inside each of us, and we all four have to learn to love each other. Otherwise there will only be more heartbreak and misery.'

'It will happen,' Laura said earnestly. 'It must. Look.' She reached into her bag and pulled out a little black box which she opened, revealing a ring with the biggest diamond Cassie had ever seen.

'Amos gave it to me when I first knew him. I've kept it all these years for Marcel, so that he can give it to the girl he loves.'

'It's beautiful,' Cassie said, gazing at the ring.

'Would you like to try it on?'

'No,' she said quickly. 'You're very kind but no thank you.'

Laura sighed and put the ring away. 'I shall hope for better things soon.'

As they strolled back together Jackson came out to call, 'Come on in! You'll never guess who's on the box *again!*'

'Travis?' Cassie laughed.

'Honestly, I swear he thinks he really comes from heaven. There's no getting away from him.'

In fact the episode was nearly over and they arrived just in time to hear Travis announce heroically, 'That's what we must all remember. Seize the moment whenever it comes. Don't let the chance slip away, or we may regret it for ever.'

Everyone in the room laughed and cheered, Travis looked sheepish and held out his glass for another drink.

Cassie cheered with the others, glancing across at Marcel to see if he shared the amusement, but he seemed sunk in thought, as though something had taken him by surprise.

But then he looked up and smiled. Someone appeared at Cassie's side, offering wine, and the party engulfed her again.

It was only later that she remembered Travis's dramatic pronouncement, because of its devastating consequences.

Next morning the family gathered on the beach for the wedding to take place. When Harry appeared she was accompanied by Darius's children, his daughter Frankie and son Mark. With them came Phantom, whom Mark led to the front and settled him where he had a good view.

Cassie watched, entranced, not only by the beauty of the ceremony and the surroundings, but by the love that blazed from the bride and groom.

She remembered Harry's words about the turning point, the moment when the road ahead became clear. Would she and Marcel ever reach that point? Or was it too much to hope for?

She stole a glance at him and found him looking at her intently. She smiled, receiving his smile in return. And something else? Had she imagined it or had he nodded? And if so, what had he meant?

Then he looked away, and she was left with her thoughts.

For a long time after that she wondered about that moment, and how differently everything might have turned out.

The reception was much as expected—speeches, laughter, happiness. Then they spilled out into the garden again and someone put on some music so that there could be dancing.

'Are you glad we came?' Marcel asked as they twirled under the trees.

'I wouldn't have missed it for the world. Everything was perfect.'

'Yes, they seized the chance when it came. Travis was right. That's what we should always do. Now, watch this!'

Plunging a hand into his pocket, he drew out the diamond ring Cassie had last seen in Laura's hand. Before she knew what he meant to do, he took her hand and slid it onto her finger.

'Marcel—'

'Seize the moment,' he said. 'This is our moment and I'm seizing it. *Listen, everybody!*'

They all stopped and looked at him eagerly.

'I've got wonderful news,' he cried. He held up Cassie's hand so that they could all see the glittering diamond.

'She's said yes, and the wedding will be as soon as possible.'

Cheers and applause. The family crowded around them, smiling, patting them on the back, embracing Cassie, asking to see the ring.

She showed it mechanically. Inwardly she was in turmoil, her mind whirling with a thousand desperate thoughts, of which the chief one was, *No!*

CHAPTER TWELVE

THE crowd waved and cheered. Harry flung her arms around Cassie, crying, 'You next. I'm so glad.'

Cassie maintained a determined smile, practically fixed on with rivets to hide her real thoughts.

She loved this man, so why wasn't she over the moon at his declaration of love?

Because there had been no such declaration, only a pronouncement without asking her opinion first. And this was the side of him that roused her hostility.

It would take a heart of stone to resist the way Marcel was gazing at her now, but she forced her heart to be stone.

'Aren't you going to ask me to dance?' she said and he swept her onto the floor.

Here there was a kind of safety. Nobody could hear them or study their whirling forms too closely.

'Well,' he said, smiling in a way that would have dazzled her with delight at any other time, 'we finally got that settled.'

'Did we?' she retorted. 'You didn't even wait for my reply.'

'I didn't need to,' he said, still smiling. 'I won't take no for an answer.'

Give in, cried a voice deep inside her. *You love him. Isn't that enough?*

But it wasn't enough to quell the indignation rising in her.

'But I won't have to, will I?' he persisted. 'You know this is what we both want.'

'If you're so sure of that, why won't you wait for me to answer?'

He sighed, humouring her. 'All right, we'll do it your way. Cassie my love, will you marry me?'

She looked into his eyes and shook her head. 'No, Marcel, I won't.'

'Oh, I see, you're going to make me beg.'

'No, don't beg. It would only make it worse when you have to accept my refusal.'

'Darling—'

'I mean it. Let's get out of here.'

The way back to the village lay along a road overlooking the sea. Halfway there, he stopped the car.

'Better if we talk here,' he said.

'Yes.' She left the car and went to stand looking out over the waves. 'I can't marry you, Marcel.'

'I know we've needed time to sort things out, but I thought we'd managed that by now.'

'But you didn't ask me. You just assumed I agreed with you and claimed me in front of everyone, almost as though the decision didn't concern me. That's the side of you I dislike so much, the side that makes you check up on me when I'm out, making phone calls to see if I'm there.'

'I never give up something that belongs to me. If it's mine, it's mine. You belong to me, and I won't give you up.'

'You talk as though I was an inanimate object, nothing but a possession.'

'You are a possession, but not inanimate. You belong to me because you once gave yourself to me of your own free will.'

'And then took myself back.'

'But not of your own free will. You yourself told me that, so it doesn't invalidate your original gift.'

'But you can't—we can't—'

'Maybe you can't, but I can. And I'm going to. All those years ago we made a verbal contract and I'm holding you to it.'

She regarded him with disbelief. She didn't know this man. He called himself Marcel, but there was a glint in his eyes that took her by surprise. It might almost have been humour, and the curve of his lips suggested a hint of teasing that went back to the other Marcel, years ago.

'A contract is a contract,' he said. 'You told me a thousand times that you belonged to me and nobody else. Nothing that's happened since invalidates that, so the deal still stands.'

'And that's what I am to you—a business arrangement.'

'Of course. But you'll find that I conduct business at very close quarters.' As he spoke he drew her close.

It was sweet to be in his arms again, but the voice of reason rose up and screamed, reminding her of all the sensible resolutions she'd made.

'No,' she said, pushing him away. 'Can't you understand? *No!*'

He stepped back. 'Then you don't love me?'

She sighed. 'Cassie loves you, but Mrs Henshaw can't stay with a man who behaves like this.'

'Isn't it time we forgot that Jekyll and Hyde nonsense?'

'But it's how things are, except that I'm content to be both people. But you aren't content. You only want one of us and you can't accept that we come as a package. But so do you. You're just as much two people as I am. One of you is the Marcel I loved. The other one acts more like Amos, or even J—'

'Don't!' he shouted. 'Don't dare to compare me to Jake Simpson.'

'Why not? He used to give me orders, and drive me up a blind alley so that there was no choice but to do as he wanted.'

Silence. Only the wind and the murmur of the waves.

'You'd better take this,' she said, handing him the ring. 'It might have fitted me years ago, but not now.'

By common consent, not a word was spoken as they returned to the hotel. Laura was already there.

'I didn't expect you two back so soon,' she teased.

'I'm tired,' Cassie said quickly. 'I'm going straight to bed.'

Laura's eager questioning look was more than she could endure. There was no way she could talk about what was happening, so she went quickly to her room and locked the door. Tonight she needed to be alone, perhaps to think, or perhaps to yield herself up to the confusion and dismay that was now all she could feel. She longed to go to sleep but could only stare up at the ceiling, longing for the night to be over.

Next day they all returned to Paris. Marcel drove Laura back to her home.

'Did you tell her?' Cassie asked when he returned.

'No. I wasn't sure what to say.'

'Tell her everything when I've left. I think I should go to London tomorrow.'

'And that's it?' he asked, aghast.

'When you see the end of the road there's nothing to do but head for it.'

'But is that really the end of the road? Cassie—'

'Don't,' she begged. 'I can't make you happy, Marcel, any more than you could make me happy. We're each of us too different from what the other wants.'

'Is that really true?' he whispered. 'I can't make you happy?'

Dumbly she shook her head.

It was as though someone had struck him a blow. He sagged, his head drooped and he turned away in defeat. Cassie reached out her hand, driven by the impulse to comfort him. But then she drew back. She had to stick to her resolve for both their sakes.

She spent the rest of the day alone in her room, tying up ends, leaving him notes. The night was sleepless. Every moment she expected him to come to her.

But he did not. He had accepted her decision.

Nor did he come next morning, and she wondered if he was going to let her go without another word. But there were surely words to be spoken at the last. She went along to his apartment and found Vera just leaving.

'He's given me the day off,' she said. 'Bye!'

She sped along the corridor and Cassie slipped inside. There was no sign of Marcel. She closed her eyes, full of confusion. Her mind and heart were full of so many feelings and impressions, and they all seemed to contradict each other.

She looked into the bedroom which, by now, she knew, with its extra large double bed that was so comfortable for the indulgence of pleasure followed by sleep. But he wasn't there. Next stood another door which she'd only half noticed before. She tried the handle and felt it give.

Probably a cupboard, she thought, easing it open, meaning just to take a quick glance. But what she found made her push the door wide and stand on the threshold, confused and trying desperately to understand.

It was a bedroom, although prison cell might have described it better. Pushed up against the wall was a bed so narrow that it sent a dismal message. No lovers could ever share that restricted space. The man who slept here slept alone. There was no wardrobe. A small bedside chest of drawers was the only other furniture.

But surely, she thought, Marcel slept in the huge bed in the other room? But this one looked as if it had been recently slept in, and only clumsily made. It couldn't be anyone but him, which meant—surely not?

She sensed the truth by instinct. The outer room was the bedroom 'for show', the place where he took good-time girls who would expect to find him sleeping in lush surroundings, no expense spared. To keep up his reputation, he provided the background they expected, wined and dined them, made the speeches they would expect of a playboy and seduced them

But then he retreated to this bleak little place, because this was where he felt he belonged. Here he could be his true self. At least, that was how he felt.

The warm, life-loving, open-hearted boy she had loved had become the man who only felt truly comfortable in retreat. That thought distressed her more than any other.

And he'd loved the same about her, she thought, remembering how he'd said only recently, 'She gave herself to the world.'

They had both changed, both been damaged. She had thought she understood the extent of the injury to him, but now she was being forced to recognise how badly he'd been hurt.

'So now you know,' said a voice behind her.

Turning, she saw Marcel in the doorway, watching her. She searched his face for anger but found only weariness and resignation.

'Why didn't you tell me?' she whispered, gesturing to the bleak surroundings.

'Why do you think? Do you imagine I wanted you to know what a hopeless, miserable specimen I'd become? Look at it!'

'It...doesn't look very comfortable,' she said, searching for the right words.

'It doesn't need to be comfortable. It serves its purpose.'

She couldn't bear any more. She put her arms about him in an embrace of comfort. She thought he would cling to her, but at first he didn't. Instead his hands reached up hesitantly, barely touching her, then down again, as though he wasn't quite sure.

But at last he seemed to summon up his courage, wrapping his arms about her, drawing her against him and dropping his head so that his face was hidden against her neck. Cassie stroked his hair softly and they stood like that for a long time.

'I usually keep this door locked,' he said. 'Nobody else has any idea. Nobody ever will.'

'Nobody?' she asked.

'Nobody at all. This is me, deep inside, where nobody else ever gets to look. Not since…well…'

She stroked his face. 'Oh, my dear, dear Marcel—how long have you had this?'

'Since I bought the hotel, five years ago. Out there is the "official bedroom", and in here is the real one.'

'You never brought me in here.'

'I was waiting for the right moment—' He looked at her.

'It's now,' she said, drawing him down.

In the narrow bed there was only one way to make love, and that was to cling together, arms holding each other close, faces touching gently. When he claimed her she felt herself become one with him as never before. When he'd finished she offered herself to him again, and felt him accept her gift gratefully. In return he gave her gifts of power and tenderness that made her heart rejoice as never before in her life.

As the storm died away and she felt peace return she knew a passionate gratitude that this had happened while there was still time.

She looked up at him, eyes shining with love, waiting for him to utter the words that would start their life together.

'Goodbye,' he said.

* * *

Later that day he took her to the airport.

'There's the line for Check In,' he said. 'You're in good time. I'll go now.'

She turned tortured eyes towards him.

'Don't worry,' he said. 'I won't trouble you any more. I'm glad we had this morning. It means we can part on good terms, and that's important after the way we parted last time.'

He was silent, searching her face for something he needed to find there.

'At least we met again and found out…well, things we needed to find out. We'll always have that.'

'Marcel—'

'I told you it's all right. You're free of me now. No one stalking you, checking up on you, trying to back you into a corner. You were right about that. Goodbye, my darling. Be happy.'

'And you,' she said.

'Happy? Without you? Surely you understand that the only happiness I can have now is knowing that I set you free. Heaven forbid that you should regard me as you regarded him, a bully who forced you to do what he wanted. It's the way I was going, wasn't it? I wouldn't face it, but it was true. Thank goodness you showed me in time.'

'Why did it have to be this way?' she whispered.

'I don't know, but I do know that if we'd stayed together you'd have come to hate me, and I'll endure anything but that. Goodbye, my dearest. Find a man who deserves you, and be happy with him.'

'You can wish that?' she asked, amazed.

'I can wish anything for you that's good.'

'And you—oh, heavens, we both harmed each other so much. If only—'

'I know. But I won't risk harming you any more.' He leaned down and kissed her cheek. 'Goodbye.'

She watched as he walked away. Last time they had been in this airport he'd cried out her name in desperate determination to stop her leaving. But now he kept walking, not once looking back.

She stood there for a long, long time before moving off very slowly.

She was numb for the journey. Only when she was at home, behind a locked door, staring into the darkness, did she finally face what had happened.

Marcel had opened his arms and set her free because it was the only way he could show himself better than her fears. By doing this he'd proved the strength of his love for her.

It was the moment she'd been secretly waiting for, what Harry had called 'the turning point, when it all became clear.'

The clarity was blinding. Marcel had done what she hadn't believed possible, behaving with a generosity that paradoxically freed her to love him completely. Now she knew beyond all doubt that he was the one. The only one.

And she had lost him. It was over. Final.

Perhaps it was the best thing for him too, she thought, trying to comfort herself. If they had stayed together she might have made him wretched. He deserved better than that. He deserved better than *her.*

And with the thought came a sense of pride and even happiness that she'd thought never to know again. Marcel had loved her enough to ignore his own needs, his own pain. His generosity raised him head and shoulders above all other men. To be loved by him was an honour.

She might never see or hear from him again, but as long as she lived she would know that she'd won the heart of the finest, bravest, strongest, most honourable man in the world. That thought would sustain her throughout the long, sad years ahead.

* * *

Back in London, she realised that it was time to be practical. She was out of a job. There was more in her bank account than she had realised, owing to a sudden infusion of funds from Paris on the day she'd left. Marcel had put in three months' wages as a farewell gift.

She texted him, *Thank you.* And received in return, *Good luck!*

Nothing else. Not a word.

But the money wouldn't last for ever, as she realised when she visited her family, and her brother-in-law exclaimed, 'Do you mean you're out of a job?'

'Don't worry,' she said, handing him a cheque. 'I'll get another.'

But what? That was the question. The business world beckoned, but it no longer satisfied her. She needed more to fill the emptiness inside.

A few evenings later she went for a walk along the Thames, sometimes stopping to lean on the wall and watch the blazing sunset over the river. As she gazed she suddenly heard the sound of a familiar click, and turned to see a man aiming a camera at her.

'Don't move,' he called. 'I haven't finished.'

'You've got a cheek,' she began, then stopped. 'Hey, aren't you—Toby?'

Toby had been the eager young assistant of the photographer who had helped to make Cassie's name ten years ago. Since then he'd become successful on his own account.

'How lovely to see you after all this time!' she said, embracing him warmly. 'Let's go and have a coffee.'

'Not just yet,' he said. 'I'm not passing up my chance of a photo session with the great Cassie.'

'She's not the great Cassie any more. Let's get back to the studio.'

The pictures astonished her so much that she yielded readily to his suggestion of a 'proper shoot'. It was simple fun until he said, 'I've had a brilliant idea. The return of Cassie, more beautiful than ever.'

'You're mad,' she said, laughing.

'Sure I'm mad. That's what's most fun. Now, here's what we'll do…'

Her return was a sensation. Voluptuous Cassie belonged to the past. This was another age, Toby told her. Lean and boyish was 'in'. Now she was in demand again.

One evening a few weeks later, there was a knock at her door and she opened to find—

'Freya!'

When they were both settled over tea and cakes, Freya said, 'I hear you're making a modelling comeback.'

'Not really. Just a few shoots. I simply wanted to be sure I could do it.'

'Cassie still lives, huh?'

'Yes, she does. That was a nice surprise, and Mrs Henshaw thinks the money's nice, so we'll see. What about you?'

'I've come back to London to get a nursing job. Amos was just getting too much for me. You'll never guess what his latest wheeze is.'

'Jackson? Leonid? Travis?'

'Still Marcel. Honestly, that man doesn't understand the word "no". He's only put a load of money into my bank account, without even asking me. He knows Marcel needs money and he thought that would sway him.'

'Why is he still in need of money? I thought that was all sorted.'

'So did Amos. He was going to squeeze it out of that man—remember him?'

'I remember,' Cassie said quietly.

'But Marcel made him back off.'

'Marcel did?' Cassie asked quickly.

'Yes, I gather there were some very tough discussions and Marcel prevailed. So then they needed money from somewhere else, and he's raised it by selling shares in La Couronne.'

'But that place is his pride and joy!'

'Yes, but his mind was made up. He raised the cash and he's bought the London hotel but he's not out of the woods yet. So Amos thought making me rich would make Marcel go down on one knee.'

'And you don't think it will?' Cassie asked, pouring tea with great concentration.

'I've warned him if he does I'll thump him. Besides, he's still pining for you.'

A pause while her heart lurched, then a shaky laugh. 'That's nonsense.'

'No, it's not. I called in on him in Paris on my way here and we had a talk. He told me how your engagement ended. Not that there was really an engagement, was there? What an idiot he was to do it that way! I told him what I thought of him. But you two are right for each other and I won't see it come to nothing just because he's made a stupid mistake.'

Cassie shook her head helplessly. 'It's too late for that.'

'You mean you don't love him any more?'

'Of course I love him. I always will, but—'

'Do you want to talk?' Freya asked.

'Yes, I need to. When I first returned to London I was sad at losing Marcel, but I could bear it because I was so proud of him for leaving me. He did it to protect me. I'm still proud of him but—'

'But there's a lot of life still to get through,' Freya said shrewdly.

'I want him back, but I can't try to tempt him back. That's not the way.'

'Right, because if he could be tempted you wouldn't still be proud of him,' Freya said.

'Right. You're so clever. I really wish you were my sister.'

'If we play our cards right, I soon will be. Tempting is out. Compulsion is in. You've got to grab him by the scruff of the neck and not give him any choice. Now, listen carefully. This is what we're going to do…'

A few weeks later Vera glanced up as her employer hurried in. His face was tense and troubled, as always these days. But she thought that might be about to change.

'You have a visitor,' she said. 'Someone has just bought some shares in this place and says they need to see you urgently.' She nodded in the direction of her office door. 'In there.'

Frowning, he went in and stopped on the threshold.

'Hello,' said Cassie.

He drew a long breath, fighting for the control that he would need at this moment more than any other. 'What… Vera said…shareholder…'

'That's right. I've bought shares in La Couronne and I thought I should tell you soon.'

'But…it must have cost you a fortune. How did you—?'

'Raise the cash? From Freya. She's made me a big loan, which I shall pay off from the money I'll make from the hotel.'

'But surely she can't have loaned you enough to—'

'No, I have another source of income. That time we visited Jake, he sneakily returned my ring to me, the one he gave me just before we married. I found it in my bag afterwards, and now I've sold it, and I've invested the money in you.

'It's only for a short while. I don't want to keep anything of his permanently. His ring sold for nearly half a million. As soon as I can afford it I'll give an equal amount to charity. By then, Jake will have served his purpose.'

'Bringing you back to me,' he murmured.

'Exactly. Jake separated us, and now Jake has helped us find each other again.'

'He'd hate that,' Marcel said with relish.

'Yes, that's the thought I enjoy most. My other source of income is this.'

She opened a magazine, displaying Cassie, centrefold. She was stretched out, in a tiny bikini, looking directly into the camera with eyes that were almost as seductive as her barely clothed body.

'Take a good look,' she purred.

'I don't need to. I have my own copy. I'm amazed. I thought Mrs Henshaw had taken over.'

'So do the people I deal with, until they learn their mistake. It's Cassie who poses but Mrs Henshaw who draws up Cassie's contracts. They're the best of friends now.'

'I'm glad to know that,' he said carefully. 'It could make life…a lot easier.'

'It certainly does. Cassie's going to have to flaunt herself for quite a while yet, to help pay off Mrs Henshaw's debts, so the two of them decided to live together in harmony. Take one, you get the other.' She slipped her arms about his neck. 'I hope that's all right with you.'

It was hard to speak, but he managed to say, 'You once told me to get out of your life, and stay out.'

'That was then, this is now.'

He was suddenly tense. 'Cassie, my love, don't do this unless you mean it with all your heart. I couldn't endure to lose you again. I must be sure—to know that you're sure. I was torn from you once, and the last time I left you because it was the right thing to do. I thought it would help me keep your love, even if we could only love from a distance.'

'Yes, I understood that. I thought you were wonderful, even though losing you again broke my heart.'

'But—you said it yourself. That was then, this is now.' He met her eyes and spoke softly. 'Another parting would kill me.'

'There will be no other parting,' she vowed. 'I'm as sure as you want me to be, but sure in a way you don't know about yet. Things have changed. It's probably your influence. I'm not afraid of your controlling side because I've got one too. You brought it out in me and now it's out it's out for good.

'You need to know this. I'm in charge. From now on we're going to do things my way.' She laid her lips softly against his. 'Understand?'

'Understand.'

She could feel temptation trembling through him, making him draw back after a moment.

'You know that we'll fight,' he said.

'Of course we will. We'll have terrible fights, call each other all sorts of names, dig up our memories and use them to hurt each other. Sometimes we'll even hate each other. But we'll do it equally.'

'Oh, really? Well, let me tell you, conquering Cassie is a pleasure, but conquering Mrs Henshaw—that's something I'm really looking forward to.'

She smiled, nodding towards the door of the little bedroom.

'Better get started then. I don't know what you're waiting for.'

He lifted her high and headed for the door.

'Who's waiting?' he said.

* * * * *

MARDIE AND THE CITY SURGEON

BY
MARION LENNOX

Marion Lennox has written more than a hundred romances and is published in over a hundred countries and thirty languages. Her multiple awards include the prestigious US RITA® (twice) and the *RT Book Reviews* Career Achievement Award for 'a body of work which makes us laugh and teaches us about love'.

Marion adores her family, her kayak, her dog and lying on the beach with a book someone else has written. Heaven!

To John and Joy, for giving life to my books as well as saving calves at midnight.

CHAPTER ONE

It was a dark and stormy night. Lightning flashed. An eerie howl echoed mournfully through the big old house.

The lights went out.

She *had* to stop watching Gothic horror movies, Mardie Rainey decided, as she told Bounce to cut it out with the howling and groped to the sideboard for candles. She especially had to stop watching horror movies on nights when a storm was threatening to crash through her roof.

Bounce, her twelve-month-old border collie, was terrified. Mardie was more irritated than spooked. The vampire had been sinking his fangs when the power went off. Now she'd never learn what happened to the fluff-for-brains heroine who would have been a lot more interesting with fang marks.

What a night. The wind was hitting the chimney with such force it was cutting off the draw, causing smoke to belch into the room. She was down to a few candles and a flashlight.

There was a leak in the corner of the room. She'd put a bucket underneath. Without the sound of the television, the steady plinking was likely to drive her crazy.

She should go to bed.

A crash, outside. A big one.

Bounce stared at the darkened window and whimpered. The hairs on the back of his neck stood up.

'It'll be one of the gums in the driveway,' she told him,

feeling sad. She loved those trees. 'That's for tomorrow and the chainsaw.'

There wasn't a lot she could do about it now.

Bounce was still whimpering.

She took his collar and headed for the bedroom. 'It's nothing to worry about,' she told him. 'We don't have trees close enough to hurt the house. Lightning and thunder are all flashy show, and I warned you about watching vampires.'

Bounce whimpered again and pressed closer. So much for guard dogs.

Normally he slept in the kitchen. Not tonight.

It really was a scary night.

Maybe she did need vampire protection, she conceded as she headed for bed. Bounce might be a wuss but the only alternative was garlic. A girl couldn't sleep with garlic.

'Bed's safe,' she told him. 'The sheep are in the bottom paddock and that's protected. The house is solid. Everything's fine. At least we're not out in the weather. I pity anyone who is.'

Blake Maddock, specialist eye surgeon, should have stayed the night in Banksia Bay, but he wanted to be back in Sydney. Or better still, he wanted to be back in Africa.

He'd wanted to leave Banksia Bay the minute he'd discovered Mardie wasn't there.

What sort of stupid impulse had led him to attend his high school reunion? Wanting to see Mardie? That had been a dumb, sentimental impulse, nothing more. As for the rest, he'd turned his back on this place fifteen years ago. Why come back now?

Nothing had changed.

Or...it had a little, he conceded as he drove cautiously through the rain-filled night. But not much. There'd been births, deaths and marriages, but the town was just as small. People talked fishing and farming. People asked where he was living now, but weren't really interested in his answer. People asked did he miss Banksia Bay.

Not so much. He'd left fifteen years ago and never looked back.

Three miles out of town was his old home—his great-aunt's house. He'd been sent here when he was seven, to forget Robbie.

Ten years ago, sorting his great-aunt's estate, he'd found a letter his father had written to her after Robbie's death.

> We don't know where else to turn. His mother never warmed to the twins, to boys. Now… They were identical, and every time she looks at him she feels ill. She's drinking too much. Her friends are shunning her. We need to get the boy away. If we can tell people he's gone to relatives in Australia so he won't be continually reminded of his brother, the pressure will ease. Can we send him to you, for however long it takes until his mother wants to see him again?

And underneath was the offer of a transfer of a truly astonishing parcel of shares of the family company.

How much had his parents wanted to get rid of him?

He knew now, how much.

So a bereft seven-year-old had been sent to the other side of the world, to a reclusive great-aunt who'd run away herself, years before, after a failed romance. Who'd been kind according to her definition of the word, but who'd lived in the shadow of her own tragic love affair and never spoke about Robbie.

No one spoke about Robbie. No one here knew.

'Don't tell people about your brother,' his father had told him as he saw him onto a plane. 'Least said, soonest mended. I know it wasn't all your fault—your brother was equally responsible. Your mother will accept that in time. Meanwhile, get on with your life.'

His life as a kid no one wanted. His life in Banksia Bay.

It was dumb to have come tonight, he conceded. This had been his place to hide, to be hidden, and he had no need of that now.

And Mardie hadn't even attended.

Mardie had been in the year below him at school. His one true thing.

He remembered the first day he'd attended Banksia Bay School, dropped off by his silent great-aunt, feeling terrified. He remembered Mardie, marching up to him, littler than he was, all cheeky grin and freckles.

'What's your name? Did you bring lunch? I have sardine sandwiches and chocolate cake; do you want to share?'

How corny was it that he remembered exactly what she'd said, all those years ago?

It was corny and it was dumb. It was also dumb to think he might see her tonight. He hadn't thought it through.

He wasn't actually in a frame of mind where he could think anything through. He'd flown in from Africa exhausted. Dengue fever had left him flat and lethargic. It was four more weeks at least before he could return to work, he'd been told.

What work?

Bleak thoughts were all over the place. He'd stayed at his great-aunt's apartment in Sydney, the place she'd kept for shopping. He'd kept it because it was convenient, somewhere to store his scant belongings. It was the only place he could vaguely call home. Listlessly he'd checked mail that hadn't been redirected since he'd been ill, and found the invitation to the Banksia Bay reunion.

And he'd thought of Mardie. Again.

For some unknown reason, during this last illness Mardie had strayed into his thoughts, over and over.

Why? She'd have forgotten him, surely, or he'd be a distant memory, a blur. Theirs had been a childhood friendship, turning into a teenage romance. She'd be well over it. But… he wouldn't mind seeing her.

Could he drive to Banksia Bay and back in a night?

The question hung, persisted, wouldn't listen to a sensible no.

He'd decided years ago that Banksia Bay, the place where his parents had abandoned him, the place where he'd been sent to forget, was a memory he needed to move on from. But now, with his career uncertain, his focus blurred by illness, the reasons for that decision seemed less clear.

And his memory of Mardie was suddenly right back in focus.

Two hours there, four hours for dinner, two hours back. Okay, he'd be tired, but he didn't want to stay in Banksia Bay. Doable.

So he'd put on his dinner suit, driven from Sydney, sat through interminable speeches, too much back-slapping and too many questions. All on the one theme. 'Isn't it wonderful that you're a doctor—have you ever thought about coming home?'

This wasn't home. It was the place he'd been dumped after Robbie.

And of course Mardie wasn't at the dinner. He hadn't realised it was a reunion for just the one class.

He'd left as soon as he could. He should have gone straight back to Sydney.

But the thought of Mardie was still there. He'd come all this way…

Could he casually drop in at ten at night?

Um…maybe not.

The trees on the roadside were groaning under the strain of gale-force winds. The windscreen was being slapped with horizontal sleet.

Mardie's farm was right here. If it was daylight he would be able to see it.

Why did he want to see her?

She'd been a kid when he left Banksia Bay. Sixteen to his seventeen. She was probably married with six kids by now.

The impossibility of dropping in was becoming more and more apparent. On a moonlit night, maybe. If he'd rung ahead, maybe. He knew her phone number—he'd had it in his head for twenty years. As he'd left the reunion he'd thought he'd see if her lights were on and then he'd ring, and if she answered, he'd take it from there.

Only of course he'd forgotten there was no cellphone reception out here. Or maybe he'd never known. He'd left practically before cellphones were invented.

Enough. He needed to get back to the highway, put sentiment aside and focus on sense.

Focus on the road.

A blind bend. Darkness. Rain.

Mardie's house was a couple of hundred yards from the road. No lights. So that was that. Maybe she'd moved.

Of course she'd moved. Did he expect her life to have stood still?

And then…a dog, right in the middle of the road.

He hit the brakes, hard.

If it wasn't wet he might have made it, but water was sheeting over the bitumen, giving his tyres no grip.

His car skidded, planing out of control. He fought desperately, trying to turn into the skid, trying…

A tree was in front of him and he had nowhere to go.

Bounce was quivering beside the bed, flinching at each clap of thunder. Growling at the weird shapes made by lightning.

'You're starting to spook me,' Mardie told him as she snuggled under the covers. 'One more growl and you're back in the kitchen.'

The next clap of thunder sounded almost overhead and suddenly Bounce was right under the duvet.

Farmer with working dog. Total professionals. Ha! She hugged him, taking as well as giving comfort.

'We're not scared,' she told Bounce in her very best Farmer-In-Charge-Of-The-Situation voice.

Thunder. Lightning. The house seemed to tremble.

Another crash.

This one had her sitting up.

Uh-oh.

For the last crash was different. Not thunder. Not a falling tree.

It was the sound of tyres screaming for purchase, and then impact. Metal splintering.

And then?

And then it looked as if she was braving the elements, like it or not.

He wasn't hurt. Or not much. There was a trickle of blood on his forehead—the windscreen had smashed and a sliver of metal or glass must have got past the airbags. But he'd hired a Mercedes. If there was one thing these babies were good at it was protecting the occupant.

One of his headlights, weirdly, was still working. He could see what had happened. The trunk of the tree had met the front of the car square on. The whole passenger compartment seemed to have moved backward. The windscreen seemed to have shifted sideways.

The tree was about a foot from his nose.

Rain was sheeting in from the gap where the windscreen had been.

He ought to get out. Fire…

That was a thought forceful enough to stir him from his shock. He was out of the car in seconds.

A dog met him as he emerged, knee height, wet, whining,

nuzzling against him as if desperate for reassurance from another living thing.

The dog. The cause of the crash.

He should kick it into the middle of next week, he thought. Instead, he found himself kneeling on the roadside, holding it, feeling shudders run through the dog's thin frame. Feeling matching shudders run through his.

They'd both come close to the edge.

He tugged the dog back a bit, worried the car might blow, but it wasn't happening, not in this rain. Any spark that might catch was drenched before it even thought about causing trouble.

The sparks weren't the only thing drenched. Thirty seconds out of the car and he was soaked.

What to do? He was kneeling beside his crashed car in the middle of nowhere, holding a dog.

He was four miles from Banksia Bay, and Banksia Bay was in the middle of nowhere. It was a tiny harbour town two hours from Sydney, set between mountains and sea. He'd already checked for phone reception. Zip.

He had a coat in the car. He had an umbrella.

It was too late for coats and umbrellas. He was never going to be wetter than he was right now.

The dog whined and leaned heavily against him. A border collie? Black and white, its long fur was matted and dripping. The dog was far too thin—he could feel ribs. It was leaning against him as if it needed his support.

He put a hand on its neck and found a plastic collar, but now wasn't the time to be thinking about identification.

'We're safe but we're risking drowning,' he said out loud, and he stared through the rain trying to see Mardie's house.

Dark.

Still, it was the closest house. It was over a mile back to his aunt's old home which, someone had told him tonight, had become a private spa retreat, but was now in the hands of the receivers. Deserted. After that… He couldn't think.

The trees around him were losing branches. He had to get out of the weather.

Did Mardie still live here?

How ironic, after coming all this way because he'd stupidly assumed she'd be at the school reunion, to end up on her doorstep like a drowned rat. Waking her from sleep.

Crazy.

His head hurt.

He had no choice.

He turned towards the house and the dog plodded beside him, just touching.

'Mardie and a husband and six kids?' he asked the dog. 'Or a stranger.' And then, despite the rain, despite the shock, he found himself grinning. 'I came all this way to find Mardie. It seems fate's decided I'm still looking.'

The phone was dead.

There was no mobile reception here ever, but she did have a landline. Not now. The lines must be down.

She was on her own.

A car crash.

This was worse than vampires. Much worse.

She hauled on her outdoor gear at lightning speed, her sou'wester with its great weatherproof hood, her waterproof over-pants and her gumboots. She grabbed her most powerful flashlight.

Bounce refused to come out from under the bedcovers.

'Watch the house, then,' she conceded, thinking she'd be better without him anyway. She'd like the comfort of his presence but if it was a disaster…

She'd need an ambulance, not a dog.

She felt more alone than she'd ever felt in her life.

'It's you or no one,' she said savagely to herself and hauled open the door.

To be met by Blake Maddock.

How could you not see someone for fifteen years and know in an instant that you were looking at the same man?

She did. She was.

At seventeen, Blake Maddock was the best-looking guy in grade school. He was tall, dark and drop-dead gorgeous. He had deep black hair and skin that seemed to tan without the sun. At seventeen he'd needed a bit of filling out, but not any more.

This was Blake Maddock all grown up.

The grown-up version of Blake Maddock was wearing a black dinner suit, black bow tie, white shirt and silver cufflinks.

His jet-black hair was dripping. His suit was sodden.

Blake.

She must be dreaming.

But it didn't pour with rain in dreams, or she didn't think it did. This wasn't an apparition. Blake Maddock was standing on her veranda.

'Mardie?' he said, and she figured he couldn't see her. She was in the hallway and of course it wasn't lit. The lightning was almost continuous now though, and whenever it forked it lit the veranda as bright as daylight. She could see him, over and over again.

Blake.

'H...hi,' she managed but she stuttered the word. She tried again but the stutter got worse.

'It is Mardie?' he said, trying to see.

'Y...yes.'

She caught herself and stepped outside. The wind practically knocked her sideways.

A black shadow moved from Blake's side to hers. It leaned against her legs as if seeking refuge.

Blake Maddock and dog. What the…?

Her mind stopped whirling. The night slid away. Blake Maddock was right in front of her—Blake, her very best of friends.

She grabbed his hands and held on, and he stared down at her and attempted a half smile. She stared up at him, incredulous. His smile twisted, self-mocking, and it was the smile she remembered. Blake…

His smile faded. He stared down at her in the weird light provided by lightning—and then he tugged her into a bear hug.

She let herself be tugged. He was soaked to the skin. He was bigger than she remembered, taller, *harder*.

She let herself be crushed against his chest. Right this minute, all she could feel was joy.

'Blake.'

It was barely a whisper. Her past had returned. Her past was dripping wet on her veranda.

Her past was hugging her as if he'd missed her as much as she'd missed him.

Another crash of thunder, deeper, longer. This was no night for standing in the sleet, hugging. He put her at arm's length, but still he held her, hands gripping hers. As if holding on to reality.

'I've crashed my car,' he said and she thought…she thought…

She didn't think anything. She was too flabbergasted.

'Where…? Why…?'

'I've come from the school reunion.'

The school reunion. Things settled. Just a little.

She'd heard what was happening—a reunion for the class above hers from fifteen years ago. Tony Hamm, the local butcher, had been organising it. Her friend Kirsty had told her about it when she was in the local store this morning.

'They're so excited. But dinner suits… That's only because Jenny Hamm wants to wear the dress she bought for her sister's wedding. You should hear the complaints.'

Tony's class.

Blake's class.

She'd thought then…

Yeah, she'd thought, but she hadn't said. She hadn't asked: *Is Blake Maddock coming?*

Obviously he was. Obviously he had.

He was on her veranda.

He'd said he'd crashed his car. There was a trickle of blood on his forehead. She struggled to get her confused mind to focus.

'There's blood…' she managed. 'Your head…'

'A scratch. I'm fine.'

'Really?'

'Really.'

She was getting her breath back. She hadn't seen this guy for fifteen years. There were so many emotions in her head she didn't know what to do with them.

'Get into the hall,' she managed. 'Out of the wind.' She pulled away, then stood aside and ushered him into the entrance porch. As if he was a casual acquaintance.

'Is anyone else hurt?' Her voice sounded funny, she thought. 'The other car…'

'Only me,' he said, and his voice astonished her. Deep and rich and growly. All grown up. 'I hit a tree.'

'A tree?'

'I'm not drunk,' he said, and he truly was Blake, his voice touched with the lazy humour she knew so well. 'I've been to the reunion dinner. They served Tony Hamm's home-made beer and Elsie Sarling's first attempt at making Chardonnay. It wasn't a struggle to stick with water.'

Her lips twitched in return, smiling back. Tension eased. An old school friend in trouble. She could do this. 'So the tree?' she said cautiously.

'It jumped out and hit me.' He sighed. 'No. The dog jumped out. I managed to miss the dog. I hit the tree instead.'

He'd hit a tree. A car crash, late at night. Blake.

So many emotions…

Priorities. 'Is the car blocking the road?' she managed and was absurdly proud of herself for sounding so sensible.

'No. I was aiming to miss the dog and I made a good fist of it. It's well off.'

That, at least, was a plus. She didn't need to get the tractor and drag a wreck from the road to stop others crashing into it.

She could focus on Blake.

Or actually…not. Focusing on Blake made her feel weird, like stepping through the wardrobe into Narnia, into another world. The world of fifteen years ago. Concentrate on the dog, she told herself. The dog seemed far less complicated.

It was a border collie, mostly black, with touches of white. It, too, was wet to the bone. She felt it shudder against her legs, and it was a far deeper shudder than Bounce's vampire-and-thunder-induced shudder.

If there was one thing that could touch Mardie Rainey's heart, it was a dog. A wet and obviously frightened dog was always going to hit her heart like an arrow. It even distracted her from Blake. She knelt down to see, to pat.

'Hey, sweetheart, where did you come from?'

But then she felt its collar, and she knew.

A ribbon of plastic.

She knew this collar.

'Oh, no.'

'Not yours?' Blake asked.

'No. This is a pound dog.' She fingered the collar, feeling ill. 'The local Animal Welfare van crashed last week and dogs escaped. Stray dogs are turning up everywhere. This collar says this is one of them.'

But this was a border collie.

Farmers round here valued their dogs above diamonds. Border collies were natural workers. For one to end up in the pound didn't make sense.

But she could only concentrate on the dog for so long. The dog was distracting, but not distracting enough.

She had Blake Maddock in her front porch.

'Mardie, I'm in trouble,' Blake said above her. The momentary emotion that had given rise to the hug had faded, leaving manners. 'Would your mother object if I came in to dry off and ring for help?'

Would her mother object?

Memories of the last time she'd seen Blake flooded back. Blake in this house, in this kitchen. Blake kissing her senseless.

'Come to Sydney,' he'd said urgently, holding her close. 'You're smart. You could get a scholarship. There's stuff we can do, Mardie. We can make a difference. Come with me. You can't be happy here.'

She remembered her whole body melting as Blake kissed her so deeply she thought she surely must say yes. She remembered his hands slipping under her blouse, and she remembered the hot, aching need.

But she was sixteen and her mother was suddenly there, confronting them with anger. Her mother was so seldom angry it jolted them both.

'Blake, it's time for you to go home. Mardie and I need to be up early, to draft the sheep ready for crutching.'

And, as she'd spoken, Mardie had seen fear.

Her mother had heard what Blake had said. She'd heard him asking her to go to Sydney.

She'd known, even then. At sixteen, the weight of this farm was on her shoulders.

You can't be happy here... Why not?

She loved Banksia Bay, and she loved farming. She'd also loved Blake, with every shred of her sixteen-year-old being.

But Blake couldn't wait to be off. He was heading to Sydney to do medicine.

She could get a scholarship? To do what? Something to make a difference? What was he talking about?

She loved her art, she loved making things, but even then she'd known Blake saw her passion as not to be taken seriously.

Even then she'd known they were moving in different directions.

'Write,' she'd told him, feeling desolate.

'Follow me to Sydney. Finish school and apply to the same university. I'll wait for you.'

She still remembered the desolation. 'I don't think I can. Blake, please write.'

'And just be friends?' he'd demanded, incredulous. Her mother was waiting stolidly for him to leave. She moved into the living room, out of hearing but not out of sight. 'We've gone too far to be just friends.'

She thought of that statement now. It had been an adolescent ultimatum: follow me to Sydney, move in my direction or cease being my friend.

All or nothing.

It had to be nothing.

She'd watched him go and her sixteen-year-old heart felt as if it was breaking.

And now he was back—grown, changed, but still Blake. He was watching her face, reading her warring emotions as he'd always been able to read her emotions. 'Is your mother…?' he started.

'Mum's fine,' Mardie said.

'She's asleep?'

'It's midnight.' She hadn't seen this man for half a lifetime. Use your head, she told herself. There was no way she should tell this…stranger…that she was home alone. Let him think her mother was still sleeping in the front room.

Even if he had hugged her.

Even if he was Blake.

'Did I wake you?' he asked. 'I'm sorry.'

'I was still awake. A tree came down and then I heard the car crash. I was coming to find out.'

'If you could turn on a light…' Blake ventured.

'No power. But come in anyway. Are you…are you really okay?'

'Shaken, not stirred.'

And at that…she smiled.

James Bond movies had been their very favourite thing. That last year together, a new movie had come out. She remembered persuading her mother to take them to Whale Cove. Dressing up. Standing hand in hand in the queue, waiting for tickets. She'd looked as glamorous as a sixteen-year-old on limited means could manage. A home-made dress, all slink and crazy glamour. Stilettos from the second-hand market. Blake had worn a dinner suit, probably not even hired. Money was never a problem for Blake. He'd looked a fairly adolescent Bond, but at sixteen she'd thought he'd looked a Bond to die for.

Shaken, not stirred.

Right now she was stirred.

She stood aside to usher him into the house. His body brushed hers as he passed.

There was no way she could feel him through her waterproofs.

She felt him. Every nerve in her body felt him.

This was weird. A teenage love affair, long over.

It was the night, she told herself. Her fear from the crash. The appalling storm. A boy she'd once loved.

A man, she told herself sharply. A stranger. She needed to be practical, sensible, and together.

'The dog…' he said.

'Dogs are welcome in this house.' Even stray and sodden ones. Maybe especially stray and sodden ones. 'Go through to the kitchen,' she said. 'It's warmer. I'll find towels and shed my coat.'

They were operating by flashlight. She lit a candle on the hall table and handed it to him.

The lightning outside was almost one continuous sheet. The house went from dark to light, from dark to light…

'This isn't James Bond,' he said. 'It's Gothic Horror.'

Gothic Horror… Her thoughts exactly. He'd always been on the same wavelength. The thought was…unsettling.

Unsettling but good. As if a part of her was suddenly restored.

There was a crazy thought.

'If you've grown fangs since I last saw you, I'm heading into the night right now,' she muttered. 'Kitchen. Go. Now.'

The dog whimpered and pressed closer against her.

'Leave her with me,' she said as he hesitated.

'She's my responsibility.'

'You brought her to me,' she said. 'One dog doesn't add very much to what I take care of.'

'Mardie…'

'Just go.'

After fifteen years, Blake Maddock had walked back into her life.

For some stupid reason, her head felt as if it was exploding.

Blake. A childhood friend. A teenage boyfriend. Nothing more.

Focus on the dog. Nothing else.

She headed for the linen closet and the dog stayed with

her, its body still just touching her leg. She crouched in the dim light and ran her hands over the sodden coat and the dog whined a little and pressed in closer.

A female. Full grown. Trembling without pause.

There was no obvious wound. She didn't seem tender to touch.

She needed to get her into the light. Into the kitchen, where she had a bigger store of candles.

Back to Blake.

Not quite yet. Her head wasn't near to accepting the weird way her body had reacted to his presence.

She gathered towels. She thought about Blake; how she could get him dry. His clothes were soaked. Towels?

Something more.

She hesitated, told herself she was stupid, fetched a bathrobe.

The dog stayed with her, sticking close, a feather-touch of contact.

This dog had done it hard, she thought. The Animal Welfare van had crashed over a week ago. Where had this dog been since then?

Mardie's heart wasn't hard at the best of times. She could feel it stretch right now.

'Yeah, I'm a sucker for dogs,' she told her. 'Especially beautiful dogs like you. But there must be some reason you were at the pound in the first place. Were you in for sheep-killing?'

That was the most common reason a farm dog ended up discarded. A dog got a taste for blood. It was tragic, but once a dog started killing sheep there was little that could be done.

Most farmers quietly put them down. If they were too attached, though, they'd take them to the pound, hoping some townie would take them on, someone with a contained yard with not a sheep in sight.

It hardly ever made for a happy ending. A working dog

wasn't meant to be contained. They pined, they made trouble for their new owners, they ended up being put down anyway.

So…she now had a stray dog, probably a sheep killer, and she had Blake Maddock.

A girl should have some protection.

A clap of thunder shook the house so loud the windows rattled.

She thought of Bounce under her bedclothes. Until the storm ended there was no way Bounce was moving.

She was on her own—but what else was new?

Having Blake Maddock in her kitchen was new.

You've faced worse than Blake Maddock, she told herself.

And…it was Blake. The thought made something inside her shiver, and it wasn't fear.

Hormones?

Nonsense. Hormones were for a teenage romance. Get over it. Be practical.

It was good advice. She took her armload of towels and her bathrobe, she took her courage in both hands—and went to see if she could follow it.

CHAPTER TWO

THE great thing about a wood-burning stove was that a power outage couldn't mess with it. Cutting wood was a pain, but Mardie had learned to enjoy it, and the stove more than paid for itself with comfort. In the small hours after a difficult lambing, when she was cold and wet, the fire was a warm, welcoming presence.

It was the heart of her home.

Blake was standing before it now. He'd put the kettle on the hob. He'd opened the toasting door so he could see the flames; so he could hold his hands out for warmth. He had his back to her.

He was so…large.

She'd known he'd become a doctor. Someone had been to a graduation ceremony in Sydney years back and had seen him.

She hadn't heard of him since. And now, here he was, big and handsome and rugged, wearing a dinner suit, a city doctor in city clothes.

She had a city doctor in her kitchen.

She had Blake in her kitchen.

See, there was the anomaly. Blake was from another life. Blake no longer fitted here, yet there was part of him that was…Blake.

And he didn't look like a city doctor, she thought as he

turned to face her. In truth, he looked more weathered than most farmers. He looked tanned and muscled, and the creases of his eyes were etched deep, as if he constantly faced harsh sun.

He also looked a bit…gaunt? That'd be the crash, she thought, but then she decided it looked more than that. She sensed deep-seated strain, and he looked too lean for health. He looked as if he might have been ill—or maybe he simply worked too hard.

City surgeon, making millions? More millions. She knew little about Blake's parents other than they'd been killed in a light plane crash when he was twelve, but she did know they were wealthy. His great-aunt had money, too.

Blake obviously had moved on in the same mould.

'I hear you're a doctor,' she said cautiously, and he nodded.

'Yes.'

'Congratulations.'

'On being a doctor?'

'Of course. You've cut your head. How bad is it?'

'It's nothing.'

'Have you hurt anything else?'

'No.'

'Promise?'

'Yes.'

'Let me check the cut for glass, then. Sit.'

'Still bossy?'

'Always.'

He sat.

He used to argue. Always.

Maybe he was hurt. Maybe he…

'I had six airbags,' he said. 'I was almost suffocated but not hurt. This has to be superficial. But I would be grateful if you could check.'

She checked. She filled a bowl with warm water, she

washed his face with care, she used the flashlight to check for glass.

It was an ugly scratch. There were a couple of metal slivers, embedded. She found tweezers, tugged them out. She put on antiseptic and a plaster.

Touching him was weird. Touching him felt…shivery.

Get over it. He was the one who should be shivery, not her. Concentrate on need.

'You need to get dry,' she said, trying to keep her voice steady. 'There's a bathrobe here that's wool and warm. Dry yourself and put it on.' Deep breath. 'I think you need to stay the night. I'd drive you into town but you've already proven it's not safe to be out. I don't see that you have a choice. You want to change now, while I towel the dog? Take a couple of candles upstairs. Same bedroom you always had. I keep the spare beds made up. You don't have a choice.'

How had that happened?

One minute he was deciding to turn back to Sydney. The next he was standing in Mardie's attic, hauling on her dressing gown.

No. Not hers. It was soft brown cashmere and it was huge. A man's.

Her father's?

He remembered Mardie's dad with huge regret. Bill was a big, genial countryman, deeply contented with his wife, his farm, his daughter. As kids, Blake and Mardie had trailed after him like two adoring puppies, helping, messing around, being with him.

Bill had died of a massive heart attack when Mardie was barely in her teens and he'd felt as gutted as Mardie. He'd felt little emotion when he'd been told his own parents were dead—he hadn't seen them for years—but Bill…

If this was Bill's bathrobe…

He smiled, remembering Bill, remembering this place as it had been.

Why had he never come back?

He knew why. Because of Mardie.

Mardie…

She'd grown up, of course she had, but she was still the same Mardie. She was short, blue-eyed, freckled and compact. Her honey-blonde curls were still tied into braids. And her eyes…

He'd always loved how they'd creased into laughter in an instant. Time had now etched those laughter lines to permanent.

Tonight she was wearing tattered jeans and an old woolly jumper. Bright red socks with a hole in one toe.

Years of tending sheep, of living on this farm meant she was wind-burned, sun-burned, cute as a button.

She was a farmer.

She could have been so much more…

No. It had been stupid to demand that of her fifteen years ago. It was stupid to think it now.

So get this over with, he told himself. Don't let your emotions get tangled up. Get in there, be courteous and thankful, accept her offer of a bed for the night, call for a tow truck first thing in the morning and get out of here. You've seen her. That was what you wanted. Now leave.

Because?

Because Banksia Bay seemed threatening, and Mardie seemed even more threatening. He didn't know why, but she was.

Or maybe he did. Maybe he was old enough to see it.

Mardie was comfort, fun, loving. She was a refuge, as she'd always been his refuge.

Mardie was all the things he could never let himself have.

* * *

What was keeping him? She towelled the little collie as dry as she could, encouraged her to lie in Bounce's dog basket, then started making toast.

The collie whined and headed back to her, once more just touching her knee.

She made toast and the dog kept contact all the time.

'What's wrong?' she asked, and offered her a piece of toast.

The dog didn't take it. As if she didn't see it was being held out.

She moved it a little closer.

The dog sniffed, sniffed again—and then delicately took it from Mardie's hand.

What the…?

She'd been working by candlelight. She flicked the flash-light back on and looked. She really looked. And in the better light…

No.

She plumped down on the kitchen chair and drew the dog to her.

'Oh, sweetheart. Oh, no.'

Blake walked back into the kitchen and stopped short.

The dog's head was resting on Mardie's knee. Tears were sliding unchecked down her face.

'Mardie…'

She looked up at him, and all the tragedy of the world was in her face.

'She's blind,' she whispered. 'She was tipped out of that van a week ago and she's blind. How's she ever survived?'

Blind.

Things fell into place.

The dog standing motionless in the road, not registering his oncoming car.

The dog touching him, staying by his side, following him here by touch.

The dog moving to Mardie, whose clothes would smell of farmyard, of the familiar, then not leaving her. Just touching.

'How do you know?' he asked, but already he knew it for truth.

'Look at her eyes.' She flicked on the flashlight.

He looked.

The dog's eyes were opaque, unfocused, unseeing. Cataracts covered both the eyes entirely.

She'd be seeing vague shapes, light and dark through thick white fog, he thought. Nothing more.

'It'll be why she was in the pound,' Mardie whispered. He'd walked back into the kitchen absurdly self-conscious of wearing a great woollen bathrobe but Mardie was oblivious to anything but the dog. 'She's only young. I'm guessing four at the most. And she's smart and so polite. She's skin and bone. She must be starving, yet she took the toast like a lady. Oh, sweetheart.'

She sniffed and sniffed again. She ran her fingers through her hair, a gesture he remembered, Mardie under stress. She'd obviously forgotten, though, that she'd tied her hair into braids. Her fingers caught one of the bands and her hair fell loose, a cascade of honey curls.

One braid in. The other free. Tear-stained, messy, freckled… She didn't care. She was totally oblivious.

Something kicked him, hard, deep inside. Something that hadn't kicked him for a long time.

'Let me see,' he said, more roughly than he intended. He knelt on the floor, cupping the dog's jaw in his hand, looking at her eyes.

The dog let him do as he willed. She was totally trusting, or maybe she'd gone past trust. Maybe she was at the point of: *Kill me now, nothing can get worse than this.*

Definitely cataracts.

If it was the same as humans… Cataracts sometimes came

with age. Sometimes they were caused by illness or injury. These, though…

'Sometimes they're genetic,' he said, thinking out loud. 'She seems a young, otherwise healthy dog.'

The dog let her head lie on his palm and sighed.

Mardie sniffed again.

'Years ago, one of my neighbours' old Labradors, Blacky, got cataracts,' she muttered. 'Roger said the cost of having them removed was too huge to consider. Blacky was a pet, though, old, fat and lazy at the best of times. He was content to live out the rest of his life in front of Roger's fire. But for a young working dog… If she can't work she'll be miserable, and useless to whoever owns her.'

She fingered the plastic collar.

The flashlight was still on. They read the collar together, Blake absurdly aware of honey-blonde curls tumbling to her shoulder only six inches away. Absurdly aware of a ragged sweater.

Mardie…

'She has a name.' Mardie seemed unaware of his distraction and Blake looked where she was looking. There was a number written in black on the collar, followed by rough script.

Bessie. Owner: Charlie Hunter.

'It's worse and worse,' Mardie said, and her face said it was.

'Charlie Hunter?'

'You must remember Charlie. He's a farmer up on the ridge. A nice old guy, keeps to himself, almost ninety. He used to be the best dog-trainer in the district. Brilliant. When he won All Australian Champion I made him…'

But then she faltered. Bit back what she'd been about to say.

'I guess…I guess whether I know him or not doesn't matter. But he had a stroke eight weeks ago and he's had to go into care. I'm guessing this is his dog.' She took a deep breath, and when she continued her voice cracked with emotion. 'So this is Bessie. He kept her even though she was blind, and when he could no longer keep her he put her in the pound. I wouldn't have thought… It would have been kinder to put her down.'

And she rose and walked out of the room.

Bessie sniffed his hand and he patted her, stroking her silky coat. The kettle whistled on the stove.

The roof was leaking in the corner, into a bucket. A steady trickle. The bucket was almost full.

He took a candle and checked the living room, the matching corner. Another bucket.

The way they were filling, it'd be a twenty-minute roster to empty them, all night.

He made tea and then Mardie was back, with another collie by her side. Bigger. Younger. Having to be towed.

'Bounce,' she said sternly, hauling him into the room whether he liked it or not. 'Get over the thunder. You're needed. Meet Bessie.'

Bounce was clearly cowed by the storm. Another low rumble filled the night. His ears flattened and he whimpered.

Bessie whimpered back.

Bounce's ears forgot about flattening. Another dog, in his kitchen? This clearly took precedence over thunder. He launched himself forward, stopping abruptly two inches from Bessie's nose. He sniffed.

Bessie sniffed back.

The procedure was repeated from different viewpoints.

Bounce gave his tail a cautious wag.

'Basket,' Mardie said.

At the side of the woodstove was an ancient dog basket. There'd been dogs in that basket ever since Blake could remember. There were never less than three. He'd been vaguely surprised not to see dogs in there tonight.

The family was down to one dog?

'Basket,' Mardie said again. Bounce gave her a *Must I?* look but turned and headed where he was meant to go.

Bessie went too, just touching.

Bounce turned in two circles, sighed, flopped.

Bessie flopped, too. Closed her eyes. Was asleep in an instant.

Bounce stared up at Mardie, doubtful as to this new order.

'Stay,' Mardie said gently, and Bounce sighed again, but he wriggled until his body was curved around Bessie's. He settled.

'That's great,' Blake said, feeling immeasurably cheered. 'Another dog…they have ways of figuring they can trust.'

'They'll both relax,' Mardie said. 'Bounce wasn't finding me the least bit reassuring against the gods of thunder but an older one who's not scared is just what he needs.'

'And tomorrow?'

'Tomorrow I'll call Henrietta, who runs the pound,' she said bleakly, sitting back down at the table. Hauling her mug of tea close and holding it, as if needing the comfort of its warmth. 'But one step at a time. Would you like toast before bed?'

She was suddenly businesslike. Brisk. Putting emotion aside.

There were still tracks of tears on her cheeks.

He found her absurdly…or not absurdly…

'I don't need anything to eat,' he said, a bit too abruptly. 'I've just had a reunion dinner.'

'So you have. You're sure your head's okay?'

'It's fine. Thank you.' She was seated right by him. So close… Instinctively he reached out to touch her hand. It was a gesture of gratitude, nothing more.

She flinched.

It was as much as he could do not to flinch in return.

'I'm staying up to eat toast,' she said, carefully focusing

on her mug of tea and not him. 'Sleep well. There's a bit to face in the morning, so get some rest.'

'Mardie?'

She did look at him then, with all the distrust in the world. His heart twisted.

'When I left…I never meant to hurt you,' he said.

'You did hurt me,' she said, flat and definite. The emotion of that instinctive hug was gone; remembered hurt was back. 'I wrote to you. I worried about you. You never wrote back.'

'I needed…to protect myself.'

'Then that's all right,' she said stiffly. 'All explained.'

'I was a kid. I was stupid, not to keep in contact with my best friend.'

'We were teenagers,' she conceded. 'Sensitivity isn't a teenager's strong suit. Forget it. Go to bed.'

'Sensitive or not, I've regretted it. More and more as I grew older.'

'It doesn't matter.'

'It did to me. It does. I am sorry. That's why I came tonight. I wanted to see you. It's what I wanted to say.' And before he could think it through—because if he had he never would have done it—he stooped and he kissed her. His kiss was light, a brush of his mouth against her forehead. It was a kiss given because he couldn't bear not to. A kiss of apology.

It was a dumb gesture. She pulled away as if he burned.

'That's enough of sorry,' she told him brusquely, harshly. 'It was all a long time ago. It doesn't matter any more; just go.'

'Are you planning on bucket-emptying all night?'

She sighed. Looked at the buckets. Didn't look at him. 'They'll be okay.'

'They'll flood.'

She'd been thinking that, in the fraction of her mind that wasn't taken up by him. An hour ago the leak had been a drip.

The drip was becoming a trickle and the trickle was threatening to turn to a gush.

'I'm sure it'll be fine.' Some things weren't worth worrying about. No way was she getting up on the roof in this weather.

'It'll be the corner of the roof, where the spouts meet,' he said. 'The water's banking up; there's too much for the drainpipe to cope with.'

'How do you know?'

'I've coped with more than floods over the last few years. Once upon a time your dad let me up on the roof with him. I can remember the set-up, and I know down-pipes.'

'You understand plumbing?' She was incredulous.

He grinned. 'Hey, I'm a doctor. Plumbing's half my med training. Plus my work has been practical in more ways than one. So now, not only am I offering my professional opinion, I'm proposing surgery. Though I'll need to put my dinner suit back on. There's no way I'm getting Bill's robe wet.'

She wasn't listening to the end of his statement. She was too intent on the first. 'You can't get on the roof. Are you out of your mind? Have you seen the lightning?'

'I have,' he agreed, grateful that here was something concrete he could do, something to lessen the emotion. 'It's sheet lightning, not fork. Fork's bad. Sheet's not great but we also have trees, much taller than the house. Plus there's two chimneys, both of which would be hit before the house itself. I'm not proposing to stand on the roof acting as a lightning conductor. I'm proposing to stick a ladder against the corner of the house while you hold the bottom, then climb up and disengage the down-pipe. I might need a hacksaw. Do you have a hacksaw?'

'I...might,' she said, flabbergasted.

'Excellent. With just a hole instead of a pipe, the water'll stop banking up under the eaves.'

'How do you know?' she said, suspicious, and he grinned.

'Trust me, I'm a doctor.'

She didn't grin back. 'You'd go outside again—into the storm?' She was still hornswoggled. 'Plus you have a lump the size of an egg on your head.'

'Hero material, that's me,' he said, trying to make her smile. 'But I'm not too heroic. The lump's already subsiding and I know what I'm doing. But I do need my sidekick—that'd be you in your sou'wester.'

'I wouldn't need to get up all night,' she said, dazed.

'There's my board and lodging paid for. What about it, Mardie? Deal?'

She struggled to shut her mouth. Stop being flabbergasted. 'You're proposing we brave the tempest?' she managed. 'With a ladder? I don't mind a bit of rain. Rainstorms are when most of my lambs seem to be born. But you… You'll need to put that disgusting dinner suit on again.'

'It's not disgusting.'

'If it's not yet, it soon will be,' she said darkly. 'But this is an offer I'm not refusing. Okay, Superman, you're on.'

He fixed the leak, by the simple expedient of climbing the ladder, hacking the drainpipe out of the spout, clearing the worst of the banked-up leaf litter and letting the water gush free. He even managed to do it so water didn't land on Mardie's head as she held the ladder below. It seemed simple, except she couldn't have done it. Balance in the rain and handle a hacksaw as if accustomed to it. Balance while not noticing the lightning.

He was steady and sure and fast.

She felt…

She felt…

She had no idea how she felt.

He came down the ladder. Brushed against her, which made her feel…as if she didn't know how she felt. Grinned, a triumphant small-boy grin she remembered. 'Flood averted,' he said. 'Much better than a finger in the dyke, don't you think?'

'Much,' she said faintly, because she couldn't think of anything else to say.

When had he got so big?

When had he got so…male?

They stowed the ladder, they came back inside and he dripped in the hall.

'Would you…' she started and then she stopped. She simply didn't know what to say next.

'Would I like another towel? Yes, I would. And then bed.'

'I… Thank you.'

'Enough of the thank yous. Let's call it quits.' He touched her lightly on her cheek—and she flinched and his smile died.

She got him his towel. He nodded his thanks and headed straight for bed. Up to the attic where he'd stayed when he was a kid.

She headed back to the kitchen. She'd told him she was staying up to eat toast.

She'd lied.

She was staying up to think about Blake.

Blake Maddock was in her attic.

Blake Maddock had fixed her plumbing. Blake Maddock had kissed her.

Blake Maddock had touched her cheek, a gesture of farewell, and her cheek still burned.

For this was a new Blake Maddock; the grown-up version. He was a guy who'd pulled away her flooding down-pipes as if he coped with manual labour every day of his life.

That was what he looked like.

Whatever he'd been doing for the past fifteen years, it hadn't made him soft. He was lean—almost too lean—but his muscles made up for it. And his body… As he'd come back down the ladder, his soaked clothes clinging, he'd looked… he'd looked…

A girl shouldn't think how he'd looked.

And he'd kissed her.

So…what? He'd kissed her for the first time when she was six years old and she'd given him her sandwich. She'd giggled and her friends had said 'kissy kissy'. They'd all giggled then. She and Blake were best of friends.

Not any more. They weren't even minor friends. Friends would have sat up for an hour or so, catching up on what had happened through the years.

He didn't want to catch up. He was stuck here because his car had crashed. He'd fixed her down-pipe because he felt sorry for her. He wanted to get the night over and get back to Sydney.

So why had he kissed her?'

'Because he's arrogant and he has more money than any-one has a right to. He thinks he's aristocracy.' She said it out loud but it didn't make sense.

He'd never acted rich. All the time she'd known him, he acted as if his family's money was something he didn't want to know about.

He never talked about his parents, then or now. Everything she knew, she knew from scant town gossip.

Tonight…she should have asked what he'd been doing. She'd assumed he was a city doctor, but he looked so weath-ered…he must have been doing something else.

Neither had asked the important questions. Neither had told.

She should have told him her mother wasn't here. He could have slept in the front bedroom.

Would he be able to sleep in the tiny attic bed?

It didn't matter, she told herself, sticking bread in the toaster without thinking. Their friendship was over. She hadn't seen him for fifteen years and after tonight she wouldn't see him again.

She shouldn't mind.

Quite suddenly, quite fiercely, she minded.

What would her life be if she'd gone to Sydney with him?

Maybe she'd be a doctor's wife. A rich doctor's wife. They'd have a gorgeous house, a couple of kids, piano lessons, mid-week tennis. Society functions. Ladies' lunches.

Um…how about that for a stereotype?

She could have gone to university as he'd wanted her to. She'd been smart enough. Maybe she could have been a doctor, too.

A doctor? Her favourite subject at school was art, and she still remembered the adolescent Blake's disparagement. 'It's all right for a hobby but not for a career.'

He'd had ambition. She didn't, or not ambition as he saw it. She'd never wanted to leave Banksia Bay.

Apart from Blake. She'd wanted, desperately, to go wherever Blake went.

At school he'd been quiet about his future, telling no one, even hugging his desire to study medicine to himself. He kept lots of things to himself. Even to her, his best of friends, he'd seldom talked of his family, his future, or his past. Maybe that was wise. His family's wealth made him different from most kids in Banksia Bay. The eccentricity of his great-aunt made him different. The fact that he had fabulously wealthy parents who never came near made him really different.

He was still…different.

He probably had a wife, she thought suddenly. He might even have cute, piano-playing kids.

He wasn't wearing a wedding ring. She'd noticed.

'Don't go there,' she told herself, and ate the toast without thinking about it.

Bounce opened one eye and watched with hope. She gave him a crust, then offered another to Bessie, but Bessie didn't stir.

She was a smaller dog than Bounce. Sweet.

Blind.

'Don't think it,' she told herself, but she knew she was thinking it.

She couldn't. It'd be cruel to keep a blind working dog. It'd be sentimentality at its worst.

'And it's not as if there's any spare money to spend on operations.' She was still talking out loud. 'Even if it's possible.'

A thunderclap rolled across the night and made her shudder. Instead of heading behind her legs, Bounce simply nestled closer to Bessie.

Bounce had a new best friend.

Which left her alone.

Bed. Alone. Without even Bounce.

'That's a dumb, sad thing to think,' she told herself. 'Ooh, who's feeling sorry for herself? Go to bed and enjoy listening to the thunder. And don't keep thinking of Blake. He's nothing to do with you and he's out of here, first thing in the morning.'

He should have sat up and talked.

He lay in the dark and counted bruises to distract himself. The crash hadn't left him completely unscathed. His head ached. Something had thumped his shoulder and that ached, too.

He'd been barely civil downstairs. He hadn't asked anything of her life for the past fifteen years. How dumb was that?

She'd think he was just using her.

He *was* using her. This was the closest place to stay out of the storm. Even if they'd been strangers he would have asked for shelter, and she might have been kind enough to say yes.

Of course she would. This was Mardie, still feeling sorry for strays after all these years.

What had she been doing all this time? Married? He should have looked for a ring.

Surely not. A husband would have made himself obvious.

Her mother? Etta hadn't appeared either, but Etta had suffered from appalling arthritis fifteen years back. She'd occasionally been bed-ridden even then. How was she now?

He should have asked.

He should have asked lots of things.

Once upon a time he'd known all there was to know about Mardie. They'd been lone children on adjoining farms. When his parents had sent him here, seven years old, deeply traumatised, he'd missed his twin as if part of him had been ripped away. Mardie had helped fill that appalling void. They'd spent their childhood together. Best friends.

And then… Six months before his final exams he'd suddenly seen Mardie differently.

Theirs had been a fumbling teenage love affair, as painful as it was sweet. But it meant, for the first time, he saw a possibility for sharing the load into the future, of having someone by him as he carried his burden of guilt and grief.

How unfair was that? He'd never even explained—how could he? *Help me make up for my brother's life?*

He'd said simply, 'Follow me to Sydney,' and she'd said no.

'Write,' she'd said.

He'd thought at first that he could, but what he hadn't realised was how much it hurt. Those first months in a huge, anonymous university college, away from anyone he knew… Losing Mardie… It had been like losing Robbie all over again.

But he had to leave. Banksia Bay was where he'd been dumped. It had become a refuge but he'd always known he had to leave.

'Stay there until we all forget,' his father had said. Even at seventeen he'd known forgetting was never going to happen. Staying in Banskia Bay seemed like a long, continuous betrayal of memory.

So he had to leave, but if he'd phoned Mardie, if he'd heard her voice, if he'd made any contact at all, then he risked crumbling. And how could he do that?

Robbie, his ghost, his shadow, was driving him.

Behind Robbie... His parents, running through inherited money as if it was water, squandering their lives, losing Robbie in the process. Consciously forgetting their son.

His great-aunt, floundering after an ill-advised love affair, locking herself away in Banksia Bay, as far from what she thought of as civilisation as she could get, using her inheritance as a shield from the world. Consciously forgetting her lover.

So many lives, wasted. Including Robbie's.

For Robbie's sake, the squandering would stop. The forgetting would stop.

So he'd decided that contacting Mardie would simply keep the wound open. Then, by the time he was settled, by the time the ache eased, it seemed too late to rekindle friendship. He'd burned his bridges, and now he had to pay the price.

The price was that tonight she'd welcomed him almost as a stranger. He'd kissed her and she'd backed away. He'd touched her and she'd flinched. And he'd gone to bed without even asking about her mother.

They'd have time to talk in the morning, he thought. He'd ask...and then he'd leave.

Again.

He stirred uneasily. The spare bed always had been too small, too hard. He ached.

The storm kept on, unabated.

He lay awake and thought of Mardie. Of a life long past.

Of a seventeen-year-old who was desperate to save the world, to do *something*, but who wanted to carry Mardie with him.

Why remember it now? Theirs was a childhood friendship, faded to nothing. He shouldn't have come.

It was just...the invitation to the reunion had seemed almost meant. He wasn't sure why he'd kept thinking of Mardie during this last long illness, but he had.

The Mardie of his childhood.

The problem was, he decided as he drifted towards sleep, it wasn't the Mardie of years ago he was thinking of now. It was the Mardie of now. Mardie hugging him joyously in that first instinctive burst of surprised welcome. Mardie in her vast sou'wester, holding the ladder as if this was the sort of work she did every day of the week. Mardie, as she was, but a thousandfold more.

Why had he returned?

Sleep was nowhere.

The night had no answers, and neither did he.

CHAPTER THREE

BLAKE finally slept—and he woke to the sound of singing.

For a moment he thought he was dreaming. He was in a tiny attic room. Whitewashed walls. A narrow bed.

For that instant he was back in his childhood, and then he was wide awake. The events of the night before flooded back.

Mardie was outside, somewhere below his bedroom window. Singing.

He glanced at his watch. Silly o'clock.

He swung himself out of bed and winced. Yes, the airbags had saved him from injury but he was still battered.

He also still suffered aches from illness. Haemorrhagic dengue did that to you. He stretched cautiously. Ouch.

The singing went on. It was something operatic, ridiculous, sung at the top of her lungs. Mardie at full caterwaul.

He found himself grinning, remembering early grade school. The whole school had been learning Christmas carols for the annual concert. An ambitious music teacher had listened to each child in turn. Divided them into sections. Soprano, alto, baritone, tenor.

She'd listened to Mardie, grimaced and given her a section of her own.

'You can be the drum,' Miss Watson had decreed. 'Stay at the back and boom along to the beat. Just sing "Pum Pum Pum Pum Pum."'

But what Mardie lacked in talent she made up for in enthusiasm. The night of the school concert, Mardie's ear-shattering "Pums" had practically drowned out the choir, and the audience had dissolved into delighted laughter.

Mardie had laughed as well.

He grinned at the memory, his aches receding as he pulled open the shutters and looked down.

She was milking the cow. One cow. This was sheep country, not dairy. She'd be milking for personal use.

Or not. One cow made a lot of milk.

Who was living in this house with her?

The house was silent. The storm of the night before was past. The early-morning sun was glittering on the wet paddocks.

Mardie was sitting in the little open shed at the back gate, calmly milking the cow in the wooden bail he remembered climbing on as a child.

This place was a time warp, he thought. All the things he'd done in the past fifteen years…

He'd seen the world. His work in Africa…

She'd stayed home and milked the cow.

'Rather than stand and stare, make yourself useful,' she yelled up at him. 'There's bacon in the fridge. Start cooking. I'll be inside in five minutes.'

Had he been so obvious?

'Is there anyone else home?' he yelled back.

'No.' Short and to the point. 'Except the dogs and they're not moving. I think they're in love.'

'Mardie…'

'Bacon,' she yelled. 'I'd like four rashers, two tomatoes, four slices of toast and I'll cook my own eggs when I get in. Or you can milk the cow. Take your pick. By the way, the pool of water under the downpipe's practically a swimming pool. If you hadn't diverted it, it'd be in my house. You deserve four rashers as well.'

* * *

His dinner suit was still sodden. Of course. Clothes were an issue. Why hadn't he brought spares? Feeling…weird…he donned Bill's bathrobe again and headed downstairs.

The kitchen was warm and welcoming and smelled of damp dog. Or a bit more. Bessie's week of being a stray had left her distinctly on the nose. But if there was one thing Blake's work in Africa had equipped him for, it was working with smells. He might bathe her before he left, he thought.

Or maybe not. Maybe he should leave fast.

Depending on Mardie.

Both dogs rose as he entered, heading out of their basket to greet him. Bessie came side by side with Bounce. Just touching. She'd learned this mechanism to cope, he thought—finding something trustworthy and sticking like glue.

She touched his hand with her wet nose and he felt his gut twist.

A blind working dog…

Don't get involved, he told himself, but he already was. He was thinking of bathing her but he was thinking much more.

Breakfast first.

He knew this place backwards. Little had changed. The kitchen had been repainted, though. Sea blue. Nice. The big old woodstove was still the centrepiece.

There were a couple of extraordinary enamelled paintings on either side. Abstract. They looked like wildfire under glass. Even when the woodstove wasn't lit, these paintings would give warmth to the room, he thought. Mardie always did have an eye for good art.

Breakfast.

The vast frying pan, black with age, seemed an old friend. The bacon was a slab rather than pre-cut rashers, just like it'd always been when he stayed here as a kid. He cut it thick, tossed rashers into the pan, and dog smell was immediately replaced by cooking bacon.

The dogs wiggled with hope, and he cut more. It was a special morning. Bacon all round.

He was halfway through making toast when Mardie appeared. She was wearing another ancient sweater with holes in the elbows. She'd pulled her gumboots off at the door and her feet were covered with bright yellow socks. No holes this morning. Sartorial elegance at its finest.

She'd done her hair, braiding it and coiling it high. It made her look a little more sophisticated than last night, but not much. Nothing could ever make this woman sophisticated, he thought. She was carrying a bucket of milk, the quintessential dairymaid. She looked…

Incredibly sexy.

That was a dumb thing to think. Since when had faded jeans, torn sweater and a bucket of milk made a woman sexy?

But there was no denying, Mardie was…sexy.

And it seemed the admiration worked both ways. 'I'm glad you've put on the bathrobe,' she said as she heaved her bucket onto the bench. 'Have you been working out? I can't remember all those muscles. Standing at the attic window showing them off…I would have thought a bit of modesty would be appropriate.' Then, as he started to feel discomfited, she grinned. 'I know. It's bad manners to comment, but manners were never my forte. And while I'm commenting… You're too thin. You want a glass of milk? Guaranteed non-pasteurised, non-homogenised, organic, still warm from its own personal milk heater, Clarabelle Cow.'

She dipped a ladle into the bucket and poured two big glasses. Handed him one.

How long since he'd drunk milk straight from the cow?

He thought of the hospital food he'd endured over the past awful weeks. Thought he should have just come here.

That was a bad idea.

He put down the glass and she smiled. 'Milk moustache,' she said and handed him a tissue. 'Nothing changes.'

Something had. They used to wipe each other's milk moustaches. That had started when they were knee high to a grasshopper. The fact that she'd handed him a tissue…

Now they were practically strangers.

It behoved a man to remember it.

'Why the cow? Can you drink a bucket a day?' he asked.

'I make cheese with a friend. Lorraine's a local potter—we help each other in all sorts of ways and we make cheese on the side. We have one cow each. It works well because if either of us is busy we do the other's milking. And we're good. We sell it at our farmer's market. You have no idea how much we can charge, and it's fun.'

Fun. For some reason the word threw him.

Mardie, with her milk moustache, having fun.

'How long have you been up?' he asked, moving on with an effort.

'Dawn. I went round the sheep to make sure none got hit by lightning, but the Cyprus hedge is a great shelter and they're fine. The gum's down across the drive, though. You had to go round it last night?'

'Yeah.' His mud-covered shoes on the veranda testified to the scrambling he'd had to do to get here.

'I'll get the chainsaw onto it. That's my after-breakfast job. Oh, and I believe your car's a write-off.'

'You've seen it?'

'I've seen it,' she said grimly. 'How fast were you going?'

'Obviously too fast.'

'You're so lucky you're not dead.'

And there was something about the way she said it… The lightness suddenly disappeared. Her words were flat, with a faint tremor beneath.

There was something about the way her face changed.

He knew this woman. He hadn't seen her for fifteen years but he knew…

'Who else has been killed in a car crash?' he asked, and it was a question and a statement all in one.

'I...' She stopped. She shook her head but he knew her denial was a lie.

'Your mother?' He felt sick. *He should have asked.*

'My mum's in Banksia Bay Nursing Home.' She concentrated on fetching eggs from the pantry, refusing to return to car wrecks. 'Her arthritis cripples her. I bring her out here whenever I can. She sits on the veranda in the sun and tells me all the things I'm doing wrong.' She smiled again then, starting to crack eggs into the pan. Moving on. And he couldn't push. *He had no right.*

'But you know something?' she said, still inexorably changing the subject. 'She's happy. She doesn't need to stay here. All these years we fought to keep her independent, she finally gave in and now she's surrounded by friends. She plays bridge, she watches old movies, she reads. She doesn't need her daughter to do the humiliating things. She comes out here and enjoys the farm but she's always ready to go back to her comfy bedroom with her music and her books and the local nurses who make her feel loved. I don't feel bad about it at all.'

'So you're here completely by yourself?'

There was a moment's hesitation. Then... 'Yes.' It was almost defiant.

'You should have gone to university.' It was an explosion.

She paused, mid egg break. Stiffened. Then she calmly went on breaking eggs. Four. She scooped bacon fat over them so they cooked sunny-side up. Slid them onto two plates. Sat at the table and loaded her plate with bacon.

'I've never regretted it,' she said at last. 'Not for a moment.'

'Look at you.' Why was he feeling so angry? Why was he feeling...that it had all been a waste? It wasn't fair to attack her, her lifestyle, but...the idea that she'd been *mouldering* here was suddenly killing him. 'I go away for fifteen years,

I get myself a medical degree, a career. I've done so much. And you…'

'Have you been happy?'

'Happiness isn't the point.'

'What else is the point?' she demanded, buttering toast. 'My mother's arthritis started when she was thirty. When she was thirty-eight she lost her husband. Yet she's happy. She had the choice. Miserable or happy. She chose happy. She still chooses happy. Pass the marmalade, please.'

'What did she do with her life?'

'She made us all happy,' she snapped. 'Including you. Don't you dare say that's a waste. Marmalade!'

'Where are you putting all this?' She was about five feet two. She was little and wiry and compact. She was eating enough to keep him going for a full day.

'Work makes you hungry,' she said evenly, and her anger had been carefully and obviously put away. 'You've been lying in bed letting your calories sink languorously anywhere they want. My calories have been bouncing all the way down to the bottom paddock on the tractor, into the bails to milk Clarabelle, over to see your car and the ruined tree, and they're all used up. Speaking of your car…' She glanced at her watch. 'I'll ring Raff, the local cop, at eight. And Henrietta.'

'Henrietta?'

'The lady who runs the pound.'

'No.'

It was an explosion, and the word stopped them both short.

Mardie paused, her bacon midway to her mouth. She gazed at him, calm and direct. 'No?'

From their basket, the two dogs watched. Or one dog watched and the other watched by proxy. Bounce had been declared Bessie's eyes.

'No?' she said cautiously. 'Are you offering her a home?'

'I can't.' That was practically an explosion, too.

'Neither can I.' She met his gaze square on. Knew what he was asking. Rejected it. 'Don't ask it of me.'

He needed to make some phone calls before he talked about the next option. He needed to know his facts. But for now… 'Why not?' he asked.

'She's a working dog. Look at her. She's beautiful, young, energetic, aching to run. She's bred to work. I've seen injured working dogs before. Without their work, they pine. Look at how thin she is. Charlie Hunter is a kind old man and he would have loved her to bits. He'll have fed her whatever she'll take. When he went into the nursing home he'll have handed her over to Henrietta at the pound, and Hen loves dogs. She'll have hand fed her if that's what it took to get her to eat. But she's still stick-thin. I know a depressed dog when I see one. She's blind and she's miserable.'

'So you'd put her down?'

'Like it's *my* decision?' She glared. 'That's unfair and you know it. But as for keeping her… Bounce would be out every day with me, working the sheep. He'd come home and Bessie would smell him, would know what we'd been doing. Border collies have arguably the highest IQ in the animal kingdom. They're not content to be lapdogs. It won't be safe for me to have her where sheep might kick her, where blind doesn't work. She's not meant to spend the rest of her life in a basket by the fire and I won't do it to her.'

'Cataracts are removable.'

'Maybe.' She spread marmalade on a second piece of toast, looked at it and then set it aside. 'I read my veterinary guide after you went to bed last night. Cataract operations in dogs are problematic. There's a high chance of failure and the cost per eye is astronomical. I couldn't even think of going there. Putting her though that…'

'But if you wanted her…'

'You found her,' she said, and her voice was back to harsh. 'She could never stay with me.'

'What's the difference between staying in a city apartment while you work all day, or staying by herself here?'

'I don't work in Australia,' he said.

'You don't work in Sydney?'

'My great-aunt had an apartment there. I'm clearing it out. From now on I'll be based in California. I really can't take on a dog. But I didn't mean to make you responsible.'

'But you did,' she said, suddenly savage. 'You're making me feel all sorts of things I don't want to feel.'

He raked his hair. 'I'm sorry.'

'Good. Excellent, in fact. Let's get you out of here.'

That was surely the best option. He glanced down at his bathrobe. Winced. Thought about his still-soggy dinner suit.

She'd followed his glance. 'I'll run into town when the shops open and buy what you need.'

'I need to get back to Sydney.'

'There's a bus this afternoon.'

'I don't…'

'Want to use the bus? You have no choice. Otherwise you're stuck here for the weekend and this house is too small. You know it is. Now, if you'll excuse me, I have work to do.'

'What needs doing?'

'I told you. I need to attack the tree across the drive with the chainsaw. Otherwise I can't get into town to get you clothes. I also need to move the sheep back into the outer paddocks. The Cyprus run's restricted—it's my safe paddock but there's not much feed. I either have to move them or hand feed them. So if you'll excuse me… Every minute you keep me here is a minute more before I can run into town to get clothes.'

'You expect me to sit in your father's bathrobe while you work?'

She stilled. 'My father's bathrobe?'

'I assumed…'

'Don't assume,' she snapped. 'My father never wore a bathrobe in his life.'

'Whose...?'

'Stay out of it.' Her anger was palpable. Any minute she'd throw something at him.

'Mardie, I need to help you,' he said, feeling his way through what seemed a minefield.

'You can help by staying out of my way.'

He rose, angry himself. 'I'm not useless.'

'You're useless in a bathrobe or a dinner suit.'

'I did fix the spouting.'

She glowered. 'So you did. I'm trying to remember it.'

'Are you punishing me for walking away fifteen years ago?'

Whoa. There was a moment's deathly silence. Her face lost colour. She closed her eyes and when she opened them something had changed. Anger had been replaced with pure ice.

'Are you out of your mind?' she demanded, speaking slowly, each syllable dripping with frost. 'You think I've been longing for you for fifteen years? Doing nothing? Grazing a few sheep, pining after my long-lost love, playing lovelorn little hayseed?'

'I didn't say...'

'You didn't have to say. What you're thinking is like a huge placard over your head.'

'All I said was that it was a waste...'

'To stay here? To live where I love to live?'

'A hundred sheep...'

'I'm a craft therapist, Blake Maddock.' She was practically yelling. 'And an artist. I did my training part-time, an art course in Whale Cove, going back and forth for almost four years. I work in the local nursing home, organising outings, craft, music, fun. I also practice my art and I'm good. It gives me huge pleasure, and I'm starting to sell. I've sold off acreage because I can't run this farm as a full-time commitment but I still love it. My sheep make me happy. I love my work in the nursing home. I make the best cheese in the district. My mum still loves coming out here. I don't earn enough for luxury but I love everything about my life. And in case you think I've been pining for you… You think you're wearing my dad's bathrobe? I bought that for Hugh. For my husband. Hugh was killed in a car accident two years ago, the week before Christmas, the week before I gave it to him. For some reason I kept it and I loved it. So you're standing there in my husband's bathrobe, accusing me of having no life, of having lived in a time warp since you left, of doing nothing. And you kissed me last night like you were doing me a favour!'

There was no *practically yelling* about it. The last sentence was truly a blast. The dogs backed to the far end of the basket and cringed.

Blake felt like doing exactly the same.

'Mardie…'

'I'm not listening to another word. If I listen to any more, you risk getting a bucket of milk thrown at you. I'm going out now. I'm going to cut the tree away from the driveway and I'm moving sheep. Then I'm going to drive into town, fetch you some clothes that aren't Hugh's and buy you a bus ticket. I believe it leaves at two. I'll drive you to the bus station and it'll be pure pleasure to see the back of you. It was lovely to see you but now it'll be lovely to see you go. So now… Take care of the dogs while I'm out. And thanks for cooking the bacon. I'd eat some more but I feel like choking.'

She stomped out of the kitchen. Bounce leaped after her and she slammed the door.

He was left with Bessie.

He was left with what he'd done.

* * *

Bessie whimpered, nosed her way across to him and lay her head on his knee.

The little collie was doing it for her own need, not his, he told himself, but he took comfort anyway as she rubbed her head under his palm.

Mardie was a widow. She'd trained as a craft therapist.

Fifteen years and he knew nothing of anything. It was a great black hole.

He should have kept in touch.

Walking away from Banksia Bay had been a no-brainer. From the moment Robbie died he knew he'd have to do something. He remembered the announcement of his final-year marks, the letter offering him a place at medical school and the relief of finally knowing he had a plan.

But then he remembered telling Mardie and watching her face pale as it had paled a few moments ago.

He'd been exuberant, exultant. 'I'm going to Sydney. I can finally do something with my life.'

He glanced out of the window at the rain-washed world, at the undulating paddocks, the vast, spreading gums lining the driveway, the shimmer of the sea in the distance.

He and Mardie had spent a magical childhood in this place. Wandering the farm, the beaches, the harbour. Surfing, rabbiting, messing round with boats, nothing to contain them.

But he needed to work. In Africa he'd made a difference.

No more.

He glanced out of the window again. Mardie was heading up the drive on the tractor, towards the shattered tree. Chainsaw on the back. Bounce running along behind.

A husband, dead. A mother cared for.

A wasted life?

It was unfair. He needed to apologise.

He already had. There was nothing more to be said. She wanted him to leave.

He couldn't leave yet. He'd work with her one last time.

He'd make amends if he could.

Bessie stirred on his knee, her blind eyes staring at nothing, white clouds of fog.

'Maybe we're both blind,' he told her.

Me, me, me. Wrong attitude. To be feeling sorry for himself when this dog was in such need.

Self-pity helped no one. He needed to help Mardie. He needed to sort the fate of Bessie. He needed to make some phone calls.

And then he needed to leave.

CHAPTER FOUR

THE tree had spilt straight down the middle. The scorch marks from the lightning formed a vicious slash down the side of the trunk still standing and the ground around the base was scorched black.

She loved the trees down the driveway, a sentinel of mighty gums a hundred years old.

She felt like crying.

Not just for the tree.

What was he doing, walking into her life again with his stupid, hurtful judgements? What crazy twist of fate had him crash his car where hers was the closest house?

Seeing him stand in her kitchen…in the bathrobe she'd bought for Hugh…

It made her feel tired and old and ill.

And also immeasurably sad. Her first sensation on seeing him again had been joy. Then, as she'd stood in the rain last night, holding the ladder while he fought her drainpipe, the joy had turned to something else. Something inexplicable.

A resurrection of what she'd once felt, or something more?

It didn't matter what she'd felt. She didn't need his judgement.

Work was her salvation. If she worked hard enough she didn't have to think. This tree would take weeks to clear, but she'd do enough now to clear the drive.

She attacked the smaller branches first, slicing them free and dragging them clear. After chopping the main branches for firewood, she'd be left with a pile of leaf litter. She'd use it eventually for mulch, but first she had to get it into a clear space so at the height of summer she didn't risk fire as it rotted and heated.

It was heavy work, heaving branches onto the trailer on the back of the tractor, but work was what she needed to defuse anger.

Work had always been her salvation. When her mother grew sicker. When Hugh died.

When Blake left.

How could she put Blake leaving alongside her grief for her mother, for Hugh?

She'd been sixteen. It couldn't have hurt as much.

She still remembered it though. Blake walking away.

She wanted to cry.

She didn't.

It was just…him walking back. Reminding her of what she'd lost.

She hadn't lost anything. She especially hadn't lost Blake.

She'd never had him.

The chainsaw sliced through a protruding branch. She stepped back smartly as it crashed from the broken trunk.

It was hauled away before it hit the ground.

She turned, and Blake was there.

He was back in his dinner suit. Or most of his dinner suit. Trousers and shirt and shoes. His trousers were still soaked. His gorgeous dress shoes were muddy. His white shirt was damp, the top buttons were undone and the sleeves were rolled up. Everything clung.

Don't look. He made her feel…

Don't feel.

He grabbed the branch and dragged it across to the trailer.

'You'll ruin your suit,' she managed.

'I can afford it.'

Of course he could. Money had never been an issue.

The old stories seeped back. Miss Maddock, Blake's great-aunt. She'd arrived here in her thirties, so gossip said, cashed up, buying the lonely house out on the headland, doing it up almost as a mansion, but seeing no one. There was money to pay for upkeep, money to keep her isolated, money enough to snub the district, take a shopping trip to Sydney once a month, be as eccentric as she liked.

Mardie was too young to remember when Blake arrived but she knew the gossip about that, too. 'His mother's ill. His parents have more money than they know what to do with. The aunt's agreed to look after him until his mum gets better, heaven help him.'

Then, as he was about to finish junior school, more gossip. 'They're dead in a plane cash in Italy. Blake'll have to stay on with the old lady. Word is the parents were really rich. It's in trust for the kid. Though how he can use it, stuck here with her…'

The town heard a little about the plane crash, learned Blake's father was a wealthy gambler who spent his life between casinos, learned his mother had been 'ill' for a long time, learned nothing else. The aunt shut up and told the town to mind its own business.

Past history. She hauled her thoughts back to now.

Don't feel.

She cut the chainsaw motor and the silence stunned her. 'Thank you,' she said.

'It's the least I can do,' he said shortly, heaving the branch with a strength that put hers in the shade. 'After offending you just about every way I can think of, I need to make amends. You want me to keep going with this while you move the sheep?'

'Chainsawing's a skill.'

'Hey, I'm a surgeon,' he said, sounding miffed, and suddenly she found herself smiling.

And how could she not look? How could she not feel?

He was standing in the early-morning sun, dressed in the remnants of his dinner suit. His hair was rumpled; he obviously hadn't stopped to worry about personal grooming. He'd grabbed another branch and was about to heave.

'A surgeon,' she said, cautiously. 'So that makes you a chainsaw expert?'

'You're saying I'm not capable?'

'If you've been practising chainsawing on your patients for the last fifteen years, heaven help them.'

He grinned. It lit his face, making him look younger. It made him look like the Blake she remembered.

She felt her smile fade. Blake…

'Mardie, I'm sorry.' He wasn't coming close; there was half a ruined tree between them. 'I barge back into your life, I make stupid assumptions, I insult you, I try and land you with a blind dog…'

'Plus you didn't make the bacon crispy,' she retorted. 'I can forgive anything else.'

'I didn't…'

'Whatever you've been doing in the last fifteen years, it's not been cooking. Are those clothes very uncomfortable?'

'They're fine.' He paused, looked down at his sodden trousers, gave a rueful grimace. 'Okay, they're appalling.'

'I could lend you…'

'I don't want any more of your husband's clothes.'

'You didn't appreciate the bathrobe?'

'The bathrobe's excellent—although dry jocks would add a little something, even to the bathrobe.'

Dry jocks…

She blushed.

How long since she'd blushed? Her blushing used to kill her as a teenager. She thought she was over it.

She wasn't. She blushed. Over the mention of jocks. What, was she thirteen again?

'Hey,' Blake said, and suddenly his attention was no longer on her. Which was just as well. The blush was taking a while to subside. He stooped and peered at the slab of trunk that had peeled away. 'Look at this.'

She looked—and she blushed some more.

At ten years old, before she had any idea of vandalism, of desecration of trees, maybe before she had any sense at all, her dad had given her a pocket knife for her birthday. It had neat little tools on the side. It had her name engraved on the hilt. She'd loved that knife.

It hadn't always been a force for good—as displayed by what Blake was looking at.

The carving was at the base of the tree, practically in the dirt so only she knew it was there. It was cut into the bark and it had scored deeper and deeper as the tree grew.

M.R. xx B.M. A heart.

Blushing didn't begin to describe what was happening right now. She was about to go up in flames.

Blake was grinning.

'So I was dumb,' she snapped and reverted to chainsawing. Really loud. Loud was her salvation.

Would her blush never subside? She cut the lowest branch free, right through the middle of the initials.

M.R. xx…nobody. A heart all by itself.

He didn't comment.

They worked on, Mardie sawing, Blake carting timber.

Her blush and her head gradually cleared, and so did the driveway.

It would have taken her half a day to do this herself, but in an hour they had the driveway clear. The rest could be done over time. Not this morning, when she had Blake to get rid of.

She was so aware of him…

Stupid, stupid, stupid.

'Sheep?' he said, as she tossed the chainsaw onto the back of the tractor.

'Yep. I'll take the trailer off and head down and get them. I'll need Bounce.' She gave a man-sized whistle and Bounce came flying to her side.

Bessie emerged from the house. Reached the steps. Stopped.

'Can you stay with Bessie?' she asked, but Blake was already striding back to the house. Instead of going inside, though, he lifted Bessie down the steps, set her down and then headed back, Bessie at his side.

Mardie was removing the trailer from the tractor. Trying to block Blake out. She needed to head down the paddock and move the sheep—without a city doctor and a blind dog.

'It's rough going down there,' she said. 'I don't think…'

'Let her come,' he said gently. 'She's breaking her heart. She could sit at your feet on the tractor. There's room.'

'And when I get down there? I need to work. I can't…'

'I'll come with you.' Then, instead of waiting for her to agree, he climbed onto the running board, set Bessie at Mardie's feet and hung on himself. He looked down at Bounce, who was quivering all over, anticipating adventure. 'Sorry, mate, you're going to have to run behind.'

'He wouldn't have it any other way,' Mardie managed. And stupidly she felt like blushing again.

He was far too close. He was right…there. His shoulder was brushing her waist.

He expected her to calmly drive the tractor with him standing on the running board?

A woman could crash.

What were her hormones thinking?

Whatever they were thinking, they had nothing to do with her, she told herself. Her hormones could go take a cold shower. This guy was rude and insulting and an echo from her past she could do without.

It was just that he was so…close.

He'd ripped his shirt. He had a smear of mud down his face. He obviously had no shaving gear with him. His five-o'clock shadow was dark and…okay, and *sexy.*

She thought suddenly of her teenage James Bond fixation. Blake as James Bond at seventeen? Not even close.

Blake now…

He looked a lean, mean James Bond, she thought. And he was right by her side. She and James, off to face adventure with their two sleek adventure dogs.

Or off to move sheep with one silly pup and one blind stray.

'We should have brought the Lamborghini,' Blake said, and she glanced up at him in amazement.

They'd always had this. The ability to read what the other was thinking, to laugh even before the other was laughing.

She couldn't stop herself smiling.

'You want me to gun this baby?' she demanded. 'In fourth gear I reckon we can hit ten miles an hour. Three minutes tops from nought to ten. Who'd look for Formula One when we have my old tractor?'

He chuckled.

She loved his chuckle.

She loved Blake.

Huh?

No! She was old enough and sensible enough to stop herself right there. Once upon a time she'd loved Blake, with all the passion of her sixteen-year-old self, but even then she'd been sensible, knowing she couldn't follow him.

Now the sensible side of her kicked in again. She'd loved a seventeen-year-old Blake, but that wasn't who was standing on her running board. This guy must be what, thirty-two? He'd lived more of his life without her than with her. He had another life somewhere she knew nothing about.

He'd made all sorts of judgements about her, and she wasn't about to do the same to him.

She didn't know him any more.

'Are you married?' she asked suddenly. He was gazing out over the paddocks towards his aunt's old house, his eyes following the route they used to travel on their bikes, sometimes half a dozen times a day.

'Why do you want to know?'

'Because it's all been about me,' she said, exasperated. 'You've got my back-story, even down to the colour of bathrobe I hoped my husband liked. I know nothing.'

'You know I studied medicine.'

'And you know what I did. Snap. Now marriage. I've shown you mine, you show me yours.'

'Was yours happy?'

'Blake!'

He grinned at that, a trifle rueful. 'Yeah, I know. Unfair. It's just…' His voice trailed off.

'You did get married?'

'No,' he said. 'I was engaged for a bit. It didn't work out.'

'Oh, Blake…'

'Old history. I'm over it.'

'Another doctor?'

'Yes.'

'That makes sense.'

'What's that supposed to mean?'

'You wanted someone to share your life.' She hesitated. 'No. It was more than that. You needed someone to incorporate into your life. A marriage was never going to work on that basis.'

Silence. Her words had been mean, she thought. She should apologise. She did in her head but not out loud.

For some reason barriers were needed. She didn't need to get any closer to this man than she already was.

She needed him to get off the tractor. She needed him to stop touching her.

They reached the gate into the Cyprus paddock. 'Leave this one open,' she said.

He jumped down, and she was jolted by the sense of loss. How dumb was that?

He swung the gate wide, waited till she was through and then jumped up again. It was a prosaic action, done a score of times a day in her life, but she could tell… His face was revealing more than he could possibly know.

There were all sorts of sensations crowding in. The sensory experience of morning on a farm after rain… Something she almost took for granted but he'd lost fifteen years ago.

He hadn't lost it. He'd set it aside.

The Blake she knew was still in there.

The sheep were grazing near the Cyprus hedge. She'd used this paddock a few times recently and pickings were lean. The sheep headed towards the tractor as soon as they saw her coming, hopeful for hay.

'You're going to have to work for it,' she told them, turning thankfully to practical and prosaic. 'There's plenty of feed in the back paddocks, so you need to move.' She jumped down from the tractor—on the far side of Blake because there was no way she was brushing past him—and whistled to Bounce.

'Away to me,' she called. Firmly. Hopefully.

Eventually Bounce was going to be a brilliant working dog. He was desperate to please, and fiercely intelligent. Right now, however, he was just a bit too eager. Full of potential and hope.

He headed clockwise round the back of the pack as per order but he rushed, he went too close to the sheep and they startled. They started scattering before he could get to the back of the mob, spreading out in bleating sheep hysteria.

She'd have to run herself to get on the other side of them. She took off…

And suddenly Bessie was beside her, like a shadow, running in tandem, keeping pace.

The sheep reacted differently with the dogs. With her they were likely to run past, spread out, but Bessie's presence gave them pause. They fell back, uncertain. Bounce finally got round the back—and they started heading the way she wanted them to go, to the open paddock gate.

'Way back,' she yelled to Bounce and he streaked further back.

He barked.

And then Bessie was gone from her side, flying across the paddock to join Bounce at the rear, but on this flank.

She had two dogs at the back.

Bounce barked again and Bessie moved further back. She was well out of reach of the flock but they knew she was there.

How had she done that? *She was blind.*

There was no time to think about it now. Mardie sprinted towards the gate to stop them veering along the fence instead of through. But Blake was already there.

James Bond in his dinner suit, herding sheep.

The sheep crowded towards him, saw the open gate, hesitated.

Bessie barked.

Bounce crowded them behind.

James Bond held the gate.

They rushed through, a steady stream of non-panicked sheep, and the thing was done.

With just Bounce that might have taken her half an hour. They'd done it in minutes.

Blake swung the gate closed. 'How easy was that?' he demanded, grinning in satisfaction. 'Two good dogs…'

Both of them looked at Bessie.

As the sheep had flooded through the gate she'd paused, stopped. She'd have followed movement, light and sound. Now, things would simply be green again.

She sat, waiting for some sensory cue to move again.

Bounce headed to her side and sniffed. Rubbed himself against his new friend. Touched Bessie as she had touched him.

The start of a canine love affair?

Oh, for heaven's sake… She really was operating on hormones this morning. Mardie whistled. Bounce ran towards her and Bessie came with him.

Wagging her tail.

Wagging her whole body.

Border collies worked for pleasure. Herding sheep had been bred into them for generations.

This dog was seriously good.

She'd kept her distance from the flock. It was a bright morning and the sheep were washed clean with the rain. White against green…it had been possible for her to help.

And if she could help blind…

How much would it cost…?

'I'll pay,' Blake said and she blinked.

'Pardon?'

'I can't keep her,' he said. 'I know it's not fair to ask you to keep a dog I found, but you've always had more than one dog. I remember three.'

'I don't think…'

'She's born to work,' he said. 'She's almost as good blind as Bounce is now.'

'Bounce will get better,' she said, distracted and loyal. 'He's a work in progress.'

'And Bessie's a work of art. You know she's good. You could use her. I can afford…'

'It doesn't always work,' she said shortly. She'd thought this through it morning, with her face against Clarabelle's flank. It was the time she did her best thinking, but the conclusions she'd come to this morning were bleak. 'You think I'd do that to her? Send her to the city, two operations, each one risky. Weeks in a strange place, strange kennels, knowing no one. She's done that already. She's been in the pound since Charlie went into care. She's been thrown out of the Animal Welfare van when it crashed and she's been wandering lost for a week. You want me to put her through more trauma?'

'Yes,' he said bluntly. 'She could take it.'

'She can't.' Mardie squatted, clicking her fingers, and the gentle little collie came to her. 'She's had enough, Blake,' she said. 'To put her through operations with no guarantee of success…'

But he wasn't accepting what she was saying. 'It would succeed,' he said, just as firmly. He hesitated. 'Okay, there's never a hundred per cent guarantee but it's close. She's a young dog. These cataracts haven't been present for all that long. I've had a good look. They're full, fluid-filled, not old and shrinking. That means less risk of scarring. Underneath, her eyes should be fine. There's a small risk of retina detachment with the operation, but with the best aftercare the risk is tiny.'

'How do you know?'

'I do the same operation all the time on humans,' he said simply. 'That's what I am, it's what I do—ophthalmology. There's a vet in Sydney who spent time with me while we were training. He's a personal friend and, Mardie, I know he'll do this for me. I'll pay all the expenses and at the end of it you'll have a fine working dog. I know she's my responsibility; I'm not asking you to take her on as a favour. I know she'll be a fabulous dog. I know she can be cured.'

She stared up at him, stunned. 'But the cost…' She couldn't think of anything more sensible to say.

'You know money's not an issue.'

Of course it wasn't. Somehow she forced herself not to look at Blake, to look only at Bessie. To think only of Bessie. So many things… To take this next step…

'I'd…I'd have to talk to Charlie,' she managed.

'Charlie?'

'The guy who owned her.'

'He put her in the pound.'

'He didn't have a choice. He was hospitalised himself.'

Bessie was being licked now by Bounce. Her week of escape had left her with interesting smells, and probably interesting tastes. Both dogs seemed deeply content.

Bessie and Bounce… Growing more devoted by the moment.

Hormones. Leave them out of this.

'How long would she need to stay in Sydney?' she asked, cautiously. Forcing herself to think past Blake. Beginning to think…maybe.

'Maybe a week. A few days before for tests and a few days after.'

'You'd be doing this because…'

'Call it thanks for the night's accommodation.'

'Then we'd be square again,' she said, a bit too harshly because suddenly…suddenly that was how she was feeling. Harsh. 'It wouldn't do to be in my debt.'

'Mardie…'

'I'm sorry, that's not very gracious.' She rose, reaching a decision. Regrouped. Tried very hard to put harsh behind her.

'Okay, so I don't want charity, but this is Bessie we're talking about. So that'd be it? You'd take her to Sydney, fix her eyes, give her back to me, no strings attached?'

'What do you mean—strings?'

'I'm not sure,' she said. 'It was only…that kiss. Blake, dumb or not, I don't want to go down the friendship path again. One cured dog, that's all this would be.'

'I never suggested anything else.'

She didn't reply.

She was being dumb.

He'd never suggested anything else. Of course he hadn't. So what…*else* was she thinking?

* * *

He hated not knowing what she was thinking. He'd always known.

He didn't know now.

He gazed around him, at the farm, at the sunlight on the wet grass, at the great crashed gum in the distance.

The shattered timber…

A friendship finished.

It wasn't about the kiss, he thought. It was about much more.

'I should have written,' he said softly into the morning stillness. 'I'm sorry I didn't. I was young and stupid and I didn't know how to handle my own grief at leaving.'

'You weren't sad to be going. You were jumping out of your skin.'

'I was,' he said. 'But I was sad to be leaving you. Gutted.'

'You didn't show it.'

'If I'd shown it,' he said simply, 'I never could have left.'

Then the outside world arrived. A police car pulled up out on the road, and Raff, the local cop, strolled across the paddocks to meet them. Someone had obviously reported Blake's crashed car.

'Hey,' Raff called. Blake knew Raff—he'd been part of the pack of local kids and he could see Raff recognised him in turn. Raff greeted him with warmth and a trace of relief. 'I heard you were at the reunion last night. When Gladys Mitchell called and said a Mercedes was wrapped round a tree I thought it must be you.' He grinned as he took in Blake's battered clothes. 'New fashion for farm work? Give the place a certain style, eh, Mardie? So what happened?'

He listened as a good cop should, but when he was told about Bessie his cheer slid away.

'Dogs,' he said bleakly. 'They're all over the place, and this one… At least Henrietta will be thankful she's found. You want me to take her back to town?'

'I'm keeping her,' Mardie said, and Raff looked from the dog to Mardie and back again.

'She's blind, Mardie,' he said, as if Mardie might not have noticed. 'I don't know how to say this but…'

'Blake says he'll fix her for me. He's an eye surgeon. He knows about cataracts. He'll take her back to Sydney and cure her.'

Raff whistled, stunned. 'You'd do that?'

'Yeah,' Blake said, feeling suddenly defensive. There was surprise in Raff's voice—amazement that an outsider was offering to help in what was essentially the town's business?

He'd never been part of this community, he thought. He'd been the rich kid. The kid who lived with the weird old lady. Now here he was, still on the outside, a guy in a dinner suit, offering charity.

But the charity, it seemed, was acceptable. 'Hen'll offer you her kingdom,' Raff said. 'Mind, her kingdom consists of lost dogs so I'd run a mile. But what about you, Mardie? Can you afford to keep another dog?'

Afford…

Were things so tight, then, that the cost of even keeping another dog would be a consideration?

'Of course I can. And she's good, Raff,' Mardie said. 'Great with sheep. I'll go in and talk to Charlie.'

'Charlie?'

'Her collar said she's Charlie's dog.'

Raff whistled at that, too. 'Of course. I remember… She'll be great, then. Charlie's been amazing,' he told Blake. 'In his day he's been the best dog-trainer in the district. Took every championship going.'

And Blake suddenly remembered.

Just before Mardie's dad died he'd taken them to the local sheepdog trials. They'd seen an elderly man in a battered coat and wide-brimmed hat take all the awards going. Charlie. Charlie's dogs had moved sheep so skilfully they might as well be attached to them by leads. The dogs simply looked at the sheep and the sheep jumped to obey.

'I'll learn how to do that,' Mardie had declared, and he couldn't help himself—he looked at Bounce. Who was still sort of…bouncing.

'He's a work in progress,' Mardie repeated defensively, and he grinned.

'I can see that. Taking a while to settle.'

'Bessie'll teach him,' she said. 'When she's better.'

'So you are serious?' Raff asked Blake. 'Will you take her to Sydney with you now?'

And Blake got that, too. This guy was interested in practicalities and he was also protecting his own. He wasn't having Mardie landed with a blind dog and a half-promise to fix her. Maybe Raff knew, as Blake did, that once Mardie took Bessie on, she'd keep her, regardless.

Once Mardie gave her heart, she didn't take it back.

And that was a kick in the guts, too.

She'd married?

What was she supposed to have done? Had he expected her to stay loyal to him for fifteen years? Pining for a memory?

He'd moved on. So had she.

'I need to contact my vet friend,' he said, but he was speaking to Mardie. He was thinking of Mardie, feeling bad. Okay, he'd let her down in the past, but on this at least he could make good. 'I don't know when he could fit her in. And I'll need to get her there. I imagine I'll need to take the bus back to Sydney and come back once I've organised a car.'

'I'll take you back to Sydney,' Mardie said.

Silence.

Mardie, driving him back to Sydney.

It was little more than a two-hour drive.

Why not?

It was just that…

He saw the corners of her mouth twitch. Uh-oh. She'd guessed his errant thought. His dumb thought.

'I'm guessing Blake's worrying that Sydney's a big, big city and I might rightfully be scared,' she told Raff, her eyes suddenly alight with laughter. 'But I hear there's folk who've visited and come out alive.' She snagged a blade of grass and started chewing. Country hick personified. 'Ain't that right, Raff?'

'He's right in that there's perils aplenty,' Raff said gravely, cop-like, catching on in an instant.

'Like what?' she said and put on an anxious face.

'Restrooms,' Raff drawled back. 'Fearsome places. They teach us in cop school. If you use a city restroom, don't sit on the seat—city germs'll kill you before you can put your shopping on the floor. And don't put your feet on the ground or you'll be hit by a syringe from under the stalls. White slave traders,' he said, his voice loaded with doom. 'You'll wake up in a harem in Bathsheba. You reckon you can risk that, our Mardie?'

Mardie grinned. At Raff, not at him.

'I reckon I'll take my chances. Lorraine'll look after my place for a while. Mum's happy right now. The forecast for the weather's settled. It'll do me good to have a few days away.'

Whoa, Blake thought. A few days? She was coming to Sydney as in...*coming to stay*?

'My aunt's apartment only has one bedroom,' he said before he could stop himself.

Mardie's grin widened. She and Raff were still enjoying their joke. 'Not a harem, then?'

'Um...' He managed a limp smile. 'No.'

'Too bad. But I have somewhere I can stay in Sydney,' she said quite kindly. 'In Coogee. I can take Bounce there. It'll be easier on Bessie if Bounce is close; a semblance of normality. Is Coogee close to where Bessie will need to be looked after?'

'Yes.' As luck would have it, the next suburb to Central Vets.

But… How come she had a place to stay in Sydney? The way she and Raff were laughing…she went often?

There were a million questions he wanted to ask.

He was an outsider. He had no right to ask.

'I'll catch the bus back to Sydney,' he said, not knowing what else to say. 'I'll let you know about Bessie's operation and you can come as soon as it's scheduled.'

'Organise it now,' Raff said, laughter giving way to cop in charge.

'You don't trust me?'

'I don't want Mardie landed with a blind dog.' Raff's smile died. 'You haven't been near the place for fifteen years. Why should I trust you? Sorry, mate, but my job's looking out for this community.'

'I keep my word.'

'I trust him,' Mardie said.

It needed only that—that she gave him a reference as well as everything else. But he glanced at her and she met his gaze and he saw…

It was more than words. She was meeting his gaze head-on, her eyes clear and steady, and he knew that a decision had been taken.

He'd lost something fifteen years ago. A tiny part of that was being given back.

He smiled at her, and she smiled straight back, a wide, cheeky smile that was almost daring.

He'd forgotten how lovely that smile was.

Or maybe he'd always remembered but he'd locked it away in a corner that had stayed locked; a corner that held things that hurt too much to take out and examine.

A corner that held Robbie?

'You have a change of clothes somewhere?' Raff asked, watching them both with a bemused expression. It was a cop expression, giving nothing away but maybe understanding more than they wanted.

'No, I…'

'There's nothing in the car except your laptop and briefcase,' Raff said. 'I searched it. I also wasted a few minutes searching in case you were dead. You might have phoned, Mardie.'

'The phone's down.'

He swore. 'Sorry, that's right, a tree crashed on the lines between town and here. It should be up by lunchtime. Okay, moving on, you need to organise the dog and then you need to organise something to wear. You go out in public like that and I'll have calls to arrest you for indecent exposure.'

Raff was right. He was indecent. His ripped shirt was hardly there.

Both Mardie and Raff were gazing at him. Raff with speculation. Mardie with…something else.

She started to smile and then…suddenly her smile turned again into a blush. He watched as she fought, but failed, to keep her colour under control.

It wasn't just a blush. It was sheer, breathtaking beauty.

Mardie…

'I'll take him into town and buy some gear,' she managed, trying to sound practical despite the blush. 'If he can organise Bessie's operation for this week I'll take them both to Sydney tomorrow.'

'Excuse me,' he said. 'Is this about me? And I can take the bus.'

'Don't look a gift horse in the mouth,' Raff said shortly. 'If Mardie's happy to take you… Sunday's the soccer bus. You don't know what you're missing.'

'I can't stay here another night.'

'There are bed and breakfasts in town,' Raff said. 'Though most of your reunion lot are staying for the weekend. You'll be lucky to find anywhere.'

'Don't be dumb,' Mardie said. 'You can stay and help me get rid of the rest of the tree.'

'Organise the vet first,' Raff said.

'I told you, Raff, I trust him.'

'Yeah, you'd trust anyone,' Raff said and handed Blake his radio. 'Satellite,' he said. 'I can get signal anywhere. For emergency cop stuff. Or, in this instance, emergency dog stuff and protecting-Mardie duty. If Mardie's putting you up for the weekend and you're imposing a dog on her, it's the least I can do. Mardie might trust you. I want proof. Ring your mate and see if you can get this operation organised. Now.'

CHAPTER FIVE

COLIN could do it. 'For no one else,' he said, 'but for you, yes. I leave gaps for emergencies. Cataracts don't usually rate but in this case I'll slot her in. I'll need her here three days beforehand for tests and eye-drops. If everything's good then I'll schedule surgery for Thursday. She'll need careful monitoring afterwards but you should be able to do that yourself.'

He'd worry about aftercare later, Blake decided, relaying the part about surgery and tests but not the aftercare. He knew it'd be complicated, and things were complicated enough.

Raff left, promising to send a tow truck for the car. Promising to let Henrietta know about Bessie.

He left grinning.

He'd backed Blake into a corner. Instant dog surgery.

He'd backed him into staying another night with Mardie.

Staying with Mardie was the biggie. He felt... It felt...

As if he was out of control, and Blake Maddock was a man who didn't like being out of control.

The trip into town made him feel even worse. Mardie had offered to buy clothes for him, but that seemed weird. What he hadn't thought through was how weird it would be to walk into Morrisy Drapers and have every person in the shop recognise him.

They already knew what had happened. Of course. Banksia Bay was like that. He was wearing his battered dinner-suit trousers and Raff's spare jacket with cop insignia. Inconspicuous R Us.

He felt like a flashing neon.

'Oh, you poor boy.' Mrs Connor, who ran Morrisy Drapers, was a gusher. 'We hear your car's a write-off. But Raff says it's a rental car so that's lucky. But you were even luckier you weren't killed. And all for a stray dog. My old dad says never swerve for animals. They're not worth losing your life over.'

'Bessie's lucky he did,' Mardie said roundly. 'How could he not try to miss her? And he didn't risk his life. He was driving a tank.'

'A Mercedes isn't a tank,' Mrs Connor said, shocked, as she handed clothes over the counter. 'A tank's what you drive.'

'My truck's not a tank. It's practically luxury,' Mardie retorted. 'Isn't that right, Blake?'

Blake glanced outside to where they'd parked the truck. It was an ancient Dodge, built, he suspected, to withstand the Huns.

Definitely tankish. Though most tanks didn't have rust.

'Um...pure driving pleasure,' he managed and he was rewarded by Mardie's smile. It was a truly gorgeous smile.

It always had been a gorgeous smile. He hadn't realised how much he'd missed it.

'It's definitely classy,' Mardie declared, eyeing Blake's pile of sensible clothes with approval. 'Like these. Jeans and T-shirt, pure class. What about boots, Mrs Connor?'

'Work boots or nothing,' Mrs Connor said.

'Excellent,' Mardie decreed. 'We have twenty-four hours before we head to Sydney and I intend to put him to work. You want to change here, Blake, before we head to the nursing home?'

'We're going to the nursing home?' He wanted to go straight back to Mardie's. Actually, he wanted to go straight back to Sydney but it wasn't happening. It was Mardie who was giving orders. He was on her turf, doing what she wanted.

The nursing home it was. Her mother, Etta.

'I need to see Mum,' she said. 'I need to organise a few days away, and we also need to see Charlie, to explain that you found his dog and you're going to save her. Mum will love to see you.'

'It might be better if you go alone,' he said diffidently, and she looked at him as if he was crazy.

'Better for who?'

'For your mum.' Etta had been so good to him. He should have kept in touch. Why make her remember what a stupid kid he'd been? 'I've been no part of your mother's life for a long time now,' he said, almost to himself. 'It's best to leave things as they are.'

She looked at him for a long, considering minute. Looked as if she was about to say something and then thought better of it. Reconsidered.

'Fine,' she said at last. 'Stay in the truck. Stay nice and uninvolved, like you have for fifteen years.'

Mardie checked in at the nurses' station first. She worked here three days a week. She needed to organise time away.

Liz, the nurse administrator, greeted her with unconcealed curiosity. She was practically vibrating with her need to know. 'So the rumours are true. Blake Maddock's back.'

'I hate this town.'

Liz giggled. 'We're fast. I hear he's hot. You guys were such an item…'

'Fifteen years ago,' she retorted. 'Will you cut it out?'

'You're not the least bit interested?'

'No!' That was a lie, but the guy was sitting out in the truck being uninvolved. It'd pay her to be uninvolved as well. Very uninvolved.

'Yet you're going to Sydney with him.'

'I really hate this town. Yes, but I'm not staying anywhere

near him. I'll stay at Irena's. He's organising the operation on Bessie's eyes, that's all.'

Liz's smile faded. 'Bessie. Raff told Henrietta you found Charlie's dog. You really think the operation will work?'

'Blake's an eye surgeon. He says it will.'

'It'll be the best gift you could give to Charlie. Did you bring her with you?'

'I wasn't sure if I should.' She hesitated. 'Would it be kind?'

Liz considered and then grimaced. 'Maybe not. He gave her to the pound, and it nearly killed him. If the operation doesn't work… For him to say goodbye again…'

'You think I shouldn't tell him we're trying?'

'He already knows she's been found. This is Banksia Bay, after all. Tell him what's happening, but it might stress him too much to see her. Operations sometimes fail, regardless of what your Blake says.'

'He's not my Blake!'

'Regardless of what *anyone's* Blake says,' Liz retorted, her smile returning. 'Get her better and bring her in then. Meanwhile, don't worry about your mum; you know we'll look after her. And even though we love your craft classes, we all know how long it's been since you've had a break. Take a real holiday. Have some fun. If anyone deserves it, you do.'

And then she paused. Someone was strolling past her window.

Her eyes widened. 'Oh, my…'

Mardie followed her gaze.

Blake.

Jeans. T-shirt. Work boots.

Body to die for.

'Oh, my,' Liz repeated, mocking fanning herself. 'If I'd known he was going to turn out like this I would have snagged him in grade school. Only, of course, you got in first.'

'I did not!'

'You did, too.'

'Yeah, well, if I did it's all in the past,' Mardie said hotly. 'He wiped Banksia Bay from the map when he left.'

'Yeah, but a woman could forgive a lot of a guy who looks like this.'

'Not this woman,' Mardie retorted. 'I have a long memory.'

'Boyfriend-girlfriend fights from fifteen years ago?' Liz chuckled. 'With that package in front of me I'd get over it fast. People change.' But then Liz held up her hands as if in surrender. 'Okay, sweetie, if anger's needed to keep you safe, then stick to your anger. But don't let it mess with fun. Say goodbye to your mum and then go to Sydney—and you keep an open mind.'

Then she glanced again at Blake and fanned herself some more.

'A very open mind,' she repeated. 'A girl'd be a fool not to.'

Mardie's mother was playing solitaire. She glanced up as Blake opened the door and her eyes grew huge. She recognised him in an instant.

'Blake Maddock. Oh, my boy…' Somehow she pushed herself stiffly to wobbly feet and held out her arms.

It took a moment to respond. He stood in the doorway, looking at the woman who'd been practically a mother to him. She'd been far more a mother than his own.

She'd been burdened with arthritis for all the time he remembered, but he'd never seen anything but cheer. She'd lived surrounded by chaos, the radio always on, her kitchen table always laden with her next creation. Her cooking trials had been truly scary. He and Mardie would appear for lunch, Mardie's dad would be looking terrified and Etta would be saying firmly, 'You can eat it or not, there's always eggs on toast, but give it three bites first.'

Chocolate pudding with chilli. Duck à l'orange, only: 'We can't afford duck so I shaped a duck with mince instead. Do you think it looks like a duck?'

Crazy stuff.

Wonderful. Fun.

He'd loved it.

He'd loved Etta. And Bill.

And Mardie.

He should have stayed in touch. He'd been a stupid kid, he'd long accepted his reasons for leaving, but still he felt bad.

Regardless, here was Etta, wobbly on her feet, standing with open arms. Tears were slipping down her cheeks and she was smiling and smiling. 'Blake,' she said again and he walked forward and hugged her.

Mardie walked in the door and her mother was hugging Blake. No, her mother was being hugged. She'd been lifted right off her feet, and she was crying, laughing and railing against him, all at once. 'Put me down, you silly boy. You'll do yourself a damage. Ooh, put me down.'

Blake and her mother…

She stopped short in the doorway and she felt as if the earth had shifted.

Her mother adored Blake. From the time he'd first been allowed past the boundaries of his great-aunt's property, Etta had welcomed him with open arms.

'You ring your aunt and ask if you can stay for lunch,' she'd say, and Blake would look at the crazy experiment on the kitchen table and jump right in.

'Yes, please. That looks…really yummy, Mrs Rainey.'

Now… It was as if she was welcoming home a long-lost son. But Mardie had watched her mother wait for news from Blake, as she herself had waited. She wasn't feeling so welcoming.

If she let herself be as welcoming as her mum… Dangerous territory. She felt as if she were teetering on the edge of some kind of abyss and she needed to step back fast.

She needed to be happy. Bouncy. Impersonal. She pinned

on a smile and forced her voice to brightness. 'Isn't it great he's here? Did he tell you he crashed his car last night?'

'No!' Her mother sank back into her armchair, looking at Blake with such an expression…

How could Blake walk away and come back and still be loved? Mardie thought.

He hadn't expected it. He didn't want it. She could read Blake's face and she could see regret and dismay.

He didn't show it in his voice. Instead, he told Etta about the crash, making it funny. He told her about Bessie, making the story sad but hopeful. By the end Etta was demanding they bring her in.

'We can't,' Blake said and told her about Charlie.

'Oh, of course. So you'll fix her and bring her back to visit him all better?' Etta's eyes were shining.

'We'll fix her and then Mardie can bring her in.'

'You come in,' Etta said, suddenly stern. 'I bet Charlie remembers you. He'd love that.'

'My life's in Sydney. And overseas.'

'People only go overseas for visits, and Sydney's a two-hours drive away. If you can go overseas you can come here.'

'Bessie will be Mardie's dog,' he said, gently but inexorably. 'I don't have a place here any more.'

'There's a place in Mardie's spare room, any time you want,' Etta said with asperity. 'That's fine with you, Mardie, isn't it?'

Maybe not. But Mardie didn't say so. She gave her mother a reassuring smile, she said of course Blake could always stay, and she knew that Blake intended nothing of the kind.

He'd walked away. He was home by accident, but it wasn't his home.

He couldn't wait to get away from Banksia Bay. Nothing had changed.

* * *

They left Etta, and walked silently to Charlie's room.

Blake was feeling disoriented, as if shadows of the past were reaching out to touch him. Mardie was silent by his side.

She'd been angry with him—she was angry with him. He'd forgiven himself, he thought. He'd figured why his teenage self had acted as he had. Justifying it to Mardie seemed harder.

Justifying it wasn't necessary. He didn't need to tell Mardie…

Maybe he did. Maybe that was the whole reason he'd come home.

Not home. Banksia Bay.

Regardless, now wasn't the time.

Charlie Hunter had once been a big man. No longer. He'd shrivelled with age, and his last stroke had left him paralysed down his left side. He lay motionless, surrounded by memorabilia. Trophies and ribbons. Photographs of dogs. A gorgeous enamelled plate showing Charlie—with dogs. Leads, collars, framed Australian Championship certificates. A lifetime of dogs.

'My Bessie,' he whispered as Blake told him what had happened, what they hoped to do. He could barely get the words out.

'If you don't want…'

But where there'd been apathy and defeat, suddenly there was fire. 'Are you dreaming?' he demanded. 'If I'd had the money, her eyes would have been fixed two years back.' Charlie's words were distorted with paralysis, but he said them loud and strong so they couldn't be mistaken. 'But these last two years, since my first stroke…well, a blind dog wasn't what I needed. It wasn't fair on her, though. She spent her life at my feet, never whining, just there for me. But when she was a pup…the joy of her…'

He paused and fought for breath. Fought for strength to go on. 'It would have been kinder to put her down,' he whispered. I just…couldn't. So finally I sent her to the pound instead. What a cop-out. If you could cure her…'

'No promises,' Blake told him. 'But we'll try.'

'You're a good lad,' Charlie whispered. 'I remember my Hilda talking about you, saying she had no idea how such a miserable old grouch as your aunt deserved a kid with such a good heart. And happy. You were happy as a kid.'

Happy. There was that word again. It caught Blake like a faltering of the heart.

Happy was for childhood. Not for now. Now was for keeping promises.

Without going back to Africa?

It wasn't the time to think of that now. Get out of Banksia Bay and then think it through.

'Bessie'll be back here soon,' he told Charlie. He was sounding too brusque but there was nothing he could do about it. 'Mardie will bring her in as soon as she gets back from Sydney.'

'That's a promise,' Mardie said and he caught another edge of anger. Fair enough. He was promising Mardie's time. He was promising Mardie would see things through.

She would, though. She was the dependable one.

She was the one who stayed at home while he moved on.

Mardie had things to do for the rest of the day. It seemed leaving the farm for over a week involved organisation and she didn't want his help.

'Find a book and give your head a rest,' she told him. 'Lie by the fire and think how lucky you were last night.'

She headed out to see someone called Lorraine, who'd look after the place while she was absent.

He was left with the dogs.

He *was* tired.

He picked up a copy of the *Farmers Weekly* and tried to read.

The dogs lay in front of the fire and tried to settle.

They were all doleful.

Enough. Yes, his head was aching; yes, there were bruises which hurt; the aches from dengue were still with him but lying around made him think of them more.

He had proper clothes now. He could do proper stuff.

He put on his boots and both dogs were alert and at the door in an instant. Together they had it figured; Bounce maintained contact with Bessie as if he realised how much she needed him.

Smartest dogs in the world. Bonding with each other while he watched.

It'd be a joy to give Bessie back her sight, he thought, a joy for Bounce as well as for Bessie.

It'd also be a joy for Mardie. A gift he could leave her with.

The thought was a good one. He headed outside, a dog at each heel, feeling better.

He intended to go for a walk over the farm. He did for a bit. Things looked the same. There was a new shed out the back, seriously big, that had him intrigued, but it was locked.

Was this a guy's shed, he wondered, locked after Hugh died? The thought of Hugh left him feeling strangely empty. Sad that he hadn't kept in touch. That he hadn't been here for her. That there was a part of Mardie he didn't know?

He didn't want to walk any further, he decided. He didn't want to end up at his aunt's crazy mansion which, according to the guys he'd talked to at the reunion, was now boarded up, after the spa operators who'd bought it had gone bankrupt.

Despite the hour, he was tired. Dengue had left him with residual fatigue that was taking months to recede.

But to sleep seemed impossible. Instead, he headed for the massive pile of ruined tree.

They'd cleared a path down the driveway, but heaped on either side were mounds of splintered timber yet to be moved.

How long since he'd played with a chainsaw?

This was a man's job. Fatigue receded in the face of a plan. He grinned and practically felt his chest expand. 'We can do this,' he told the dogs and he felt their quiver of excitement, responding to his enthusiasm. Man with chainsaw.

'So chainsaw, tractor, trailer. I hope she's left the keys. Let's see how much we can get done before she gets back.' It was a small enough token of his thanks, he thought.

Chainsaw. Excellent.

He found the chainsaw in the unlocked shed by the house. On close inspection it seemed a truly excellent power tool. He'd been frankly jealous of Mardie wielding it this morning. 'Nothing to this,' he told the dogs, who both gave rather dubious wags of their tails.

'Okay, you guys can stand back,' he told them. 'You count the logs as I stack 'em for firewood.'

Bounce looked at Bessie and whined. She moved in close and both dogs headed off to the bottom paddock.

Getting some exercise, or abandoning the *Titanic*?

'Dumb dogs,' Blake said. He heaved his chainsaw across his shoulder and headed for the tree.

She hadn't meant to be away for so long, but Lorraine was aching to show her a vase she'd created and to demonstrate a technique she felt could take her in another direction.

Lorraine was a potter. Mardie was an enameller. Together they'd just invested everything they owned and a bit more into a state-of-the-art kiln—a kiln to die for. They could both do so much now they had it.

Lorraine's enthusiasm was infectious, and at home was… Blake. It was worth talking enamelling, talking potting, so she didn't have to go home to Blake. Blake, whose mere presence had her discombobulated.

But she couldn't stay away for ever. Finally she said goodbye to Lorraine. She headed home.

She turned into the drive and slowed.

They'd cleared the driveway this morning, but there'd been a mass of timber left on either side.

Blake must have worked like a man possessed. The pile of logs beside the woodshed was four times what it had been this morning.

And the remains of the trunk… She was close enough to see. Close enough to…

No!

For what was left of the trunk, still standing tall this morning, had now crashed to the side of the driveway.

And worse…

Behind the massive trunk she could see…Blake on the tractor, slumped over the wheel. Unconscious?

She was out of the truck before she knew it, screaming without words. Or maybe there were words, just the one.

No. No. No.

Running.

'Blake…'

She was clambering across fallen branches, stumbling, ripping branches aside. Feeling cold, empty terror. 'Blake!'

She thought…she thought…

'Blake!'

He lifted his head from the steering wheel. Pushed himself up. Spoke.

'Mardie?'

Alive…

Her heart kick-started again. Just.

Blake. Alive.

He sounded dazed. Half asleep? 'I got it down,' he said. 'The whole thing.'

There was even a tinge of pride in his voice.

He got it down.

Terror receded, leaving a void where things didn't make sense. She was struggling to take it in.

She was in the middle of a crush of timber.

Blake was alive.

'I thought you were dead,' she said stupidly, not believing what she was seeing. 'I thought…'

'I went to sleep,' he said apologetically. 'I cleared the branches that fell, and then I thought I could get the rest of the trunk down. It took more than I thought.'

Asleep.

'I thought…' she said and then stopped.

He'd seen her face now. She knew she wouldn't have a vestige of colour left.

'I had dengue fever,' he said apologetically. 'It takes it out of me. I really wanted to get it down. Then I brought the tractor and trailer close to clear the mess but I thought…' He gave her an apologetic smile. 'The sun felt great. I thought I'd take a quick nana nap.'

A nana nap. He'd been taking a nana nap while she thought he'd been brained by a tree.

She gazed around her, taking great gulps of air. Maybe she'd forgotten to breathe.

He'd cleared half a tree.

Then he'd had a nana nap.

'I might have been slightly ambitious,' he conceded. 'I had this idea of clearing the lot before you got home, and it's a great chainsaw.'

'It…it is,' she agreed. Paused. Took a few more breaths. Then had to say it out loud. The thing that was hammering in her head. 'You could have been killed. I thought you had been.'

She started to shake.

She couldn't stop.

She couldn't…

And suddenly he was stomping across the pile of crushed wood and leaf litter until he reached her.

He held her shoulders and he held her tight.

'Mardie, it's okay. Nothing's hurt. I knew what I was doing.

The tractor and I were on the other side of the driveway when it came down. It only looks bad because I brought the trailer in close to start clearing up.'

She couldn't hear. His words were a buzz.

The events of the past, surging back. Moments that had transformed her life.

Her father, folding as he walked in from out in the paddocks. Dead in an instant.

Hugh. One stupid moment, stupid kids in a too-fast car, and his life was over.

And again… The instant she'd seen the fallen tree and Blake slumped over the wheel.

Reaction took over, leaving her no choice in how she responded. She tried to shove back from his hold and she yelled, as she'd never yelled in her life.

'You stupid, stupid moron. You used a chainsaw when no one was home. Don't you realise the first rule, *the first rule*, is to have someone with you when you use big power tools? You just chopped. Macho, macho stupidity. You've given me half a winter's full of chopped wood and what good would that have done if you were dead?'

'You'd have been warm,' he said cautiously. Still holding her.

She wasn't responding to humour. She couldn't. 'It's cold in the cemetery.' She was still yelling.

'Yes, but it's me who'd have been there, not you. But it didn't happen. Mardie, it didn't happen. It was never going to happen. Believe it or not, I knew what I was doing. I'm sorry I didn't finish clearing it. I wanted to. I'll pay to…'

'*Pay?* I don't care about payment.' She was still hysterical. 'I'm not in this for money. I'm not the one who walked away to make money.'

And suddenly it was about more than the tractor. More than this moment. Much more. She was out of control and she was saying it like it was. Years of hurt, welled up and finally released.

'I walked away to make money?' he said cautiously.

'You never looked back,' she said, still out of control. 'Not once. You and your aunt and your stupid, rich family who couldn't even look after a kid, and your stupid money making. If you'd been killed now it'd be no less than you deserve. Of all the stupid things…' She caught her breath on an angry sob. 'I could have lost you again. And now you've brought down the rest of the tree and we'll have to clear this and all you can think of is paying.'

She'd almost lost him again.

She heard her words echo, reverberate. They'd come straight from her heart.

They both knew it.

She was shaking as if she'd stepped out of an ice box. Her teeth were chattering so hard she could hardly get the words out.

There were tears tracking down her face. The night Hugh died… The day her father collapsed…

The day Blake left.

The dogs moved close to the base of the mess of tree and whined, worried by her yelling. *She* was worried by her yelling. She didn't get out of control.

She was out of control now.

She was still in the middle of the leaf litter. Blake was still holding her.

The branch under them sagged.

And suddenly Blake was in charge. He took her by the waist and lifted her free, tugging her down to solid ground. He set her in front of him but didn't release her.

He held her round the waist as she trembled. Holding her tight. Not saying a thing. She tugged away, but not very hard. Not enough to succeed.

'What…what do you think you're doing?' she managed.

'Waiting until you get over the shock. Trying to reassure you that it's okay.'

'It isn't.'

'Tell me what happened, Mardie,' he said softly. 'The car crash. Was that how your husband died?'

'I… Yes.' There was nothing else to say.

'Here?'

She didn't want to tell him. She never talked about it.

She told him.

'We were driving home from Lorraine's, up the road. A Christmas barbecue.' Her voice was still shaking. Her world was still shaking. 'Six o'clock on a warm Sunday night. A carload of kids came round a blind bend on the wrong side of the road and that was…that. I ended up with a fractured pelvis. But Hugh…my gentle, loving Hugh who'd give me the world, who gave me the world, was gone in an instant. And the dogs. All our dogs. They were in the back.' Another sob. The urge to yell was back, but she couldn't raise the energy. She felt desperately tired. 'And you…you play with chainsaws as if it doesn't matter one bit. You just…risk…'

It was too much. She choked on a sob, her knees gave way from under her and he drew her into him.

For a fraction of a moment she resisted, holding herself rigid. He could feel her anger. He could feel her fear.

But he could feel her shaking and it was the shaking that killed her resistance. She crumpled and he gathered her against him and held and held, as if there was nothing more important than to hold her against his heart and let the world go on without them.

Nothing was more important.

The dogs stood beside them, silent sentinels. Neither moved, as if both realised this moment couldn't be interrupted by a wet nose; it couldn't be interrupted for the world.

He simply held her.

Had she had someone to hold her when Hugh died? he wondered. Two years ago.

Had Mardie buried her husband and come home to an empty house?

The dogs…

He thought of them now. Minor in the scheme of things, minor compared to a husband, but still…

Every time he'd been to this place there'd been a dog pack. 'You need generations of dogs, training each other.' He remembered Mardie's father saying it. 'You lose a dog, it's a heartbreak. You lose all your dogs…' He'd shrugged. 'I don't know how a man could go on without them.'

Bounce was Mardie's only dog, and he was only about twelve months old. That meant it must have been twelve months before she could even bear to get another dog.

He'd have been in Africa. He scanned Australian news on the internet, but never in such detail as names of car crash victims. If he'd known…

The shaking was starting to subside. She tugged away a little and he released her to arm's length, no further.

'Tell me about Hugh,' he said softly, and she managed a ghost of a smile. Realising he was trying to haul her from shock. Trying to respond.

'He was from Whale Cove. Practically a foreigner.'

He smiled, straight into her eyes. It was a smile he couldn't remember using before. Or maybe he had. It was a smile just for Mardie.

'You met him at Whale Cove?'

'That's where I did my art course. He was a paramedic, an ambulance driver. He was gentle, kind, loving…all I ever wanted in a husband. We were friends for ages, were engaged for two years, married for three.'

'He lived with you here?'

'There was Mum.' She was recovering a little but her voice was still shaky. 'We couldn't leave her, and Hugh was happy to transfer to Banksia Bay. Then, when she finally decided to move to the nursing home, Hugh said he loved this place as much as I did. It would have been a great place for our children…' She broke off. Closed her eyes.

'Enough,' she said. 'We have stuff to organise.' She stared at the driveway. 'This to clear, for a start.'

'No.'

'No?'

'I think,' he said apologetically, 'that neither of us should use the chainsaw for a while.'

'You want me to come home to this mess?'

'I've fixed that.'

'It doesn't look fixed.' Indignation was returning. Indignation versus shaking? He almost smiled. Indignation any day.

'That's what I was talking of when I mentioned paying,' he said. Whether or not the shaking had stopped, he was still holding her and she was still allowing herself to be held. 'I rang Raff. He gave me the name of a guy who chops wood for a living. Tony Kennedy'll be here at eight on Monday to clear the mess.'

'But you're already covering the cost of Bessie's operation,' she managed, sounding stunned.

'You know I can afford it.'

There was a moment's silence at that, drawn out, tense, loaded with something he didn't recognise.

'I don't…take charity,' she said at last.

'I don't believe I'm offering charity. I'm responsible.'

'You're not responsible for Bessie.'

'I'm not paying for Bessie for you. I'm paying for Bessie for me. But, regardless, I owe you.'

'Why do you owe me?' she asked in a strange, tight voice.

That, at least, was easy.

'You and your parents made my childhood bearable,' he

said simply and firmly. 'I owe you a debt I can never repay. I should have been here for you two years ago. That I wasn't…'

He let the sentence hang.

Silence. More silence. He wasn't sure what to say next. How to begin to make things better?

There was no way.

Mardie was watching him. Her face was calm. Assessing.

Very calm. And suddenly he thought…it was like the eye of the storm.

He could almost feel the other side.

'Do you think I needed you?' she asked, almost diffident.

'I assume…'

'Assume nothing.'

'Sorry?'

'Do you think I spent the last fifteen years pining for you?' she asked, still in that strangely calm voice.

'I know that's not true.'

'You do,' she said cordially. 'Yes, at sixteen you were my boyfriend. I wept for weeks when you left. But weeks, Blake Maddock, not years. And then you know what? I got angry. And then I got over it.'

'Good for you.'

'Don't patronise me,' she snapped, and the storm moved closer. With the potential to build. 'Of all the…'

'I didn't mean to patronise.'

'Yes, you did,' she said. 'You do. You're sorry you weren't here for me two years ago. As if somehow, magically, you could have made it better.'

'I never meant that.'

'Good,' she said. 'I'm glad you didn't mean it. Because it wouldn't have made one whit of difference. Do you know how surrounded I was?'

'No, I…'

'I was loved,' she said. 'I *am* loved. Don't you dare think of me as poor, lonely Mardie, facing the big bad world because heroic Blake Maddock wasn't here to take care of her. This place is my home. I'm loved. When people are in trouble here, we help. I had a broken pelvis and my husband was dead but I had my community to surround me. My freezer still contains so many home-cooked meals that I could live on tuna bakes for years. My sheep were cared for, my fences fixed, my house painted. My garden was replanted so that I've had veggies and flowers ever since. I have a friend who came and stayed for two months—Irena. I was cosseted to bits. And here you are saying you're so sorry you weren't here for me, as if it would have made a blind bit of difference.'

She took a deep breath, the calm façade cracking wide open. 'And you know what? It's great that you've organised this tree to be cleared, and I accept with pleasure. But I don't depend on it. If I'm in trouble, I have a town full of people who'll help. If I rang up a few friends and said I can't cope with a fallen tree I'd have a working bee here in minutes. You know…'

Another breath.

'Last winter I got the flu. I didn't let anyone know because I hate fuss, only then I ran out of wood. The place was cold, and I was too tired to get out of bed and chop some. Then Liz arrived. She's the administrator of Mum's nursing home. I'd rung and said I had a cold and couldn't come in, but Liz thought she'd check anyway. She practically called out the army. An hour later the house was a furnace, there was food, fuss, heat packs, every home remedy known to man. I was so coddled I had no choice but to get better.'

'That's…great.' It was a pathetic comment but what else was he to say?

But she hadn't stopped. She'd barely paused for breath.

'And you know what?' she snapped. 'It all happened without you. And now… I love it that you're helping with Bessie. I'm grateful you've organised the tree. But don't you dare think I'll fall in a heap without you. I spent a few weeks in tears as a lovesick teenager and then I moved on. Now, if you don't mind, I have things to do to get my life in order before I leave. And, believe it or not, I can do all those things by myself.'

CHAPTER SIX

THE power came on.

Mardie headed down the paddocks to do one last run around the sheep before dinner.

He suspected she didn't need to. He suspected she didn't want to be in the house with him.

The tow-truck driver arrived and shook his head over the Mercedes. Blake had already rung the hire-car firm; insurance would sort it from here. He retrieved his laptop and briefcase, watched the wrecked Mercedes be towed away, and then went back to the house and set up his laptop in the attic.

It might be wise to lie low for a while, he thought. Leave Mardie to settle down.

He was due to speak at a fund-raising dinner on Monday. It was his first foray into public speaking since his illness.

He read his prepared speech and frowned. Surely he could do better.

He thought of Mardie and he thought…passion. The world could do with more passion. So could his speech.

He squared his shoulders and pulled up a blank document. Try again? He couldn't quite match Mardie in the passion stakes but he'd give it his best shot.

* * *

The sheep were as safe as she could make them. They had feed and water, the hens were happy, the place was secure.

Back in the house, she looked—tentatively—for Blake and was relieved when she realised he was upstairs. She could hear him on his computer. Working.

Good. He was out of her hair.

He wouldn't have the internet up there. She should have offered him access to her computer.

She might make the offer, she decided, but not until after dinner. She hauled a tuna bake from the freezer. A nice easy fix. Plus it would underscore what she'd yelled at Blake. Excellent.

She picked a lettuce and a couple of tomatoes from the veggie patch. Practically gourmet. Blake Maddock would be used to five-star restaurants. How would he react to defrosted tuna bake?

She really had yelled at him.

Maybe she'd overdone it, just a little.

She should call him down. Have a drink before dinner.

Maybe not. She was, she discovered, still seething.

She should check the weather forecast. She hit the internet and confirmed there was not a storm in sight. Excellent.

She went to close the computer and then…

A thought.

She just happened to type *Blake Maddock, Ophthalmologist.*

She'd never searched for him. For all these years, she'd never enquired. She hadn't wanted to know.

She wanted to know now.

Blake Maddock, Ophthalmologist. Enter.

She entered Africa.

She stared at the screen as if it had grown two heads.

For Blake was right in front of her, but not the Blake she knew. This was the face of some major foundation, Eyes For Africa. Blake as a professional.

Blake working in desperate conditions. Blake, surrounded by queues of kids. Blake operating. Blake standing in the background as a nurse removed bandages from a little boy's eyes. A clip of a documentary describing Blake's work.

On the front of the website there was a blurb for a black-tie dinner this coming Monday in Sydney. *Head of Eyes For Africa, Dr Blake Maddock, will be addressing...*

She'd known nothing.

This town knew everything there was to know about everyone. Surely…

No. Banksia Bay knew everything there was to know about its own, and Blake no longer belonged. His aunt had scorned the town, and when Blake left that was the end.

She read on, her head spinning as she flicked through screens of information.

He'd headed to Africa almost as soon as he'd finished his specialist training. His work there was groundbreaking.

He'd said he worked overseas. But…Africa? *All this time...*

'I guess you know all about me now, too,' Blake said from behind her and she froze. She didn't turn. To say she was dumbfounded would be an understatement.

'Africa,' she whispered.

'It's where I keep my harem. Stocked by my white slave traders.'

She managed a smile but it didn't reach her eyes. This was too astounding for humour.

'You work for charity,' she said, finally spinning to face him.

'Yes.'

'You're not rich.' It was…an accusation?

'I am,' he said diffidently. 'My family made a fortune in tin mining—I still own shares. My great-aunt had extravagant taste in home renovation but for the rest she was miserly. My parents died before they could spend their inheritance. I can afford to pay for a dog and a bit of tree clearing.'

'That's not what I meant,' she said, thoroughly confused. 'I thought you studied medicine to make money.'

'Why would I do that, when I already have far more than I need?'

'I don't know,' she said miserably. 'How would I know? Blake, why?'

The question was almost a wail.

'Does there have to be a why?'

'Yes,' she managed. 'There does. I thought I knew all about you. Then I thought I didn't know anything. Now…' She shook her head. 'Sorry. It has nothing to do with me, what you do. I don't have the right to ask.'

She closed her eyes. She counted to ten because she didn't know what else to do.

Opened them. Thought of a long-ago question.

Asked it.

'Who's Robbie?'

The question hung.

Robbie.

'Why—' he found it hard to speak '—why do you ask?'

There was a long silence. The question hung.

And then she told him, 'There was someone called Robbie.' It was a statement, not a question, and it left him winded.

There was someone called Robbie.

Not according to his parents. Or his great-aunt. No one.

There was someone called Robbie.

'Yes,' he said. 'How did you know?'

'It's the only thing I've been able to think of,' she said, sounding unsure. 'When you left…I thought I knew everything about you, my best of friends. But that last night… You were so excited about leaving, about studying medicine. But you'd never said what you wanted to do until then. It was like there was some part of you you'd kept hidden. I couldn't figure it out, but after you'd gone and I was trying to make sense of it…Robbie was the one thing I couldn't ask about. He was the one thing I didn't know.'

He tried to think of something to say. He couldn't.

'How…?' he managed again at last.

'When we camped out in the tent on the back lawn,' she said diffidently. Unsure. 'As kids. You cried out in your sleep. Nightmares. Stuff like "Robbie I can't… Robbie, don't…" I got Mum and she brought us both inside and cuddled you back to sleep. Then, another time when you were sleeping over, I heard you crying, "Robbie, Robbie", and I knew Mum went up to you. I asked you once, "Who's Robbie?" and you said no one. I asked Mum, and she said kids who lived alone often have friends in their head. She said if you didn't want to tell us then I wasn't to ask. But I thought… Whenever you had the dream…you sounded terrified. I heard Mum tell Dad once, "That boy has demons". For some reason when you left I thought…I thought the demons might be Robbie.'

Robbie.

For all these years he'd done what his father told him.

'Don't tell people about your brother. It makes your mother ill.'

And then, when he couldn't stop crying, he'd been packed off to Australia, to an aunt who barely said Blake's name, much less his twin's.

Robbie...

The sound of Mardie saying it was a release all by itself.

The demons might be Robbie. It was suddenly unbearable that she thought that a moment longer.

'Robbie was my brother,' he said, and the words sounded strange, as if they were coming from some dark recess that had been locked for years. They were.

'Your brother?'

'My twin.'

She was on the swivelling computer chair. The chair wasn't

moving. She was totally motionless, her eyes not leaving his. Trying to read him.

'He died?'

'Before I came here.'

'How old?' It was scarcely a whisper.

'When I was…when we were seven. We were living in a beachside mansion in California. My mother's birthday. A party, so many people. It was hot, we couldn't sleep so we decide to go for a swim.'

'Night?' she whispered.

'Midnight. It was a stupid time to go for a swim, but there was so much noise…'

'Your parents let you go for a swim at midnight?'

'They didn't know. We were supposed to be sleeping, but it was hot. And the nanny…' He shrugged. 'I don't know where she was. Anyway, we crept down the back stairs. The noise… I remember one woman was laughing like a hyena. Robbie copied her. He was giggling.' He paused. 'And then he dived into the pool, into the shallow end. His neck…'

He broke off. How to go further? He couldn't. Even to Mardie.

'Enough,' he said. 'It's ancient history. My parents never talked of him, didn't want me to talk of him. My aunt didn't speak of him either. That was fine by me. It hurt, so I didn't. But it seemed… When I got into medicine…'

'You did that for Robbie?'

'I did it for me,' he said savagely. 'To stop the hurting. I thought…if I could help kids…' He raked his hair. 'Sorry. I'm not going to burden you. Robbie's my shadow, and he's always with me. Working in Africa helps, makes up in some way for Robbie having a life. I know now that trying to forget him made it worse. It seemed a betrayal but I had no choice. I was a kid and decisions were made for me that were bad. I've moved on. Or maybe I'm still moving on.' He hesitated, regrouped, somehow hauled his thoughts back to now. 'Can I smell fish?'

'Tuna,' she said, looking stunned.

'Tuna bake?'

'Y...yes.'

'Excellent,' he said. 'My favourite.'

'Liar.'

'I don't lie,' he said and then he smiled. 'Okay, maybe I'm stretching the truth a little when it comes to tuna bake. How long is it that it's been frozen?'

They ate dinner in near silence. Tuna bake. What's not to like? Mardie thought, though maybe it was time she did a bit of freezer-clearing. Time had made the noodles crystallise, and even though they'd reheated looking fine, they tasted... well, cardboard might be a good way to describe them.

Even Bounce and Bessie seemed a bit dubious.

Thinking about clearing freezers was okay. Thinking about dogs was okay, too. If she thought about a seven-year-old called Robbie, her head might explode.

'You know, I reckon the dogs need to get used to these tuna bakes,' Blake said as he helped her clear. 'How many more do you have?'

She smiled, but absently, circling the subject of Robbie. Knowing she should go back to him. Thinking she couldn't.

She was feeling as if this man beside her was suddenly who she'd thought he was—a part of her. It was a dumb feeling, but there it was.

Blake... How she'd felt... How she was feeling... It was muddling into emotional turmoil.

She wanted to put her arms around him and hug him.

She wanted...

No.

'The internet said you're in Australia fund-raising,' she managed at last, cautiously.

'Yes.'

'When are you going back?'

'I'm not sure.'

'You're not…?'

'Is there anything else that needs doing? If not, I should get some work done before bed.'

She was finding it hard to speak. She'd known this man so well, once upon a time. How strange that Robbie, Africa, these two great unknowns about him, were making her feel that, at some deep level, he was still…hers?

He'd always kept his inner thoughts to himself, but she'd guessed stuff. She'd even guessed that someone called Robbie was important, but she'd accepted her mother's explanation.

And when he'd left? Hormones had messed with how she'd reacted, she thought. She'd been too busy seeing her needs, her loss, that she hadn't begun to probe what he needed.

Okay. She attempted an inner regroup. She did know this man. Pressing him for answers would never work. She needed to come at him sideways.

He'd asked her if anything needed doing. She met his gaze then, and for the first time she really looked at him. Really saw him. She was looking for the boy behind the man, the Blake she knew. She'd been disconcerted by his size, his deep, sexy voice, his dinner suit, his crashed Mercedes.

Now she just saw Blake.

And she saw the strain. Something lost. Something more than a long-ago grief.

He'd tell her in time, she thought. If she could regain a little of what was lost.

Okay, moving sideways… She looked down at her feet to where two dogs were slumped side by side. Alternate universe. Dogs.

'Bessie smells,' she said.

Blake looked startled. 'Sorry?'

'She's been lost for a week. Before that she was in the

pound. Tomorrow we're taking her to Sydney. My truck's a four-seater so she can sit in the back with Bounce, but it's going to be a pretty pongy journey.' She managed a grin. 'If it was Bounce I'd wait until a warm day and put the hose on him. Bessie, though, needs tenderness. That means warm water in the tub in the wash-house, towels and my hairdryer. You just asked if you could help. Here's your answer. I'm not sure how Bessie feels about personal hygiene but if she's anything like Bounce, heaven help us both. You hold and I'll wash. Let's go.'

The wash-house was a lean-to bathroom-cum-laundry at the back of the house. The bath was huge.

Mardie filled the bath, and Blake tried lifting Bessie in.

A lot of farmers never washed their dogs. They either made them stay outside or in some cases they were so used to smell-of-dog in their living room they didn't notice. Fleas were dealt with by dumping the dogs in the sheep dip.

Maybe that was all Bessie had known. It was certainly all she wanted to know. When Blake lowered her into the water she responded as if this was death-by-drowning.

'It's okay, it's okay, it's okay,' Mardie said, frantically soothing, but frantic and soothing didn't go together. Bessie opted simply for frantic. She lurched upwards, managed to get her paws onto Blake's shoulders and heaved.

Blake was suddenly prone, backwards on the floor, with sodden collie all over him.

Mardie tried hard to keep a straight face.

She failed.

'Oh, dear...' she said, convulsing.

'You try,' Blake said, staggering upright. Glowering. Dripping.

Mardie grinned. Excellent. Blake might be a highly trained eye surgeon, but this was her territory. She could wrangle a ram if she must. A gentle collie...

Nothing to it.

There was, actually, something to it. She ended up as soaked as Blake, but pride was at stake, and Bessie stayed put.

'Shampoo,' she said bracingly to Blake. 'You soap her.'

'I'm wet enough.'

'Wet doesn't stop the smell. Pull yourself together. A bit of willpower.'

'Right,' he said and staggered back to the fray. Laughing.

Things had changed. Something about wetness and laughter and a shared challenge. The tension of the past few hours peeled away.

Blake and Mardie and a dog. Two dogs, for Bounce was cautiously out of range, anxiously supervising as his new love was turned into a sudsy mop.

Things were suddenly okay again. Or more okay than they'd been.

They were back to…

Friends?

By now Bessie had figured they weren't trying to drown her. She'd figured suds meant no harm. So she settled. Except for the shaking.

She wasn't shaking from terror. She was shaking as an intelligent dog got rid of water. No matter how hard Mardie held, she sent suds flying all the way to Bounce at the door.

Blake was doing his best to massage the suds. Every time she shook he got coated.

Every time she shook Mardie subsided into giggles.

'It's fine for you; you have a change of clothes,' Blake retorted, massaging on with grim determination.

'I have a clothes dryer,' she said. 'It's not great for dinner suits but it's fine for work gear. You can go back into the bathrobe while I clean your clothes.'

'Domesticity at its finest,' he said dryly—and then chuckled.

She loved his chuckle. She loved… She loved…

Bessie chose that moment to shake again, which was just as well. Because suddenly Mardie wasn't sure what she loved. Or where the boundaries were.

The boundaries were deeply scary.

They dried Bessie as best they could in the sodden bathroom, then took her into the living room. They towelled her in front of the fire and Mardie fetched her hairdryer.

There was a moment's alarm from Bessie; hairdryers were also something she'd never met. But the warmth of the fire, Mardie's reassurances, Bounce's presence—Bounce knew what a hairdryer was and was intent on sharing the hot air himself—was enough to make her relax.

Mardie and Blake were wet but the room was warm, and what was a little damp between friends? They sat by the fire, with Bessie draped over their knees, Mardie drying and combing, and Blake cutting tangles.

They worked in silence, but the silence wasn't tense. It was as if they were getting to know each other all over again.

Coming together. Merging.

They swapped ends and worked on.

Bessie relaxed completely. She was warm and cared for and the safest she'd been since she'd been put in the pound. She practically purred.

'I hate the thought of taking her to Sydney,' Mardie murmured. She was drying her tail, a lovely feathery black-and-white wag machine. 'Uprooting her again seems cruel. I just want to let her settle.'

'She can't get what she needs in Banksia Bay.'

'Same as you?'

'This was never my home,' he said simply.

'So where's home now?'

No answer. She didn't press.

They finished drying. Bounce gave Bessie an encouraging lick, as if to say, *Job done, wake up, your place is with me now.*

Bessie heaved herself to her feet. Bounce waited until she was steady, then headed for the sofa.

The living room sofa was forbidden to dogs except on the rare occasions when Mardie needed comfort, or when a dog could sidle in unnoticed and curl up before Mardie saw…

Bounce edged to the sofa, Bessie by his side. He glanced nervously at Mardie—and then he was up, Bessie with him.

The two dogs were practically grinning as they dived between cushions. They wriggled under, and hid. Not very well.

Mardie should yell.

It was all she could do not to laugh.

'I take it by Bounce's demeanour that the sofa's forbidden,' Blake said, smiling with her.

'It certainly is. I'm sure Bessie knows it, too.'

She must. Both dogs had nosed under cushions, determined on invisible.

Mardie giggled. She felt…

As if she was standing on the edge of something momentous. Huge.

How she felt about Blake.

'We're both wet,' Blake said, sounding regretful. 'I need to get these clothes into the dryer.'

That'd mean going to bed. They both knew it.

Neither of them moved.

The fire was crackling, sending out gentle heat. They weren't cold. Wet or not, staying right here seemed an excellent option.

She was like the dogs, Mardie thought. She was blocking out the world, revelling in comfort, hoping she wouldn't be noticed.

She was taking comfort from Blake's presence, hoping it wouldn't end.

'Tell me what Hugh was like,' Blake said softly and it had ended.

Or…not, she thought, confused. It should hurt, telling this man about the man who'd been her husband, but suddenly it didn't.

It seemed right.

'Hugh was my friend,' she said softly. 'He was ten years older than me. He was big and quiet and solid. He laughed when I did. I loved him.'

'Would I have liked him?'

'He wasn't like you.'

'That's not what I asked.'

'No.' She considered.

Hugh. A man supremely contented with his lot.

He was the youngest of seven brothers. He'd been brought up tough.

He didn't have an ounce of toughness in him.

He had the best smile.

'Yes, you would have liked him,' she said and she knew it was true. And then she thought…if Hugh could see her now, curled up by the fire, covered in dog hair, smelling of dog shampoo, talking to her friend from childhood…

'He would have liked you, too,' she said. 'He'd be glad, for me, that you're here. I used to tell him about you. He liked it. He didn't have all that happy a childhood himself and he was hungry for happy.' She hesitated. 'He would have been really interested in what you do. "Tell me," he'd say. So that's what I'm saying. Tell me about Africa.'

He hesitated. Unsure. 'I suspect you've read all you need to know,' he said diffidently.

She thought about that, of the countless documentaries she'd seen, of the wildlife, of the humanitarian crises, the sheer scope of human tragedy.

Yes, she'd read about it. But to be there…

'What does it smell like?'

'Smell…'

'Smell. First impression.'

'Dry and sparse and wind-blown,' he said, frowning. 'I used to stand on the cliffs here and smell the salt. In Africa I smell the sand. The wind… The locals call it *arifi*, meaning thirst, a wind that scorches with many tongues. It rips the heart out of a man. It doesn't give a smell, it takes it away. It leaves you sucked dry. And the people…the kids…the damage…' His voice died. 'There's no point thinking about it.'

'You're doing something about it.'

'Not any more.'

'You're not going back?' she asked, astounded all over again.

'Not,' he said harshly, feeling the frustration build. 'I can't. I might be forced to go back to something like you're doing.'

'Um…' she said cautiously, stunned by his sudden anger. 'Are we back where we started? Mardie Rainey, born in Banksia Bay, headstone for the local cemetery ordered at the same time as my birth certificate?'

'I didn't mean…'

'I'm sure you did mean.' She might be shocked into sympathy but she wasn't letting him get away with this. 'You're summing up my life as worthless?'

'I didn't…'

'Yes, you did,' she said, but she wasn't angry. She was simply sad. 'How do you think that could make me feel?' she said, meeting his gaze square on. 'Seeing my husband die and watching my mother fade. Living here by myself, in my childhood home, and then opening the door to my ex-best friend who tells me what a waste my life has been. You're right, I haven't saved a single African child. We all can't.' Deep breath. 'Why do you keep trying to hurt me?'

'I'm not.'

'I believe you are,' she said steadily. 'I thought…I thought I didn't know you any more but it seems I do. I remember when Mum used to try and hug you, you'd turn yourself rigid, pushing her away. It took her ages to be able to hug. I think you're doing exactly the same thing now. Why?'

'Are you trying to hug?'

'I'm not trying to hug,' she said simply. 'I'm asking what's wrong. One friend to another. You've told me about Robbie. Now tell me about the next big thing. The thing that's put the strain behind your eyes. The thing that's making you want to lash out.'

'I…'

'Just say it, Blake,' she said softly. She put out her hand and touched his—and she waited.

For however long it took.

The fire crackled in the grate. Bounce started snoring. Bessie wuffled and nudged cushions so the two dogs were closer.

She waited.

And finally he closed his eyes and said it.

'I can't go back to Africa,' he said, and he tugged his hand from hers, as if he no longer had the right to the contact. 'It seems I'm taking my frustration out in all sorts of inappropriate ways. It seems hurting you is one of them.'

'Why not?' she said at last.

'I've had dengue fever three times. They tell me three strikes and I'm out. I've had my three strikes.'

'You can never go back?'

'Nowhere there's dengue'

'Or you die?'

'I know the odds. I believe them.'

'So what will you do?' She managed a half smile. 'Unless you're serious about running sheep?'

He shrugged, not returning her smile. 'Who knows? Feel sorry for myself. Go to school reunions. Hurt my friends.'

'There's three strikes,' she said. 'You've done them all. Now you're out again. So the next thing is…'

'I have no idea.'

She thought for a little. Thought about touching his hand again. Thought better of it.

The fire did some more crackling. Bounce did some more snoring. Bessie just seemed to…listen.

There was no hurry for what had to be said.

'Burying yourself in anger would be the fourth thing,' she said at last. 'When Hugh died, I yelled at trees, at rocks, at my friends, at the kids who crashed into us, at anything. It didn't help.'

'Neither did anyone telling you to get over it.'

She smiled at that, wryly. Agreed with a vengeance. 'All that did was make me want to slug someone even worse. Like I wanted to slug you when you criticised me.'

'So now it's you who's angry?'

'Maybe I am,' she said. 'Why wouldn't I be angry? You're judging my life as worth less than yours. You're saying if you can't go to Africa you're nothing. But you can't see what I get and what I give.' She met his eyes, challenging. 'I like my life, and I do good things. I make people happy. I make me happy and I don't need to defend myself to you or to anyone.'

'I know you don't.'

'Then stop beating yourself up about something you can't change. You do the best you can. No one should expect you to do more than that, including the ghost of Robbie, including yourself.' She hesitated. She wanted, quite badly, to take his face in her hands and kiss him. As comfort?

If it was only that, she thought, she'd do it in a heartbeat, but there was that between them…

'Go to bed, Blake,' she said instead. 'Relax. Think of all the excellent things you can do in the world. There's lots, I'm sure there are, in places where there isn't dengue. Figure it out.'

She pushed herself to her feet.

He rose with her. Came too fast.

She was too close.

His hands came out and steadied her.

And the need grew.

A need from fifteen years ago?

That night in the kitchen…a kiss interrupted. It was between them now, a tangible thing. Fifteen years and a kiss unfinished.

Fifteen years of need.

A need that was as great now as it had been then. More so.

A need that seemed a compulsion, an aching void that had to be filled.

Two halves of a whole, meant to be together.

The fire hissed at their feet, sap catching, making tiny explosions, fizzing to nothing.

A need so great…

'Do you want me to kiss you?' Blake asked, and the world held its breath. The world including Mardie.

'Properly?' she asked.

'With your mother not watching.' He was smiling, a smile that turned her heart.

'I've spent fifteen years figuring out how that kiss should have ended,' she whispered, trying to keep her voice steady. 'I wouldn't mind knowing…'

She wouldn't mind knowing what?

He had no chance to find out because he was no longer listening.

A prophecy carved in a ruined tree. *M.R. xx B.M.* Carved when she was ten years old.

Finally happening.

And fifteen years were gone, just like that. They were a man and a woman grown, but at some basic level they were still who they'd been, friends who'd spent half a lifetime together, who'd grown from boy and girl to man and woman, and who'd moved to this, the next and natural level.

It felt natural. It felt inevitable and it felt right.

Her lips melted against his. Her body curved into his, and she moulded into his hold, tilting her chin, taking as well as giving.

He tasted her kiss.

He tasted her mouth.

He tasted her body and he loved her, as he always had, as he always would.

She smelled of dog shampoo. In truth, maybe she tasted of dog shampoo.

She was wonderfully, miraculously perfect.

She was Mardie. His friend. His home.

She was too great a temptation to resist. She was too sweet to think of pulling away.

She was too much his Mardie to do anything but kiss her.

For this moment he surrendered absolutely. He let himself hold her as he wanted to hold her, to be in this place, by her fire with her dogs nearby, to have her in his arms and to feel her loving him.

Mardie of the loving heart…

He'd fallen in love in the school playground all those years ago and he'd never fallen out. He loved her with every shred of his being.

Forget the dog shampoo. She tasted of nectar, ambrosia, more. She tasted…

Of Mardie

Mardie. His Mardie.

He hadn't known he was off centre but he knew it now. Mardie. His centre.

She was on tiptoe, deepening the kiss, demanding as well as giving. Surrendering but besieging. Wanting as much as he wanted.

She wasn't close enough. He was tugging her against him,

her breasts were curved into his chest and she felt as if she was melting into him.

He wanted her closer.

Part of him.

Her hands were in the small of his back, clinging. He was still damp. The fabric between them felt as if it was nothing. There was only a vestige of decency.

The vestige of sense…

He couldn't think that.

But…he had to think it or he'd sweep her up and take her to bed, this instant. It was all he wanted to do. For it felt so right, so meant. After fifteen years, finding his home.

Her hands were slipping to his hips. Tugging him closer still.

Sense.

All he wanted was to take her. All he wanted was to give.

Sense!

Somehow he found the strength to pull away, to break the contact, and heaven knew it broke more than that.

He did it. He held her by her shoulders, at arm's length, gazing down into her dazed and bewildered eyes.

'Blake…' she whispered and her hands covered his. 'You don't want…'

'I did want,' he managed in a voice he scarcely recognised. 'I do want. But I should never… I can't have.'

'Why can't you have?' There was suddenly a trace of indignation in her voice, the feisty Mardie surfacing under the lover. 'It's not as if I'm unavailable,' she said. 'Is it the thought of Hugh?'

She was suddenly glaring at him. Self-sacrifice, it seemed, wasn't in her vocabulary. He wanted to smile.

He didn't.

He'd wanted to kiss her and he had, but now…he felt as if he was at the edge of a deep, sweet vortex, being tugged inexorably into its unknown centre.

Away from everything he'd worked for.

'I'm not giving up,' he said, hardly aware he was speaking. 'I can't. To escape back to Banksia Bay… I no longer need to escape.'

She tugged back so his hands could no longer hold her shoulders. She looked confused. But then his gaze locked on hers and there was anger behind the confusion. Anger growing.

It seemed she was waiting for an explanation. It was as if he'd kissed her under false pretences.

Suddenly she was practically tapping her foot.

So explain. If he could.

'Mardie, my parents sent me here after Robbie died because it made my mother ill to look at me,' he said, trying hard to make sense of what he hardly understood himself. 'My great-aunt took me in. This place had been her refuge for years and it became mine. My parents were…dysfunctional, to say the least. My great-aunt was little better, but once I met you, and your parents… This was safe as I'd never been safe. It was home as nowhere had ever been home. Even after ten years here I still felt overwhelming thankfulness that I'd found you. I could have stayed. But I had things to do, my Mardie-girl. I still have things to do, and I can't do them here.'

'Don't call me Mardie-girl.'

Mardie-girl.

He hadn't meant to.

Her father had called her Mardie-girl, and in private, as they'd grown older, it had started slipping out. Mardie. His Mardie-girl. No. She was right. Its use now was inappropriate.

And it had rekindled anger.

'I'm only Mardie-girl to people I love,' she snapped—but then she flinched and she closed her eyes. 'Though that's dumb,' she whispered. 'Because I do love you. You know I always have. Though not…not like this. Not like tonight. What

I had with Hugh was real and wonderful, and the thought of you didn't get in the way for a moment. But we've always… meshed. Only I never saw myself as a safe harbour. An escape. I saw myself as an equal. A friend. Fun, happy, silly, sad—you and me, mates.'

'We were. I hope we are.'

'Then why are you spouting nonsense about escape?'

'I don't know that, either.' He raked his hair and raked it again for good measure.

'Then I guess that makes two of us not understanding,' she said, more mildly now. 'I thought you wanted to kiss me. It seems I was wrong. Okay. You've stopped kissing me, so let's leave it at that. You need to strip off and put those clothes in the dryer. You can't do that with me around. I might get the wrong idea. No. That's nuts. It's all nuts. I'm confused, you're confused. So let's focus on what we know for sure. We have two happy dogs, one of whom needs medical help. Tomorrow we're going to Sydney. So tonight I'll leave you to your convolutions and your plans for the future, which doesn't include kissing, and I'll go to bed. Goodnight, Blake. Happy plans.'

And that was that. She clicked her fingers for the dogs and she headed out of the room and down the passage to her bedroom.

She walked inside, the dogs following her—side by side, Bounce glancing back at him with what looked like reproach—and she slammed the door behind them.

She left and he stood by the fire until it died to embers.

Once again he'd hurt her. He should walk away now.

She was driving him to Sydney. She'd have to put up with him the whole way. She'd see him during the week as they cared for Bessie. Then…

Did he really want to walk away?

No. But what was between them…

It wasn't friendship. It was so much more.

That she'd guessed about Robbie left him winded. That she and her parents had respected his privacy, had guessed he was hurting, had let him be…that left him awed.

They'd loved him.

Love. It was a strange concept.

In medical school he'd met a girl as committed to aid organisations as he was, passionate about saving the world. They'd studied together, worked together, become lovers almost as a side issue. Become engaged.

Six months later she'd met an African aid worker and fell hopelessly, helplessly in love. 'I'm sorry, Blake, it's the way he makes me feel. I really love him.'

They were still friends. But…love?

The way a heart twisted?

The way he makes me feel...

The way he felt tonight, when he'd held Mardie.

No. Stop, right now. This is Banksia Bay.

Banksia Bay was never an option.

He didn't think Mardie's life was worthless, of course he didn't, but…could he imagine himself working here? Taking care of coughs and colds? Playing with sheep on the side?

Being with Mardie-girl.

Just Mardie, he corrected himself. Not his Mardie-girl. What had once been granted to him with love, had now been withdrawn.

He couldn't pursue it.

Because of Robbie? He'd forgiven himself years ago for Robbie's death. One seven-year-old could never be held responsible for another's moment of risk-taking, regardless of what his mother had thought and said. But still that sense remained, to do something worthwhile, to somehow compensate for the waste that was his brother.

He should be able to walk away from it. See a shrink. Move on.

But it had been with him for too long, was too great a part of his life. He had no hope of ever moving on.

And that meant walking away from Mardie? He knew it did.

The door swung open, almost of its own accord. He glanced across and it was Bessie. She'd managed to push past the loosely hinged doors. For some reason she was nosing her way across to him, following his scent. Finding him. Putting a paw up, as if asking for a pat.

As if offering comfort.

He'd always wanted a dog. He'd always been so jealous of Mardie and her dog pack.

If he stayed here…

No.

'You don't belong with me,' he told Bessie, more roughly than he intended. 'Bounce is just down the hall. So's Mardie.' And before he could think further about it he led her out of the room, down the passage.

Mardie's door was open. Bessie must have pushed it wide again.

He could just call…

He didn't.

He propelled Bessie silently into the room and closed the door after her.

And went up to bed without saying a word.

She heard him return Bessie

She heard him close the door.

She lay awake and thought.

About two little boys swimming at midnight. About Blake's parents. Packing him off to Australia. Loading him with guilt. The legacy they'd given their son…

Anger was no use.

That was the problem. Nothing was any use. What had

been done was done, and Blake was living with the consequences for ever.

It was doing her head in. Anger, sorrow—there was even a touch of humiliation tossed in there as well. She had it all.

She thought and thought, until sleep finally gave her release.

She dreamed of twins.

She dreamed of Blake.

She woke to the sounds of chopping.

Blake. Doing his manly thing again. Sigh.

At least it wasn't the chainsaw, she thought grimly, throwing back the covers and heading for the window.

The first weak rays of dawn were barely filtering over the horizon. Even Clarabelle wasn't at the gate yet.

Blake was chopping.

He was back in his jeans, but he was bare to the waist. He was lifting the logs he'd sectioned yesterday, putting them on the block beside the woodshed and attacking. The axe came down over and over, with strong, rhythmic strokes.

The wood was green. It took three, four strokes to strike each log through.

He didn't falter. One after another. Stacking the pieces and moving to the next. No pause.

She should call out that she had enough wood to last her for the winter. She wouldn't be burning it green anyway, and next winter it'd split with half the effort.

But she knew without being told that he needed the physical effort.

Demons. Her mother had surely been right.

Not demons. Robbie.

He didn't look up. Every ounce of energy went into smashing the axe into the wood.

She wanted to walk out and take the axe from him. She wanted to hold him, just hold him, the child inside the man.

She couldn't. Whatever harm his parents had caused had gone so deep she couldn't touch. His harm would just hurt her.

Fifteen years ago he'd walked away and she'd lived without him ever since. She could do it again.

With demons like his, there didn't seem a choice.

CHAPTER SEVEN

THE journey to Sydney was made mostly in silence. The truck had an excellent radio, for which Mardie was profoundly thankful. She tuned it to a discussion on nineteeth-century circuses. She tried to be fascinated.

For Blake had gone somewhere she couldn't reach. He was silent and grim, hardly speaking at all.

'Hitchhikers are supposed to entertain the truckies who pick 'em up,' she said at one stage.

'Would you like me to talk?'

'I'd like you to tell me about Africa,' she suggested. 'More than it has a truly appalling wind.'

'You don't want to know.'

'Fine, then,' she said, grittily cheerful, and went back to her circuses.

When they reached the city she needed facts. 'Where's your apartment? Where can I drop you off?'

'It's on the harbour,' he said shortly. 'But you don't want to be caught in city traffic, and we need to take Bessie to the vet clinic. We'll go to your place, dump your stuff and take her straight there.'

'Yes, sir.'

'I didn't mean…'

'To be brusque? Of course you did,' she retorted. 'But I like brusque. Least said, soonest parted. Let's go.'

* * *

Least said, soonest parted... He wouldn't have put it like that, but then he wouldn't have put it at all. He was simply doing what he needed to do.

If he told her what he thought of the pompous historian spouting circus stuff, if he joined in, he might relax, and if he relaxed then they'd end up where they were last night and he'd end up hurting her. Hurting her more.

Shut up and move on. Do what needs to be done. Leave.

To go where?

He'd figure it. Eventually.

'This is Irena's,' Mardie said, pulling up outside a tiny weatherboard cottage overlooking the cliffs of Coogee. 'She has cats. Bounce is used to them. Let's see how Bessie reacts.'

He climbed from the truck as Mardie negotiated the garden path and rang the bell.

Irena's house. A friend of Mardie's. If he'd thought about it, he'd probably have guessed Irena to be a Banksia Bay local who'd moved on.

Country girl made good?

That was the kind of thinking that was getting him into trouble.

It might also be a little bit wrong.

For the woman who opened the door was…magnificent. Fiftyish. Six feet tall. Black leggings, high black boots, a purple sweater that reached mid-thigh and a tiny skirt. Strings of amethyst and topaz. Oversized earrings.

A Cleopatra haircut.

She greeted Mardie with a cry of delight, enveloped her in a hug and Mardie practically disappeared.

The hug over, Mardie was held at arm's length and inspected.

'Look at you.' It was a cry of dismay. 'If you haven't brought anything decent to wear…'

'I have brought clothes but I don't want to get dog on them.

Irena, meet Blake Maddock, the guy I was telling you about. Blake, Irena's my agent.'

Her agent?

'How lovely,' Irena purred, and smiled a totally bewitching smile that said she knew exactly what personable men were made for and she knew exactly what to do with them.

Mardie giggled. 'You're scaring him,' she said.

'Not him. He's a big boy.' She grinned at Blake and turned back to Mardie. 'Did you bring them?'

'Yes, but…'

'I want to see them. Now.'

'We need to get Bessie to the vet's.'

'Colin's not expecting us for another hour.' Blake was fascinated.

'An hour's great,' Irena said with satisfaction. 'And you said it's right by here. Excellent. Bring them in.'

'The dogs…?' Blake ventured.

'Bring them in, too,' Irena said with ill-concealed impatience. And then she gave a rueful smile. 'Sorry. Your dog's why we're getting the plates early and I should be grateful. I am. So I'll take Bounce inside, and the memory box—is it in the tray? Mardie, you bring Bessie and introduce her to the girls. Blake, you bring the plates.'

'The plates?'

'It's the box on the back seat,' Mardie said, taking pity on him. 'The memory box is the big one in the tray. The plates are smaller. But please be careful. If you drop them I'll have to shoot myself.'

'You and me both,' Irena said. 'And Cathy.' She glanced at her watch. 'I hope you don't mind but she's been desperate to see. She should be here… Oh, great, here she is now. Come on in.'

And then they were in Irena's huge kitchen, which seemed to take up half the house. There were two Siamese cats, circling the dogs with care. Bessie seemed cautious but not overwhelmed. She stuck close to Bounce and seemed fine.

It was Cathy who looked overwhelmed.

Cathy was a middle-aged woman, mousy, wearing a twinset and a tweed skirt, looking scared. She'd received one of Irena's hugs as well, which could, Blake thought, overwhelm anyone.

'Blake doesn't know what's happening,' Mardie announced, looking bemused. 'Sorry, Blake, I should have told you.'

'You didn't tell him about the memory wall?' Irena demanded. 'It's only the most beautiful thing you've ever done.'

'Blake and I have been too busy for chat.' She was opening what Irena was calling the memory box. Tugging out assorted…things.

A battered seaman's cap. A container of model trains. A box of fishing flies. Photographs. Letters. Boots. An ancient pair of scuffed slippers.

A rat-trap?

What the…?

'Cathy's husband was drowned when a pilot boat tipped at the harbour mouth twelve months ago,' Irena told him and Cathy flinched as all eyes turned to her. She reached out and took the rat-trap, and held it as if it were a shield.

'I'm so sorry,' Blake said, because there was nothing else to say. 'What happened?'

'It was an awful night,' Mardie explained, as Cathy hugged her rat-trap like a talisman. 'An oil tanker was threatening to flounder on the rocks past the heads. They sent tugs and pilot boats out. They saved the tanker, but one of the tugs and one of the pilot boats were lost. Six men and two women were drowned. Cathy's Bernard was one of them.'

'Bernie was a crewman on the pilot boat,' Cathy whispered. 'He went out…and he didn't come back. It's been awful. But now…we're going to have a memorial wall, at the harbour where their boat used to be tied. Mardie's making plates. Nine plates for each one lost. Seventy-two plates in all. Mardie asked me to choose things that were important to Bernard, things the kids and I want him remembered for. Funny things. Silly things. Like the rat-trap.'

'Why the rat-trap?' Blake was totally caught in the emotion in the woman's face. The grief. The pride.

'We were friends at school,' she whispered, and pride prevailed. 'One day I told him there'd been a rat in my bedroom and the very next day Bernie brought me a rat-trap. We were both fourteen and I went to bed that night with my trap under the pillow. No way was I using it for rats.' She hesitated. 'Isn't it dumb, to have kept a rat-trap. Did…did you use it, Mardie?'

'I surely did,' Mardie said. 'Can you unpack the plates?' she asked him. 'Each panel's on individual padding.'

He lifted the plates free, one after another.

Nine enamelled plates.

He couldn't believe their beauty.

Each one was about twelve inches square.

The first was a portrait, glass, fired onto a copper base. A seaman.

It wasn't exactly a portrait, he thought. It was slightly abstract, an impression, but it was wonderful. The strength of the man came through—a battered sailor, his face creased against the weather, the sea behind him.

Cathy choked back a sob. She let the rat-trap fall to take it. She just…looked.

He lifted the next plate free. It was like a collage. A thing of exquisite beauty, but built from images of ordinariness. Here was the rat-trap. A football. Fishing flies.

A second plate was trains—a whole panel of trains Bernard had obviously loved. The real trains, the models, were spilling from the memory box, but their image on the plate was just as real. Bernard's face was on this plate again, as a faded background, a man watching with pride as his trains circled a track of crimson glass.

The colours were extraordinary. The depth of field, the layering of objects upon objects. Each one was saying this man had such depth…

Nine plates, representing a man's life.

Cathy was crying openly now, moving from plate to plate, touching them with awe, with reverence and with love.

'You guys need to get Bessie to the vet,' Irena said, a bit more roughly than she needed to, sniffing a bit, but Blake wasn't ready to surface yet.

He turned to Mardie—who was watching Cathy. Smiling a smile he'd never seen before.

'You did all these?' he managed.

'I've done seven sets,' she said. 'Sixty-three plates. I have Robyn Partling's story left to do. Another month and I'll be finished.'

'You should see where they're going,' Cathy whispered. 'They've made a wall at the harbour. Every person will see my Bernard. They'll see he loved trains. They'll see that letter he wrote to the paper about the turtles. They'll even see my rat-trap.'

She choked, and Irena put a bracing arm around her.

'Whisky,' she decreed. She turned to Mardie and Blake and sent them a silent message. Go. 'I'll dry Cathy up, but I suspect she'll like to be alone with these. So off you go and save your dog. Cathy and I will phone the harbour master. He's the one organising this. The other six have blown him away. This one will be no different.'

It took ten minutes to drive to the vet's. It took almost that long for Blake to catch his breath.

He remembered the plates over the fire-stove and knew now where they'd come from.

He'd seen the plate in Charlie's nursing-home bedroom and knew it was Mardie's as well.

Brilliant.

They pulled into the car park. Mardie went to get out of the truck but he caught her hand. There were things he needed to get clear.

'I always knew you could draw,' he said slowly. 'I never dreamed…'

'That I'd do enamelling? There you go, then. And I never dreamed you could be a doctor in Africa.'

'You never said…'

'You knew I loved drawing.'

'Yes, but not like this,' he said explosively. 'These plates… I'm not an expert but…with your skill you could make a fortune.'

'I do make money,' she said diffidently. 'But not with these. My friend Liz is a nurse I work with. Liz's brother, Mike, was one of the men who died that night. I came to the memorial service. I saw Liz clutching an old fire engine Mike loved when he was a kid and I thought…I could do something.'

'But you've been enamelling before?'

'For years. I run the sheep to keep the grass down. I work three days a week at the nursing home because I love it. The rest of the time I do this.'

'Raff said you were broke.' He was trying to get things clear. 'You couldn't afford to help Bessie. I assumed…'

'There's a lot of that about,' she said. 'Assumptions. You always saw my art as my hobby, not the passion it is. While I had no idea you were striving for medicine and why.'

'So you've been enamelling since school?'

'It's what I do,' she said gently. 'I don't make millions but I do make a living. The problem is the cost. There's always something. For these plates I needed a bigger kiln, a good one. You need an even temperature over the entire surface or the glass cracks. Lorraine's a local potter. She and I went halves but it still cost a fortune.'

She turned to Bessie and Bounce on the back seat, moving on with decision. The two dogs were sitting bolt upright in their harnesses, both looking nervous. 'Okay, Bessie, you're next. Do you think we should take Bounce in?'

'I think we should,' Blake said, because a man had to say something and that was all he could think of.

Concentrate on the dogs.

Anything else was too difficult.

Colin was waiting for them, a big, confident vet who oozed professional competence. In the veterinary clinic, with its strange smells, Bessie reacted with even more nervousness. Colin, however, was amenable to Bounce staying beside her. He could see that together they were settled.

A bond was growing between these two dogs that was starting to seem a tangible force.

Like me and Blake, Mardie thought, and scared herself by thinking it. Glanced at Blake and thought…for once, don't know what I'm thinking.

Luckily, both Colin and Blake were intent on Bessie's eyes. Colin was cautiously optimistic and once he examined her he became even more so.

'It's looking good. We'll need blood tests, scans, the works, and I need to start her on anti-inflammatory eye-drops. Can you leave her with me today, pick her up about five?'

'Can Bounce stay with her?' Mardie asked, and Bounce looked up with sudden distrust. 'I know, smarty-boots,' she told him. 'You understand. But today you're the sacrificial lamb. If I could hop into the cage with Bessie to comfort her I'd do it in a heartbeat, but I suspect I wouldn't fit.'

Everyone laughed

They left the dogs and walked out into the sunshine.

Laughter died. Silence.

No dogs. Nothing.

Sunshine, beach, nothing.

Without speaking, they headed towards the beach. Found themselves on the sand. Just walking.

Just walking.

There was something about Bessie and Bounce…

Togetherness. He hadn't felt like that even when he was engaged to be married.

Maybe that was why he was no longer engaged. He didn't know how to do it.

So what was the problem with that? He'd always been an outsider.

Except when he was with Mardie.

He was with Mardie now.

The difference was, Bessie and Bounce connected. They belonged together, in a way he and Mardie never could. Mardie had been his escape from reality. Banksia Bay. Mardie. They were part of his past, the part that had been used to 'get over Robbie'. Neither were part of his real world.

He could, Blake realised, walk away right now. He could pay Colin's bill. Take a cab into the city to his apartment. Leave Mardie with Irena, with her life that didn't include him.

No. There was a growing part of him that was denying his outsider tag, that was hungry to come in.

'I'd like to talk over what Colin says this afternoon,' he said diffidently. 'I have this fund-raising dinner tonight…'

Don't go any further. A voice was raging in his head. Don't! To be an outsider was the life he was accustomed to, the life he'd chosen.

A life where the pain of losing Robbie could never be repeated.

'Talking to lots of strangers,' Mardie said sympathetically. 'Ugh.'

'Would you like to come?'

He couldn't believe he'd said it.

He'd said it.

'It won't be all that interesting,' he said. 'Corporate money, politicians, people wanting to look charitable while contributing as little as possible. But…' He hesitated. 'You did ask about Africa.'

'So I did,' she said. 'You'll be talking about Africa?'

'Yes.'

'Then I'll come.'

Just like that. She glanced at him and their gazes locked—and then they looked away. A step taken…

Regretted?

'I'd like to be there, but inconspicuously,' she said hastily. 'Can you arrange for me to slip in at the back?' She ventured an uncertain smile. 'But, as for coming… It's only fair. You've seen my plates; I wouldn't mind seeing your work.'

'Great. I'll pick you up at…'

'No,' she said, suddenly definite. 'I have a truck. You have a mangled Mercedes. And, besides, I'm not coming as your partner. I'm coming as me. If you could organise a ticket I'll collect it at the door.'

'And you'll wear beige and blend into the wallpaper.'

'Something like that.'

'You're not an inconspicuous woman.'

'I am, too,' she said. 'Five feet two in socks. Favourite footwear, gumboots. Favourite perfume, wet dog.'

'In this crowd that'd be conspicuous,' he said and grinned. Feeling suddenly absurdly happy. Not knowing why but suddenly not caring. 'Would you like to have lunch now?' he asked before he knew he was going to.

But she was shaking her head. Looking a little…scared? 'Irena wants me to talk to the harbour master,' she told him. 'And I imagine you have things to do as well. If we need to discuss Bessie… Ring me in the morning if you don't get a chance to speak to me tonight.'

'Of course I'll get a chance.'

'It doesn't matter if you don't,' she said softly. 'We live in different worlds, Blake. They've collided today and it's lovely. But, apart from this one collision…we both need to get on with our lives.'

He did have things to do.

There was the small matter of insurance and a crumpled Mercedes. That took most of the afternoon.

He checked the cost of hiring another. Crashing hire cars did appalling things to premiums.

He gave up, found a car yard and bought one.

He headed back to his apartment. Ran through his presentation.

Passion.

He rewrote and rewrote. Thinking of Mardie.

Tell me about Africa…

What was she doing now?

She was due to pick the dogs up at five. She had a cellphone. He'd ring…

She answered on the second ring, and he thought: how easy was that? He could have rung her any time over the past fifteen years.

Why hadn't he?

He knew why.

'We're on the beach.' She was yelling into the wind. 'The dogs have spent all day in a cage. They have energy to spare.'

He wanted to be with them. Badly.

Not happening.

'How's Bessie coping?'

'She's running with Bounce, still just touching, but they're going as fast as each other. They look fabulous. I think they're in love.'

Love.

Don't go there.

Mardie would look fabulous too, he thought. Her hair would be flying every which way. She'd have bare feet, he guessed. Jeans, T-shirt, freckles, curls…

He was standing in his great-aunt's faded apartment.

He wanted to be on the beach with Mardie.

'What did Colin say?' he managed.

'He'll have the results of the blood tests back on Wednesday. There's a couple of other things, but he's really optimistic.' She hesitated. 'He's willing to do both eyes at once, if you'd like.'

'It's not up to me.'

'It is, because you're paying.'

'So pros and cons?' His emotions were all over the place. He seized on the professional with gratitude.

'It's cheapest to do one eye only,' she said. 'Dogs manage well with one eye.'

'They manage better with two. But if there's infection…'

'He said that. He said if he operates on two at once there's a tiny chance of cross infection; that something going wrong with one can mess with the other. But he says the chances are minuscule; he's almost willing to guarantee success in a dog as young and healthy as Bess. And here's the thing. He also says it wouldn't put her under additional stress. She'd have it done, it'd be over, I could take her home and she never need come here again.'

Excellent. But why did that make him feel…wrong?

'So that's that, then,' he said, more harshly than he intended. 'Two eyes. Decision made. Are you still coming tonight?'

'I… Yes, if it's okay.'

'I've organised a ticket.'

'I'll come just as the dinner ends,' she said. 'I'd like to hear you speak but you don't need to pay for my dinner.'

'Speeches are through dinner. There's no choice.'

'Then can I have a nice quiet seat down the back where I can sneak away?'

'It's all arranged,' he said. 'I'll see you then.'

'Then I'd best go and get the sand out from between my toes,' she said. 'Oo-er. And I just bet Irena will make me put on a frock.'

The dinner was formal. Very formal.

If Mardie had known how much the tickets cost, she'd never have agreed to come, Blake thought, as he greeted what seemed like the complete *Who's Who* of Australia. Politicians. Celebrities. There were a few professionals who were here to learn, like the doctors from North Coast Rescue—a division of the Australian Flying Doctor service—but they were in the minority. Most people were here to see and be seen.

Maybe he should have warned her. Even sneaking into a dark corner, she wouldn't want to look like a country mouse.

She *was* a country mouse.

She was also one of the most brilliant artists he'd ever met.

Mardie.

He felt like shouting it to the rooftops. Hey. The Mardie I knew… The Mardie I disparaged… She's kind and loyal and clever—and she's talented beyond belief.

She was nothing to do with him.

One of the most eminent politicians in the land was waiting to be introduced. He needed to get a grip. Work the room. Remember why he was here.

'I'm very happy to meet you, ma'am. We certainly appreciate what you've done for us. Let me tell you about Sharik. She's five years old—here's her photograph. Through your funding, she can now see. If I could just tell you about the rest of the children in her village…'

* * *

She hadn't thought this through.

They had fund-raising dinners at Banksia Bay. Yes, she knew it'd be a bigger deal than that, but this… This was breathtaking.

The venue was right on Sydney Harbour. There were queues of cars lining up. Rollers. Bentleys. Porsches. A Lamborghini!

Maybe there was something else on in the same building, she hoped nervously, thinking it was just as well she'd caught a cab. Imagine driving up in her truck.

A security guard was at the entrance. 'Your ticket, ma'am?'

'I… Dr Maddock said he'd leave a ticket for me at the entrance.'

'You're Miss Mardie Rainey?'

'Yes.' *Aargh.* Was it too late to cut and run?

It *was* too late. The man took her arm. 'Take over, Pete,' he called to his colleague. 'Miss Rainey's arrived.'

Had she decided against coming?

The head table needed to sit first. Guests of honour were seated before the riff-raff—if you could call two-thousand-dollar-a-head ticket holders riff-raff.

Regardless, Blake was being ushered to his seat and Mardie wasn't here yet.

'Sir…'

He turned and the security guard was guiding her forward.

Mardie.

But different.

She took his breath away.

He thought suddenly of the night years ago, of the premiere of the James Bond movie in Whale Cove. Etta had made Mardie a dress they both thought was the last word in sophistication.

This, though…

Every woman in the room was gowned in sophisticated

splendour. Gowns that clung, satin, silks, sleek this-year's fashion.

Not Mardie. She was dressed…as Mardie.

Her dress did cling. And yes, maybe it was silk, but that was where the comparison ended.

It was tiny, deceptively simple, and it was breathtakingly lovely.

It was a sheath of shimmering fabric that resembled nothing so much as a jewel box straight from the Ottoman Empire. Crimsons, purples, deep pinks, with threads of gold. Simple yet exquisite. It fitted her from breasts to just above the knee as if it was a second skin. It was as if she was wearing a perfect jewel.

She wore a dainty filigree choker around her throat, embedded with stones to match the dress. Enamelled? A Mardie Rainey original? He guessed it was.

Her legs were in shimmering silk stockings. Her stilettos made her legs look as if they went on for ever.

Her curls tumbled over her shoulders, arranged with simplicity and a style that made every other woman's hairstyle seem overdone.

She smiled a greeting to him and he realised everyone in the room had stopped talking.

Why would they not, in the face of this smile?

Mardie…all grown up. Not a country mouse at all.

Mardie, grown past him?

'I'm so glad you could come,' he managed, and the politician's wife he'd been speaking to gave a delighted cry.

'It's Mardie Rainey. Oh, my dear, your work's divine. Are you here with Blake?'

'She is,' Blake said promptly, before Mardie could confirm or deny, and he stepped forward and took her hand.

'Hi,' he said and smiled. He felt like keeping on smiling. Not letting go of her hand.

'Quiet corner?' she said.

'Top table's the quietest.'

'You didn't...'

'I hate going to these functions as a singleton. It messes with the seating plan. The organisers were relieved.'

'Blake...'

'So you've saved the day. Where did you get that dress?'

'I made it.'

Of course. His breath was taken away all over again.

And...these people knew her?

The politician's wife did, at least. 'I've been trying to have Mardie make me some jewellery,' she said. 'Like the choker... Oh, my dear, it's to die for.'

'I'm caught up at the moment,' Mardie said.

'With the memorial wall for the pilot tragedy,' the woman said. 'Yes, but it won't make you money. I'm prepared to pay...'

Mardie smiled politely, made some air promises, turned once again to look at the two empty seats at the top table.

'They're waiting for us,' Blake said.

'I can't believe you did this.'

'You don't enjoy sitting between the gov...'

'No. Don't tell me who they are; I don't want to know,' she said. 'The only way to survive this is to spend dinner telling myself everyone's ordinary.'

He smiled, ushering her to her place. His hand touched the small of her back as she sat. It felt... It felt...

'Blake?'

'Mmm?'

'Remember that time I let you try my bath-boat on the dam?'

'I... Yes.' He did remember.

Back to being eight years old. A wide dam in the back paddock. An ancient bathtub.

Mardie's method of getting from one side of the dam to the other was to seal the bath's open plughole with clay and paddle like crazy. She'd offered to let him try. She hadn't actually told him that the clay plug disintegrated and time was of the essence.

He therefore paddled to the middle and paused to see if there were tadpoles.

The next moment he was neck-deep in tadpoles.

Her lips twitched as she watched him. 'You can remember,' she said.

'I might just…'

'I'm just thinking,' she said, softly but surely. 'Top table, huh? Is this revenge? I'm thinking there has to be an even better fate for you than tadpoles.'

She ate a magnificent dinner, feeling more than a little overwhelmed. Feeling a bit…as if she was pleased she'd dressed up. Initially she'd gone for simple, but when she'd emerged from the bedroom Irena had sent her straight back to change.

'You go anywhere near a guy like that wearing a little black dress, you're out of your mind. You have clothes that could knock his socks off.'

'I don't want to knock his socks off.'

'Then there'll be other women who do,' Irena said bluntly. 'Would you be happy to see him head off into the night with someone else?'

Of course she would. She had no claim on him.

But she'd changed anyway, and she didn't regret it.

She was being treated as Blake's partner. He didn't have time to spend with her. Most of his attention was taken by the Very Important Persons on the far side of him. But every now and then he glanced at her, their eyes met, and it was enough.

He was still Blake. Her friend.

The guy she'd dressed up for.

The people around her—politicians, celebrities—were making small talk. Inanities.

Boring.

So… So why not help? Blake was here for a purpose, she thought suddenly, and she'd been given a free ticket. So why not work the room as Blake was doing?

'I've come to Sydney this week to have my dog's eyes operated on,' she told the guy beside her, slipping the words neatly into a pause in the conversation. 'Cataracts. It's the most marvellous operation. My collie will be back to herding sheep, running on the farm, doing all the things she loves. It's such an amazing operation. And did you know how little it costs in Africa, for a person? Compared to here, it's tiny.' She'd read this on the foundations's website. She knew her facts.

'How awesome would it be?' she said softly. 'To make a blind person see? To give the gift of sight…? How great must it feel to be able to give that gift?'

She sensed, rather than saw, Blake's body stiffen beside her. Whatever he'd been expecting, it hadn't been her taking up the cause.

But she was getting little response. The people around her were hardened to appeals.

The politician's wife was still looking at her choker with longing.

Okay, go sideways. Ignore Blake's stiffening. Do what seems right.

She thought of the pictures of Blake in Africa. The work that could be done…

'My next piece of jewellery…' she said, thinking out loud, eyeing the wife of the Very Important Politician, 'is a choker like this one. If I sell it, I'm thinking that might raise enough for thirty eye-operations. Or more.'

'I'd buy it,' the woman said. 'In a heartbeat.'

'I'll pay more,' the woman opposite said.

'Raffle it,' her partner said, looking amused.

'You'd get more if you auctioned it,' another man said. 'If you're serious?'

'I… Yes.' And she discovered she was.

'How long would it take you to make one?' the politician asked, pushing inexorably forward. 'My wife's been looking at it since you walked in. If I covered the basic cost…'

'I'm donating it,' Mardie said.

Conversation at the far end of the table had stopped. Blake put a hand on her arm. A warning? 'Mardie…'

'I know what I'm doing,' she said. She returned to the politician doing the dealing. 'I need to complete a project I'm working on, but I could easily have the choker made by November.'

'Deal,' the guy said. 'Blake, it's time for you to tell us what we need to know. I'm thinking your lady's offer comes afterwards.'

'Knock 'em dead,' Mardie said and managed to give Blake a smile.

This was what she'd come for. *Tell me about Africa.*

The people around her faded to nothing. She wanted to know.

He'd never been much of a public speaker at school. Was he nervous?

She was nervous on his behalf.

He smiled back at her. Then he touched the choker lightly, a feather touch, and his finger just grazed her neck. Sending a shiver… 'This is to do it justice,' he said and that was exactly what he did.

And she needn't have worried, for this was a Blake she'd never met before.

He greeted his audience with ease, he made a wry observation about the day's political events which made everyone smile—and then he took them to Africa.

Tell me about Africa.

She'd asked and he'd been curt to the point of rudeness.

But not because he didn't care. Not because he couldn't tell it.

Because it was a part of him?

He had a screen behind him, a half-hour documentary where a cameraman had filmed Blake treating children's eyes.

Sound had been recorded along with sight, and the moment the video started the sound of the wind echoed through the room.

They were working in a makeshift tent under a canopy of half-dead trees. The wind sounded appalling. What had he called it? *Arifi...*

It made her shudder. She could feel it through the flimsy fabric of the children's sparse clothing. She could sense it, blasting sand into those vulnerable eyes.

She watched as Blake and his assistants fought to keep the equipment clean, fought to keep the sand at bay, fought to help.

The people...the kids...the damage... That was all he'd said to her when she'd asked. It was practically all he said here. His words were an aside to what was happening on the screen—simple explanations, nothing more.

The cameraman was focusing on the children's faces, and then closer. To eyes that were so damaged...

Blake's commentary was a word at a time, saying what was necessary. Nothing more.

'This is Afi. She's better now, practically a hundred per cent vision in her left eye. Moswen's not so good. Look at the scarring. We're hoping for funding for complex surgery for her but we're not holding our breath. Here's Tawia. Four years old. We caught her early, but where she lives...the flies... She gets infection after infection...'

She was, she discovered, crying. She groped for a tissue and the politician's wife handed her one. The woman had a handful and was using them herself.

Blake was touching these people—influential, wealthy people who could make a difference.

This was Blake fighting for what he was passionate about.

How could she ever have thought he'd gone to medical school to make money?

The presentation finished. Every person in the room was still in Africa.

Blake cleared his papers from the rostrum. Prepared to step down.

A thought…

There was this one moment before people turned back to their wine, their social conversations, before they returned from where they'd been taken.

She slipped the choker from her neck and pushed it to the man who'd asked if it was for sale.

'Take this,' she said simply. 'I should have thought of it. Auction it now.'

'What are you doing?' Blake demanded.

'What I want to do.'

There was no better time…

If these people left, their world would catch up with them. The dinner itself had raised money. Blake's presentation would raise more. But if she could find an outlet for the distress in the room right now…

'There's more where that came from,' she told Blake. He looked as if he'd protest and she reached out and took his hand. Linked her fingers in his.

'Hush,' she said. 'I want to do this.'

So he hushed. They both hushed, while a small and beautiful choker, of copper and semi-precious stones, maybe three hundred dollars of materials and a week of Mardie's work, was sold for an amount that took her breath away.

For Africa.

'And there's another for the losing bidder in November, if she wants it,' she whispered to the auctioneer as the room applauded. 'The same but different. I'm happy to consult on colour and style.'

Bemused, the auctioneer made the offer and the woman accepted, signing a cheque on the spot.

Leaving Mardie hornswoggled.

She'd just sold jewellery for a sum she could scarcely comprehend.

Only Blake's hand was holding her to earth.

'So…so you think we did all right in the fund-raising department?' she managed.

'We did.'

'You were wonderful.'

'Not as wonderful as you,' he said softly. 'But now… You're minus jewellery. I'm thinking… Mardie, would you be interested in a diamond to take its place?'

'A diamond…?'

'Mardie, you are my very best friend. I can't believe what you've just done. To marry you… It would be my honour.'

Her world stilled. He was…proposing? Where had that come from?

He'd taken her breath away.

He'd taken his own breath away. She met his gaze and realised he was as shocked as she was.

Had he meant to say it?

In this crowded room… *A proposal?*

'I don't think…' she said and then found courage. Also a certain amount of indignation. 'No. I don't need to think. Diamonds aren't my style.'

'Not?'

'Hugh gave me the only diamond I want,' she said and she met his gaze squarely. She glanced down at her left hand and it lay there still, her tiny solitaire.

Her armour against future hurt.

'I'm guessing yours would be bigger,' she said. 'But it would come with strings.'

She took a deep breath. Regrouped. She knew his proposal had been instinctive, a spur-of-the-moment response to current emotion. One of them had to be sensible.

'Blake, you asked me once before to become part of your life. That couldn't happen then and it couldn't happen now. For if you were serious—about giving diamonds—I'd be asking you to give yourself. And I don't think you know how.'

'I didn't mean…'

'I know you didn't mean.' Indignation was great. Indignation helped. 'Forget it.'

And then the world took over. The woman who'd bought the option on the second choker came surging forward, twittering her excitement. People needed to speak to Blake. Chequebooks were coming out. He had to work the room.

They glanced at each other and, by mutual consent, turned back to what was important.

His work. Africa.

The work he was doing was breathtaking.

He'd just asked her to marry him?

Be part of his life?

All or nothing. Just as it had been fifteen years ago.

It was surely a mistake. An aberration. He looked as shocked as she was. She concentrated on staying social, doing some ego-massaging, trying to make those chequebooks produce more.

Wondering how soon she could get away.

Blake was mid-negotiation with the head of a huge airline corporation. Something about transport for children who needed specialist care…

One of the Outback doctors was waiting to talk to him.

She could slip away. She must.

She needed to get back to her dogs. Ground herself.

She rose and slipped to the Ladies, then, instead of returning to the crowded dining venue, she just happed to edge outside.

There was a cab rank just…

'Where do you think you're going?'

Blake. Of course. He had eyes in the back of his head, and he'd always been a mind-reader.

She didn't look back but waited for him to come up to her.

'I'm going home.' She fought to sound commonplace. As if he hadn't just asked…*about marriage*? 'I'm worried. Irena's out for the night and I have two dogs locked in her too-small laundry. I need to give them a run.'

'I'll take you.'

'You're needed here.'

'There's no more to be done,' he told her. 'I've organised to meet people from the Outback Medical Service on Thursday—something about mutual knowledge sharing—but they were pushed for time tonight and couldn't stay. The rest is duelling chequebooks. Tonight was every fund-raiser's dream. One person donates on such a grandiose scale—i.e. for your choker—and no one can be seen to be outdone. Even the corporates. It was brilliant. If you knew how many eyes tonight will save…'

'I'm glad.'

'Then let me take you home.'

'The diamond…' she said tentatively.

Their gazes met. Locked. A silent message. *Don't go there.*

'The diamond was a mistake,' he said firmly, as if it really was. 'Said on the spur of the moment because I thought you were wonderful. I still do think you're wonderful, but of course you have Hugh's.'

'Of course.' Why did that make her feel desolate?

Because that was all it was. A diamond with no Hugh behind it.

Nothing.

'So can I take you home?'

'Yes,' she said, and she should have thought of Hugh—but she didn't.

CHAPTER EIGHT

ONCE again they drove to Coogee in near silence. There were so many words between them, but there seemed nothing to say. It was as if there was a chasm between them, with no one courageous enough to step near the edge.

'So you decided against another Mercedes?' she asked, thinking at least his choice of car was a safe enough topic for discussion.

'Do you know how much insurance premiums go up if you crash a Mercedes?' He shrugged. 'It was hired. I decided it was cheaper to buy this time.'

'And you're not a man who wastes money.'

'Are you criticising my choice in cars?'

'Who, me?'

But maybe she was. The car he'd ushered her into was an ancient model, a bit rusty, almost as old as she was.

She glanced across at the man beside her, looking absurdly handsome in yet another dinner suit. How many men had a spare dinner suit?

And drove a Mercedes, followed by a rust bucket.

And looked cool in all of them.

A man of parts.

'So you see this as a long-term investment?' she said cautiously and got a ghost of a smile in return.

'Not too long-term. I'm probably leaving Australia in four weeks.'

'Where will you go?'

'I'm thinking back to California.'

'Back?'

'That's where we used to live,' he said. 'All those years ago. My grandfather set up a charitable trust there. That's what I've expanded—the foundation. Our CEO quit last month. Given…my limitations, it seems sensible that I take on his role.'

She frowned. 'I thought you were the CEO.'

'I'm chairman, because of the family connection. Administration's never been my forte. I far prefer working in the field. I've done the occasional fund-raiser, like this one, but mostly I've left the administration to others. It'll be a good fit for me now, though.'

'Now that you can't do fieldwork?'

'Yes.' Short. Harsh. Desolate.

'You sound like Bessie,' she said softly. 'Charlie said it'd be kinder to put her down if she can't work. Is that how you feel?'

'That's melodramatic.'

'Not so melodramatic if you love your work. Like me if you took the art out of me.'

'It means so much to you?'

'I suspect not as much as your work.'

'So if you were to think of coming to California with me…?' But he said it tentatively, as if he already knew it was out of the question. As they both knew it was.

'That'd be two of us miserable,' she said. 'Why are you asking? For the same reason you asked fifteen years ago? Because you wouldn't mind a security blanket?'

'I would never think of you as a security blanket,' he said vehemently. 'What you did tonight…'

'Was fabulous,' she said, deciding—with a fairly major effort—that she needed to cheer up. Or at least sound as if she'd cheered up. 'It pays to be different. All those diamonds, all those floor-length gowns, and I walk in wearing a home-made tube and costume jewellery. I sit next to the most gorgeous guy in the room and suddenly I'm cool and my choker's desirable and the whole room wants what I'm having. But the money it produced… Can you believe it? How much money do those guys have to play with?'

'You needn't worry,' Blake said. 'Those cheques will be lodged as tax deductions, used to gain all sorts of corporate advantage. The chokers themselves are just icing on the cake. They're not as important as image.'

'That's put me in my place.'

'It was a very nice tax deduction,' he said kindly.

'Oh, the praise. I'm all a-flutter.'

He grinned and suddenly the atmosphere in the car lightened. The stupid issue of diamonds receded. 'It was more than the choker,' he said softly. 'If you knew how much of a difference your actions made…'

'To the kids in Africa?'

'Of course.'

'Do you ever think of anything else?' she ventured.

'It's what I do. It's what I am.'

'Because of Robbie?'

'I don't know any more,' he said simply. 'Yes, when I started it was about Robbie. Now, I love what I do. I believe in it and I'll keep working towards it.'

'So no holidays?'

'Not so much,' he admitted.

'You know,' she said softly, 'maybe you should take some time off before you take on this very important job you have in California. Cut yourself some slack.'

'I don't need slack.'

'You don't do slack. That doesn't say you don't need it. Your face says you haven't done slack in a very long time.'

'I haven't relaxed,' he admitted. Hesitated again. Regrouped. 'So you'd never think about coming to California?'

'Why would I?'

'We could do good.'

'No,' she said. 'We wouldn't. We'd self-destruct. This is a dumb conversation, Blake. It's unsettling. Leave it. Once upon a time we were friends. Now we have a dog in common and nothing else. We both know it can't ever be any more than that so we might as well stop now.'

Irena was out, at the opening of an art exhibition. 'Don't wait up for me,' she'd told Mardie. 'These things can stretch out for days. Mind, if you get caught up, too…' She'd eyed Mardie thoughtfully. 'Which I hope you do. If my neighbour doesn't see my car, she'll come in and feed the cats. Shall I leave a note saying feed the dogs as well?'

'No!' Mardie had said, revolted, so here she was, back home at eleven at night, not even pumpkin hour. Home to her dogs and Irena's cats.

So much for Irena's hope. Blake hadn't even as much as suggested he'd like to…she didn't know…have crazy, hot sex? Anything.

He'd simply asked her to marry him.

Which was much easier to refuse.

Blake was standing on the doorstep with her. 'I don't like you going into an empty house,' he'd said curtly as she'd told him there was no need. 'And I need to check the dogs are okay.'

The dogs were okay. She opened the door and they practically knocked her over in their joy. Bouncing with excitement.

The cats were a picture of smouldering resentment, perched precariously on the curtain rails.

Uh-oh.

It seemed the laundry door hadn't closed properly. She gazed around in dismay at the chaos.

That lamp looked…expensive.

'You'll have to make another choker fast, to pay for this,' Blake said, his lips twitching, and she found herself chuckling.

What was it with this man? He drove her nuts. He was driven by demons she could never hope to compete with, yet underneath…

Underneath he was still just Blake. A boy she'd loved.

A man she could still love?

Should she take his proposal seriously?

Maybe he had been serious, she thought. He wasn't a man who took things lightly.

He'd asked because he meant it?

If he had…

If he had, there was part of her that ached to accept. Only of course it hadn't been a proper proposal. It was just like that invitation to come with him to university all those years ago. Come to California. All or nothing. Be subsumed by his life.

Share his demons?

She had no intention of sharing his demons. No way. She had enough of her own.

He was helping her fight down the over-excited dogs. He was too near.

How to tell him to go home?

How to tell him he was far too distracting?

'I…I need to change and take the dogs for a walk,' she said. 'I need to get rid of some energy.'

'You're not walking in the dark.'

'It's Coogee,' she said patiently. 'It'll be lit like daylight. Security patrols. The works. I've done it before. The security guys even know me—at this time of night they'll turn a blind eye if I let Bounce off his lead.'

'How often do you come down here?'

'I sell my enamelling,' she said patiently. 'I live in two worlds.'

'So you could come to California…'

'No, Blake, I couldn't,' she snapped. 'Have you forgotten my mother? Have you forgotten how much I love Banksia Bay? And have you even begun to realise how much I don't know you? Enough. You're welcome to come for a walk on the beach with me, but that's the extent of it. If you have time to wait until I put some jeans on. If you don't mind walking in a dinner suit.'

'Lately I've been doing all sorts of strange things in a dinner suit,' he said, sounding grim.

'Maybe your life's changing in more ways than one,' she said. 'Think about it. California doesn't sound like much fun to me. How about some lateral thinking?'

As if… When had this man ever changed direction? Was it possible that he ever could?

He stood and waited until she put on jeans and windcheater and trainers, and when she came back to the sitting room he couldn't figure whether he loved her more in her wonderful home-made dress or in her casual jeans.

Love...

It was a simple word but it was resounding more and more.

Mardie.

Mardie herding sheep. Mardie tackling the tree with her chainsaw.

Mardie loving her mother, loving her community.

Love.

But he didn't truly know what love was and how he was feeling now… He didn't know what to do with it. There was nowhere to take it.

He'd asked her to marry him. What if she'd said yes?

He'd make it work.

She wasn't taking the risk. She was being wise for both of them.

Beach, walk, dogs.

He tossed his jacket and tie, rolled up his sleeves, pretended to be casual.

Pretended he could fit into Mardie's world.

He knew that he couldn't.

He'd expected a stroll. He didn't get one. Mardie walked as if there was a sheep in trouble down the back paddock and she wasn't wasting time getting there.

The tide was far out. The foreshore was well lit but even if it hadn't been, the full moon made walking a pleasure. They could walk for miles on the ribbon of wet sand and on the paths around the cliffs—and maybe she intended just that. She was striding as if she meant to leave him behind.

That was okay. It felt okay that she was simply on the beach beside him.

More—it felt good.

It felt good to the dogs, too. Strange smells. Shallows to run in. Humans to herd. Both these dogs must know the sea. Bessie stuck to Bounce's side, but she seemed almost the leader, egging Bounce on.

Blake let his attention stay on the dogs. It was easier to think dogs rather than think Mardie, for every time he thought about Mardie…

Mardie tonight, glowing, sophisticated, beautiful, generous. Every man in the room watching her. His Mardie-girl…

To walk away…

Not his.

Don't think about it.

Think of Bessie.

To cure her would give such pleasure. It wouldn't feel so bad going back to California knowing he'd left Mardie with two dogs instead of one.

Why had he asked her to marry him?

He hadn't been serious. If he seriously wanted this woman to marry him, he needed to get down on bended knee and do the thing in style.

The answer would be the same. The idea was, as she'd said, unworkable.

Unthinkable.

Except he was thinking it.

Marriage on his terms?

Marriage for him; not for Mardie.

Bad idea.

'So what were you about, offering diamonds?' Mardie asked, still striding, and he wondered if she was angry. She'd never been one to sulk in silence. Bring the elephant into the room and inspect it from all angles.

'Thinking aloud,' he said. 'Wishing our worlds could collide.'

'Would you really want our worlds to collide?' she asked. 'Or is it more that in your world you don't have anything of my world? And my world feels safe.'

'Safe…'

'Why did you come back to Australia after your illness?' she asked. 'I know there was this fund-raiser, but someone else could surely have handled it. If home's in California…'

'It's not.'

'Home has to feel somewhere.'

She slowed. She'd kicked off her sandals and was walking in the shallows.

He'd been walking a little up the beach where it was drier. As she slowed he tugged off his shoes and hit the water, too. Her anger seemed to have dissipated. He flinched as the first wave hit and she smiled.

That smile… Marriage… Why wouldn't a man ask, even if the concept was impossible?

The dogs came tearing back to them, crazy circling, as if making sure their flock of humans stayed in a tight knot.

He wouldn't mind staying in a tight knot with Mardie.

Home was…

Here. With this woman.

It always had been. Ever since that first day in the playground. Sharing lunches.

Why had he come back to Australia?

It had been his refuge after Robbie died. He'd found peace here. He still thought of Australia as a refuge.

He couldn't stay somewhere because it was a refuge. He couldn't love somewhere because it was safe.

He couldn't love a woman for the same reasons.

Mardie was much, much more.

'Ooh, there's some stuff going on in that head of yours,' she said. 'For heaven's sake, Blake, let it go. Race you back to the headland. You could always beat me, but you've been sick and I've been training. One, two, three, go…'

And she was off, flying along the wet sand, her dogs hurtling along behind her. Dogs and woman…

He'd never met someone so…free.

She had her demons. Of course she did.

She chose to let them take care of themselves.

Maybe he, too…

No. Too hard. It was far too hard.

She beat him—of course she did—he'd spent the first half of the race in stupid, unproductive thought—and when he did finally catch her, she seemed angry again. They were at the start of the path up to the house. She didn't pause; she went right on up, and when they reached his car parked out the front, she fussed over dog leads and didn't look at him.

He waited until she straightened. Tried to figure what to say.

She held out her hand. A formal gesture of farewell.

'I've had a lovely night,' she said, a trifle too stiffly. 'Thank you.'

'That's… I've enjoyed it, too.'

'I can manage on my own now, with the dogs.'

'I'll be here on Thursday when Colin operates.'

'There's no need.'

'I'll be here.'

'Thank you,' she said simply. 'That would be lovely. Goodnight.'

And before he could react, before he could reach out a hand and take hers—she slipped into the house with her dogs without another word.

Tuesday and Wednesday, he didn't see her. There was no reason.

She needed to take Bessie back to the vet's for a couple more pre-op tests, but she lived close and for him to take the half-hour trip there…

As she'd said, there was no need.

He had things to do. There were always things to do.

One of the cheques for Mardie's chokers bounced. He was used to that. Guys big-noting themselves among their peers, then letting the charity cope with the consequences.

He made a few enquiries, discovered the guy did have serious money, discovered he'd tried this on before.

He made a couple of calls to the media, had a journalist do a dig story and he had a phone call from the bank within the hour.

The cheque had magically been cleared.

There was no way the scum-bag was getting Mardie's choker without paying.

He could do good, he thought, as he tallied the figures for Monday night. He could make the foundation much bigger than it was now. He could make it huge.

He wanted to work in the field.

But that was dumb. The cause was what counted. To die of dengue because he wanted to be indispensable… How would Robbie feel about that?

His twin. The guy who questioned everything he did.

How would Robbie feel about Mardie?

There was a dumb question. A dumb thought.

Put her out of his mind.

Then suddenly he thought…Irena. Irena was Mardie's agent. If Mardie had an agent then there must be more sales.

Mardie had looked him up. He could do the same. He did an internet search for one Mardie Rainey, looking for stockists. Discovered a tiny gallery that specialised in three-dimensional art.

He just happened to walk past. He just happened to walk in, expecting rings, bracelets, maybe even chokers like he'd seen on Monday night.

Instead he found tiny enamelled pictures. This then, was how she'd landed the job commemorating the pilots. Where she'd gained her reputation.

These pictures were extraordinary.

They were of…nothing. Glass on copper.

A blade of grass against a weathered fence post.

A piece of driftwood on a beach.

A raindrop.

Nothing.

Everything.

He looked at them and thought of Africa. A child's sight.

So little. Everything.

He thought of Mardie's life.

And he thought of his own.

Thursday. 'Have her here at eight. No breakfast,' Colin had decreed and Mardie had Bessie there at seven forty-five. She stayed in the truck until the clinic doors opened, hugging Bessie, wishing they'd elected to have only one eye done today and not both. Both eyes seemed scary.

Even one seemed scary.

She'd left Bounce with Irena and the cats. Bessie had to do this alone.

She had to do this alone.

Bessie seemed bereft, and she felt exactly the same.

But then… Her truck door swung open and Blake was there. Just…there.

Deep breath. This was good. Wasn't it? Two of them could feel bad about Bessie together.

He was so close.

He'd asked her to marry him. The question had hovered in her head for two days.

Stupid.

She was so happy to see him again she could hardly speak.

'S…so tell me again why we're doing both eyes?' she managed.

'So we won't have to spend another night like last one,' he said. 'Staring into the dark thinking of all the things that can go wrong.'

'You, too?'

'I know the odds,' he said. 'Healthy dog, healthy eyes under the cataracts, great surgeon, tried-and-tested procedure—this is as good as it gets. The biggest risk is retina detachment and that's a risk no matter whether we do one or both. It'll be fine.'

'Yet you still sat up all night.'

'Yep,' he said and lifted Bessie from her arms. 'I'm a sucker for a lady with facial hair. Colin's here. All systems go. Let's get our Bessie's sight restored so she can get on with her life.'

'Blake?'

'Mmm.'

'Did you come…just to wish us luck?'

'I'll stay close until it's done. I've agreed to meet a couple of guys at the airport in an hour but that's close enough to here. If you'd like me to stick around…'

'I would.' She hesitated. She shouldn't need this man.

'I definitely would,' she said.

They stayed with Bessie until the anaesthetic took hold, but then they had to leave.

'You're not watching,' Colin told him. 'Blake taught me,' he explained to Mardie. 'If there's anything guaranteed to make my hands shake, it's my teacher watching. Take him away and don't let him come near until I've finished.'

'Fine by me,' Mardie said, feeling bad. She hugged Bessie and left. Feeling…watery.

She pushed open the door to outside with more force than necessary.

Blake ushered her through. Closed the door after her. Offered her a tissue.

Went a step further and hugged her.

'I don't cry,' she managed. Not pulling away.

'You shouldn't. Bessie's about to be cured. What's there to cry about?'

'Do you get emotional about patients?'

'Never.'

'Liar.' She knew this guy.

'I shouldn't.'

She sniffed. She managed—with a pretty big effort—to pull herself out of his arms. Blew her nose, hard.

Got a grip.

'So you want me to stay here while you have your meeting at the airport?'

'Stay with me,' he said softly and took her hand.

She gazed down at their linked hands.

Thought, inexplicably, of Bessie and Bounce. Practically Siamese twins.

She didn't pull away.

What was he doing, meeting these guys? He was wasting time.

He'd met them the night of the dinner. Riley and Harry. Doctor and pilot with an Outback Flying Doctor medical service based at Whale Cove. Squeezing the dinner in between care flights.

It seemed Harry was a friend of Raff's, the Banksia Bay cop. Raff had told them about him. They'd come on Monday night to listen. Asked if they could talk to him.

A job offer? Questions about fund-raising? Normally he'd decline but he'd been feeling…disoriented. As if he didn't know how to say no.

Now…he and Mardie watched as the light plane came in to land, a patient was transferred to an ambulance headed for a city hospital, and then Harry and Riley were free.

They didn't speak. They simply waited.

With their patient transferred, the men came over to them. Big men, tough, in the uniform of the Flying Doctor Service.

'Raff says you're looking for a job,' Riley said bluntly, straight to the point.

Raff. Banksia Bay. Of course. Everyone knew everyone.

'He has his wires crossed. I'm not.'

But it seemed Raff had done some research. He'd worked fast and he had it right. 'Raff says you've been in Africa treating eyes,' Riley said. 'He says you can't go back because of dengue. Now he thinks you're planning to be a pen-pusher. That'd be just plain dumb. We could use you, right here, right now. There's no dengue where we work, just a whole heap of need.'

* * *

It wouldn't work.

They drove back to the vet clinic and the silence in the truck was almost tangible.

Blake was staring straight ahead.

'I'm going back to California,' he said at last. 'I think I have to.'

'So you met them why?'

'I thought they might want to talk mutual fund-raising.' But he hadn't. He'd known the minute he'd met them that there was a job on the line. If he and Mardie…

No.

'You wouldn't consider it?' she ventured. 'Robbie doesn't give you that option?'

'I should never have told you about Robbie.' It was an explosion.

'I should have guessed.' She hesitated, and then went on. 'Blake, that night, all those years ago,' she said softly. 'I can only imagine. Two little boys, lying in that great big house. Following rules. But then…the joy of sneaking out to play in the pool. Two little boys having fun. And tragedy. But surely that doesn't mean you need to follow rules all your life, especially if those rules are ones you've set up for yourself. If those rules were meant to make up for Robbie, they never can. They never will.'

'This is…'

'None of my business? Maybe not. Or maybe it is my business, because you're my friend.' She took a deep breath. 'On Monday you even suggested I marry you. It was offhand, like something I wouldn't even consider, but you know something? I would.'

'Mardie…'

'Only not with your shadows,' she said, with only the faintest tremor behind the words. 'For I'm not sharing.' Another deep breath. 'Blake, have you ever talked to seven-year-old Blake?'

'What do you mean?'

'It's a thing you do,' she said diffidently. 'It's a thing I learned. When Hugh died...I was a mess and our local doctor organised a shrink to see me. You know what was going round my head? That I hadn't put the dogs in their crate. I'd cleaned it and then we were running late so I thought—why bother putting it back? So they were fussing in the back seat, and Hugh was telling them to pipe down, and the kids came round the bend. He didn't have time to swerve. If he'd had that extra split second... I thought... Well, you know what I thought.'

'It wasn't your fault.'

'Yeah, you say that. Everyone says it but you can hear it as many times as you want and not believe. You know that better than me. But the shrink... You know what he did? He made me find a picture of me from before the accident. And he said I needed to treat the hurting me as separate. The Mardie-Before and the Mardie-After. And the Mardie-After needed to talk to the Mardie-Before, talk through exactly what happened that day, tell her that what she did wasn't criminal or even stupid. He said I should give that Mardie a hug and move on. And you know what? Eventually I did.'

He didn't say anything. Nothing.

'So...could you look at a photograph of your seven-year-old self, and tell him he has to pay for the rest of his life?' she ventured. 'Or would you look at that seven-year-old and give him a hug and weep for what he's gone through already? Robbie's death. Your parents' abandonment. And then...could you tell the little boy that you were to live his life as he ought to live his life? To have fun. To do good if that's what you want, but only if that's what you want, not because you're paying back shadows. To...' She paused. Thought about it. Finally said it. 'To allow yourself to be happy.'

'I think we should leave it,' he said heavily, and she thought, yes, she should. She'd said everything she could say.

Or…not quite.

Just say it.

'And, as for Monday… As for the diamond…I would marry you,' she said simply. 'In truth, I decided when I was ten that I wanted to marry you. And it seems I've never stopped. I loved Hugh, but in a different way; he was a different man. It doesn't take away what I felt for him, what I feel for you. It seems I've loved you all the time and I guess I always will. Shadows or not. But if you can't get rid of your shadows I guess our loving will keep us at a distance. Because there's no choice. For both of us.'

They met a beaming Colin.

'I couldn't ask for better,' he said. 'Textbook perfect. It's gone brilliantly in both eyes. She's on the way to recovery. All she needs is absolute quiet, to wear the cone collar all the time, no barking, drops twice a day, total care, and in four weeks I'm thinking you'll have a magnificent working dog. Do you want to see her? She's still heavily sedated.'

They went in and saw her.

Her eyes were still closed. Colin gently lifted a lid and the awful milkiness was gone.

Mardie felt… She felt…

Good. Excellent. Dog-wise, at least, this was job done. She could get on with her life with two dogs.

Blake would go back to the US. Things would return to normal.

But, despite her tumultuous emotions, Colin's words were starting to sink in. Quiet. Cone collar. No barking. Total care…

She didn't quite have a handle on this.

'No barking at all?' she said, faltering.

'I thought Blake would have explained post-op care,' Colin said, frowning.

'Blake did mention it,' she said. 'I just thought… I can

handle eye drops.' She took a deep breath. 'No. Sorry. I can handle everything. I'll take Bounce to the boarding kennels for a month. It won't kill him. If Bessie's locked inside, she'll stay quiet.'

'You're hardly ever inside.' Blake said.

'I guess loneliness is the price she pays for her sight.'

'It's not,' Blake said.

'Not?'

'I have an apartment here in the city,' he said. 'I'll be working here for the next few weeks. I do some online teaching,' he explained as they both looked at him in surprise. 'I can do that while I keep Bessie at my feet. I know she'll miss Bounce but it'll work. I'll bring her back to the farm in a month, just before I go.'

There was the solution, just like that. Easy.

Mardie looked down at the sleeping dog. Bessie.

It should feel great.

It was an eminently practical solution.

She could walk away. Go back to Irena's, collect Bounce, go back to the farm.

Blake would return Bessie to her in a month. And then… nothing.

It was a neat solution all round.

It felt…

It felt…

Not neat.

'That's great,' she said, sounding feeble. 'I… You have your car here, Blake? I can go, then. I really would like to get back to the farm this afternoon.' She put her hand on Bessie's soft head, taking as well as giving comfort.

'Take care of her,' she whispered. 'Thank you, Colin. And…and thank you, Blake. You're both wonderful.'

'I'm not wonderful,' Blake said.

'Yes, you are,' she said, gaining strength. 'Yes, you are, if you let yourself be.'

CHAPTER NINE

FOUR weeks was a very long time in the life of Mardie.

She did exactly what she'd been doing a month ago. She spent three days a week in the nursing home, helping aged fingers give pleasure to their owners, having fun. She worked furiously on her last plates, and then slowed because Robyn Partling's life refused to be told in a rush. In a month they were done and she loved them.

She could take them to Sydney this weekend and deliver them.

Or not.

This weekend Blake had said he'd bring Bessie home, and something inside her—the silly, hormonal something—was saying, *Last chance, Last chance, Last chance.*

He rang, friendly but curt. 'She's done brilliantly,' he told her. 'Colin's taken the cone off. Her eyesight's amazing. He says she's ready for farm life again. Can you be home at two on Saturday?'

'Of course,' she said simply—and then she was nervous.

Really nervous.

What was she doing, thinking *last chance*? There never was going to be a chance. He'd drop off Bessie and say goodbye and fly out to California and that'd be the end of an unsettling period of her life.

She had to settle.

Which meant…normal.

Saturday.

She went to see Charlie and told him Bessie's latest news. She told her mum.

'We'd love to see her come home,' they both said, and she thought—normal; I can do that.

Two o'clock on Saturday.

Blake was coming home.

No. Bessie was coming home. Blake was merely the delivery man.

He turned into the farm gate, expecting the old Mardie. Mardie in her jeans and an ancient sweater—the Mardie who belonged here, not the unsettling Mardie who'd blown him away in Sydney.

He wanted it to be the old Mardie. He'd take the thought of her back to the States with him, he thought, as he'd carried her in his thoughts for years. She was a warm part of his heart that had stayed safe, that was used for comfort but not permitted to interfere with what he had to do.

He wanted that part of him to stay unaltered.

He looked to the veranda and there she was, on the top step, Bounce beside her.

Bessie was harnessed in the back seat but he heard her whine.

'Home,' he told her and the word felt…

Yeah, like the word he wasn't allowed to feel. He needed to hand Bessie over and get out of here, memories intact.

He pulled up. Bounce tore down from the veranda, Mardie following a trifle more sedately but not much. She was smiling.

What cost that smile?

'Bessie.' He let her out and Mardie was on her knees, hugging, and Bounce was going wild, trying to reach his friend. He watched the group hug and felt his heart twist.

'Bessie.' It was a quavering voice from the veranda and Bessie froze. Pulled out from the group hug in an instant.

Looked up.

Really looked.

Her eyes worked fine. Her hearing was even better. She knew who was on the veranda and she was gone, flying across the yard, up the steps, reaching the old man in the vast padded hospital chair. Skidding to a stop. Not jumping. Just sitting, hard beside him.

Charlie's gnarled old hand dropped to her silky head and she quivered from nose to tail. She put a paw up, as if in entreaty. Quivered some more.

'Up,' he whispered and she needed no more persuasion. She was up on his blanketed knees, licking his face, her paws on his shoulders, doing what an untrained, out-of-control dog would do when reunited with her beloved owner.

Only this was no untrained dog. Charlie chuckled and submitted to licking, and even hugged back himself, but he was frail and he knew it.

'Enough,' he said, and Bessie was off his knee in an instant, sitting beside him, looking adoringly up at him. Charlie was smiling and smiling.

So was Blake.

And Mardie.

And so was her mother, and the nurse who stood silently behind. Groping for tissues all round.

He'd thought he was bringing Bessie back to Mardie. Instead… Here were Charlie and Etta and a nurse with a name tag that said she was Liz, administrator of the Banksia Bay Nursing Home. He was bringing Bessie home to Banksia Bay, to be enveloped once again in this all-embracing town.

'Welcome home,' Mardie said as he reached her, to him alone, and she hugged him unself-consciously, as if it was the most natural thing in the world.

Could he accept that welcome?

He thought suddenly of that night all those years ago, shut in the house, bored, tired, fed up with listening to the grown-up party downstairs. One moment's breaking of the rules. *Let's go out and swim.*

That moment felt like now.

'You want to see what she can do?' Charlie asked, his voice cracked with age and pride, and the moment when he could have hugged Mardie back was past. When he could have whirled her round and round in his arms and held her to him and declared he, too, was truly home…

It was a fantasy. A stupid, dangerous longing.

'Of course,' he managed and put Mardie aside, and heaven alone knew the effort that cost him.

'Charlie's wonderful with dogs,' Etta said placidly from her chair, looking from Mardie to Blake and back again, and Blake knew she was asking questions in her mind that couldn't be answered.

'Charlie's the best dog-trainer in the district,' Liz said. 'Half the dogs in this town have been trained by Charlie, or by guys Charlie's trained to train, and the younger dogs have reached the stage where they seem almost to have been trained by Charlie's dogs. Generations of dogs, teaching each other, courtesy of Charlie. His legacy will live for ever.'

Charlie's wrinkled face worked; he tried not to smile, tried not to look as if he wasn't moved. But he was.

Even in the past four weeks Charlie had slipped; Blake could see that.

Liz was giving him a gift. An affirmation.

As maybe in his turn Charlie had gifted each of them.

Banksia Bay. His refuge. Blake felt…

Mardie took his hand and squeezed, but it was a message, nothing more.

He couldn't feel.

The offer from the Flying Dotor… An insidious siren song.

Not as insidious as Mardie.

'I've put some sheep in the home paddock,' she said. 'You want to help take Mum and Charlie down to watch these guys strut their stuff?'

To be drawn further into this emotion?

He had no choice. There was no escaping, but did he want to escape?

Yes. He told himself that harshly.

Only not yet. All eyes were on him. He was their audience.

He was Charlie's affirmation.

So they took the two big hospital chairs across to the gate into the home paddock where Mardie had herded six sheep. They were young ones, yearlings, wild and silly, ready to run any which way.

She'd set pegs up at intervals and a tiny corral in the centre of the paddock, with an entrance about the width of a man. Or a sheep.

'Walk up,' Charlie said to Bessie and Bessie's eyes, the eyes that had been hidden for so long, lit with excitement and pure instinctive pleasure.

'Stay,' Mardie told Bounce and Bounce quivered and stayed.

'In here,' Charlie said, his voice scarcely a whisper, but Bessie heard. 'Look back. Get back, take time, come by…'

And in moments the sheep were transformed from a bunch of silly youngsters to a beautifully controlled, collie-trained flock. Bessie moved almost without command, glancing back at Charlie every so often, a tiny glance, watching Charlie's hand. Watching each and every one of the sheep. Weaving them seamlessly through the pegs, out and back, out and back, and then into the tiny gap and into the makeshift coral.

Done.

As a display of sheer skill, of communication between man and dog, it was breathtaking.

'That'll do,' Charlie said gruffly and Bessie came flying

back to his side and sat again, totally attentive, waiting for the next order.

'He's... Charlie's been teaching me,' Mardie said in a voice that was none too steady. 'Want to watch?'

So they watched as Bounce gave it his best.

He wasn't close to as slick as Bessie was. The communication between Bounce and Mardie wasn't as great. At one stage he saw Bessie half stand, as if aching to help. Charlie's hand rested on her head.

'Stay,' he said softly. 'Young 'uns have to learn.'

And Bounce was learning and so was Mardie. The sheep were eventually back in the corral and Mardie's beam was as wide as a house.

'How's that?'

'They all clapped and laughed and Bounce bounced back to Bessie. Charlie released her, and the dogs did a wide joyous circle of the whole paddock. Not touching. There was no longer need for touch. Bessie had her eyes back. Still they didn't leave each other. Siamese twins. Touching at the heart.

Mardie's hand was suddenly in his, and this time there was no pressure. No message. It was simply because...she wanted her hand to be in his.

'Thank you,' she said softly. 'Thank you from all of us.'

He wanted to kiss her.

He wanted to kiss her more than anything else in the world.

Robbie... Don't go near the pool...

Mardie deserved more than being used as a refuge.

'I need to go,' he said and glanced at his watch. 'I... There's things to do. I leave for the States on Tuesday.'

'Of course.' She tugged back, reminded of reality. 'You can't stay for...'

'No.' Blunt. Curt. He watched Etta's face fall.

He didn't see Mardie's face fall. He carefully wasn't looking at Mardie. He'd pulled right away.

'I'll walk you to your car,' she said.

'I'll put the kettle on,' Liz said. 'You guys play with the dogs for a few more minutes,' she told Charlie and Etta. 'Mardie and I'll push you inside when the kettle boils.'

Liz had thus given them privacy. It meant Mardie could walk him back to the car and they didn't have an audience,

Mardie slipped her hand back into his as they walked.

He should pull away. He didn't.

'I'm sad you're going back,' she said softly. 'You could have made a difference with North Coast Rescue.'

'I'll make a difference with what I'm doing.'

'By sitting in an office?'

'I'm good at fund-raising.'

'Yes, but does it give you pleasure?'

'That's not the point.'

'No.' She pulled her hand away.

They reached the car. He should get in and go. Leave. Drive away and never come back.

'I should never have come,' he said.

'I'm glad you did. It's like…closure.'

'I've always hated that word.'

'Me, too,' she whispered and she turned into him. Looked up.

And he didn't get into the car.

For first there was something he had to do. Something he had no choice in, for every nerve in his body was telling him to do it.

He cupped her chin with his hands, he stooped and he kissed her.

Her lips met his. Merged.

Heat, want, need. It exploded between them, surging at the point of contact and spreading.

It was as if his world had suddenly melted, merged, fused. All centring round this one point.

This woman in his arms.

He held her, gently and then more urgently. She was on tiptoe to meet him and he lifted her, hugging her close. Melting.

Mardie. His Mardie.

Not his Mardie. He'd made his decision.

But to walk away would hurt. Why not savour this last piece of surrender, for surrender it surely was? Surrendering himself to what he wanted most in the world.

This woman in his arms.

This woman he was kissing.

This woman who was kissing him. For the roles were changing, the delineation was blurring.

A man and a woman and a need as primeval as time itself.

History was disappearing. History and pain and even sense. Especially sense.

His defences were crumbling as he held her, as her breasts crushed against his chest, as she merged into him.

Mardie.

He'd met her when he was too young to know what a woman was. She'd become part of him in a slow, insidious process that now seemed inevitable, unalterable. She was like part of him, part of his childhood, part of his teens, but…part of who he was right now.

She knew him as no other woman could know him. She'd exposed parts of him he'd hidden with years of carefully built barriers, because behind the barriers…pain.

Where was the pain now?

Not here. Not with this kiss. Not with this wonder.

It was waiting. He knew that, even as he surrendered to the here and now, to the pure loveliness of this moment. Self-recriminations were right behind him, waiting to take over. But he had this one moment. His kiss intensified, became more urgent, more compelling.

Mardie…

But she was suddenly withdrawing, just a little. He felt her body stiffen. Her hands fought to find purchase between them, and she pushed him away.

It felt as if part of himself was being torn, to let her go.

He had to let her go.

'This…this is *some* goodbye kiss,' she said in a voice that said she was shaken to the core.

'It is.' He wanted to reach out and touch her again. Gather her back into his arms.

Surrender…

Stay here. Stay safe. Banksia Bay. Mardie. Its own sweet siren song.

Staying safe couldn't last. The world was out there.

To retreat… To come home…

It wasn't his home.

'Thank you…for being you,' he said simply. 'I've loved this time.'

'No, you haven't. It's torn you in two.'

'Maybe it has,' he said simply. 'But at least now, when I walk away I know there's truth between us. Friendship.'

'Like that will help.'

'Mardie…'

'I know,' she said bleakly. 'You can't help it. You need to save the world and somehow you think you can't do it here. You can't think that I do it, that my mum did it, that Liz up there does it, that Charlie does it, too, in his way.' She paused. Closed her eyes. Took a deep breath.

'Sorry. You don't understand and you'll never understand. Off you go and save the world in your own way, my lovely Blake, and know I'll always think of you. With love. Because I can't help myself. But there'll always be a little part of Banksia Bay that's home for you, Blake, whether you want it or not. Don't forget it. Don't forget us.'

* * *

They were waiting for her. Her mother, Charlie, Liz and the two dogs.

Bessie whimpered as if she realised what she'd lost and Charlie hushed her.

Her mother held out her hand and she took it and then stooped and let Etta hug her. Her mother's hugs… Once upon a time they'd made things better. Not now.

'He's not coming back?' Liz asked.

'What do you think?'

'Sorry, girl,' Charlie said.

There was a moment's silence while they all thought of something to say.

Then… 'That dog of yours needs work,' Charlie said roughly. 'You want a quick lesson before Liz orders us all in for scones and tea?'

'Yes, please,' she said, trying valiantly not to…well, not to stand and wail. A girl had some pride.

'Well, let's get on with it,' Charlie said. 'Time's short. We've got things to do. Get yourself together, girl, and move on.'

'You're tired,' Liz said.

'Not too tired for what she loves,' Charlie retorted. 'Never too tired for that.'

He drove back to Sydney feeling empty.

So what was new? He'd had this emptiness in his gut for ever.

Not when he was with Mardie. When he was with Mardie she filled his life.

It was a dangerous, insidious sweetness.

Why couldn't a man just give in?

And do what…?

North Coast Rescue would give him a job in a heartbeat. 'We fly clinics three days a week,' Riley had told him. 'We almost always fly north. It'd be a snap to detour through

Banksia Bay—there's a light airstrip at the back of the town. We could pick you up on the way, drop you off on the way back. Long days, but, mate, they're so satisfying.'

Three days a week. The rest… Writing? Teaching online? Doing some foundation work?

Helping Mardie train Bounce.

He'd never change the world.

He'd change a little bit.

It wasn't enough to stop this fierce, desolate drive within him.

How could he let it go?

See a shrink in the States? Come back cured?

No. He'd come back with the guilt in recess. He could never live with Mardie on those terms—she deserved so much more.

Get over it.

He thought of what he'd left behind. Mardie. Etta and Charlie. Bounce and Bessie. Sheep and hens, beach and farm.

It had been a refuge when he was a child. It had been a refuge now as he came to terms with dengue.

A man couldn't stay in a refuge for ever. He had to face his demons on his own.

He returned to Sydney.

He spent time consulting with two Australian doctors who'd volunteered to spend a year each in Africa.

He packed up the apartment, and put it on the market. It had been stupid to keep it all these years. He was never coming back.

Two more days… The loose ends were being tied.

Monday night. At one in the morning, he was staring at the ceiling, waiting for sleep that wouldn't come.

A phone call.

'Blake?'

Mardie. He was upright in an instant, flicking on the light. Her voice…

'What's happened?'

'No…no drama,' she said but he could tell by her voice that she'd been crying. 'It's just…Charlie died yesterday. In his sleep. It's…it's fine. It was his time. Liz…Liz knew he was slipping. She came out and got Bessie, and Bessie was asleep on his bed when he died. He knew she was there. He knew she was safe, and well and happy.' She caught her breath. Struggled to go on.

'It's just… I wasn't going to tell you, you don't need to know, but then I thought…I couldn't sleep so I thought I'd tell you and you can do what you want with it. His funeral's this afternoon. No one's expecting you to come. It's…it's nothing to do with you but I thought…I thought I'd let you know and let you decide whether it's anything to do with you or not.'

She shouldn't have told him.

She sat in the front pew, with her mother in her wheelchair beside her and Bessie at her feet. The Banksia Bay vicar saw nothing wrong and everything right with Charlie's dog being here, being part of the ceremony.

Charlie's coffin was loaded with every trophy, every ribbon, he and his dogs had ever won. There were photographs everywhere.

Charlie and dogs. He'd never had children but his dogs lived on.

Mardie was almost totally focused on Charlie, almost totally focused on what the vicar was saying. But a tiny part of her was aware of the door.

This one last chance…

He wasn't taking it. He wouldn't come.

'It's okay, sweetheart, you have us,' her mother whispered, taking her hand, and she flushed. Was she so obvious?

'I don't need anyone.'

'Nonsense,' Etta said sharply. 'We all need everyone.'

He came. He'd meant to go in. At the last minute he stopped himself. He still felt as if he had no place here.

Going in would be a statement he had no wish to make.

Instead he parked his car on the hill overlooking the church. Watched people go in. Watched people gather outside. Many, many people, most of them attached to…dogs?

The service was being broadcast on loudspeakers so the crowd outside could hear. The day was still and warm, and the sound carried.

He heard people talk of Charlie, with respect and with affection.

He heard Mardie. Had they asked her to speak the eulogy, then? Her voice came over the loudspeaker, true and clear. 'Charlie's dog, Bessie, is here. If Bessie has a voice, here's what she'd like to say about Charlie…'

Laughter. Murmurs of agreement, of affection, of wistfulness from the congregation.

Old hymns. Favourites he remembered from when Mardie's mum had bossed them into church.

They felt like something he missed. Like part of him, cut off.

And then a blaze of bagpipes, the ancient tune, "Dawning of that Day," signalling the end of the service.

The crowd parted so the pall-bearers could carry their burden out.

But they didn't just part.

They formed a guard of honour, all the way from the church door to the graveyard at the foot of the hill where he stood.

A man or woman or child was suddenly standing every step of the way, on either side of the path where the coffin was carried. And beside each man, woman and child…

A dog. Not just a dog, but a trained dog. Mostly working dogs—collies, kelpies, blue heelers, but the occasional poodle, spaniel, mutt.

Every dog was sitting hard on his owner's heels, rigidly to attention, eyes straight in front as the coffin passed, a last and loving respect to the man who'd spent his life training them. Who'd passed on his skills from dog to dog, from generation to generation.

Mardie was walking behind the coffin. Bessie was beside her, not on a lead, heeling beautifully, steady, sure.

Behind Mardie, others—friends, relatives, more dogs. Liz was pushing Etta's chair. Bounce was heeling by the wheelchair as if he realised the significance of this day.

A community, mourning its own.

He thought suddenly of Mardie's plates. Her skill in creating things of wonder, the pilot's wife's awe and gratitude.

He thought of Etta, Mardie's mother, her crazy cooking, the way she'd welcomed a stray little boy into her home.

He looked at Liz, who ran one of the best nursing homes he'd ever been in.

Of Raff, the local cop, who cared for this community with firmness and with love.

Love…

He thought of the children he'd treated in Africa. All those lives, altered because of what he'd done.

He thought of what he could do…

He could go back to California. Make Eyes For Africa bigger.

Others could do that. Others would do that. He could keep an overseeing role.

He could stay here and make Mardie happy.

She was already happy. She didn't need him.

He should…

No. Enough of *should.*

The procession had reached the graveyard now. Mardie was

standing by the open grave, Bessie by her side. She looked… alone.

Enough.

He walked down the hillside to join her.

Not because he should. Not because it'd save the world.

He walked down to join Mardie because it was what he most wanted to do in the world.

If he could make Mardie love him… If he could be part of this community…the world would be his.

She'd been aware of him for a while, high on the hill, just watching.

He was too far away for her to be sure, but she knew. A sixth sense…

Or the fact that he was part of her and she knew her own heart.

The vicar was about to speak as he arrived, but the crowd parted to let him through and the vicar hesitated, giving Blake time to be where he needed to be.

By Mardie's side.

Holding Mardie's hand.

The vicar smiled a question—okay to go on?—and he nodded.

It was as if he had the right to be here. As if he had the right to be part of the ceremony for this old dog-trainer, a man who was loved by so many.

Charlie belonged.

As Blake finally belonged.

Mardie's hand tightened on his and he knew it for truth.

It took the rest of the day before he found some time alone with her. The wake was enormous, the pub crowded, and the day turned into an impromptu dog trial.

The football oval was taken over, hurdles, pegs, pens set up. Charlie's dogs versus Charlie's dogs.

Someone thought of a barbecue; parts of the crowd dispersed, came back with supplies. Day turned to dusk turned to dark. The stories of Charlie were legion.

Mardie moved through the crowd with Bessie. It was as if Bessie was part of who Charlie was; it was important that she stayed.

But finally only the diehards were left—old men who'd sit and remember their friend over a beer or six, Charlie's mates.

Mardie was free to leave.

Blake drove her home in her truck. His car was still up on the hill and it was likely to stay there.

There was a thumping sound in the engine. Ominous. He might need to do something about that.

He would. He'd put it on his list. His list for after he'd asked what he needed to ask.

Once again, there was silence in the truck, but it was different. Peace. Acceptance.

The beginning of joy?

He pulled up in the yard. They climbed out, the dogs jumping wearily down after them and heading straight inside, to their basket by the fire. Side by side again.

Joined at the heart.

Like him and this woman by his side.

Mardie let them in and then turned. Blake was right behind her. Close.

Watching her in the moonlight.

'I'm glad you came back,' she said simply.

'I should never have left.'

'You had to leave,' she said softly. 'You know, if you'd told me about Robbie, I would have understood. I understand now how important it was to you. How important it is.'

'It was a process,' he said simply. 'Something I had to work through. Something that started when I was seven, went full circle, then came back to you.'

She stilled, except her heart hadn't stilled. Her heart was hammering as if it might explode.

'You've come back?'

'I love you, Mardie,' he said simple and true. 'Like you… I've loved you all the time without stopping. Things got in the way. I couldn't get perspective. But now…'

'Now?'

'The funeral today,' he said. 'Hundreds of dogs, a funeral procession for one old man. A pilot's wife weeping over a plate. Raff, looking after his community. Harry and Riley at North Coast Rescue. You're all doing what you do, what you love to do, what makes you happy. But you don't destroy yourself in the process.'

'Is that what you've been doing?'

'No,' he said sharply. 'I left here when I was seventeen, and yes, I felt like a martyr then. Heading off to make up for my brother's life. But it changed. It became a passion, a love all on its own. It was only when I couldn't do it any more that shock and illness and a lack of perspective made me go back to the martyr bit.' He reached out and took her hands. 'It took one dog. One dog and one beautiful woman. It took my best friend, Mardie Rainey, to set me right.'

'So…' She was scarcely able to breathe. 'So you're set right now?'

'I have a plan.'

'A plan…'

'It's in its infancy,' he said. 'A bud of a plan. It needs work. It needs an artist to tweak the edges. But you want to hear?'

How could he doubt it? Her face must have answered for her.

'I teach online,' he said simply. 'I'd like to expand that. Medics in remote areas… I'm learning to use Skype so I can talk doctors through procedures. Video links. There's so much. If I stay in the one place, I can be connected all over the world.'

'You'd…be happy with that?'

'No,' he said. 'Not completely. So I will accept Riley and Harry's job offer. Three days a week they do their Outback clinics and they'll fly via here. I can work with them. I can still make a difference. I might,' he added diffidently, 'need to go overseas a couple of times a year, to conferences, to teaching clinics and to keep in touch with the foundation. I can still do fund-raising. And…if you wanted to…you could come with me.'

'Come with you?'

'Not to be taken up with my life,' he said. 'Not to follow my passion. But to follow your own. There'd be things you could do, techniques you could learn. We could learn together. We could…'

He paused. Thought about it.

Dropped to one knee.

'We could marry,' he said.

'Blake…' The whole world held its breath.

'I offered you diamonds,' he said simply. 'In Sydney. It was a stupid, crass thought, nothing more. And you know what? Tonight I don't even have a diamond. I've come unprepared. All I have to offer…' He shrugged. 'No. I don't have anything to offer, Mardie, but I do love you. All I have to offer is my love. I want to share your life. I want to be a part of your life. I love you, I want you, and I want to come home.'

And Mardie stared down at him and felt so much love that she must surely be dreaming.

He was waiting for her to answer. A girl had to think of something.

'So no diamond, huh?' she said cautiously.

'I… No. I can get one, but…'

'And an ancient rust bucket of a car that's still stuck on the hill overlooking Banksia Bay cemetery.'

'I guess…' He sounded confused.

'And the mere possibility—not even confirmed—of a part-time job. Part-time? Haven't you heard the saying? For better or worse but not for lunch.'

'I could…I don't know…take a packed lunch down the paddock every lunchtime. Bounce and I have some learning to do. That could be Bessie's teaching time.'

'So you wouldn't be underfoot?'

'Not very much.'

'But you want to stay here?'

'Wherever you are,' he said simply. 'That's where I want to be, for the rest of my life.' Deep breath. 'Mardie, love, I don't want to hurry you, but this veranda's hard.'

'Is it?' She dropped on her knees before him. 'Oh, yes, so it is. You think we should put some padding on it?'

She sounded hysterical, she thought. She felt hysterical.

He took her hands in his. Hysteria faded.

'No padding,' he said. 'Just a fast answer. Yes or no. Mardie Rainey, I love you with all my heart. I want to be part of your life and I want you to be part of my life, for ever and ever. So there's no ring. I'll buy you one in the future but for now it's just me. Just me, Mardie, nothing else. No shadows. No regrets. Just us. Mardie Rainey, my love, my heart, will you be my wife?'

And she looked into his dear face, the face she'd grown with, the face she'd loved once and loved for ever.

Her Blake.

Her past and her future.

Her best friend.

Hysteria was gone. Doubts were gone—there was nothing but Blake.

'Why, yes, Blake Maddock,' she whispered, 'I believe I will.'

'He's home, too,' Blake said with deep satisfaction.

A simple ceremony on a driveway into a Banksia Bay farm. A driveway lined with ancient gum trees. A man and a woman, husband and wife, with their two dogs pressed together beside them.

The Banksia Bay vicar presiding.

Robbie's ashes had lain in a memorial wall for twenty-five years. Blake had hated them there, so now they'd brought him home, to a place where an ancient gum had once stood, a tree with linked initials, split in the storm.

Robbie's ashes were now scattered in the sunlight, on the earth around a sapling already reaching for the sky.

'No carving,' Blake said sternly to Mardie.

'Not me,' she said virtuously. 'But our children might not be into rules.'

The vicar frowned them down. This was a serious business. He read the blessing and then he smiled.

'This is a good thing to do,' he decreed as he gazed out over the farmland to the sea beyond. He'd heard the simple story and he approved. Now he motioned to the bump Mardie was proudly carrying under her smock. 'The bairn…if it's a boy, will you name him Robbie?'

'She's a girl,' Blake said, hugging his wife close. 'Already confirmed and her name's Oriane. It means dawn.'

'Lovely,' the vicar said, beaming. 'For I don't believe in looking back more than we need. Love continues. As for the rest… The past can get in the way of the future.'

Then he glanced at his watch. 'Speaking of the future, I must go.'

'So must we,' Blake said, smiling and clicking his fingers for the two dogs to join them. 'We have dog trials this afternoon. Today, my wife thinks her dog, Bounce, will beat my dog, Bessie, at the Whale Cove Sheepdog Trials. She's dreaming.'

'He'll do it,' Mardie said. 'If not this month, then next.'

'Only because Bessie needs to retire next month. We're having pups,' he told the vicar. 'Babies all over the place. But, pregnant or not, she'll still beat any dog, hands down. Our Bessie's brilliant.'

'We're all brilliant,' Mardie said. Smiling and smiling. 'Together we can do anything.' She hugged her husband and he hugged her back.

'We can do anything we want,' she said simply. 'Together we're home.'

* * * * *

THE BOY IS BACK IN TOWN

BY
NINA HARRINGTON

Nina Harrington grew up in rural Northumberland and decided at the age of eleven that she was going to be a librarian—because then she could read *all* of the books in the public library whenever she wanted! Since then she has been a shop assistant, community pharmacist, technical writer, university lecturer, volcano walker and industrial scientist, before taking a career break to realise her dream of being a fiction writer. When she is not creating stories which make her readers smile, her hobbies are cooking, eating, enjoying good wine—and talking, for which she has had specialist training.

CHAPTER ONE

MARIGOLD CHANCE scrolled through the images on her digital camera with her thumb, and cringed. Of all the crimes against photography she had ever committed for her sister Rosa, of which there had been many, the past few hours had been a low point.

Mari might be forgiven for the portrait of the dry cleaner's miniature dachshund in a cute beaded princess sweater, or even the popcorn-puff hooded jacket Rosa had made for the hairdresser's Pekinese. But persuading the newsagent's fox terrier to pose with a knitted plaid waterproof raincoat with the name 'Lola' in gold chain stitch on the back was the last straw.

Her sister Rosa had a lot to answer for.

'Oh, you are such a genius.' Rosa grabbed the sleeve of Mari's coat and squealed so loudly that two elderly ladies in the street looked across in alarm. Mari gave them a smile and a small wave with the hand that was not firmly in the fierce grip of her sister, the budding internet entrepreneur, who was wrestling to see the back of the camera.

'Lola looks amazing. You see? I knew it would be useful to have an IT expert in the family one day. You told me how important it was to have great visuals on the website you made for me and now I have. It was hard work but so worth it.'

Mari snorted in reply and lifted the camera out of her sister's reach. 'You spent most of the time lying on the floor playing with the puppy and feeding her treats. I was the one doing the hard work.'

Rosa waggled her fingers at her dismissively. 'What can I say? Some of us are blessed with the creative touch. Animal models are hard to find in the world of Swanhaven pet fashion and Lola wasn't too keen on posing for more than a few seconds. I think bribery is acceptable in the circumstances. After all, it's not often my big sister has a chance to be a fashion photographer for the day. The least I could do was sacrifice my dignity in the name of your future career. You might need that extra line on your résumé one day soon.'

Mari sighed and gave her head a quick shake. 'I should never have told you that my department is laying off technical staff. I'm fine. *Seriously.* There are lots of hardware engineers who want to take the package and do other things with their lives, but not me. I love what I'm doing and don't plan to change any time soon.'

'Um…fine. Right. Is that why you were looking for IT jobs around Swanhaven on the internet this morning?'

'Hey!' Mari play poked Rosa in the arm. 'Were you spying on me, young lady? I can see behind that sweet innocent face, you know.' Mari paused for a moment and decided to give Rosa a half version of the truth. 'I wanted to compare the freelance rates in Dorset compared to California, that's all,' she replied with a smile and shrug. 'Things have certainly changed a lot in the years since I last lived here. Apparently there's Wi-Fi in the yacht club. Could this really be possible?'

And the moment the words had left her mouth, Mari instantly felt guilty about not telling her only sister the full truth. But she couldn't reveal her secret just yet, no matter how much she was looking forward to seeing the look on Rosa's face when she broke the news that she was buying back their childhood home. Rosa had been inconsolable when their little family of women had been evicted from the home where they'd once been so happy, and Mari knew how much she'd wanted to live there again.

But she couldn't even hint that the house could be theirs until she was certain that everything was in place.

Rosa was sensitive enough to pick up that Mari was worried about her job security and with good reason. Mari Chance had been the provider in this family since the age of sixteen, when their father had left and their mother floundered in grief and despair.

It had been Mari's decision to sacrifice her dreams of university so that she could leave school as soon as she could to work for a local business and become the breadwinner for Rosa and their mother. And she felt even more responsible now that Rosa was on her own and she had a high-flying job with a salary to make sure that Rosa was taken care of. Even if it did mean that they were apart—her sister had to come first before anything that Mari wanted in her own life.

Rosa was the only person in Mari's life who she truly trusted but this was one time when she wasn't ready to open up and share her fears and dreams for the future. She had worked too hard to give Rosa hope, only to see it replaced with bitter disappointment.

Luckily her sister was distracted by a lovely spaniel who dared to be out in the cold air without one of her knitted coats and, spotting a potential customer, Rosa pulled Mari closer and whispered, 'See you back at the cottage. I'm on a mission. Bye for now. Oh—and thanks again for the photographs. I knew I could rely on you. We'll talk more later.' And with that, she released Mari all in a rush and scampered off in the direction of the spaniel, her hand already in her pocket looking for dog treats.

'You're welcome, sweetie,' Mari replied in a low whisper nobody was going to hear as she watched Rosa laugh and smile with the spaniel's lady owner. 'You know you can always rely on me.'

Marigold Chance was never the girl called for sports teams or talent contests. She'd left that to her brilliant older brother Kit and her little sister Rosa. Both extroverts to the core. No, Mari was the person who'd stayed in the background and made the teas and watched the other people having fun. Usually at events she had organised and made happen. Every family needed a Mari to keep things working behind the scenes to make sure that everyone was safe and well and had what they needed. No matter how great the personal cost.

Especially in times of crisis when the whole world fell apart.

Mari shrugged off a shiver of sad memories, turned the corner and started down the narrow cobbled street towards the harbour, and was rewarded by the sight she never grew tired of—Swanhaven bay stretched out in front of her.

The sea was a wide expanse of dove-grey, flecked by bright white foam as the waves picked up in the icy wind. A bright smile warmed Mari's face despite the cold. Swanhaven harbour had been built of granite blocks designed to protect the fishing fleet from the harsh English Channel. Now the long wide arms held more pleasure craft than local fishermen, but it was still a safe harbour and delightful marina which attracted visitors all year round, even on a cold February afternoon.

But that was not where she wanted to go before the early winter darkness fell. There was somewhere very special she wanted to visit now she was free for the rest of the day. The one place that meant more to her and Rosa than anywhere else in the world. She could hardly wait to see her old home again. Snow or no snow. Nothing was going to stop her now. Nothing at all.

'Well, you know what your father's like. Once he gets an idea in his head, nothing is going to stop him.' His mother chuckled down Ethan Chandler's cellphone, her voice faint and in snatches as it was carried away in the blustery wind. 'He's out by the pool at the moment and quite determined to experiment with all of the fancy extras on his new barbecue, even if we are in the middle of a mini heatwave. Which reminds me. How *is* the weather in Swanhaven at the moment?'

Ethan Chandler took a firm grip with his other hand on the tiller of the small sailing boat he had hired from the Swanhaven sailing school and let the fresh wind carry the light boat out from his private jetty into deeper water before answering. A spray of icy sea water crashed over the side of the boat and he moved the phone closer towards his mouth and under the shelter of his jacket.

'You'll be delighted to know that at the moment it is grey, wet and windy. And cold. Cold by Florida standards at least. You're going to freeze next week.'

Her reply was a small sigh. 'I did wonder. I remember only too well what February can be like. But don't you worry. Your father and I wouldn't miss seeing our new holiday home for anything. We are so proud of you, Ethan.'

Ethan inhaled a slow calming breath. *Proud?* Proud was the last thing his parents should be.

Far from it.

Apart from a couple of one-to-one sailing classes he had run as a personal favour to his old mentor at the Swanhaven Yacht Club, he had made it his business to keep out of sight and hide away at the house. The work that needed to be done was an excellent excuse for not socialising in the town but, the truth was, in a small town like Swanhaven, people had long memories. Ten years was nothing, and Kit Chance still had a lot of family in the area and the weight of the accident which killed Kit had become heavier and heavier the longer he stayed here.

Proud? No. The minute his parents were settled, he would be on the first flight back to Florida.

Luckily his mother did not give him a chance to reply. 'And how are you managing at the house on your own?'

Ethan turned his head back towards the shore and enjoyed a half smile at the sight of the stunning one-storey home which hugged the wooded hillside on one side and the wide curve of the inlet on the other. Now that was something he *could* be proud of.

It was a superb location. Quiet, private and secluded

but only ten minutes drive to Swanhaven, which lay around the headland in the next bay, and even faster by boat. Perfect.

'Everything's fine. I'm just heading out now to Swanhaven to pick up some groceries. But don't worry, Mum. The team have done a great job and it will all be ready for next weekend.' *I hope.*

'That's wonderful, darling. You've been so secretive these past few months; I can hardly wait to see what you've done with the place. And don't you worry about your father. I know he was reluctant at first to let you manage the project, but you know how hard it is for him to hand over control of anything to anybody. He's so pleased that you agreed to finish off the work for us. We both are. Who knows? With a bit of luck your father might actually start slowing down and think about retirement one day soon.'

Ethan fought down a positive reply but the words stuck in his throat.

It had taken a few years before his parents understood that their only son had no interest in becoming the fourth generation architect in Chandler and Chandler, Architects. Ethan had no intention of spending his life in an air-conditioned office looking out on the ocean when he could be on the waves himself, pushing himself harder and harder. He felt sorry to let them down but they eventually accepted the fact that he had his own life to lead and they had supported him as best they could.

The least he could do was come over to Swanhaven and finish off their retirement home for them. It was ironic that his mother had chosen to come back to Swanhaven of all places, but she had grown up in the area and they had some happy memories of the summers they spent here before the accident which changed all of their lives. His most of all.

They had talked about Swanhaven many times and he knew that, although his mother loved this bay, they had chosen not to come back here because of the accident and how he felt about it.

But now they were ready to move on and this house was a symbol of that.

And if they could cope with having a holiday home here, then he would have to learn to live with that. It was the moving part that he had a problem with. But that was his problem, not theirs, and there was no way he was going to spoil his mother's delight in her new house.

'Good luck with that one, Mum. If anyone can do it, you can.'

'Well, thank you for that vote of confidence. Oh, I'm now being called to ogle some gizmo or gadget. Keep safe, darling. And see you next Saturday. Keep safe.'

Keep safe. That was what she used to say at the dockside before he set out on a dangerous sea journey. They were always her final words. Only a year ago they had been squeezed out through tears when he left for the Green Globe round-the-world race. Now he could hear warmth and an almost casual tone in her voice through the broken reception.

So much had changed. Now she was saying it before a short shopping trip across the bay to Swanhaven, not months spent alone battling the most treacherous oceans in the world where a simple mistake could cost him the boat or his life. Or both. Where he could be out of contact with the world for hours. Perhaps days.

Now she could call him from the kitchen of their lovely Florida home and know precisely where he would be for at least six months of the year. Safe and out of harm's way. Running sailing courses at the international yacht club where troubled teenagers from all over the state could receive the help they needed to rebuild their lives.

And she was happier than he had seen her for a long time.

How could she understand that he had chosen to abandon his comfortable car in Swanhaven and come out in wild wet weather in a boat which was smaller than the one he used to have as a boy, just to feel the wind and the spray? To sense the reaction of the rudder under his hand as the tiny sail stretched out to the fullest it had probably ever seen as he angled the craft into the wind at just the perfect inclination to squeeze every drop of speed.

He knew this stretch of water like the back of his own hand. Kit had shown him where the currents lay over shallow water and the best place to turn into the wind so that they could practice how to use the sails.

Ethan smiled to himself and shifted the tiller just a little more. Just seeing this part of the bay again on his first day had brought back so many fine memories, and some sad ones. Those summers spent sailing every day with Kit Chance had been some of the happiest times of his life. And he still missed him.

Over the past year or two his mother had dropped not so subtle questions about when he planned to stop pushing himself harder and harder with each yacht race. He had always laughed it off. But she had a point. Maybe there was more to life than competitive sailing? But he had not found it yet. Teaching kids to sail for a few months a year had done nothing to lessen his need to be at the helm of a boat, on his own, testing the boundaries, running faster and faster. But it was a start.

Kit would have loved it. But he couldn't. Because he had died in a freak accident nobody could have predicted or prevented. And Ethan had survived. The burden of that guilt still lay heavy on his shoulders. Especially in this town where Kit had grown up. So far he had managed to keep a low profile and focus on the work at hand.

Ethan shrugged the tension away from his shoulders.

He had seven days to finish the house before his parents flew into London, then he would get back to honouring Kit in the only way he knew how. By sailing to the max and teaching young people how to live their lives to the full, just as Kit had done.

With a bit of luck his parents might actually like what he had done. Especially when they found out that he had made a couple of alterations to the original plans. Instead of an extended parking area, Ethan had built a solid garage, workshop, boathouse and jetty. These were his personal gifts to his parents. And particularly his father.

Maybe, just maybe, they could find the time to sail out on their own boat together from their private jetty, like they used to, when he came back in July to make good his promise to open the Swanhaven regatta.

Now that was something worth looking forward to.

A squall of icy sleet hit Ethan straight in the face and he roared with laughter and dropped his head back in joy. That was more like it. Bring it on. Bring. It. On.

* * *

Marigold Chance thrust her hands deep inside the pockets of her thick padded down coat and braced herself against the freezing wind, which was whipping up the sand onto the path that led away from Swanhaven and out past the marina and jetty to the wild part of the Dorset shoreline.

Leaving the village behind, she walked as fast as she could to get warm, her target already in sight. A slow winding path started on the shore then rose slowly up and onto the grassy banks onto the low chalk hills which became cliffs at the other end of the bay.

Steps had been cut into the cliff face from the beach, but Mari paused and closed her eyes for a moment before she stepped forward, desperate to clear her head and try to relieve the throbbing headache which had been nagging at the back of her neck for the past twenty-four hours.

This part of the beach was made up of pebbles which had been smoothed by the relentless action of the waves back and forth to form fine powder sand in places and large cobblestones in others. It had been snowing when she arrived in Swanhaven and the air was still cold enough to keep the snow in white clumps on top of the frozen ice trapped between the stones at the top end of the beach where she was walking. The heavy winter seas carried with them pieces of driftwood and seaweed that floated in the cold waters of a shipping lane like the English Channel.

For once Mari was glad to feel the cold fresh wind buffeting her cheeks as she snuggled low inside the warm coat, a windproof hat pulled well down over her ears.

The relentless pressure of her job as a computer systems trouble-shooter was starting to get to her, but exhaustion came with the job and it was all worth it. In a few years she would be able to start her own business and work from home as an internet consultant. With modern technology, she could work from home and run an online internet advisory business from anywhere in the world, and that included Swanhaven. This small coastal town where she had spent the first eighteen years of her life was where she wanted to make a life and create a stable, long-standing home, safe and warm, for herself and Rosa. A home nobody could take away from her. From either of them.

Mari inhaled slowly to calm her breathing and focused on the sound of the seagulls calling above her head, dogs barking on the shore and the relentless beat of the waves.

She could still hear the flap of the pennants on the boats in the marina and the musical sound of the wind in the rigging of the sailing boats.

This was the soundtrack of her early life, which had stayed with her no matter where she might be living and working. Here she could escape the relentless cacophony of cars, aircraft engines, noisy air conditioning and frantic telephone calls in the middle of the night from IT departments whose servers had crashed. In her shoulder bag there were three smartphones and two mobile phones. But right now, for one whole precious hour, she had turned everything off.

And it was bliss. Her breathing tuned into the rhythm of the ebb and flow of the waves on the shore and for a fraction of a second she felt as though she was a girl again and she had never left Swanhaven.

Sailing and the sea had formed a fundamental part

of her childhood. She loved the sea with a passion. She knew how cruel it could be, but there was no finer place in the world. And Kit would understand that.

Turning her back to the wind, Mari slipped the glove from her left hand and reached into the laptop bag she carried everywhere. Her fingers touched a precious photograph and she carefully drew it out of the bag, holding tightly so that it would not be snatched away in the gusty wind. It was only right that she should look at this photograph here of all places, even though it had been around the world with her more than once. Not like Kit's best friend Ethan Chandler, on the deck of some horrendously expensive racing yacht, battling the ocean for his very life, but inside a bag which went into the cabins of aircraft and hotel rooms and even restaurants and offices and computer server rooms.

The smiling face of her mother looked back at her from the photograph. She was a tall, slim, pretty woman with freckled skin illuminated by the sunlight reflected back from the water in the sunny harbour of Swanhaven. One of her arms was draped around Rosa's shoulders. Rosa must have been about fourteen then and so full of life and fun and energy. Her baby sister was always ready to smile into the camera without a hint of embarrassment or hesitation. But this time Rosa and her mother had something to laugh about—because they were watching Kit playing the fool. As always. Seventeen years old and full of mischief, Kit was their hero, full of life and energy and funny, handsome and charming—everyone loved him, and he was indulged and spoiled. Kit would not sit still for a moment, always jumping about, always wanting to be in the action, especially when it came to the water and sailing.

Mari remembered the day she'd taken the photograph so well. It was the Easter holiday and the sailing club had been open for a training day. Of course Kit was the instructor, yet again, but he was not content to simply smile for his younger sister, but had to leap forward onto one knee and wave jazz hands at her, which, of course, made Rosa and her mother laugh even louder. This was her happy family she loved, so natural and so unrehearsed. Just a typical shot of a mum having fun with her three kids on a trip to the marina.

Looking at the image now, she could almost feel the sun on her face and the wind in her hair on that April morning when she'd captured the precious moment in time when they'd all been so happy together. It was hard to believe that she had taken the photograph only a few months before the yacht race in the annual Swanhaven Sailing Regatta when they lost Kit in a freak accident and the thin fabric of safe, loving little family was ripped apart.

He had been the golden boy. The much-loved only son.

Oh, Kit. She missed him so much, like a physical ache that never truly went away, but somehow over the years she had learned to push it to the back of her mind so that she could survive every day, though the pain of the loss was still there. Coming back to Swanhaven, and seeing the boats in the marina and young people finding such joy in the water, brought back all of those happy memories so vividly.

They had been such good times with her family all around her.

Mari ran her fingertip down her mother's face on the photograph, just as the wind picked up and almost whipped it away, and she popped it back into her bag, made sure that it was safe and pulled on her gloves as quickly as she could.

Perhaps she was not as ready to see her old home as she thought she was? It had been her mother's dream that one day she should be able to buy back the home she had loved so very much, but she'd died before Mari could help to make that dream come true. And it broke Mari's heart to think that she had let her down when they had come so close to making it a reality.

But she still had Rosa to take care of, so she drove herself to work harder and longer to help her sister, no matter what the cost to her own dreams of running her own business.

Turning away from the cliff, Mari faced the wild buffeting wind from the sea and skipped down the path back onto the shore, walking faster and faster along the rough large boulders, sliding on the wet surface, squelching against kelp seaweed, until she was at the end of the jetty and in front of her was the curving bay and the rising cliffs of chalk towering above in the distance.

She took a couple of steps further along the beach and there it was, the low dip in the cliff made by a small river and the sloping grassy bank and the winding path from the shore which led to the cottages where they used to live. Bracing herself, Mari lifted her head, back to the wind, and looked up towards the houses she could see quite clearly now. At this distance, the aged and weathered old roofs blocked the view of the actual house itself, but she could see a large placard from the local estate agent announcing that the house was soon to be sold by auction and the contact details. She had talked to the elderly couple who owned it a few times, but they had not been interested in selling. Until now, when a broken hip had forced them to move into the village.

Tears pricked her eyes and she wiped them away with the finger of her glove. Cold wind and regret assaulted her eyes. But her mouth sheltered a secret smile.

It had taken years of working nights, weekends and public holidays for the extra salary she needed to build up savings but she had finally done it this week after her bonus for working over the whole Christmas and New Year holiday had been paid. It was hard to believe that she finally had enough for the deposit she needed to buy back the house their father had built brick by brick. This was probably the only chance she would have to make this house a home again for herself and her sister, where they could live and work side by side one day.

Other people had social lives. Lovely homes and designer clothing. Even boyfriends. Instead, Mari Chance had become the 'go to' single girl who was willing to work when her colleagues spent precious holiday time with their families. Promotion after promotion had meant travelling to some far-flung parts of the world at a moment's notice. But she did it. And most of the time she loved her work. Loved the idea that she could arrive at a business office where the staff were panicking and walk out with the IT system working perfectly. That was deeply satisfying. Besides, she did not have any personal commitments, not even a pet. But all that travel came with a price.

The crushing loneliness.

And now the one thing she had been dreaming about for the last three years was finally going to happen—it was so close, she could almost feel it. Everything was ready. She had the funds, her place at the auction had been booked, and she knew the going rate for the property from recent sales figures.

This was the house she had been born in. The house she had loved and been so happy in, and now she could make the offer—in cash and above the expected price with a loan facility already agreed at the bank, if the price was higher than she had budgeted for.

She had to have this house.

She had to.

This was where her travelling and relentless activity and exhausting work was finally going to come to an end. This was where she was going to spend the rest of her life. Building a routine with Rosa in the place where she had grown up with extended family all around her. She was ready to come home to Swanhaven.

At that moment an icy blast ran up inside Mari's coat and a deep shiver crossed her shoulders and down her back, making her stamp her feet and clap her hands together to restore some circulation. Time to get back to hot tea and toasted crumpets—Rosa's favourites. She could come back and see the house any time she wanted—but perhaps not today.

Indulging in a brief smile and a final lingering look, Mari turned back into the wind as she strolled back towards the marina and the stone terraced cottage Rosa had made her own. Instantly Mari's eyes were drawn to a small sailing boat which was coming towards the jetty from the west. It was the only boat on the sea and was too small to have crossed the Channel so it could not have come very far.

For a moment Mari wondered who was brave enough,

or foolish enough, to be sailing in open waters on a day like this. Icy blustery wind and grey skies did not equate in her mind to a pleasant sailing experience. She continued walking, her head angled down against the wind, but she could not miss the small craft as it came closer and closer towards the shore and the safety of a berth in the sheltered marina. She walked swiftly to try and get warm but, even with her fast pace the stiff wind in the small white sail sped the light craft faster than she could walk.

It was coming in too fast. Much too fast. The closer she got to the marina, the faster the boat came towards her. He had not even lowered the sail and, oh, no, the crosswind was gusting now across the entrance to the marina. There was no way this boat could stop itself from being smashed against the jetty or the stone breakwater of the marina.

No! She had to do something. Shout. Call for help.

Mari looked frantically around—but there was nobody close enough to hear her call and the wind would snatch away any chance of being heard in the town.

The cellphone was useless—the lifeboat would never come out in time. There were only seconds to spare before the boat collided with the dock.

She started jogging, running for the shore, waving her arms above her head, trying frantically to attract the attention of the sailor, who seemed to be totally oblivious to the danger he was in. Mari was shouting now, over and over, 'Watch out, watch out,' but the words were flung back into her face by the bitterly cold winds which attacked her cheeks and eyes so that she could hardly see with the tears of winter blurring her vision. Her hat was long gone, blown away in the wind.

Her heart was beating so fast that she thought she was going to pass out. Heaving lungfuls of cold air tipped with icy sleet, she reached the edge of the water and had to bend over at the waist, a hand on each knee, not daring to watch as the small boat was tossed violently from side to side like a plastic bath toy.

She knew exactly what was going to happen next and the horror of what was to come filled her mind. She could not watch.

Her face screwed up in pain, ready for the terrible sound of the hull smashing against the jetty, her hands ready to press against her ears to block out the horror and the cries of anguish from the lone sailor. Eyes closed, she knew what was coming and yet felt so powerless to prevent it that the horror of the moment washed over her with a cold shiver which ran across her shoulders and down her back.

She waited and the seconds seemed to stretch into minutes.

And then the minutes grew longer. And all she could hear was the smashing of the waves on the shore and the screeching of the herring gulls as they swooped down into the harbour in the wind.

Slowly, slowly, hardly daring to look, Mari lifted her head and pushed herself to a standing position.

Just in time to see a tall sailor step off his boat onto the jetty, coil the rope around a bollard on the pontoon one-handed and use his other hand to rake his fingers from his forehead back through his hair as if the wind had made a nuisance of itself by messing up his hairstyle.

The sail was down and neatly wrapped, the boat was perfectly aligned in a berth in calm waters and the sailor looked so composed he might have just stepped from a cruise ship on a lazy summer afternoon.

Stunned and totally bewildered, Mari could only watch in amazed silence as the man double-checked the rope, glanced at his watch and then turned around to stroll casually away from her down the walkway which led back to the town. And just for a second she saw his face for the first time.

Her heart missed a beat.

Ethan Chandler was back in town.

CHAPTER TWO

MARI lifted her head so she could look at Ethan again, just to make sure that she was not mistaken, except this time with her mouth half open in shock.

But of course it was him. Nobody else came even close to Ethan in looks or ability. He had sailed on his own around the world non-stop! Little wonder that he could moor a small boat on a floating pontoon in an English winter.

Ethan… She was looking at Ethan Chandler.

A bolt of energy hit her hard in the stomach and punched the air from her lungs. The blast was so physical that Mari clutched hold of the edge of the stone wall of the marina with both hands to stop herself from sliding onto her knees. Frozen with shock.

She could not believe this was happening. It had to be some sort of crazy nightmare brought on by lack of sleep and far too much caffeine and wine last night over dinner with Rosa.

There was nothing else to explain it.

The man-boy she had last seen ten years ago looking back at her from the backseat of his father's car as they drove out of Swanhaven, leaving her behind, clinging to the wreckage of her life, was blocking her way back into town. Mari sucked in oxygen to feed her racing brain and the frantic pulsing of blood.

This must be what it felt like to have a heart attack.

The last person on the planet she had expected to see again was dressed in chinos and a pale blue shirt, under a luxurious all-weather jacket the colour of the smoothest latte.

Ethan Chandler. International Yachtsman of the Year. The boy whose family had rented the house next to her home each summer holiday and in the process became part of Swanhaven and the star of the sailing club for a few weeks and her home town's only true claim for a celebrity. The village shop even sold bottles of the delectable designer aftershave he'd promoted a few years earlier.

The stylist who had chosen his shirt had done an excellent job and that particular shade of blue was a perfect match for the colour of his eyes, even in the grey February light which took the edge off a suntan cultivated under the Florida sunshine.

At the age of seventeen Ethan Chandler had been the best-looking boy in town. A natural athlete and champion yachtsman destined for greatness. Ethan at twenty-eight was a revelation. Of course she had seen his photo on TV and on the cover of magazines, clean and polished and with all of his rough edges smoothed out to create the perfect image. Male-model handsome, rugged and broad-shouldered.

But there was a world of difference between seeing Ethan standing behind the wheel of an ocean-going yacht, or modelling board shorts on the cover of a sailing magazine, and having the man himself standing so close that she could see the stubble on his cheek on the side of his face.

Ethan had always had that cocky and easy confidence in his own charm—but this was taking it to a completely new level. Six feet of broad-shouldered, tousle-haired hunk could do that to a girl.

The blood rushing to her cheeks and neck was so embarrassing. And Marigold Chance did not blush. Ever.

And then, almost as if he knew that someone was watching him, Ethan stopped walking, paused, and started to turn around to look in her direction.

Instantly, without thinking about what she was doing or hesitating more than a split second, Mari pulled the hood of her coat high over her head and whirled on one heel so quickly that she was walking back the way she had come along the beach path before her hands were back by her sides, punching the air with each step.

Determined to get as far away from Ethan Chandler as possible.

Grains of sand flew up beneath her feet as she strode forward, too terrified to look back just in case Ethan had recognised the crazy woman power walking along the beach. Her head was spinning with a confusion of thoughts and feelings. Some deep part of her was secretly hoping that he had seen her, and he was even now running to catch up with her, ready to calm her nerves and tell her that he'd never meant to hurt her feelings all those years ago when they had kissed and he had walked away without a single word of goodbye.

But that would mean that he had cared about her back then. And still did. This was impossible.

No. Ethan was always destined to be her brother's

unobtainable best friend and the boy who'd survived the accident when Kit had not.

Her feet slowed but her heart was pounding inside her chest and she felt the blood flare in her face despite the icy-cold wind from the sea. A few more steps and she would be around the corner of the bay and out of sight from Swanhaven marina. And Ethan would not be able to see her tears.

Mari's left hand pressed against the damp cliff wall.

After all these years, she had fooled herself into thinking that she had finally come to terms with Kit's death.

Idiot.

All it took was one sight of Ethan—not even a word—just seeing him again, and she was right back to being sixteen again and those terrible few months after the accident when all she wanted to do was be alone. Grieving, scared, frozen and numb and so very alone. Trapped inside her thoughts, withdrawn and traumatised.

Only one person had been able to challenge her enough to break through the prison doors of her anguish and that person was Ethan. He had done something no one had ever done. He had kept challenging, kept on asking her forgiveness, kept on forcing her to engage with him, until her self-imposed barriers had finally broken down. And for one hour of one day she had clung to Ethan like a drowning girl with every single emotion raw and open and exposed for him to see. This was the boy who had made her brother go out in a race he was not ready for. This was the boy who had teased her and ridiculed her every summer holiday. This was the boy she had secretly had a crush on, but said nothing. Because he was so perfect, so admirable and so very, very unobtainable.

And in that moment when she had been most vulnerable, he had kissed her. And she had kissed him back. And she might have been sixteen, and this was her first kiss, but she knew that he meant it.

And it had destroyed her.

The guilt of kissing and wanting Ethan after he had brought about her family's ruin had been too much for her to bear. She had felt so weak and angry and disgusted with herself.

When he'd left town the following day, without even saying goodbye, she knew that she had deluded herself into thinking that Ethan could ever care about her. She wasn't even worth taking the time to speak to.

Mari closed her eyes and took a couple of long breaths. She was twenty-six years old, a trained IT professional and an adult who was used to handling computer crises. Ethan was probably only passing through with his parents. She could cope with seeing him again over the next few days before she went back to work. It was all going to be fine. Just fine.

Only at the exact same moment she allowed herself to breathe normally, there was the sound of footsteps on the cobblestones and sand and, as she turned her head sideways, Ethan Chandler jogged around the corner.

He tried to slide to a halt on the uneven path, arms flailing at the same time as Mari pushed herself back against the wall.

So the only thing he had to grab hold of to stop himself from falling…was her.

Seconds later, Mari's brain connected to the fact that Ethan Chandler was holding her by both arms, pressing her against his jacket, and she looked up into the blue eyes of the boy who had broken her heart. Words were impossible. Mari inhaled a heady mix of aromatic spices, leather and freshly laundered linen as her own hand moved instinctively to press against the soft fabric and feel the warmth of the man beneath.

'Hello, Mari. Are you okay there? I wondered if it was you.' Ethan flicked his head back towards the shore. 'I only caught a glimpse so I couldn't be sure but… wow…I had no idea you were back in town. I…er…' he broke off as their eyes locked; it was only for a second but she knew that he had recognised the total confusion and disbelief and anger that was whirling around inside her head at seeing him again '…wasn't expecting to see you.'

His iron grip relaxed on the sleeve of her jacket and she almost fell back onto the rocks.

'Ethan,' she whispered, her voice hoarse and pathetic, 'I didn't know that you were around.'

She swallowed down an ocean of nerves into a bone-dry throat, looking for something to say to break the silence. 'That was quite a performance. I thought you were in trouble out there,' and she gestured to the waves breaking over the harbour wall.

'Trouble?' He coughed nervously and stepped back. 'No, I wasn't in trouble. I suppose it is a bit blowy.'

Mari blinked a few times and shook her head in disbelief.

'Blowy? Right. I hope you know that you scared the living daylights out of me just now. How do you do it? How do you get into that boat and go out on the water in weather like this? I simply don't understand it.'

His reply was a twitch at the side of his mouth which

told her more than a lengthy answer. Oh, yes. She had been right. The boy who had become the man was still as annoyingly arrogant and self-confident that it shone out of him like a beacon to all those around him who were still trying to find their way in the dark. And straight away she was back to being the plump, geeky girl who was the constant target of his incessant teasing.

It was so aggravating she could scream.

She was different now. She could handle this man who had become a star. They had both been so young the last time they spoke—teenagers trying to find their place in the world.

So how was it that the last time she had felt like strangling someone as badly as she did now, her client had just uploaded a virus onto the brand-new server she had just installed?

Ethan took it to the next level.

Grinding her teeth together in frustration, Mari pressed her fingers into her palms and slowly closed her eyes, then opened them while her blood pressure calmed.

'I've got used to bad weather over the past few years, and Swanhaven bay is positively calm compared to the seas in the Southern Ocean. But I'm sorry if I scared you.'

And with all of the extra confidence and self-assurance that ten years of a life spent in the spotlight and hero worship could bring, Ethan took one step closer and casually slid his left hand up and down the sleeve of her padded coat. 'Are you okay now?'

And it annoyed her so much that it sucked any chance of logical thought out of her mind, rendering her speechless. A blinking, wide-eyed creature. Just as she had been all those years ago when she'd hero-worshipped him from afar and he'd ignored her for most of the time and teased her the rest.

'You've changed your hair,' Ethan said softly, his sea-blue eyes focused on her face. He grinned the kind of white smile that would make toothpaste companies queue up to arrange sponsorship deals. 'Looks great.'

Yes, this makes my day, she thought, and found something interesting to look at on her gloves. *How dare he look even better with a few years on him? When she felt positively shop-worn and decrepit? And her hair had been squeezed under a hat for ages and must look a total mess.* For a moment she couldn't think or move. Nor trust herself to look at him again, never mind talk to him in joined up sentences.

Why did he still have this effect on her? Why? He had always had the confidence, the natural charm of the handsome, gifted people who had sailed through life on a warm breeze. And knew it. Nothing had changed in that direction.

'Thank you.' Mari cleared her throat, lifted her chin a little higher and tried to ignore her pounding heart, while forcing her mouth and head to reconnect long enough to say something intelligent when they had zero in common. 'It's been a while.'

'I was sorry to hear that your mother passed away. She was a remarkable woman,' he said in a low voice. 'I was racing solo in the Southern Ocean when it happened or I would have been there. You should know that.'

'Of course,' Mari said, desperate to take control, and managed a closed-mouth smile. 'Did you know that

Rosa is still in Swanhaven these days?' She shook her head in amazement. 'She loves being here so much. So at least one of us is still in the old town.'

Before he had a chance to answer, Mari made a point of pulling her scarf tighter so that she wouldn't have to look into those blue eyes. She was a mature woman. She could do polite to a visiting celebrity who used to be close to her family. 'What brings you here on a Friday morning in February? I thought you lived in Florida.'

'I do, but for some reason my mother has decided that she wants to retire back home in Swanhaven. So I've been building them a retirement place in the next bay,' Ethan said with the husky tone in his voice that made her very glad that she was leaning against the jetty because her knees had suddenly decided to take on the consistency of blobs of jelly. 'Dad and I designed it together but I'm here to finish the house before they move in next week.'

He was going to stay in Swanhaven for a whole week? No, no, no. How could this be happening?

Mari whipped back towards him, blinking in astonishment, and managed to link enough words together to create a sentence. 'Are you moving back here with them full-time?'

Then he smiled with his own unique, closed lips, one-side-of-his-mouth special smile. 'That would be a no. I have a life back in Florida, thanks all the same. But I'll be around for a few weeks. Things to do. Some business to take care of. Then there is the Sailing Club.'

She swallowed hard and tried to come up with something to say but was saved when the icy wind sent another shiver across her shoulders.

'Well, good luck with that. But right now I'm freezing and I promised Rosa that I wouldn't be out long. It was nice seeing you again, Ethan. Maybe we can catch up another time?'

When Swanhaven harbour freezes over.

He turned away and started strolling away from her towards the cliff path which led towards her old home and smiled back at her over one shoulder, one eyebrow raised as he gestured towards the path.

'Looks like I just got lucky. If you're heading home I'd love to catch up with Rosa again. With a bit of luck she might find me a dry crust or two to nibble on, since I'm starving. Would that be okay?'

And then he started up the cliff path, away from Swanhaven, and straight for her former home. The home which was now up for sale. The home she was going to buy back.

He carried on walking and it took a second for her brain to process what he was doing.

He didn't know. Ethan had no clue that they had lost their home when her father left the family. But she was not going to tell him the whole bitter saga. He would soon find out for himself if he stayed around—and preferably when she had gone back to work. Rosa would tell him.

Oh, Ethan. There have been a lot of changes since the last time we spoke.

Instinctively Mari took one step forward, then stopped and called out in a loud voice, 'Sorry, Ethan, you're going the wrong way. Rosa lives in the town these days. And I hear the harbour café does a great range of snacks.'

He stopped and turned back to face her, the wind ruffling his hair into a set designer's dream of rugged and his eyebrows came together in a puzzled look. 'You sold the house? I thought your mother loved that place?'

Her breath caught in her throat as it tightened in pain. *Get it over with,* she told herself. *Just tell him and you won't have to explain yourself again.*

She looked up at Ethan, who was standing, tall and proud and so bursting with life and vitality and all she could think about was that Kit should be standing there. Her lovely, wild, adventurous brother who loved to break the rules. She had lived her early life in Kit's shadow, but she would have given anything to see him smiling back at her at that moment. Alive and well and so full of energy and potential.

Instead of which, she saw Ethan Chandler. Kit's best friend. The boy who was sailing the boat on the morning Kit went over the side and died. And it broke her heart. Worse. It broke through the veneer of suppressed anger which she had kept hidden.

'Yes, she did. Don't you know? We lost the house when my dad had his breakdown and his building firm closed down owing thousands of pounds. We haven't lived there since the summer you left. The summer Kit died. The summer we lost everything. Goodbye for now, Ethan. See you later.'

And she turned away from this god-handsome man who she had idolised as a girl and walked as fast as she could in the biting wind, back to Swanhaven and the world she had created for herself when everything around her was crumbled and destroyed.

CHAPTER THREE

'How about this one?' Mari asked as she tapped Rosa on the arm, then pointed at the laptop screen. '"Looking for a grumpy old man to nag? Try *Hire a Haggard*. Smart men aged sixty-plus. Guaranteed to last a good couple of hours if fed and watered. Dancing and friskiness at your own risk."'

Rosa put down her knitting and peered at the head and shoulders photos of older men displayed on the screen. Her face lit up with a stunned grin. 'That. Is totally perfect. I hadn't thought about renting a wrinkly. We can tell Aunt Alice that we've organised a male escort for the evening. She'll be thrilled! And at seventy-nine a man of sixty-plus has to count as a toy boy. Valentine or no Valentine.'

Mari grinned back and winked. 'I live to serve. A toy boy! I like the sound of that. Although the idea of a male escort might come as a bit of a shock to the more snooty members of the Swanhaven Yacht Club.'

'They'll survive,' Rosa sniffed. 'Besides, we only have the Valentine's Day party once a year and Aunt Alice does manage the clubhouse. It's only right and proper that she sets a fine example to the younger generation with a dapper date. Especially when my big sister has flown all the way back to Dorset especially for the big day. This calls for posh frocks. Shoes. Bags. Plastic baubles. The full works.'

She rubbed her hands together in delight, then looked hard at Mari over the top of her spectacles. 'Unless of course you have a love slave hidden in the attic of your tiny flat, but there hasn't been much evidence of that lately. Has there?'

'Guilty as charged,' Mari replied as she shut down her laptop, 'but I have been a tad busy. As well you know.'

There was a snort before her sister answered. 'Work, work. Travel, travel. What a pitiful excuse. Anyone would think that you actually preferred living in California to coming home to Swanhaven now and again.'

Mari stared back at her open-mouthed, then tutted several times before answering her baby sister. 'Perish the thought. Why do you think I booked time out for the Valentine party this weekend?' She smiled warmly before going on but her mouth closed slightly as she murmured in a lower voice, 'I do feel guilty about leaving you here on your own to clear Mum's things after the funeral. Thank you again for helping me out this last year. It hasn't been easy.'

Rosa reached across and squeezed Mari's hand before unfolding herself from her old squishy sofa and walking the few steps across to the picture window of her terraced cottage and the view down the cobbled lane towards Swanhaven harbour.

'Aunt Alice has been making an effort to persuade me to spend more time with her at the club but things haven't been the same, have they?'

Mari shuffled off the sofa and came to stare out of the window, her arm wrapped around her sister's shoulders. 'No,' she whispered. 'Not the same at all.' And they stood in silence, both gazing down towards the sea and the cliff path.

Directly across the lane was the parallel row of white-painted two-storey terraced houses which stretched down from the church and small primary school to the harbour and the yacht club, which served as the village meeting place. This was the temporary house which she had moved into with Rosa and their mother when they had to sell the home they adored. And here they still were, stuck.

'Do you know, it's almost ten years since we moved here? I still feel that I let her down, you know. About the house.'

Rosa turned and shook her head. 'That's ridiculous. Don't do that to yourself. She was so proud of your success and how hard you were working to make it happen. I have no doubt about that whatsoever and I was here with her every day. You did the right thing.'

'But I promised her, Rosa. I promised her that I would do whatever it took to get the house back for us. And she never lived to see that happen. And now our old house is finally up for sale when she's not here to enjoy it.'

'I know. But we tried. We really tried.' Pain flashed across Rosa's lovely face for a split second before she beamed across at Mari. 'Of course there is one small news item that I have been keeping from you all day and the suspense is killing me. I can't hold it in a minute longer.'

There was a groan and Mari's shoulders dropped

petulantly. 'Please, not another walk around the harbour looking for dogs without coats so you can sell your wares,' she whimpered. 'It's freezing out there! Jet lag. That's it. I still have jet lag.'

'Protest all you like, but I am determined to show off my talented computer guru of a sister to all and sundry.' Rosa moved closer to Mari. 'As far as this town goes, you are officially one of the local celebrities who have actually made good in the outside world.'

'Me? A celebrity?' Mari clutched the back of the nearest chair and pretended to faint at the idea. 'I mend company servers and design tailor-made software systems, and design websites in my spare time,' she finally managed to squeak. 'That does not make me a celebrity. Believe me, the company head office is in California and the celebrity culture is alive and well.'

'What can I say? Standards here have slipped. But not for much longer. Because there is something I have to tell you.' A cunning smirk lifted one side of Rosa's mouth and she waggled her eyebrows a couple of times before taking a breath and speaking so fast that her words all ran together. 'Ethan Chandler is back in town and I really wanted you to meet him on your own at the harbour but you haven't and he is probably going to be at the club tonight so you should know about it before you get there.'

She sucked in a deep breath, chest heaving. 'There. I'm glad I finally got that out. It's been a nightmare keeping Ethan a secret for these past few days but I was so sure that you would see him around and it would all be fine. And why are you shaking your head like that?'

Mari took hold of her sister's shoulders and forced her to make eye contact.

'I saw Ethan this afternoon on the way back from my walk. He was coming into harbour in a boat smaller than your bath tub and he frightened the living daylights out of me. There. Satisfied?'

She gave Rosa's shoulders a gentle shake before dropping her hands back onto the chair. 'What were you thinking? You should have told me.'

There was a hiss as Rosa bared her teeth. 'I know, but you were always so intense when he was around. And when Kit died…you were so hard on him, Mari. And now, with all of this media interest… Stay there; I kept the article for you.'

Rosa dived back into the living room and rooted around in a basket overflowing with yarn, knitting paraphernalia, old newspapers and unopened mail until she finally found the magazine she was looking for.

She flicked through the pages, her eyebrows tight with concentration, and then she grinned with delight and held up the page with a thumb and forefinger at each corner and waved it from side to side in front of Mari's face.

Splashed across two pages of the colour supplement of a national newspaper was a stunning photograph taken of a racing yacht in full sail on a choppy sea under hot blue skies. And standing at the helm was a tall imposing man, broad-shouldered, tanned, with handsome features and body language that screamed of total confidence in what he was doing. Ethan was wearing an impossibly clean white T-shirt with a designer logo on the breast, navy shorts and baseball cap. No shoes.

His tanned sinewy legs were spread for stability, his bright blue eyes focused on the sea in front of him, alert and intelligent, and his arms stretched out on the wheel. Mari scanned his left hand for a wedding ring without even realising what she was doing, but it was covered up with an article praising him for his work on a charity for disadvantaged teenagers.

'Isn't he dreamy?' Rosa was almost sighing with delight and swaying from side to side.

Mari breathed out slowly, blinked several times to break out of his hypnotic gaze, then peered at the page and almost snatched it from Rosa's hands. 'And you forgot arrogant, bossy and the bane of my life. As far as Ethan Chandler was concerned I was the nearest geeky girl with her head in a book who he could tease and torment whenever he pleased. And then ignore the rest of the time. Oh, yes, I certainly made a big impression on Ethan.'

Then she took a closer look at the date on the newspaper. 'Wait a minute. Ethan never lived here. He only came for the summer holidays with his parents. That hardly makes him a local.'

Rosa took the magazine back with a cough and smoothed out the page. 'His mother came from around here, which makes it close enough. Besides, his parents are building a retirement bungalow in the next bay and Ethan is certain to visit them now and again. That makes him a local as far as we are concerned. And the really good news is that he's back in town for a while working on his parents' house.'

Rosa paused and tapped one finger against her chin. 'The way I see it, it would be a very friendly gesture if *someone* would invite him to the Valentine's Day party at the yacht club. Just to welcome him back to Swanhaven, you understand. I would do it myself but, seeing as you had *such* a special relationship...well, it does point one way. And now where are you going?'

Mari wound one of Rosa's hand knitted scarves around her neck a couple of times before replying. 'Down to the harbour to clear my head. I've started to hallucinate. For a moment I thought I heard you suggest that I ask Ethan Chandler to the Valentine party. Which is obviously ridiculous. And no. We did not have a *special* relationship. Okay? I don't want to go there.'

Her fingers fumbled with the buttons on her cardigan and Rosa came over and fastened them for her. 'That was a long time ago, Mari.'

Mari swallowed down a denial but couldn't. 'I know. But it doesn't change the fact that Ethan Chandler always has to win. No matter what the risks are or who gets in his way.'

Rosa smirked in reply, then tipped two fingers to her forehead. 'He always did make you frazzle. There are plenty of girls around here who think men like that are God's special gift to women on earth because we deserve treats like Ethan now and then.'

'Ethan does not make me frazzle,' Mari chortled. 'I am a goddess, and as a goddess my special power is that I am immune to handsome men. My problems are far more to do with the sixty-five e-mails which have come in since three this afternoon, and all of them are desperately urgent.'

She glanced back at the magazine and gave Rosa a faint smile and a gentle tap on the nose to wipe away the sadness in the room. 'So let's forget about Ethan and start on the really important business of planning party outfits and organising a date for Aunt Alice, shall we?'

Rosa winced and flicked a glance up at Mari. 'Drat.

Um…there is one more *tiny* thing. I sort of promised Ethan that I would help him decorate his parents' house if he agreed to open the summer Sailing Regatta. And he said yes, thank you. More hot chocolate?'

Mari grabbed Rosa by the waist as she stood to go back to the jug warming on the hearth of her open fire. 'Oh, no, you don't. Sit. Do what your older sister tells you.'

Rosa faltered, but sat back down and looked at Mari sheepishly over the rim of her mug before shrugging a little as she replied. 'It seemed like such a good idea at the time. He was in town ordering building materials and hanging out at the yacht club just after he arrived. We got talking and it was pretty obvious that Ethan might be brilliant at carpentry and the like but he had no clue whatsoever about colour charts or layouts. So I sort of took pity of him and traded a week's work for two days of his time in July. His folks will be here over the summer and he's happy to have his photo taken for the TV cameras and the whole media circus. The publicity would be amazing. Swanhaven needs celebrities like Ethan more than ever. And the sailing club needs a boost.'

Mari sat back on the arm of the sofa, stunned. 'Rosa the interior designer? Well, this day is turning out to be full of surprises. I think I need to sit down.'

The doorbell sounded. 'Who can that be at this time of night in this weather?'

Mari stood to clear away the cups as Rosa chatted to someone at the door, then turned at the sound of footsteps.

'I can always make myself scarce if it's a customer or one of your new boyfriends,' she said, and turned to find herself staring into the chest of Ethan Chandler, who was grinning down at her.

Mari crossed her arms and glared at Ethan, stone-faced.

The sheer bulk of him seemed to fill all of the space in the cosy living room, and she had to fight the urge to step back into a corner so that she had room to breathe.

He was overwhelming in every way possible.

This was not helped by the fact that Rosa was peeking out at her from behind Ethan's shoulder and nodding with her head towards Ethan, flapping her face with her hand and fluttering her eyelids. Oh. Yes. Apparently she had to be polite. She could do polite.

'Hello, Ethan. Nice to see you again so soon. Is there anything that we can help you with?'

He bowed slightly. 'First, I just wanted to make sure that you got home safely. And secondly, the snow is still falling and I'm on my way to the clubhouse. Thirdly, I'm here to warn you that you may be accosted by the local TV station on your way out. So, if my favourite two ladies require an escort, personal security or a lift home, I am at your service.'

He raised his head and glanced around the room, inhaling appreciatively. 'And what is that fantastic smell? Blueberry muffins? Or cinnamon?'

Rosa groaned and rolled her eyes. 'Two. That's all I can spare. Blueberry and cinnamon. And I do have to get to the club early so a lift would be great.'

Ethan responded by lifting the back of Rosa's hand to his lips. 'I would be delighted to have your company.'

'Oh, you are terrible.' Rosa grinned, then looked from Ethan back to Mari, then back to Ethan again, her eyes wide. 'Dress. Coat. I'll be five minutes. Maybe ten.' With a quick nod, she turned around and fled upstairs.

There was an uncomfortable silence in the room for a few seconds, broken only by the crackling of the logs in the open fire and the ticking of the old mantle clock while Mari busied herself filling a bowl with hot water and started washing the cups, aware that Ethan had strolled up to watch what she was doing, his back against the wall.

'We have to find a way through this situation somehow, Mari. And I can't do it alone. My parents are going to be regular visitors to Swanhaven, the press are in town and I will probably visit them when they are here. Can we work together to put the past behind us? Or at least agree to a truce. Any ideas would be welcome at this point.'

'A truce?' Mari laughed with a shake of the head, then sighed. 'That is quite a concept. But I do have a few questions,' she said quietly over one shoulder.

'Anything. Just shout.'

Mari took a breath and turned to face Ethan, who was looking at her with such total focus that she felt like the most important person in his world at that moment, and wanted to squirm at the same time. 'Why has the local TV station come all this way to talk to my family and neighbours, Ethan?' she asked. 'And why are your parents flying all the way here in winter when they could stay in the sunshine in Florida? Why are you really here? I don't want my sister or this community to be dragged into some part of the Ethan Chandler Reality TV show or some major marketing campaign that we don't know about. I care too much to see it ridiculed like that. And please tell me the truth.'

Ethan's arms unfolded and he pushed one hand deep into his trouser pocket. 'Okay, I asked for that. No TV show or marketing campaign, but you are right about one thing. I've just heard that TV cameras and journalists are heading this way and are about to descend on Swanhaven. And they are all looking for exclusive interviews and feature articles.' He held up one hand. 'I did not invite them. You can blame the PR company we use for that.'

'PR company? When does a yachtsman need a PR company?'

'I frequently do,' he stated, and then his smile faded. 'But this isn't about me. It's about the sailing charity I set up just over a year ago after I got back from the Green Globe round-the-world single-handed yacht race.'

Ethan paused and licked his lips. 'I'll give you the short version. There were three captains leading the race for months. It was tight all the way. By the time we reached the Southern Ocean at the bottom of the world I was in the lead by half a day but the seas were the worst we had ever seen. Every second was a fight to stay upright.'

Mari's breath caught and she realised that she had stopped breathing.

His face was dark, eyebrows tight together. 'This was a place you don't go to unless you have to, and when you get there you stay awake for as long as it takes to get out. I still don't know what happened, but in the middle of the night I was on deck fighting a storm when my yacht hit a freak wave so hard that I went flying onto the deck. Part of my mast sheared and crashed into the cabin. I was knocked out for probably five or ten minutes and woke up with one mighty concussion and a boat that was taking in water.'

Ethan wandered over to the window, drawing back the curtains and peering down the narrow street. 'It was about as bad as I could get without sinking. And I knew it. The only good news was that my radio still worked.' His voice was softer now, as though talking to the window was easier than talking to her, but Mari could still hear the tension in his voice.

'What happened? Did the organisers launch a rescue mission?'

He nodded. 'The Australian coastguard had overall responsibility with the race organisers and they called in any commercial shipping in the area, including the other yachts in the race.'

He shook his head. 'It took six hours of some crazy sailing in which he almost damaged his boat to reach me, but my friend André was the first to arrive.' Ethan laughed low in his throat. 'I've never been so glad to see anything in my life. I managed to get into the water and across to his yacht. My boat was only fit for salvage and, by taking me onto his, André was out of the race. So we had a lot of time to talk about our lives and how we got started. We realised that both of us had learnt to sail in junior sailing clubs run by volunteers in small coastal towns like Swanhaven. It was strange, but the more time André and I spent together, the more we both came to the same conclusion. We both owed our passion for the sport to those sailing clubs.'

There was just enough change in Ethan's voice to make Mari look up and pay attention. Suddenly he sounded excited and energised. Enthusiastic.

Mari could not help but smile. 'Kit and his friends lived for that club. They did amazing work.'

'I know. I used to be so jealous that Kit lived here all year round and could sail any time he wanted. He had more freedom than I ever had back when we lived in London.'

Ethan's smile broke through the tension in the air and she blinked several times to break free from the intensity of his stunning grin.

'Did you really think that I had forgotten about Kit and the summers I spent with him here? He would have loved to run a sailing school. I know it and so do you. When I got back to Florida I took the decision to retire from competitive sailing to create a charity teaching disadvantaged teenagers to sail. I bought a huge old wooden schooner and it has taken a lot of work to fit it out as a training ship, but it's a fine vessel and does the job.'

'When did you start teaching?'

'About six months ago. The results have been amazing. The charity is turning the lives of those teenagers around. In a few weeks they can find self-confidence and skills they did not think possible. We're giving them a chance to show what they can do.'

Ethan moved closer to Mari and she leant back against the sink as he rested his hand lightly on her arm. When he spoke his voice was low and warm. 'Look, Mari, I'm here to finish the house for my parents. My mother has always loved Swanhaven. She's stayed away for ten years but this is where she wants to spend her summers. But some researcher is bound to pick up on the accident and start asking around town about what happened to Kit. And I'm sorry if they do. I really am.'

'Then you shouldn't have come back here.'

'You're right. But my mother wants to spend more time here when she retires, and I want to give something back to the town which got me started on this amazing life. That's why I agreed to give a few classes and open the regatta for Rosa. And if that means extra publicity for the charity and the town? Then I can put up with being reminded about the accident. But what about you? Are you okay with my being here?' he asked in a low voice, and Mari shot him a sideways glance.

His head was tilted to one side and there was a look in his eyes that she had never seen before. A look which shouted out regret and concern and sorrow in one single glance, and her heart contracted so tightly she could only nod quickly in reply and turn back to her washing-up. 'I don't have a lot of choice, do I?'

His hand reached out and took hold of her wrist. 'You asked me why I came to Swanhaven, Mari. And I've told you. But if it's going to cause too much trouble or bring up too many painful memories, you just let me know and I can be out of here any time you want. As for now? Sorry about scaring you earlier. I can promise you that I will try my best to keep a low profile and try to see that Kit is not mentioned. And I always keep my promises.'

Mari looked deep into those intense blue eyes which still had the power to enthral her and was still working on a reply when Rosa skipped down the last stair with her shopping baskets, hat, scarves and gloves bundled in her arms.

'Ready when you are, Ethan.'

Ethan's mouth twisted up at one side as Mari turned to face him. 'Something tells me that this weekend is going to be one to remember. I can hardly wait.'

CHAPTER FOUR

COLD night air filled Mari's lungs as she gingerly made her way across the cold footpath to the Swanhaven Yacht Club, where the normally staid club sign had been decorated with sparkly illuminated hearts ahead of the Valentine's Day party.

Strange how it managed to be fun and stylish instead of cheap and tacky.

Unlike her shoes. She might share the same shoe size with Rosa, but she certainly would not have chosen sparkly sandals with three-inch heels to crunch through the thin layer of ice covering the snow. Rosa had taken one look at the elegant black shift dress that Mari usually wore for a casual evening and insisted that for once she should wear party shoes like a proper grown-up and she was going to choose some for her.

Fairy lights leftover from Christmas twinkled in the metal railings on the balcony of the yacht club, illuminated by the warm glow of light from the windows. As she moved closer, Mari could see people clustered around the huge log fire burning in the hearth of the old stone house. It was as though every precious, warm feeling she had ever associated with Swanhaven had come together in one place. Concentrated in one room.

Inside were most of her old school friends and extended family. These were the people she had known all of her life—and in turn they knew her. Good and bad.

This was the community she had left behind—but not for much longer if her plans came true.

Almost by magic, there was a rush of movement from the entrance and Rosa stepped outside, grabbed her arm and pulled her through the door and into the hallway.

'It's freezing out there! Ethan has already started on the buffet so you'd better work fast if you want something to eat!'

There was nothing else for it but allow herself to be dragged to the kitchen where the long pine table was groaning under the weight of enough food to feed half the town, which was probably necessary, judging by the crush of people who had squeezed themselves into the small rooms.

Mari followed Rosa past the crowds and looked around, grateful that she was tall enough to see over the heads of most of the other people there, especially in these heels.

She made her way slowly into the dining room, chatting and greeting friends and neighbours on the way, and then she saw Ethan in the small office the harbour master had once used.

And her heart let her down with a quick beat that made it pound. Palms sweaty, she gawped at the best-looking man in the room. He was wearing black trousers that had clearly been made to measure, especially around the seat. And a crisp white shirt open at the neck, designed to highlight his deep tan and the whiteness of his smile and eyes.

Oblivious to her ogling, Ethan was chatting to the chairman of the yacht club, who was standing with his arm around the shoulders of a teenage boy she did not recognise. As she watched Ethan pointing to a group photograph from one of the regattas where he had won the junior race, Mari suddenly knew exactly what she would be giving Ethan as a house-warming present for his parents. Over the years she had created a collection of personal photographs from the summers he had spent with his family in Swanhaven. She had nothing but respect for Ethan's parents and they had been totally amazing after the accident. Her mother would never have got through without their help.

The last thing she wanted was his parents to feel that she had forgotten about them or that they were unappreciated or unwelcome in the town.

And oh, the camera loved Ethan.

All she needed was a scanner to create a digital slideshow from the dozens of photographs she had taken over the years in those dreamy holidays. That way, Ethan could choose the prints he wanted from the film and have them framed! Yes! She could give them to Rosa before she left and her sister could pass them on as the final touch when she went to help Ethan decorate. And she knew exactly where the old photographs were kept in Rosa's house.

Mari gave Ethan a fleeting smile as she started to weave her way towards the bar, only to be stopped by one neighbour after another, all anxious to catch up with her news and hear all about her exciting life in computing across the ocean.

Ethan glanced over his shoulder at that moment and caught Mari smiling at him. And his breath caught in his throat so hard he could only manage a nod before turning back to chat to Henry Armstrong, the instructor who had taught Kit and himself to sail all those years ago and who was now retired and Chairman of the Swanhaven Yacht Club! When Ethan had arrived in Swanhaven, Henry had asked him if he would give his nephew Peter a few extra sailing lessons as a personal favour while he was in town. Ethan had hesitated, as his plan had been to keep a low profile. But after chatting to Peter he'd agreed to help him with some things he was struggling with.

Peter was a shy boy who held back in group lessons, but it was clear that he was passionate and talented and ready to learn. Over the past week he had grown fond of this fatherless boy who was prepared to go out on a bitterly cold day and get wet.

The only embarrassing part was how grateful Peter's mother and uncle were, and now he nodded away their thanks before watching them melt back into the crowd of friends and neighbours, some of whom Ethan recognised from the family parties he had been invited to at the Chance house when he was a teenager. Mari's aunts certainly had not changed much—they were still as eccentric as ever. Rosa was certainly cast from the same stock. But Mari? She was so different.

She certainly was not the awkward, gawky sixteen-year-old girl that he remembered.

When had Mari finally learnt to stand ramrod-straight with her head upright? What had happened to the girl who had been so cripplingly shy that she'd found it impossible to look at a boy eye to eye? And the old Mari certainly would never have had the confidence to wear a fitted dress like that! A dress designed to make best use of her stunning figure. Elegant, sophisticated and formal, it was the perfect dress for a professional woman who wanted to get the message across that she would not tolerate any form of unwelcome familiarity.

If it had not been for Kit, Mari would probably have stayed a complete mystery to him. Just another girl, who happened to be living next door to their holiday home.

And yet… Marigold Chance was the girl he *could* have asked out a thousand times, if the words had not choked in his throat each time he'd almost said them.

Ethan winced at the memory of how inadequate his best friend's younger sister used to make him feel. Mari could never be interested in him as anything more than a friend of her late brother. Why should she? Mari was a loner. Unapproachable. Contained. She didn't need to be part of a gang or play team sports to make a connection. She was happy in her own company—and he had envied her that. He had resorted to teasing her simply to get a reaction—any reaction—which meant that she took the time to notice that he existed.

What an idiot! He should have had the courage to ask her out at least once. Or at least explain that he was teasing her because he was attracted to her and was simply desperate to make her notice him.

And now Kit's sister Mari was a lovely talented woman. In an amazing dress that fitted her in all of the places guaranteed to press the right buttons in the perfect sequence. Buttons he knew he had to turn back off. And fast. And those legs!

Gorgeous and intelligent. Now that was a killer combination.

She would never forgive him for being on the boat with Kit the day he died. Just as he would never forgive himself. Each of them had found their own way to get through each day—but it never went away.

All the more reason for him to keep his distance, finish the house then get on with the work he had come here to do.

Mari shook her head in exasperation as Ethan dazzled her uncle and cousins with tales of derring-do and sailing adventures. He really did have the charm offensive down to a well-practised art and it took several minutes of manly back-slapping before Ethan glided up to Mari with her flute of champagne and his glass of cola, as though they were on the deck of a cruise ship, and started to say something.

Except that, just as she leant closer to try and hear what he was saying against the party noise, the laughter and chatter dropped away, Ethan stopped mid-sentence and looked over her shoulder in silence towards the entrance. He was white-faced with alarm, his eyebrows drawn tight together in concern and dismay.

'What is it?' she asked, concerned. 'Has something happened?'

And then Mari turned and saw why everyone had gone silent. Rosa was standing just inside the side door, her face ashen, holding her left forearm out in front of her. Her dress was covered in mud and slush and her stockings were ripped. Her hair was dripping-wet, she had lost a shoe and all in all she looked a dishevelled mess.

Mari rushed forward faster than she thought possible and grabbed hold of Rosa around the waist. 'What happened. Are you okay?'

'It's snowy. I slipped.' And then Rosa's legs collapsed under her and she slid towards the floor in an ungraceful faint as Mari tried to take her weight and failed.

It was Ethan who got there first and took Rosa in his arms before she hit the carpet, a fraction of a second before the entire crowd of people surged forward, pushing past her to help Rosa into a chair. Someone brought water. One of the lifeboat crew took a quick glance at Rosa's arm, looked back at Mari and her aunt and mouthed, *'broken wrist'*, then reached for his mobile phone to call the hospital.

A wave of nausea and dizziness hit Mari, forcing her to press her hand down on the nearest table for support. The wine. She should have eaten something before the wine. Now just the thought of food made her dizzier than ever, and she closed her eyes and fought air into her lungs.

She couldn't believe it. Only a few seconds earlier Rosa had been laughing and jigging along to the jukebox. Her aunt Alice grasped hold of Mari's arm for a second before rushing forwards from the bar to be with Rosa.

Rosa had to be okay. She just had to.

Ethan stood back, watching the scene from the back of the room, as his place at Rosa's side was taken by her family.

Rosa was surrounded by the people who loved her, while Ethan felt very much the outsider. Oh, the family were friendly and everyone here had welcomed him but, when it came to it, he was still just a visitor.

This was what he'd felt like after Kit had died. Mari had become even more withdrawn. Distant. Solitary. She had disappeared into her studies. Driven. Obsessive. Trying to take care of the family as best she could.

Mari had been sixteen going on thirty and on her own.

He had seen it and not had the skills and power to do anything about it.

How could he? His family were moving to Florida full-time, he was set for university in America and the world of sailing, and the happy summer holidays he had spent here as a boy were over for good.

Rosa had told him that Mari had decided to use her education to get out of Swanhaven. He recalled asking Rosa if she would do the same, and she'd said she'd tried, she really had, but compared to Mari? No way. Besides, she loved Swanhaven and had wanted to stay with her mother and the aunts and cousins. This was where she felt she belonged.

And then he had to leave Swanhaven and Mari and her family.

Of course everything had come to a head on the night of her sixteenth birthday party. She had waited all day for her father to turn up. But it had been Ethan who'd followed her out onto the beach and held on to her as she'd raged against the unfairness and cruelty of what he had done, talking and shouting in an explosion of suppressed emotion and crying and hanging on to him for strength until the dawn. Then he'd kissed her good-bye.

And then he had watched her pale silent face grow smaller and smaller as his family had driven out of Swanhaven. It had been one of the hardest things he had ever done. For one night he had felt an unshakeable bond with Mari which was so special. So unique. And he hadn't had the emotional tools he needed to talk to her about Kit and make her understand how truly devastated he was.

It had been easier to leave with his parents and start a new life. And he was sorry for that.

It had hurt to see her in pain then. And it hurt now.

Ignoring the other people moving towards Rosa with coats and offers of a car to the hospital, Ethan wound his way around the room, looped his arm around Mari's waist and half carried her as far as the hall, where she had some hope of catching her breath, or at least passing out with some dignity.

She looked up at him in surprise, then, as though recognising that something in him she could trust until her dying day, she stared, white-faced, into his concerned eyes.

'The ambulance is on its way, but can you take me to the hospital to be with Rosa? Please? I don't have a car and…'

'You got it.'

As Ethan grabbed his own jacket from the hall stand and wrapped it around her shoulders, he knew it would take more than a coat to stop this precious woman from shivering. He had watched when her world had fallen apart once before, and he had been a boy. Powerless to help her, he had been forced to just stand back and watch her pain.

No longer.

She faltered on the icy steps and as he held her tighter around the waist, taking her weight, he felt her heart beating under her thin dress in the cold night air and he knew his fate was sealed.

Doomed.

In that fraction of a second it took for his arm to wrap around Mari's body, he knew that there was a chance that she could forgive him for Kit's death—a small chance, but a chance nevertheless. And that meant more to him than he could say.

Ten years ago he had walked away from Mari without telling her how he felt about her. How could he? She had accused him of being reckless and not caring about anything but winning the race the day that Kit died. And she had been right about that. He had wanted to win. And maybe he had pushed the boat and Kit beyond what they were capable of doing, but no one could have predicted that wave hitting their boat so hard that it capsized. It had not seemed possible.

A series of unexpected events were responsible for Kit dying that day while he survived and he had relived those few minutes so many times in so many ways to know that there was not one thing that he could have done differently.

Strange how it didn't make any difference. His life had been changed forever since that morning all those years ago. And perhaps Mari was right to blame him. Because he certainly blamed himself and had gone on blaming himself, year after year, to the point when the only way he could escape the pain was by relentless action. Kit would never have the opportunity to sail in the great yacht races around the world—so he put himself through every extreme to win. For both of them.

He had run away from Mari on the morning after he had kissed her, filled with guilt and self-reproach.

Well, he wasn't running now. Mari needed him and it was obvious that she still linked him to Kit's death. It was time to make a stand.

He was making a commitment to Marigold Chance. All over again. And this time it had nothing to do with Kit and everything to do with Mari and how he felt just seeing her again.

He had his arm around Mari at precisely the time when he should be concentrating on getting back to Florida to plan the next phase of fund-raising for the charity. And the feeling was so amazing and yet so crazy and foolish that Ethan almost laughed out loud.

Her life was in computing in California. His life was in competitive sailing in Florida. In a few days he would leave Swanhaven in good hands and get back to a full workload teaching teens to sail for the next six months.

He was no good for her. All he had to do was make his heart believe it.

Mari turned over and pulled the duvet a little closer around her shoulders as she snuggled down into the cushion and gave a little sigh of contentment.

Mmm. She had enjoyed such a sweet dream where Ethan Chandler had sat with her on this very sofa until she fell asleep. Lovely. This was such a comfy warm bed. She could lie here all day.

Her eyes creaked open and some part of her brain registered that daylight was peeking in around the corner of the thin curtains, which looked different somehow. And it was strange that her alarm clock had not gone off. It was the last thing she checked every night without fail.

She stretched out her arm towards the bedside cabinet and her fingers scrabbled about in vain to find the clock. Her right eye opened just a little more.

It wasn't there. And her arm was covered with something pink and fluffy, which had certainly not come from her suitcase.

She pulled her arm back under the warm duvet and closed her eyes for one complete millisecond before snapping them open and sitting up in the bed.

And then collapsed back down again onto the cushions with a groan and pulled the duvet over her head.

No wonder she hadn't recognised the curtains.

This was not her cool airy apartment in California. This was Rosa's living room and she had fallen asleep on the sofa.

And Ethan had carried her inside last night because she had turned into a pathetic weeping creature the minute they had brought Rosa home from the accident department. The rest of her family had been so wonderful and encouraging while she had been totally pathetic and embarrassed herself.

She had not even managed to reach her own bedroom.

'Are you decent in there? I have coffee.'

She glanced down at her clothing before answering Ethan. She was wearing the same black dress she had put on the night before, which luckily was not creased beyond redemption, plus a long-sleeved pink sweatshirt with fluffy kittens on the front belonging to Rosa. In fact the only thing missing from her outfit were her shoes.

Yes, she was decent. And Ethan Chandler had put her to bed. And what else? She couldn't remember anything past being lowered onto the couch and someone tucking the duvet in around her. Oh! Was that part of a dream? Help!

'Coffee would be good,' was her feeble reply as she pushed herself up on the sofa and drew the covers up to cover her chest inside the sweatshirt. Pathetic indeed.

Ethan breezed into the room carrying a tray with two steaming mugs of the most wonderful-smelling coffee and a paper bag, which he opened and presented to her as he collapsed down on the other end of the sofa, completely unfazed by the fact that she was lying on it.

The tray was made from the lid of a cardboard packing box, each coffee mug had a picture of a puppy on it and there was a marked absence of napkins or plates but, strangely, this was the kind of room service she could get used to.

'Morning. I stopped by the bakery on my way in. The lovely Rosa is awake and in her kitchen and managing quite well considering the strapping on her wrist. Apparently these are her favourite cupcakes—oh, and I found these in my truck this morning. Yours?'

He held up the pair of gold, high-heeled sandals she had borrowed from Rosa the night before, and Mari gave him a look. 'Ah, I didn't think so. Feel free to help yourself to a takeaway breakfast. I brought enough for three.'

Mari reached inside the bag and pulled out a muffin in a bright pink paper case. It was covered in heart-shaped pink sparkles with a small blob of white icing at the centre.

Mari and Ethan both stared at the muffin for a second in silence before he laughed. 'Well, that definitely suits Rosa.'

Luckily the next cake looked like double chocolate chip and Ethan grinned and clutched it to his chest in delight. 'Your sister does have style. Coffee? The café was open.'

All Mari could manage was a single nod, and it took several delicious sips of the hot bittersweet blend before she was ready to speak. 'Oh, that is just what I needed. Perfect.'

They sat in silence for a few minutes, but it was Mari who found the courage to break the truce and say what she needed to say. One adult to another.

'Ethan.'

'Um,' he replied, between mouthfuls.

'Thanks for last night. Sorry about the crying jag. I'm…embarrassed about…well…what I must have looked like. Sorry.'

He shook his head and pursed his lips. 'You've no need to feel sorry. You only have one sister. If she hurts, you hurt. I get that. Things will look better in a few days.'

Mari gulped down a surge of emotion which threatened to overwhelm her. Ethan had come to Rosa's aid when she needed it, stayed with them when he did not have to, and now he was offering her understanding. Suddenly it all seemed too much to take in, and she covered it up by blowing on her coffee.

'Thank you. Although—' and she dared to look up at him with a thin smile '—I'm not sure if things will settle down in a few days after last night. What did the doctor say? A couple of weeks? That could be a problem for a girl who knits for a living and works in a bar.'

Ethan sipped his coffee before answering. 'Sprained wrists are a common injury in sailing and she will struggle for quite a while but things will be fine. She was lucky it wasn't broken.'

Mari dropped her head to focus on folding the muffin paper into tighter and tighter V-shaped angles. 'I almost feel guilty about leaving so soon when she needs help—but I must get back to work next week.'

'She knows that you came a long way to spend time with her. In the snow. And you even had to put up with me for a few hours. That's quite a sacrifice. Your sister is going to be fine.' And he reached for his second muffin.

'Hey!'

'What? I missed my dinner too. And breakfast. Did you know it's almost ten?'

'What?' Mari gasped, almost spraying coffee all over the duvet.

'Relax. You were exhausted. Sometimes it pays to let your body have a rest. I'll go and check on your sister. And try to wake up.'

Mari looked up just in time for her face to be inches away from Ethan's middle, as he lifted his left arm above his head and stretched it out towards the polystyrene ceiling tiles, rolling his shoulder to shrug off a mighty yawn. And she almost dropped her drink.

Tight, perfect six-pack. Deep tanned abs. No muffin-top hanging over the top of these jeans. A faint line of dark hair ran down between the bands of muscle below his belly button and, as he stretched up to grasp both hands behind his head, she noticed a touch of silky elastic waistband. Silk boxers. Navy check.

He still smelt wonderful.

Only now that outdoor, aromatic cologne was mixed

with something else. Sweat. Plus something unique to Ethan she had almost forgotten about.

Oh, yeah. Ethan smell.

Starched white shirts and shoe polish.

She used to make a point of sitting as close to him as she could manage without being a stalker, just so she could smell his laundry. Her own clothes had never seen an iron, because they did not actually own one that worked, and every surface in their house was usually covered in a mixture of cat hair and sometimes paint and linseed oil splatters.

He stopped moving.

She kept staring.

He just smiled and brushed the crumbs from his fingers onto the tray.

Mari moistened her lower lip with her tongue. 'Ethan. One question. Did you put me to bed last night? That was you, wasn't it?'

She watched him slip off the sofa and head for the door, only to turn at the last minute and grin.

'Maybe. Maybe not.' And he dived out.

'How can you still look fabulous with your wrist all strapped up like that? It is so totally unfair.'

Rosa kissed Mari on the forehead and waggled her elbow before wincing a little. 'It's a burden I shall have to get used to. The pretty scarf helps. And the painkillers are really most excellent. I feel quite giddy. Remind me not to drink any wine tonight or there'll be more contorts…tortoises…sprains to go with this one.'

'Oh, I will.' Mari smiled and sat down next to her sister at the dining room table. 'You are not leaving this house today, young lady, that's for sure.'

'Bossy boots,' Rosa hissed at Mari, then sat back in her chair and grinned at Ethan, who was just finishing off his second breakfast of cheese on toast washed down with scalding-hot tea. 'I bet you wouldn't make me stay inside for days, lovely man. Would you?'

Mari lifted her eyebrows and stole a sly glance towards Ethan, daring him to side with Rosa before he replied. 'You are grounded, young lady. Better get used to it. The last thing my house needs is a crazy one-armed girl going mad with a paint sprayer.'

Rosa groaned and dropped her head onto her outstretched right arm. 'Oh, no. The decorating. What are you going to do? I'm so sorry. I forgot. What still needs to be done?'

'The building work is done. Utilities, water, the lot.' He raised his right hand. 'I still need to finish the decorating and the final detail with the furniture and textiles. Everything that's going to encourage my dad to finally take a rest and retire while he's still fit enough to enjoy life. And there is the small matter of the fact that I promised my mum that the house would be ready when they get here next weekend.'

He dropped both elbows back to the table, clasped his hands together, lifted his chin and stared at Mari, his eyes never leaving her face as he spoke. 'I already called three decorating firms and they're booked solid until the end of February. I need help now.'

There was a stunned silence in the room, broken only by the crackling of the logs in the open fire. Then Rosa blew out a whistle and waved her bandaged wrist towards Ethan.

'Ethan, I can't do much except give directions. Unless…' Then she pushed herself slowly off her chair, slid around the table so that she was sitting next to Ethan, and leant her elbows on the table and gave him a conspiratorial wink.

As though they had rehearsed their movements in advance, Ethan and Rosa lowered their chins onto their cupped right hands in perfect coordination and both of them just sat there, staring into Mari's face.

'Your mother was the best home decorator this town has ever seen.' Ethan paused and added in a low, calm, matter-of-fact voice, 'I already have the paint and supplies Rosa recommended, and the house is full of stuff. What I don't have is an extra pair of hands and someone to make it all come together. If *only* someone would volunteer to take Rosa's place and help me out, it would make all the difference to my parents.'

Mari realised what was happening and held out both hands palm-forward in denial.

'Oh, no. Don't even go there! I'm here for one long weekend, and then I have to get back to work next week. There's no way I can take on a big decorating job in two days. There is also the small matter of my total lack of artistic talent. Computers. I like computers…and two against one is totally unfair.'

Rosa smiled sweetly at Mari before speaking. 'This is your time to shine, Mari. And don't give us excuses about your lack of talent. You were always the better artist at school—and everyone in the family agrees that you are totally brilliant at photography.'

'Family! Great idea. Why don't we call the cousins?' Mari gushed as she felt the ground slipping away from under her feet. 'Maybe they can take time away from work for a couple of hours? And I'm sure one or two of them can hold a paintbrush!'

Rosa gasped at Mari. 'If you like black! Aunt Lucy's twins are into Goth and are both at college at the moment.' She paused. 'Of course, both of Aunt Alice's sons are colour-blind, but they would help! There could be a few spare minutes between shifts behind the bar at the club.' Rosa's voice faded away as she shrugged towards Mari, who dropped her head to the table and knocked it a couple of times on the cloth.

Mari sat back and looked from her sister to Ethan and back to Rosa again, closed her eyes for a second, then shook her head before sinking back into her chair in resignation. 'Yes. Okay. I will do it. I will help you decorate your house. But under protest. I don't like emotional blackmail.'

'Understood, but thank you, Mari, all the same. In that case, I'll pick up the supplies we need and be back here in about an hour,' Ethan replied, leaping up to go before anyone changed their mind, but he could not resist turning back and giving her a warm smile. 'No time like the present. And who knows—by the end of the day, you might even enjoy it!'

Ethan ducked as a half-eaten muffin came flying towards his head. Only the plan backfired as he caught the cake one-handed, stood back up and took a huge bite. 'Mmm. Not bad. Not bad at all. Any more for the workers?' And then he dived out of the door before Mari could find something harder with more bounce potential.

Leaving the two girls looking at one another in silence.

'What?' Rosa asked in all innocence. 'You want to work behind the bar at the yacht club all day? No, I didn't think so.'

She glanced at her watch. 'Better get some rest, because it sounds like you're going to need it, Mari. Put the cake knife down, Mari. I am wounded, remember? Ouch!'

CHAPTER FIVE

The snow had stopped during the night, leaving a crystal-clear blue sky morning.

Mari stared out of the window of Ethan's four-wheel drive, peering through the thick pine trees and mixed forest to the inlet before they reached the shore.

The branches of the low fir trees had been painted silver and white by the heavy frost and looked like something from a Christmas card. She should have brought a camera and made some greeting cards for Rosa, like she used to when she was younger. Rosa would love that.

Great. More guilt. Just what she needed.

'You've gone quiet on me again. Is this so terrible? It's a nice day. The sun's shining. The snow has stopped. Want to give me a hand unloading the car?'

She looked at him, shook her head. 'You really hate to take no for an answer, don't you? And using my own sister to help you decorate! Shame on you.'

'For what?' Ethan replied, raising both hands away from the steering wheel for a fraction of a second. 'I was telling you the truth! I need the help. It's that simple. And who else am I going to ask? Your mum was a goddess in home decoration and you did more than help. I was there, remember? Lugging cans of paint and wallpaper all over the county in your dad's old van. You can't fool me, Mari. I saw you in action too many times. Who knows? It could be fun.'

He glanced over at her just before she turned away to gaze out of the window.

Or maybe not.

'Did Rosa tell you about the house? We have three bedrooms en suite. Air con. Triple glazing. And the best view this side of the bay with a private jetty.'

'Didn't there used to be a cottage down that way?'

Ethan nodded. 'A derelict fisherman's shack. The planning authority didn't want the land used for a hotel on the protected seafront. And it was too far out of town for a restaurant or the like. So when it came on the market, I bought it with permission to rebuild that one house on the shore. Plenty of other people wanted to develop the site and build a private housing complex and offered a whole load of money for the privilege. But I outbid them. This is where my mother wants to retire to, so this is what she gets. And here we are.'

Whatever mental picture Mari had created of a house by the shore, she was totally unprepared for the image she found at the front of the house. They had driven through a single break in the tree cover onto a paved driveway, leading to one of the most stunning buildings she had ever seen in her life.

The house itself was one storey, hugging the shoreline, with an attic floor above, the peak of the tiled roof just low enough so that the pine trees on either side still towered above it.

But that was not the killer. It was the view.

The house was not just near the sea. It was on the

shore. From the drive, she could see the long glass panels of a conservatory built on stone pillars extended a few feet over the water. To her right, the drive continued down to what looked like a solid wooden boathouse, the roof heavy with snow. On the left a double door garage below a curving extension, which seemed to fit seamlessly into the forest. The cold air was filled with a wonderful combination of pine needles, sawdust and a tang from the choppy ocean which spread out in front of them to the other side of the bay.

Ignoring the fact that Ethan had started unloading his car, Mari walked towards the boathouse so she could get a clear view across the water to the snow-covered hills. A low line of housing on the other side of the shore and the town of Swanhaven was hidden by the angle of sight.

It was a different world. Magical, private and serene.

And totally stunning.

Ethan came up and stood by her side in silence, his hands stuffed into his jeans' pockets as the icy sea breeze buffeted their faces.

They stood only inches apart until Mari shivered. She looked at Ethan and said in a calm voice, 'You win. It's fabulous. Now I understand why your folks are willing to leave Florida for a few months every year.'

The silence opened a gap between them. Their smiles locked.

And just for a fraction of a second Mari allowed herself to relax and enjoy being with Ethan as an attractive man who had been her first kiss all those years ago, and the feeling shocked her so badly that she was the first to look away.

She covered up her discomfort by rubbing her hands

together for warmth. The sooner she got on with the job, the sooner she could be out of here and back in town to take care of Rosa. 'Okay. Let's do this. Show me what you need help with.'

'Come right this way. I have three rooms with bare plaster. Three large rooms. And paint. Lots of paint. Then they need fittings and furnishings. Rugs, curtains, cushions. Everything.'

Mari whistled. 'I see what you mean. We had better get started then.'

Ethan leant forward very carefully and peered around the corner of the lounge towards Mari to make sure he did not disturb her. Kit's little sister was wearing an old, navy, extra-large boiler suit and a pair of sailing boot socks to protect the fine wooden floor as she cleaned and polished, and at that moment he thought she looked just fine.

As he spied on her, Mari started to sing along to some tune or other she had in her head like she used to do when she was happy. He had forgotten about that. Forgotten how comforting it was to have Mari around. Simply being in the same house and the same room.

Of course he would never admit it, but sometimes he missed being part of the Chance family show. Kit had been the eldest child—the gifted and special boy. The apple of his parents' eyes and a true sportsman, like his dad. But Rosa and Mari were the characters, the deep and interesting people who kept their dreams and their ideas inside and preferred home or study to getting soaked in Swanhaven harbour at every opportunity, like Kit.

They might have had the same parents, but he could

not imagine meeting three more different teenagers. And things were never organised or boring in the Chance house.

Rosa was always the soft-hearted charmer who was almost incapable of offending or upsetting anyone. An artist like their mother; like her, she appeared to have no ambition or drive to be anything other than what she was—they were completely happy to live their lives in Swanhaven. He envied Rosa that serenity. She certainly was totally different from Kit, who'd excelled in pushing the boundaries on a daily basis.

As for Mari?

On the surface, the Marigold Chance he was looking at now was very different from the geeky, self-conscious girl who had been the star pupil in high school compared to Kit, who'd adored her just the same. Back then her long hair had been as wild and uncontrollable as her sister Rosa's. Now the glorious, glossy, curly auburn hair had been tamed into a straight shoulder-length style, so that her fringe just covered the dark curves of her eyebrows.

Last evening at the club she had looked a lot more polished and confident. A lot taller than her five feet eight inches. He had watched her chat with old friends and relatives but, at the same time, he could not help but notice how she still drifted away into a corner unless one of her family was around. Mari may have changed on the outside, but he could still see the girl he had known, who liked to stay in the background, watching other people. Usually on the other side of a camera lens.

Perhaps that was why he had been so shocked at the transformation when Rosa hurt herself and the fear and deep emotion that she was capable of peeked out from her slick outer persona?

That could explain why he had sought out any opportunity to be in physical contact with her the previous evening. Helping her out of the club, into and out of his car, holding her next to him in the hospital waiting room and then hunting out a bed cover so that he could cuddle it around her on the sofa.

He was pathetic! But it had meant that he could really look at Mari close up.

There was a crease in her forehead, which showed her years of work and stress. No doubt the Swanhaven gossip network would update him with each and every achievement and promotion, but to him it was all there, written in that face.

That so very beautiful face. The pale skin. Untouched by sunshine or make-up. Plain. Natural. Cold. She might be living in California, but this girl wasn't spending her time in the sun.

The pain in his chest, which had winded him at the shock of seeing her again out of the blue, meant that it almost hurt to look at her.

Mari was still a girl living inside her head. Contained. His best friend's clever sister. The girl who had tried so hard to take over the reins when her brother drowned in a freak sailing accident and their father deserted them. He knew that in her eyes she had failed and her little family had been torn apart in pain and grief.

The ghosts of the past still ruled the closed interior world where Marigold Chance spent her life. Those dark days were still there, acting as a barrier between them.

And there was no getting away from that—they

could not go back to the people they had been as teenagers. And maybe he didn't want to.

His life was in Florida. Not a small coastal town in Dorset. It had been his decision to launch the sailing school in Florida. Now he had to prove that André and the charity could rely on him to stay the course. And that was precisely what he was going to do. The faster he could finish the house and get back to his new life, the better.

Mari and Ethan lay on the floor of the conservatory, with their bodies stretched out in opposite directions. Both of their heads were resting on the same small lounger cushion so that Mari could just feel Ethan's head move as he looked around. Dusk had fallen over the shore outside the window and the light fittings were still bare wires hanging loosely from the ceiling.

Ethan shuffled his jeans-clad bottom on the thick cream tiles Mari had just spent an hour buffing to a lustrous shine. 'This truly is the best way to test that the under-floor heating is working properly. Seriously. Temperature sensors are just not the same.'

'I shall have to take your word for that—but it does sort of make sense. Radiators would look totally out of place in here.' Mari raised her head towards the ceiling. 'This is a truly excellent viewing position.'

She dropped her head back so that she could just feel the contact with his short-cropped hair, and looked up to the slanting clear glass roof of the conservatory. Snow had slid from the special glass and most of the clouds had been blown away during the past hour to reveal patches of sky, already twinkling with stars. There was no moon, and the constellations were clear and sharp, as though newly painted.

'Come here often?' Mari asked, chewing the inside of her mouth to block the smile in her voice. 'Or do you bring all of your lady friends here to impress them with the view?'

Ethan chuckled. 'This is the first chance I've had to actually enjoy the place. The wooden floor went down three weeks ago. I only had a weekend to get the job done, then I had to get across to see André and finalise our sailing project plans for the rest of the year. Busy, busy.'

'Ethan the carpenter. This is going to take some time for me to get used to. Tell me about southern Florida. What made you stay there?'

'Accident. Serendipity if you like. My first major sponsor ran an upmarket hotel and apartment complex on the coast, and I just loved it down there. Climate. Lifestyle. The whole package. And plenty of work. The world-class yachting fraternity love Miami and the Caribbean. Add in the small fact that my dad has built an amazing architectural firm back in his home town and suddenly Florida ticks all of the right boxes.'

'Ah. Does that mean you had a lot more to prove?'

Ethan's answer was a low chuckle that made the floorboards vibrate beneath them. 'Oh, yes. Still working on that one. Although I think he still hasn't totally recovered from the shock of me actually offering to stay in one place long enough to teach sailing. How about you? Silicon Valley I can understand, but you could work anywhere. Why stay in California?'

'I actually went to Los Angeles because of a boy, but California has everything I need. There's a lot going on at the moment, which is why I'm flying back on Tuesday.'

Ethan swung his legs up and turned around so that he was facing Mari.

'Whoa. Hold it right there. You. The famous No Chance girl, moved to a city because of a boy? This I have to hear about.'

She shrugged. 'There you go, jumping to the wrong conclusions. I never said I was there for romance, did I? The boy in question was a placement student at the IT company I worked for in Swanchester who casually mentioned that he had been invited to a recruitment interview with a major Silicon Valley firm, but he was on his way to cancel. He had already accepted another offer closer to home.'

'What happened?'

'I sweet-talked my way into taking his place, had a great interview and got the job. Right place, right time. And I've been there ever since.'

'Hmm. Funny how things happen. Great opportunities love to just fall out of the sky. Would I know the name of the firm?'

Mari reached into the back pocket of her trousers with much squirming and passed Ethan a creased and slightly warm business card.

He gave a low whistle. 'You weren't kidding. My dad has used this company. Not bad for a girl from Swanhaven. Not bad at all.'

'Why, thank you, kind sir,' Mari replied in her best Californian accent. 'The surfing dudes just love my cute accent on the telephone.'

She fluffed up her hair, and then remembered that the estate agent was supposed to be e-mailing her after 4:00 p.m. to confirm the time for the house auction. 'Speaking of which, I suppose I should be getting back. I need to check my messages.'

'Surf dude?' And he made a sliding motion with his hands. 'Is some hunky youth polishing his board until you get back? Seeing as you are so cute.'

Mari rolled her eyes. 'Strictly business. Let's just say I'm between boyfriends at the moment.'

His smile faded. 'Seriously?'

'Work is crazy. The company pays me to respond to other people's emergencies. That's my job, and I do it very well, but it's a killer for any kind of social life. I did have a long-term boyfriend, if you must know, but businesses need software in a crisis and he eventually got fed up with me cancelling on him at the last minute. It's as simple as that. Could you do your work without internet or e-mail or computer technology?'

'No, I couldn't. But that sounds like a pathetic excuse to me. Damn shame. But I suppose you are right. Speaking of cancelling at the last minute,' Ethan hooted as he pulled on his shoes, 'have you seen what time it is? At some point this morning I foolishly promised Rosa that I would have you home in plenty of time for the no doubt delicious dinner your aunt has cooked. And you've done your share today.'

Mari sat up from the hard floor at the same time as he did and grasped his outstretched hand to pull herself up. And kept hold of it.

Both of them knew where any conversation about boyfriends was going. They were adults.

'And what about you, Ethan? Do you have a lovely girlfriend waiting for you back in Florida, or is it more of a case of a girl in every port?'

Her tone was fast and jokey, only Ethan still had her hand in his and started to run the pad of his thumb up and down the centre of her palm and wrist, his eyes locked on to her. Mari sensed his breath quickening. His palms were getting sweaty.

'As a matter of fact, I don't have a lady in my life at the moment,' Ethan replied, taking her question seriously. 'Long sea voyages don't do much for relationships and I know how hard it is for the sailors to say goodbye to their loved ones. And it's a nightmare for those left on the shore. Competitive sailing is a selfish and dangerous sport.' He shrugged, then he smiled that lopsided smile that made her feel giddy. 'A bit like rally driving on snow. Ready to take the risk?'

CHAPTER SIX

THIS was just a ride home from an old friend of her brother's.

It had started to snow heavily soon after they had arrived and the roads were now covered with several inches of compacted snow and ice.

No big deal. *All she had to do was trust him.*

There was silence. She stared out of the side window, aware that they were both reflected against the dark night. Ethan glanced across at her.

'I don't like it when you go quiet, Mari. What's the problem?'

She paused, and then turned to look at him.

'I was just thinking back to all the times you argued black was white that you would hate to stay in one place for more than a few weeks. And now you're teaching in Florida. Wow. You've had such an amazing sailing career and well, that is…quite a change in direction.'

He sniffed and shrugged his shoulders. 'I was at the top of my game. Best time to walk away.'

'It's still a brave decision.'

He turned off the main road and started onto the unlit tarmac before speaking, the windscreen wipers moving slowly to clear the light snow, which was still falling.

'Maybe. And how about you, Mari? What's brought you from sunny California this weekend?'

He glanced across and scanned her body, from her scuffed boots to fleece jacket. 'Not that I'm complaining, you understand. Looking good.' And he winked before focusing on the road.

She couldn't help but grin back. 'You noticed,' she said, and pulled her jacket tighter around her shoulders. 'This time I flew in from Denver. But, to answer your question, I was working all over the Christmas holiday so I promised Rosa that I would pop back to celebrate Valentine's Day. I have some business in the town, and then I'm on the last flight from London on Tuesday. And that's it. Short visit, but that's all I can squeeze into the diary at the moment.'

There was a snort from the driver and Mari turned in her seat to stare at Ethan as he shook his head in disbelief.

He slapped both hands hard against the steering wheel, making Mari jump.

'How could I forget the Valentine's Day party? What an idiot. That's the day after tomorrow, isn't it?'

Mari looked at him in disbelief and chuckled out loud. 'You forgot? How could you forget Valentine's Day? It must be serious.'

'I've been working on a completely new sailing course back in Florida. The idea is to take a whole crew of troubled teenagers on a voyage lasting a couple of weeks. A sort of summer camp on water. It will take the next few months to set up and finance and the admin is horrendous. I thought racing was busy until I started this project.'

He glanced at her quickly before going on. 'The sailing side I can handle and my parents are helping with the project management. But there is a lot at stake here, and scoping out the project is taking a lot longer than I expected.'

He stopped talking, and Mari frowned. 'Ethan, I can hear the cogs clunking inside your brain from where I'm sitting. And there's a strange burning smell. Out with it.'

'I was just thinking how great it would be if some computer guru created a totally flash website for us that would totally sell the project to sponsors. And it would have to be free. Any idea where I could find a specialist like that around here? Mari?'

And he glanced across at her with the kind of smile designed to make old girls blush and young girls squeal.

Mari couldn't help it. She put her head back and laughed out loud.

'Thank you, but no. You should be ashamed. There are brilliant PR companies who do charity work for projects like yours. Go and find one!'

'Oh, there has to be something I can do for you as a trade? Here's an idea. In return for a few days pro bono work, I shall be delighted to escort you to the Valentine party tomorrow and defend you from the amorous clutches of the half dozen single men still left in Swanhaven. What do you say? Do we have a deal?'

Mari sat open-mouthed for a few seconds, her eyebrows high. 'Are you asking me to go with you as your date? Or a paid escort service? That is disgraceful. The old Mari might have done it but not this new girl. See you at the party.'

She paused for a second and gestured at the window towards the cottages down in the village beneath them.

'I've changed, Ethan. When are you going to understand that?'

'I don't think you've changed that much,' he whispered eventually, and gave her a small smile. 'Not where it matters.'

'Well,' she answered, 'it's good to know that the great Ethan Chandler can be wrong about some things. There is hope for humanity.'

That made him laugh, and it was so contagious she smiled back in return. And something flickered between them as his eyes briefly met hers. Something that made her want to get out of this car as soon as she possibly could.

Chemistry. Chemistry as bright and as spectacular as a meteor shower.

Instead of which, she turned her head away and pretended to focus on the buildings either side of the main road into the town.

Her eyes blinked several times as she tried to clear her head. And persuade her heart to slow down before they reached Rosa's cottage.

Focus. That was the key. She needed to focus on why she was here.

She had forgotten how dark it could be on the country roads without streetlights. Occasional drifts of snow lifted up on the open fields on one side of the road but she knew that on the other side was the shoreline and the long pebble and sand beach which led down to the sea. It seemed to take only minutes for Ethan to drive the few miles to the brow of the hill she knew so well.

She reached up with her left hand in an old familiar gesture and clasped her seat belt, ready for the long descent into the bay and the stone harbour that led into

Swanhaven, but instead the car slowed and Ethan pulled into the viewing spot on top of the hill where tourists could take photographs of the picturesque fishing harbour below them. She could almost visualise the curve of the old stone harbour wall, the new marina with the pretty sailing boats and the ocean beyond stretching out to the horizon.

He turned the car so that they could look down onto the lights of the town below and make out the curvature of the bay. Mooring lights in the tops of the yacht masts in the marina twinkled in the cold, crisp, clean air. They had left the snow clouds behind them and stars were shining bright in a deep black freezing sky. It felt as though they were on top of the world looking down from the heavens like some strange Greek gods.

Mari released her seat belt and shuffled forward so that she could rest her chin on the back of her hands on the dashboard and look out over the view.

And all the time her body was hyper-aware that Ethan was sitting only inches away from her, his strong arms outstretched on the steering wheel. Every inch of her skin prickled with being so close to him, and she could feel their connection growing tighter and tighter.

Oh, no. She was not going there again. She still felt guilty about kissing Ethan the last time. She *had* to change the subject and break this silence. She just had to.

'I do have something up my sleeve which might cheer my sister up. I'm planning to move back to Swanhaven for good.'

* * *

'Move back?' Ethan's voice was low and deep and resonated around the car. 'Wait a minute. Why didn't you mention this earlier? Rosa didn't say a thing!'

'That's because my lovely sister doesn't know anything about it. So please don't breathe a word about it or I will never be forgiven.'

The crease lines at the corners of Ethan's mouth lifted, white against tanned skin and afternoon stubble. 'Okay. Your secret's safe; I owe you for this work. But why are you keeping this to yourself? She'd be thrilled to know that you're even thinking of coming back.'

'Okay,' she replied, flicking her tongue out over her lips, and something in Ethan's gut turned over and kept spinning like plates on a stick. 'You remember the house we used to live in, the house on the shore on the other side of town?'

'Of course. I loved that house. We had to walk past it every day from the place we rented. I'll never forget that amazing mural your mum painted on your bathroom wall. All blue, covered with tropical fish, wasn't it?'

Mari chuckled out loud. 'Rosa painted sea horses, and I just about managed a Picasso version of a starfish. It was amazing. I miss that house. A lot.'

Ethan noticed that the corners of Mari's eyes were glistening as she spoke but she gave a brave smile.

'Hey! You'll make a home for yourself like that one day. Give yourself time,' he murmured, suddenly wanting to reassure her.

'You're right. I could buy a cottage in the town like Rosa's, except for one thing. I don't want a house *like* that one. That's not good enough. I want *that* house. My old home. And I mean to get it.'

Ethan kept on rubbing his thumbs up and down the base of the steering wheel, but something was badly wrong as he looked into her eyes and he dropped his hands onto his knees as she went on. 'Did you know it was up for sale? Well, guess what? I'm going to buy it. I'm going to buy my old home back.'

Both of her hands clutched Ethan's arm now, her face bright with energy and excitement, her body jazzed to the point of jumping around in her seat.

'Isn't that the craziest thing you've ever heard of? I've worked every hour and every vacation I could to raise the money, but I've done it. I've saved enough to make a respectable offer for the house and land at the public auction and the bank is giving me the rest. Don't you see? I have a chance to move back here and live with Rosa in our old house. What do you think of that?'

Ethan slid back in his seat against the car door, swallowing hard.

'Well? Say something!' she said and shook her head at him.

'I guess I'm just a little confused here. I thought that you had made a new career for yourself away from Swanhaven. I mean, your old house? I haven't seen the place, but I should imagine that it would cost you serious money to make it a home again.'

She nodded furiously in reply. 'I know. I've worked the numbers. It will take time and money to restore the place and update it so I can run an online IT business from the house. I'm thinking four years at most. Maybe three if I get the Denver contract and sell my place in California and stay in my job long enough. The company are laying off technical staff but I have to hope for the best. And in the meantime Rosa could live there and work her decorating magic.'

Ethan breathed in through his nose. *What was she thinking?* Her company was laying off staff and she wanted to buy a house in a pretty tourist area close to the beach.

A cold feeling developed in the pit of his stomach. She was setting herself up for bitter disappointment.

'I'm sorry to hear about the job worries. Land prices have shot up around here over the last two years. You could be outbid. What are you going to do then?'

'That's why I didn't tell Rosa,' she answered in a low voice tinged with sadness. 'She was so traumatised when we lost that house. If I am outbid?' She inhaled sharply. 'It would be hard. I don't even know if I could handle that disappointment. But Rosa would be destroyed all over again. It would be like losing it twice. I couldn't do that to her, Ethan, I just couldn't. But I can't think that way. Because I'm not going to lose that house again. Three years, Ethan. Three years from now I can be living in my own lovely home again. And in the meantime Rosa has a house which nobody can take away from her. This is our security for the future. That's why I'm determined to win that auction tomorrow morning.'

'Tomorrow? That's cutting it fine. I thought that you were leaving on Tuesday.'

'I am. But it's all going to be fine. I've already organised the legal side and Rosa and the family can look after the details.' She paused and tilted her head to look at him. 'What is it? You look worried.'

He blew out a long breath, misty in the cold damp

air, and took hold of both of her hands and pressed them against his chest.

'Moving back here could be a mistake, Mari. A big mistake.'

Mari blinked several times as the impact of what he was saying hit home. 'Mistake?' she said, hardly believing what she had just heard. 'What are you talking about? I vowed the day we had to move out that somehow I would find a way to get that house back. And this is the first chance in ten years. Isn't it worth trying?'

He squeezed her hands tighter together. 'Of course. But I wonder if you've really thought this through. Things are so very different. Everything has changed.'

Mari gulped down a sense of dread at the chilly tone of Ethan's voice.

'What do you mean?' she whispered.

'Let's say your offer was accepted,' Ethan replied, and this time his voice was calmer and more reassuring. 'And you bought back the house your dad built for his family. Rosa would still be living in town and working at the club and you would be working every hour in California to find the money to pay the bills—if you had a job. And all that time the house would stay empty and unheated and deteriorating while you tried to find builders and tradesmen who could repair ten years' worth of neglect before you could even think about designing improvements. It would be a nightmare of stress, Mari. Is that what you want?'

'I thought you would be happy for me,' she murmured, her eyes locked on his.

He smiled sadly. 'I do want you to be happy. But your old loving and happy home is gone, Mari. Kit is gone.

Your mum is gone. Your dad is gone. And Rosa has her own life and a job she loves. Have you even asked her if she wants to move back into that house? I'm sorry, but all I can see is a lot of pain and disappointment.'

'What?' Mari pulled her hands away and slid back and away from Ethan.

'Look, I didn't mean to upset you. I mean...' Ethan paused and dropped his head back.

'Oh, do carry on,' Mari said in a hoarse whisper, trying not to sound too bitter or angry and knowing that she was failing miserably. 'Why stop now when you're so bursting with good advice for other people? I would hate to hold you back.'

There were a few seconds where all Mari could hear was Ethan shifting on the leather seat but, when he answered, his words rang out clearly in the small space that seemed to have suddenly become even smaller around them.

'This is coming out wrong, What I meant to say was that it sounds like you're going backwards in your life. I don't understand why you would want to lock yourself away in that old house with Rosa and all of the ghosts from your past and throw away the key.'

Mari's eyes sparked ominously. 'Well, I'm glad to say that you are totally mistaken, Ethan. About me, about Rosa and, most of all, you're totally wrong about what we're going to do with our lives.' Her words were coming in fast, angry, loud bursts and she reached out and slapped her hand down hard on her seat. 'How dare you? How dare you tell me how to live my life? Perhaps you should take a look at how well you have been doing these past ten years.'

'I've been doing just fine, thank you.' He nodded, his brow furrowed.

She lifted her chin. 'Have you? All those fine trophies for doing the one thing you seem to excel at. Running away. Or is that sailing away? Take your pick. Because it's all the same to me. When was the last time you came here? Oh, yes. Just before you ran out on me and left me to clean up all of the mess that you left behind in my life. No.'

Ethan had moved forward to try and comfort her—but she pushed both hands palm-forward and turned to stare out of the car window at the view.

'After everything we've been through together, I actually thought that you would understand why I want this house for Rosa. Well, it looks like I was wrong. Very wrong. It looks like we've both changed more than you know.'

She sensed his movement and turned her head towards him.

'Mari,' he said in exactly the same voice she had always known, only deeper and more intense than ever, and she looked up into his face. 'I'm sorry. I understand more than you can know.'

In that second their eyes met and any lingering thoughts she might have had that she could stay away from Ethan and walk away from this town without having her heart broken flew out of the window and into the cold night air.

And, almost as if he was feeling the same thing, his arm slipped away from the steering wheel and both his hands reached up to cup her chin so that the thumbs could swirl gentle circles on her cheeks.

Time slowed to a dead stop so that her entire senses were focused on Ethan's breathing and the warm scent of him filling the tiny space that separated them.

With one small shift in his seat, Ethan closed the space between them and his lips touched hers, warm and strong and tasting of all her forgotten hopes and dreams. All of her buried emotions surged back into life as if they had never been away but had kept dormant, waiting for this moment. And her heart swelled with such an overwhelming combination of anguish and love that when she pulled back she was afraid to open her eyes in case this was all some mirage, a dream.

'It seems that some things haven't changed at all. Have they?' Ethan said, his mouth half pressed against her temple.

'Yes, they have,' she replied in a low and trembling voice, her eyes focused on his shirt as she fought to remember how to breathe again. 'I've changed my mind. I won't be helping you out at the house after all. I quit.'

The auction house was already half-full when Ethan sauntered in and found a seat at the back of the room. Curiosity about Mari had won out in the end and he quickly spotted her sitting in the front row.

She had brushed her shoulder-length auburn hair into a shiny straight column held back by a single barrette. The stiff formal look was completed by a dark grey skirt suit and, from what he could see from this position, the same dark laptop bag she had been carrying everywhere. So this was what she looked like when she was in business mode. Impressive.

The ugly duckling of a girl he had once known truly had become a swan.

Beautiful to look at, serene and calm, and pedalling like mad under the water where nobody could see how desperate she was.

Oh, Mari. You're better than this cold, impassive creature of your own making.

Yesterday he had seen glimpses of the girl he used to know when the real Mari slipped out from beneath the weight of the past and the huge unspoken barrier that lay between them.

And it was magical.

So why did she truly want to buy back the house where she used to live with her family? He remembered it well. The house itself was fairly basic, with a stunning view over the bay from its position on the cliffs, but he had never truly paid much attention to the house. It was the family who'd lived there that was remarkable, and Marigold Chance had been the real star of the Chance home. He had never understood why he seemed to be the only person who saw that.

The auction room was filling up now and people were starting to block his view, so Ethan quickly moved forwards and took a seat directly behind Mari where she could not see him—but he could see her.

He could see how her shoulders stiffened and lifted a little when the auctioneer arrived and took his place at the podium. There was still twenty minutes to go before the start of the auction, but she was already tense and nervous.

There was the faintest whiff of the same perfume that she had been wearing yesterday in the air, mingled with heat and moisture from cold, damp clothing and a dusty room. Ethan sat back in his chair, but just at that moment the lady next to him dropped her handbag and the contents spilled out around him.

And Mari turned around to see what the commotion was, and saw him. He didn't know who was more shocked. But her wide-eyed astonishment said it all.

She stared at him through narrowed eyes, shook her head from side to side just once, checked her watch and picked up her bag, leaving her coat on the chair to reserve her place, and then tipped her head towards the entrance.

He got the message. And followed her outside.

'Are you stalking me? Because I have to tell you that one kiss last night does not entitle you to follow me around. And don't you dare try to interfere in this auction.'

Then Mari stopped, pressed her forefinger to her chin and took a short intake of breath before Ethan had a chance to answer. 'Oh. Oh, silly of me. I forgot. Why should you? I'm the one who's planning to stay in one place long enough to make a home. But you wouldn't know about that, would you?'

'Are you quite finished?' Ethan asked in a calm quiet voice as he leant with his back against his car.

'No, actually I'm not. But I only have a few minutes before the auction starts and it's freezing and you get me all frazzled when I'm trying to be calm and in control. So please. Just tell me. Why are you here?'

Ethan pushed both hands down into his trouser pockets and steadied himself.

'Good question. Long answer. Let's start with the stalking.' He raised an eyebrow. 'Someone clearly has a very high opinion of themselves.' Ethan did not react to Mari's instant cough of dismissal but carried on. 'But you have a point. I am here to see you. I'm here to see just how far you are prepared to go to move right back to where you were ten years ago.'

There was a sharp intake of breath from the woman standing in front of him with her arms crossed before she answered with a look of total disbelief on her face. 'You know why. I'm buying this house for my sister. She needs a secure home. And…' Mari stretched out her neck a little. 'It's an excellent base where I can create business at some future point. Do you have any further questions or can we go inside now?'

'Only one. How long are you planning to keep that excuse up? Because, the way I see it, you aren't buying this house for Rosa—you're buying it for yourself.' He pushed himself off the car and reached out and fought off her protests to wrap his sheepskin coat around her shoulders.

He pulled the front of the coat towards him, with her inside. 'You can fight me all you like, but I just hate to think that you're going to come back here to lock yourself away from other people. Oh, I know. People can leave, people can hurt your feelings and people can break your heart, but sometimes it is worth taking the risk.' His voice dropped even lower and he gave a half smile as he smoothed down the front of his coat.

'You don't need to be so afraid. You can live anywhere you want and go anywhere you want. And you'll be fine.'

She looked up at him and her jaw tightened. Her eyebrows came together but she forced them apart and licked her lips before answering. 'This is all I know.

This is what I want.' And she quietly slipped off his coat and strode, head up, back into the auction room.

Oh, Mari. I do hope that you know what you are doing.

The first three properties seemed to take forever to sell and there had been several breaks in the bidding when Mari had felt like screaming. Didn't they know that she had been dreaming about this moment for years, and been awake half the night worrying and the other half reliving the moment when Ethan had kissed her in the car?

How dared he turn up this morning and ruin her day with all of his questions? How dared he kiss her and give her a glimpse of all of the things she could not have? He was leaving, she was staying and he *still* kissed her. Worse. She had liked it. Stupid girl.

Either way, she was exhausted, her hands were shaking in anxiety. And the bidding was just about to start.

She didn't know whether to be sick into her laptop bag, stand on the chair and scream at everyone that this house was *hers* and they'd better not even think about bidding, or calmly sit there and make her bid at the right time.

She went for option three.

Her real worry was the size of the deposit she had to put together before the bank would agree to offer her a loan for the maximum she could afford on her salary. The constraints meant that she had a working budget with enough left over to do the repairs and create a home office. And that was all she had. Anything else would mean going back to the bank for a bigger loan, and they had not exactly been impressed by her proposal in the first place.

Without the extra cash deposit from her overtime and all of her cash savings, she could be in trouble.

And the prices so far had been a lot higher than she had expected.

But of course that would not happen with her. The photographs and house details had made it clear that a lot of work was needed. That was bound to drive down prices.

Right. Mari lifted her chin. Three. Two. One. Go. She was about to buy back her home.

Ethan clutched tight hold of the back of the chair in front of him, two rows behind Mari, his fingers wrapped around the hard metal rungs, knuckles white with pressure.

As the auction started, he felt himself being caught up in the electricity and excitement. Bids were flying everywhere from all corners of the room so quickly that it was hard to keep up. The numbers were higher than he had expected, which could be a problem. But Mari was calm. Her head fixed in place. Waiting. Waiting for the perfect time to place her bid to buy back her old home and start a new life. Back where she'd started.

And there it was. Mari raised her hand and bid a startling amount of money for her old home. But there was one more bid. From a middle-aged man at his side of the room, sitting next to a woman and three children, each of them almost bouncing with excitement and enthusiasm. A family wanted the house.

Ethan's heart sank. If he was in that position, with his wife and children around him, all looking forward to a new home by the sea—he would move heaven and earth to make it happen.

And without warning an icy chill hit Ethan hard in the stomach with such speed and ferocity that he had to take several long breaths to calm his thumping heart.

She was going to lose this house and it would destroy her. It would be better in the long-term if she made a future somewhere else, he believed that now, but it would still cause her huge pain if she thought that she had let Rosa down.

Mari immediately raised her hand again and increased her bid by another ten thousand—and was instantly outbid again.

She was so startled that it took her a full second to recognise that the family man had increased his bid by not ten thousand but another twenty thousand.

The astonishment and alarm on Mari's face said it all. She clearly had not expected to pay anything like this much and Ethan recognised by the telltale way she chewed her lower lip and bent her fingers into the centre of her palms that she knew she was at her limit.

She hesitated, her hand almost shaking, before increasing her bid yet again.

And the longer Ethan watched Mari, the more he thought that this was not the action of a woman looking for a home back in Swanhaven with her sister. This was a desperate act driven by a need to come back to the security of the past life she had once known.

The life which he had played a part in destroying.

And he knew exactly how that felt.

Because, sitting here amongst these strangers in a dusty, cold auction room, it was as obvious as a slap in the face that he was no different from Mari whatsoever.

Watching Mari struggling with her decision at that very moment, the answer screamed out at him from Mari's startled hazel green eyes. He *was* running away from the pain and the guilt that was Kit and Mari Chance and everything that happened in Swanhaven ten years earlier. It had been easier to leave and not come back and start over again in Florida with his father's new job, and he did feel guilty about that—his whole family had—but they had made the decision and acted on it. While Mari had stayed trapped right here.

It was ironic that he should only realise that fact when he was right back *in* Swanhaven. Looking at Mari. Who had stood up and was winding her way towards him, her face lined and grey and tense with concern. The weight of disappointed dreams hung heavy on her sagging shoulders.

Part of him was pleased. Her agony was over. Now she could start moving forwards, not backwards. And perhaps give him a few tips on how to do that along the way. He started to get up, ready to take her home.

Only she grasped his arm in a powerful grip, leant forwards and pressed her mouth close to his ear. 'I need another forty thousand. Will you lend me the money? Please. I'm desperate. If you don't lend me this money I will lose the house. This is my dream. This is what I want more than anything else in the world. Please help me.'

Ethan shifted his body back just far enough to look into her eyes. And saw such terror of the unknown and a deep-seated pain and anguish in that one single look that his heart broke all over again.

His actions had helped to bring her to this place.

Now he had to be strong enough to risk the fragile

bond that had grown between them. Because giving her his reply was one of the hardest things that he had ever had to do. It was wrong in every way. But he had to do it. To make Mari's dream come true.

'Yes, Mari. I will lend you the money. As much as you need.'

CHAPTER SEVEN

'WELL, it looked to me like you'd been crying ten minutes ago when Ethan dropped you off. That's all I'm saying. *Crying.* Okay? So where did you go this morning?' And then Rosa gasped and pulled her chair closer to the table. 'Of course. I should have realised. Ethan kidnapped you and whisked you off for a romantic date somewhere. That has to be it. That is *so* totally brilliant. Now, tell me everything.'

Mari sank lower into her chair at the cottage and admitted defeat for the second time that day. Once Rosa was determined to discover something, there was no point in fighting her. She would find out eventually. Half of Swanhaven had been at the auction, out of curiosity if not to bid, and the small-town gossip factory was alive and well in the yacht club. It would be around the whole town in an hour that Marigold Chance had just bought the old Chance house for twenty per cent above the expected value.

She was going to have to tell Rosa. And soon. All she had to do was pick her moment.

'I spent the morning with Ethan at the property auction in Swanchester and—' Mari took another sip of tea and considered making up an elaborate tale of love and debauchery but she simply did not have the strength to go along with anything but the truth '—Ethan and I had a bit of an argument. But in the end, he helped me out. In fact, you might almost say that he came to my rescue.'

'Ethan Chandler came to your rescue. At a property auction. Right. Well, that makes total sense. One minute you're all over him and this wonderful house he's built for his parents, and the next minute you're crying over your baked beans on toast.'

Mari hugged her tea close to her chest and stared out of the window.

Rosa bristled and gestured towards the door. 'Ethan's probably down at the harbour giving Peter Morris his sailing lesson. I can march down there in two minutes and find out what happened for myself if you don't tell me right now.'

She sighed dramatically and waved a piece of toast in the air. 'Of course it would make a terrible scene and half the town would be on the dock in a flash, but nobody upsets my sister and gets away with it. You just give the word and…'

'Stop right there. Yes, Ethan didn't upset me. He just…' Mari shook her head and bared her teeth '…has this amazing talent for doing something totally unexpected and getting me all worked up in the process.'

'Nothing new about that. And did I mention that I wanted details?'

Mari looked up at Rosa. This was it. This was the wonderful moment she had been looking forward to when she finally, finally, told her baby sister that their dream had come true.

'If you must know—' she grinned '—I asked him to

loan me some money so that I could buy a house this morning. In Swanhaven.'

Rosa collapsed into a chair, mouth open.

Mari nodded, and took Rosa's hand between both of hers. 'Yup. It's all true. I set my heart on a particular house, I didn't have enough, so Ethan loaned me the extra I needed to make the winning bid.'

And that shut her sister up for all of ten seconds before Rosa asked quietly, wide-eyed and incredulous, 'Are you really telling me that you have bought a house in Swanhaven?'

Mari nodded and tried not to look elated, but a bubble of happiness was welling up inside her and threatened to burst out in the form of spontaneous laughter. They might even be dancing.

'Not just any house. Our house. The beach house where we grew up and were so happy together as a family. I've been planning it for months, Rosa, but I didn't want to tell you in case I got your hopes up for nothing.'

Mari was almost bouncing with excitement, her shoulders practically jiggling as all the nervous anticipation and excitement of that morning came flooding out. 'I came so very close to losing it and if it hadn't been for Ethan I would have. I made a bit of a fool of myself by doing the one thing I promised myself I wouldn't do. I bid everything I had. Only it still wasn't enough. But I did it, Rosa. I finally did it. We have our house back. Isn't it wonderful?'

Rosa slipped her hand out from between Mari's and took in a sharp breath between her teeth. 'Oh, Mari... what a mess. I was going to tell you tomorrow, but now I'm sorry I waited.'

Rosa started pacing back and forth across the

kitchen, pulling one cookery book out and then putting it back on the shelf before picking up another and all the time carefully avoiding looking at her sister.

As Mari watched Rosa, a growing sense of concern slowly, slowly, pricked at her bubble of happiness and the longer she watched, the more her sense of happy excitement faded with it. 'What is it? I thought you would be totally thrilled. This is what we both want. Isn't it?'

Rosa stopped pacing, turned back to face Mari and took a firm hold of the back of the dining room chair before speaking but, far from being thrilled, the tone of her voice was sad and filled with regret.

'Do you remember taking all of those photos of my scarf collection last autumn?' she asked. 'I talked to each customer who came into the newsagent's to model a different scarf for me? Well, it was a bit more successful than I had expected.'

Mari smiled into her sister's face before replying. 'Let me guess. You have to knit like crazy for a bulk order for some fancy shop. That's wonderful. We're going to have all of the studio space you need at the house.'

Rosa held up her unstrapped hand. 'Please let me finish. This is hard to say so I need to get it all out in one go. It's more than an order, Mari. One of the customers runs a handcraft design centre in an expensive part of London. She got in touch through the website a few weeks ago. There are workshops, design studios, everything. And she asked me to manage the craft shop for her, Mari. Full-time.'

Mari looked up into the face of her sister, unable to speak.

'I said yes, Mari. I want this job—it's so perfect I

could have designed it myself. I'm going up to London next week to make sure that it is everything she claims. But if it is? I plan to move to London straight away. And I don't know when I'll be coming back.'

Mari's mouth fell open in shock.

'What? Rosa! You can't be serious. I thought you loved Swanhaven.'

'I do—and I probably always will,' Rosa replied, clutching at Mari. 'But this is my dream job, Mari. Crafts are my passion and the thought of working with them full-time makes me so excited that I can hardly believe it. I did the research ages ago but there was no way I could afford to take three years out of my life to study textiles in a city like London. It's way too expensive. This way, I can work, study and have somewhere to live.'

Rosa's eyes implored Mari to understand. 'You were the person who told me that I should grab on to any chance for happiness I could find—and this is it. This is my chance to show people what I am capable of. If I don't take this job now I'll regret it for the rest of my life, Mari.'

'But you don't need to move to London now. You could work at the house, build your business and sell on the internet. It would be fantastic.'

'Yes, I could.' Rosa nodded, her mouth thin and sad. 'But I don't want to. For once in my life I want to do something different. I want to go to London and find out about the craft business. I want to go to college and learn from the best. And I'm not going to do all of that in Swanhaven. I'm so sorry, Mari, but you really should have involved me in your plans.'

'Wow,' Mari breathed and sat back. 'You're serious

about this, aren't you? But what about our dream of moving back to our old house? I thought you wanted that more than anything. Are you going to give up on that so easily?'

Rosa shrugged. 'You're right. I did want to move back when Mum was still with us, but that's all changed now. Have you been up to our old house recently?'

Mari shook her head before replying in a low voice. 'Not for a couple of years. It hurt too much. Oh—I know it needs work. The house details made that quite clear, but we could restore it together. Just the two of us. It would be great.'

'No. It would not be great.' Rosa shook her head, then lifted her arms and let them fall down. 'This is a total disaster, Mari! I cannot believe that you didn't ask me before you bought that old wreck of a house, expecting us to live in it. It's a shambles, and I certainly don't want it.'

'How can you say that? That was our home!'

'No, Mari. It's a house that used to be our home.' Rosa looked around and waved her good wrist. 'This is my home—at least for another few weeks! And then I'm leaving to start a new life and new future. And it is not in Swanhaven.'

Then her voice softened as she flicked Mari's hair behind her ear. 'Oh, sis. What have you done? Was this for me? Yes? Oh, Mari, I love you, you know that, and you are my one and only sister, but I don't need a babysitter any more. I'm looking forward, Mari, not back. It hurts me to think that you can't do the same.'

'What? Have you not been listening? We could make this house work, we could make it like our home used to be…' Mari started to form the words to tell her all about her wonderful plans for buying their old home back and that Rosa did not have to move to London at all.

Rosa could stay here. And be with her and live the life...she had imagined for them both.

And suddenly the selfishness and stupidity of that idea jumped up and bit Mari hard on the ankle. There was no work in Swanhaven. Rosa was right. There was nothing for Rosa here but more of the same things that she had been doing with her life so far. She'd thought that her sister was happy and fulfilled here, *and she'd been wrong.*

Staying here would mean that Rosa might never find another way to fulfil her own dreams and potential. And that was just too sad to think about.

Rosa was able to find happiness living somewhere else. Living her passion.

Mari swallowed down tears and blinked hard to cover up her distress. 'Well, it looks like I have to get used to the fact that my baby sister is all grown-up with ideas of her own. It's come as a bit of a shock.'

Her reward was a one-armed hug and a kiss on the top of her head. 'I'll leave you to work out what you're going to do with this house you've just bought,' Rosa said, then laughed out loud. 'Marigold Chance is back in town. That has to be worth celebrating. See you later.'

Mari managed a small wave in the vague direction of her sister's back. 'Later.'

Perhaps coming back to Swanhaven for the Valentine Day party had not been such a good idea after all. *She could hardly wait to find out what more wonderful news the rest of the day would bring.*

* * *

The pale winter afternoon sunshine was trying to break through the clouds as Mari strolled down the narrow cobbled street towards the harbour and the yacht club.

The annual Valentine party had always been a special time in Swanhaven and, judging by the street banners, bunting and displays in the shop windows, this year was going to be no exception.

It was almost like old times, Mari thought as she turned the corner from the yacht club onto the quay. Then suddenly stopped, mesmerised by what she was looking at.

An old wooden sailing ship was moored in the harbour. It was a single-masted traditional brig with a lovely wooden hull and decking, which must have docked that morning. She could have looked at the stately and gorgeous ship all day, like many of the locals on the quayside who had gathered around to admire the brig.

But that was not the only cause of her fascination.

Mari stared in amazement at the man who was kneeling on the deck of the ship, holding a thick rope in one hand and showing a teenager how to form a special knot with the free end of the rope. The boy was gazing in rapt attention at the complicated knot that Ethan was showing him for a second time, and looked so much like Kit at that age that Mari's heart contracted.

But it was not Kit. It was a boy in a bright yellow life jacket who was so intent on twisting the rope into this special knot against a piece of rigging that when he had finished and stood back, it was Ethan who laughed out loud and broke the tension.

'You must have been practising, Peter. My arms are getting tired just holding on! Ready to test it yet?'

His question was met with enthusiastic nodding from the boy, who stretched out far enough to tug hard on the rope several times to make sure that it was firmly attached. 'All done, Captain,' he said with a jaunty salute to Ethan, who sat back on his heels to salute back.

'Well done, first mate. Stand at ease.'

Ethan was back on his feet in seconds, but not before he had slapped the boy firmly on the back and given him a warm hug across his shoulders.

But it was Ethan's face that Mari was focusing on.

And what she saw on that smiling, happy face hit her squarely on the jaw and sent her spinning. The intense pleasure, the happiness, his own delight in bringing such joy to the child, was reflected in that open-mouthed grin for all to see.

Ethan would make a wonderful father.

How had she not seen it before?

He wanted to show his *own* children how to tie ropes on a ship and how to sail. And he wanted it so badly it hurt her just to see it on his face and know that he had no idea how open and totally exposed that need was for all to see—or was she the only one to see it?

Any child with a father like Ethan would be a very lucky child indeed.

What a shame that he would never have the chance to settle down and be a father with the life he led.

Well, she would know about that.

Over the years she had often thought about having children of her own, but she had always kept that dream carefully locked away inside a stout box labeled: Later. *When I'm back living in Swanhaven in my old home. That's when my life will start and I can be happy. That is when I can think about children and a family of my own. And maybe even a husband to go with them.*

And in a flash the true impact of those ideas jumped up and slapped her firmly across the back of the head.

Wake up! She had done it! She had actually done it! She had bought back her home.

She had signed the paperwork in a daze and knew that it would be days before the legal documents were ready to be processed and money had to be transferred, but this was it.

Telling Rosa was one thing. But seeing Ethan working with this young man? The true impact of what she had done—no, what *they* had done, hit home and hit her hard.

Suddenly everything was different. She felt as though a huge door to a secret chamber had been opened and all of the dreams and goals she had kept hidden for ten years were suddenly exposed to the light and released from their captivity.

And a family was one of them.

She had chosen to put her personal happiness and her dreams of having her own children on hold, and now—now she didn't have to. She had just bought a huge family house which would be heaven for any child.

Of course she would be living there on her own, alone on the cliff, trying to create an online business, so meeting men could be a bit of a problem. But she could do it. Couldn't she?

Perhaps there was still time for a relationship—she was only twenty-six. She could make an effort if she was ready to change. If she was prepared to take the risk.

Perhaps that was why she'd always made sure that

she was the one who broke up with any man who dated her more than a couple of times, because that way *they* never had a chance to break up with *her*. The truth was, she had driven her last long-term boyfriend away because she was not ready to open up her emotions and heart and let him into her life.

Mari looked up just as a pretty woman in a long woollen coat walked along the jetty to the brig and the boy practically flew off the deck towards her. They looked so much alike that there could be no doubt at all whose son he was, and the woman wrapped her arms around her son's shoulder before twisting around to face Ethan.

'How is Peter getting on? Almost ready to go out on his own?'

'Mum!' Mari heard Peter reply, but it was Ethan who smiled reassuringly. 'Not there yet. We have a couple more sessions before the main season starts. Right?'

The teenager just grinned back, his face full of hero worship.

Well, she couldn't blame him for that.

The memory of Ethan's hands on her body, his mouth on hers, only the evening before, had her heart racing just to look at him.

As for Ethan? Maybe he was right. Maybe the life of a competitive sailor was too selfish and way too hard for the people they left behind. But surely the good times would make up for the time apart?

Mari watched Peter and his mother stroll further down the jetty towards a smart little boat with a distinctive red sail. Leaving Ethan alone on the brig.

Deep breath. Had she really asked him for money? Then cried with happiness all the way back to town in his car? That was so embarrassing. He must think her even more of a fool than he had before.

So why was it that something in the back of her mind told her that she might kid some of the people some of the time but, when it came to it, she just couldn't kid herself?

His kiss last night in the car had been so annoying precisely because it had given her hope that there could be something between them after all of these years.

But, in the cold light of a February afternoon, the gulf in their choices was only too clear to see.

He was going back to Florida and a life of sun and sea.

While she had just bought a house in Swanhaven and she would have to work every hour of every day for years to come just to pay off her debts.

There was no future in a relationship between them.

It was time to leave before either of them said or did something that could not be unsaid or undone. Something that would make one of them choose to change their lives. And she was way too scared by the emotional turmoil that had been building up inside her since the moment she'd seen him sail up to the jetty to have any hope of logical thought or rational decision-making.

He would be here until the end of the week and she had so much to organise with the house before she flew back to California. She simply didn't have the time for distractions like Ethan Chandler. No time at all. She had things to do. People to see. Some photographs to scan. And only a few more hours to do it.

In the meantime, nobody had warned her that having her dream finally come true after so long would be so bewildering that she felt giddy just at the thought of everything she had to do and the life ahead of her.

She needed to talk to Ethan. His father was an architect. He would know the next steps she needed to take to make her new home safe and sound.

As for Rosa's little bombshell?

Her shoulders slumped. He had been right about Rosa.

So. Time to pull on her big-girl pants and go and eat humble pie.

She needed Ethan's help. *Again.*

Ethan had just thanked the captain of the brig when he noticed Mari strolling along the jetty towards him. She had changed out of her suit into more casual trousers and fashion boots below a light jacket and smart scarf. Her hair was loose around her shoulders, her laptop bag slung over one shoulder and she looked every bit like the tourist she most surely was.

Gorgeous, infuriating, stubborn, irrational and absolutely lovely. His palms were sweating and his mouth went dry just at the sight of her.

He had been quiet in the car on the short journey from Swanchester back to Swanhaven for one simple reason. She had been crying every single second of the way. The intensity of the tension inside the car had been in such contrast to the almost friendly attitude and sense of connection of the previous evening that he almost regretted agreeing to the loan.

Almost. He had made the right decision—this was what Mari wanted. He knew that. But it didn't make it any easier when, deep inside, he could not shake off the fear that this girl was setting herself up for a life of lonely isolation with only the ghosts of the past for company. She was going to have to work hard to create a secure future for herself, but she was strong enough to make it happen. Even if she had to pay a high price for living here.

Perhaps it had been a mistake to offer her the money—but the Mari he was looking at now was not a girl who had lost her centre, but a lovely adult woman who knew what she wanted and was determined to get it, even if it had meant waiting all of these years.

He admired her for that. And there was the added advantage that they were locked together now by bonds more than the past. He was part of her present and her future. No interest. Just connection. Good enough.

And at the very least she had stopped crying.

Smiling to himself and more than a little curious about what she needed, Ethan walked slowly away from the town along the jetty towards his boat and waited for her to catch up.

'Mari, I hope that you're feeling better now,' he managed to whisper, and then coughed to cover up how nervous he felt.

'Much. Thank you.' Mari looked around and nodded towards Peter, who had slipped onto the boat and was practising with his sails as his mother looked on. 'So he's one of your students?' she asked.

Okay. She was making an effort to break the ice after the crying. The least he could do was go along with it. 'Peter's uncle was one of my instructors and when he found out I was in town he asked me if I could help Peter with a few coaching sessions as a personal favour. I wasn't too keen but actually it's been great. Peter is a shy boy who doesn't do well in groups but he has talent. He'll be fine.'

He turned back to face Mari and tipped her chin up so that he could see her eyes. 'And what about you, Mari? Are you fine? You had a busy morning. Buying a huge family house is an exhausting business.' *Are we fine?*

Mari shrugged. 'It certainly is. I've just told Rosa the good news.'

Ethan nodded and winked. 'Well, that explains the smile on your face. She must think it's Christmas morning in her cottage. I suspect elaborate celebrations are now being planned.'

Mari sucked in a breath to calm her nerves before speaking in a voice which emerged as a long sigh. 'Not exactly. Rosa and I had a long overdue chat just now and it turns out that she's planning to leave the town for a new job in London.'

Mari flashed him a glance when he half snorted in surprise. 'Yes, I know. Looks like I was wrong.' She licked her lips and pushed her shoulders back. 'In fact, it seems that I've been wrong about quite a few things. Starting with the fact that she doesn't want to stay in Swanhaven, and she certainly doesn't want to live in our old home with me. How about that?'

Ethan stared into Mari's face. She was trying to be brave. When the one thing she had been working towards for so long had turned out to be a damp squib instead of a glorious rocket display. She was holding it together better than he had thought possible.

And his admiration and respect just went up a notch.

'That must be hard when you've taken care of Rosa for so long. But I suppose she has to make her own decisions. You should be proud of giving her the courage to want to lead her own life. It won't be easy.'

Mari had been playing with the strap on her bag but, as he spoke, she looked up and her face brightened. 'I hadn't looked at it like that. Thanks. You're right. She should lead her own life. And she'll always be home for the holidays.'

'Absolutely. So you'll be living there on your own?' he asked and, when she gave a way too fast nod, he simply smiled. 'Well, in that case, I'd better ask my dad if he could design you a fine-looking IT studio. Home office, big glass windows overlooking the sea. Oh, yes, that would be something.'

His reward was a closed-mouth smile. 'Yes, it would. But perhaps I should start with plumbing and electricity? In fact, do you mind if I pick your brains about the repair work?'

'No problem, but phone calls may be needed.' He paused and got busy with the rope holding his boat to the jetty. 'Speaking of which, I'm going to need your bank details to transfer the money. Just drop me an e-mail. That would be fine.'

Mari stepped closer towards him so that, even on the empty jetty, only he could hear what she said next.

'That's why I've come to apologise, Ethan. I should never have put you in that position this morning. I am sorry. You were more than generous. I thanked you then, but thank you. Really, I don't know what I would have done if you hadn't been there. And if you're still looking for help at your parents' house I would be happy to get involved. If you want me to.'

She was looking at him now, almost hopeful.

And something very close to excitement and happiness hit Ethan hard. This was turning out to be quite a day.

'Well, in that case, we'd better get started, but there's one slight change of plan. My car is back at the house. I came in by boat.' And he looked at her and then tipped his head towards the sailing boat bobbing on the water, then back to her again.

Mari sniffed and crossed her arms. 'Oh, that is so cruel. You know why I've not been on a boat that small for a very long time.'

Ethan nodded slowly. 'If you want me to accept your apology you're going to have to get into that boat. It'll take ten minutes to get back to the house. Come on, Mari. Let's get this over with. Look, I will even start the outboard motor. Now that's some dispensation.'

Her arms slowly uncrossed and she started to speak, then looked into his boat in silence and bit her lower lip.

'I can't, Ethan. I just can't. I can't get into that boat. I can take a taxi.'

Mari. He watched her walk as calmly away from him as she could, down the jetty towards the beach and the cliff road, her head down against the wind, shoulders high inside her jacket making her look thin, small and fragile and almost childlike in so many ways.

Well, that had been a mistake! And he was a fool for even suggesting it.

She had been so happy this morning and in an instant he had wiped all of that joy away.

What had he told Mari? That she would be making a mistake in coming to Swanhaven? How ironic. He was the one who had made the mistake coming back here. He should have let his father complete the house in his own way and stayed where he was until the redevelopment project was complete.

That way he would not have met Mari again. He would not have talked to her, laughed and joked with her, worked by her side, and he certainly would not have made a connection.

Ethan slapped his hand palm-down on the side of his boat, hard enough to make him wince with pain.

Stupid! He should have known that coming back here would reopen old wounds and feelings that he had thought long dealt with. Especially now Mari had bought back the wreck that had been her old house and wanted to make some kind of home there.

Mari.

Ethan quickly wiped down his hands and shrugged back into his jacket.

Time was up. He strolled casually down the jetty to where Mari was standing, frozen, staring out across the bay, facing away from the ocean and peering up onto the cliff-top where Ethan knew her old home was.

She had wrapped her arms around her body as though trying to warm herself and block out the bone-penetrating icy wind, now flicked with faint sleet.

He walked slowly over, unfastened his own sheepskin jacket and stepped behind her, so that he could reach out and wrap the warm jacket around her body, pressing his shirt front against her back, his arms crossed in front of her coat so that she was totally enclosed inside his embrace.

Neither of them spoke as Ethan followed her gaze out to the dots of light which were flicking up on the far shore, his head pressed against her hood.

He closed his eyes. There had to be five layers of

clothing between their skins, and the freezing wind howled around his bare hands. And yet… He was holding Mari Chance in his arms and it felt so right. So very right that it was madness.

Slowly, slowly, he dropped his hands to her waist, cuddling against her, and started to turn her around to face him.

As though awakening from a dream, Mari realised that she was not alone and her head twisted towards him inside the huge coat. As her body turned slowly, his hands shifted so that when her chin pressed against the front of his shirt, his arms were now around her back, pressing her forwards.

His eyes closed as he listened to her breathing, her head buried into his body, protected from the icy wind and the sound of the waves lapping against the stones on the shore.

Her arms, which had been trapped inside his coat, moved to wrap around his waist so that she could hold him closer.

A faint smile cracked Ethan's face. She was hugging him back. Taking his warmth and devotion.

He dared not risk taking it any further. Dared not break that taste of trust she was offering him.

Hugging her tighter, Ethan dropped his face a little so that his lips were in the vicinity of her forehead.

Mari responded immediately and looked up as he moved back just far enough so that he could see her face under the hood.

Their eyes locked. It was a moment in time. But, just for that single moment, everything that had gone before meant nothing. They were a man and a woman who cared for one another very deeply, holding each other.

It seemed the most natural thing in the world for Ethan to run his lips across her upturned forehead, then her closed eyes, her breath hot against his cheek. He felt her mouth move against his neck. Stunned with the shock of the sensation, he almost moved away, but paused and pressed his face closer to hers, his arms tight on her back, willing his feelings to pass through his open hands, through the clothing to the core of her body.

This was unreal.

A single faint beam of light streamed out from the lively harbour that was Swanhaven in the early dusk and caught on Mari's face like a spotlight in the gloom of the dock. The faint golden light warmed her skin. They were both cold, but there was no way Ethan would break this precious moment when the barriers were down and he could express what words would fail to convey.

His hands slid up and down her back. His mouth moved across her cheek, and he felt her lift her chin. Waiting for his kiss. The kiss that could warm that frozen centre her deep loss had created.

Adrenaline surged through his body, his senses alive to the stunning woman he was holding in his arms, his heart racing. He could feel her warm breath as they looked into each other's eyes, both of them open-mouthed. Nose almost touching nose. His head tilted. Ready.

Ethan opened his eyes to look into the hazel-green eyes of this remarkable woman who he felt he had known all of his life. His dream was about to become a reality.

CHAPTER EIGHT

SUDDENLY, out of the corner of his eye, Ethan saw something on the bay.

It was a sail. A small boat with a red sail with a black symbol on it.

It was Peter's boat, and he could just make out a small figure standing at the tiller, turning the boat into the wind so it sped across the water, faster and faster. Too fast. Way too fast. And he was on his own. Almost at the same time, he caught a glimpse of Peter's mother running towards the yacht club for help.

Ethan jerked back, his hands pulled away from Mari and he frantically grabbed her hand and half dragged, half pulled her back to the jetty and physically lifted her onto the boat without asking permission or forgiveness.

It took precious seconds for Ethan to untie the rope, start the engine and rev it to maximum speed so their small craft bobbed violently against the waves as it raced towards the red sail.

'Ethan, what is it? Please. You're frightening me. Tell me what's happening!'

'It's Peter. That boy I've been teaching to sail these

past few days. He's out in the bay on his own and something's gone wrong. Look! The red sail!'

Every time he took his eyes off the water to look at Mari in the fading light, all he could see was a small huddled figure with her eyes closed, clinging on to the side of the boat. Teeth gritted, flinching with every wave that struck the boat side-on.

Then out of the still night there was a shout, then the unmistakable sound of a human body crashing into water.

Then silence. Absolute silence.

Peter's boat was stationary, listing to one side. And there was no sign of the boy.

Ethan slowed the engine and coasted a good distance from the sailing boat and, just as they got close enough to see what was happening, the boat came to a juddering halt which made Mari scream out in alarm.

Ethan scrabbled over the side to see what they had hit, then took a gentle but firm hold of Mari's arm. 'It's okay. It's a piece of wood. A tree trunk. It's just below the water level. We're not damaged. But Peter is not in the boat. I need you to take the tiller for a while. Please.'

Mari looked terrified but, with a silent nod, she carefully made her way to the back of the boat and took control.

Ethan frantically fought to get his balance at the side as he looked back and forth along the waves for any sign of the boy, calling his name louder and louder. 'Peter! It's Ethan. Peter!'

'There! In the water! Ethan!'

Ethan whipped around. Mari was pointing into the waves a few yards ahead of the boat where there was a splash of red in the surf.

Without a moment's hesitation, Ethan stripped off his boots and dived into the freezing waves, the shock of the cold paralysing him for a few seconds before he could swim the few short strokes until he reached the small figure, who was splashing about with his arms above his head in the choppy, icy water.

Ethan grabbed both of Peter's wrists and dragged him upwards until he could take the boy's weight around his shoulders. He tried to calm the teenager, who was grabbing, scrabbling onto Ethan. Peter's sodden clothes and boots almost pulled them both headfirst into the waves, but Ethan was too quick and leant backwards, taking the full weight of the coughing, spluttering and panicking boy towards him.

In a few exhausting strokes, Ethan managed to drag their two bodies closer to the boat, where he could see that Mari was already at the side, waiting. Even so, it took precious few minutes to swim close enough so that he could support the thrashing boy around the waist and hoist Peter into his own boat and Mari's waiting arms, where he collapsed onto his side, coughing and heaving water, but alive and breathing.

Ethan waited until they were both safe and out of the way before hauling himself, painfully and slowly, over the side and onto the deck, where he forced air into his lungs, before looking around for Mari. Hoping that she could get them back to shore on her own.

To his relief Mari had already moved over to the outboard motor and they were underway. The light from the cellphone pressed to her mouth illuminating her terrified pale face. Her coat was gone, wrapped around Peter, who was crying and shivering with shock and cold. Her hair was wet and hanging in strings around her face and her clothes were ruined.

And she had never looked more beautiful.

Ethan thought he heard her calling for help before the cold shakes hit him hard and he wrapped his arms tight across his chest. Cold. But with an icy fury burning inside of him.

Mari stood outside the emergency room where Peter was laughing about something with two younger-looking boys while his mother watched, her face tired and lined. She peeked through the slats in the window at the smiling teenager hooked up to the monitors, and the cluster of people around him.

Peter had given them all a terrible scare—her most of all.

Almost back to normal. That was how the nurse described her patient.

Well, that was not how she was feeling. *Far from it.*

She slumped against the wall, exhausted. And very angry with herself for being so weak and feeble that a simple accident had the power to destroy her completely.

It was all so confusing. She had turned against Ethan for surviving the accident that killed her brother, and yet she was so grateful that he had been there at that moment last night when she'd needed help, and he had not hesitated for one second to dive into the icy water to do what he could to rescue a boy he had only come to know a few days earlier.

Shaking, Mari staggered the few steps to the waiting area and collapsed, her head back, eyes closed, trying to catch her breath and persuade her heart to return to a normal beat. Adrenaline, fear and concern surged through her.

She was immediately taken back to the moments they had shared on the shore, and the tenderness of Ethan's touch. Ethan had recognised what she needed at that moment and offered it to her, before she knew it herself.

He truly had become a very special man.

She had trusted Ethan. Without thinking about it, or judging him, she had wanted to kiss him, back then, at the water's edge, and stay in the warmth of his embrace. She had wanted it very badly.

And why not?

They were adults. They were single. This wasn't the school holidays any more. All she had to do was put the past behind her and forget the pain that they both had suffered together and maybe they had a chance…

But what about the fact that she had three or four years of hard work ahead of her in renovating the house, working to earn the money she needed, and then, eventually, setting up and running her own IT business in Swanhaven? While Ethan's life was in Florida. Thousands of miles away.

Long-distance relationships were impossible.

A cold sense of reality washed over Mari. As cold as the air at the harbour.

Maybe, just maybe, there was a chance that they could spend more time together—but that was all it could be. And the sooner she realised that, the better for both of them. They could still care about one another as old friends, and she could treasure that friendship during the long months and years of lonely work she had ahead of her.

That was it. They could meet up now and then when

he came to visit his parents at their retirement beach house and have a few drinks. No strings.

No strings?

And just who did she think she was kidding with that idea?

In the space of twenty-four hours she had bought the home she had been dreaming about and working towards over the past years, was in debt to Ethan for loaning her the money and had then found out that her sister had no intention of staying in Swanhaven. Oh—and then she had to go out in a small boat to rescue a young sailor who seemed to idolise Ethan as much as she had. If that were possible.

All in all, not the quietest of Valentine weekends.

Mari sighed out loud, but turned it into a smile as the doctor strolled out of the cubicle where Ethan had been checked, leaving the curtain partially open, and from her waiting area Mari could see that the great hero was up and about, pulling on the collection of clothing that Rosa had brought in, courtesy of their extended family.

Of course Ethan had tried to make her feel better and had laughed away the threat of hypothermia and frostbite on the way here in the ambulance. Just testing the water before deciding it was a tad cold for a skinny dip—*but roll on the summer, eh?*

And all that came only a few hours after she had accused him of not knowing who she was. Stupid girl. He knew exactly who she was. Because he was her friend. Perhaps, if she tried hard enough, she might be able to see him in that way.

Time to face Ethan—and everything he had done for her. And see how looking at him as her new best friend worked.

Well, she could try! For both of their sakes.

She took a deep breath and strolled over to the door jamb and knocked once before peering around the curtain of the cubicle across the corridor.

'Nice pullover!' She grinned and folded her arms in as casual a pose as she could manage, considering that this was a hospital and the man she was looking at had been holding her not so very long ago.

Ethan pulled the pale blue and white-check V-neck sweater down over his hips, and then bent over to slip on the golfing shoes, complete with tassels.

'Only if you like the golfer look. And, believe me, after living in Florida for so many years, this is my idea of style. Plus it's warm and dry and I think the shoes go particularly well.' He glanced up at her as he pushed himself off the bed.

'How are you doing, Mari? Warmed up a bit?'

She grinned at his roughly dried hair. 'More than a bit. How about you?'

'I'm good. All my fingers and toes are intact and apparently I have the constitution of a small ox. Have you talked to Peter?'

'Mild hypothermia from finding out just how cold the water can be, and swallowing quite a lot of it in the process, but he got a nasty shock—and so did his mother. They'll keep him here overnight, but he should be discharged in the morning.'

She paused and then glanced into his face.

'I can't remember if I thanked you last night. Isn't that terrible? You saved that boy's life and I might not have thanked you. You were amazing. Thank you, Ethan. He owes you. We all do.'

He was standing now, shrugging on a ski jacket several sizes too small which probably belonged to one of the cousins, but he looked up as though startled at her question, and stepped forward so that they were only inches apart. His voice was low and trembling with emotion when he spoke.

'I should be thanking you for staying with me, Mari. I know that it doesn't change the past. But thank you.'

The shock of those words, and the intensity with which they had been spoken, acted like a detonator under a firework.

Mari looked up into Ethan's face in amazement, her sore red eyes brimming with tears, and what she saw there broke her heart.

In that moment she recognised the compassion, and the good man that he had become. Had always been. He had gone into the freezing water to save a boy he barely knew who needed his help—but that was not what he meant at all. He was talking about Kit.

She had no words to express her feelings. Words would not be good enough.

Mari raised both hands open-palmed and pressed her fingertips against the sides of Ethan's face, as though she was holding a precious porcelain object, the stubble on his chin prickling against her wrists as her eyes locked on to his.

She moved her body forward so his back was tight against the sludge-green painted walls of the hospital room, pressed her chest against his, closed her eyes and in one smooth movement tilted her head just enough so that when she kissed him their bodies were a perfect fit.

This was what she'd wanted on the shore.

This was what she had been denying herself with pathetic attempts to pretend that Ethan was nothing more than an old childhood friend, every doubt and hesitancy had been blown away by a few simple words which expanded her world into areas where rational thoughts about where this could take them in the future did not matter any more.

The thrill of his warm mouth on hers quivered through her body, warming, relaxing, exploring. Her heart thumped and her breathing became hot and ragged as she moved into his embrace, her entire body revelling in the wonder of the experience.

Ethan's head moved sideways to lock with hers as she took a breath, and his hand pressed the back of her head towards him for a second deeper kiss.

His other hand was around her back now, drawing her closer, and the pressure of his fingers seemed to lift her higher and higher, her heart racing as Ethan returned the kiss, his mouth harder, wider and hotter.

He was kissing her back with a passion and intensity she had only dreamt about as a girl and in those lonely dreams through all of the years since.

It was everything she could have imagined, and every nerve in her body sang with the thrill of the feel of his warm mouth on hers.

The first time they'd kissed they'd been teenagers, and this was a world away. This was a powerful, handsome athlete of a man who held her in his arms with such delight and passion it was ridiculous to resist. And she didn't want to.

It was Ethan who broke the kiss, the palms of his hands sliding down to her waistline. His head moved forward as she lifted away, and she was stunned to see that his eyes were still closed, his mouth open, as he tried to keep contact as long as possible.

His lips pressed into her forehead as his arms circled her waist, as though determined to keep the physcial bond between them as long as possible, so that his lips could move from her hair to her brow in one smooth motion.

She felt she could stay there for ever. Locked in his embrace.

He was her rock, the support she had been looking for all of her life.

This was the Ethan she had dreamt of.

His hands moved from her waist to her head and gently drew her back, away from him so that he could look into her face.

Her straggly hair. Her red eyes.

'Perhaps I should learn to swim after all?' She smiled. 'Just in case you're not here to rescue me.'

He said nothing. He stroked her hair back behind her ears as his eyes scanned her face, his thumbs brushing her cheeks, and he just breathed, breathed and looked into her face as though it was the most fascinating thing he had ever seen.

As though looking for something.

Whatever it was, he found it.

Ethan pressed both hands tight around her face and hair, took half a step forward, their eyes still locked. And he drew a deep breath.

As though by magic and some unspoken signal, Mari's mouth opened just in time as Ethan kissed her harder than any other man had ever kissed her, the passion of the connection so intense, so forceful, Mari automatically flung her arms around his neck to stop herself from falling backwards, the power of this man's body concentrated, focused into one single connection between two mouths.

She couldn't breathe, couldn't think of anything except kissing him back, pressure for pressure, movement for movement, her hot panting breath fighting to keep up with his.

He moved position, sliding his mouth across her lips, lifting her face with his thumbs and locking it to his.

Something in the back of her brain registered that there was movement and female voices in the corridor and, as the curtain twitched, Ethan broke the kiss. And she opened her eyes.

His eyes were wild, carnivorous. Full of passion and love. And questions.

Neither of them said anything but just stood there, her arms still wrapped around his neck, his hands now pressed into her back, then slowly, slowly, he started to breathe and the fire in his eyes calmed as he drew her closer, pressing her head into his shoulder, one of his hands moving up and down her back, the other still at her waist.

Mari closed her eyes for a second, revelling in the heat of the sensation, listening to their breathing, feeling his heart still thumping hard under his chest.

And she knew. If they had been alone in this room she would not have stopped kissing him.

She wanted to feel his touch on her skin. She wanted him to show her how much he cared about her in the most intimate way.

And if this was any indication of the passion this man

could feel, he wanted the same. He wanted her just as much as she wanted him.

Which meant only one thing.

She was in serious trouble.

CHAPTER NINE

MARI spread the bundles of photographs out across the sofa and tried to make some sense of the collection. It had been her father's idea to give Mari a grown-up camera for her twelfth birthday, and it had immediately become one of her trademarks. Whenever she left the house, the stiff brown leather camera case came with her, stuffed into pockets, satchels and school bags with a spare roll of film, just in case.

In fact people used to joke that Mari was always the one at the back of the room taking the photographs of other people enjoying themselves while she looked on. She never thought that funny or odd, just a fact of life that was all part and parcel of being the academic one. The quiet one. Not a bit like her brother or younger sister.

She hadn't minded really. It gave her a reason to be there and not have to talk. And here were the prints to prove it. Her parents, her extended family, so many Christmases and birthdays—it was all there, including some lovely ones of her mother which she set aside to scan for her own album.

Mari quickly sorted through the last bundle, selecting group shots of Ethan and his parents at a prize-giving, a summer party, and what looked like the end of the Regatta dance.

Her fingers lingered over two photos of Kit and Ethan from some junior yacht club event. Gangly, awkward limbs and wide smiles. But it was their energy and passion for life which beamed out at her from the photograph. They were both so young and happy and bursting with enthusiasm with a brilliant future ahead of them.

Ethan had come a long way and had realised his dreams. While Kit had had his snatched away from him in an instant. Just like Peter almost had.

Mari closed her eyes for a second and pressed the photograph against her chest. Ethan had saved Peter's life last night and the horror of that moment when she had seen Peter in the water was captured forever in her mind; had been there every time she had drifted in and out of sleep.

It shouldn't matter that Peter was shy and quiet, and that she saw a little of herself in him too, but it did. He had been brave enough to take a boat out on the water alone—but there was no way that he could have seen the heavy tree trunk which was lying almost submerged, just under the waterline. Until it was too late.

Her eyes pricked with tears. She had tried *not* to compare Peter's accident with what had happened to Kit, but it was impossible. She had been there last night and had seen how confused and disorientated Peter had been. Alone and in shock, he'd been too bewildered to help himself in those few crucial minutes in the icy water and his heavy clothes had dragged him down.

And just for a second she had an insight into how Ethan must have felt that day at the regatta when the wave had hit their boat. Only last night Ethan had dived into the water to try and save Peter, instead of being thrown into the water. Ethan the man had taken control, while Ethan the boy would have been just as confused and shocked as Peter had been.

Why had she not seen that before? Ethan was blaming himself for an accident that had not been his fault. And that was just wrong.

Just as she had been wrong about a lot of things.

Wiping away a tear from the corner of her eye, Mari put down her photo albums and settled on the couch with her feet tucked under her, the unheated room quite chilly now the light was fading.

The past few days had been unsettling; her mind felt giddy and out of control. As though she was spinning round and round on a carousel, unable to get off even though it was making her feel dizzy and shaking and unable to hold back her feelings and emotions.

And right at the centre of that carousel was Ethan. Somehow he was able to strip away all of the carefully constructed barriers which she had created around her heart. He had always had that power and the intensity of how she felt about him scared her. And thrilled her beyond measure.

She exhaled slowly. Tasks. Work. That was the answer. She had to focus on working through these photographs as a leaving present.

Leaving? Last night at the hospital had felt like the start of something. Not the end.

Mari sat up straighter on the sofa and blinked to clear her head.

She had just opened the first album when there was

a knock on the kitchen door and a loud, 'Hello,' in a man's voice—Ethan's voice.

'In here,' she called out, trying to sound casual and failing miserably, probably due to the thumping of her heart and the lump in her throat.

He stuck his head around the door and smiled.

The sight of his face hit her in the bottom of her gut like a punch, leaving her breathless and dizzy. The blood rushed to her head. Hot. Thumping. Her heart racing with delight at seeing him again.

'You left your laptop bag in my boat yesterday!'

She had to laugh at that. Just when she'd thought he might be here to offer his undying love and beg her to run away with him to the sunshine, and all Ethan wanted was to return her bag—the bag she usually carried everywhere with her, but somehow she had totally forgotten about it in the rush to get Peter and Ethan ashore.

'Yes, I suppose I did. Can you leave it in the hall? Thank you.'

'No problem.' He looked at the albums on the sofa. 'What have you got there?'

Mari took the plunge and gestured him over with one hand.

As he collapsed down onto the sofa next to her and stretched out his long denim-clad legs, she passed him the first volume.

To her delight, he extended one of his arms along the back of the sofa and she felt instantly warmer and somehow safer inside that embrace.

'I've decided that you need some personal photos in that splendid house of yours from your wicked and evil past. I'm sure your parents would love to have a record of Swanhaven through the ages,' she lied confidently. 'So, if you've got a minute, I could use the help.'

'Now why didn't I think about that? Of course I need personal photographs. Great idea.' Ethan started flicking through the pages before yelling out a, 'Wow!'

Mari practically leapt back in recoil. 'What?'

She leant sideways to look at the page Ethan was holding out as though it was toxic.

'Well, just look at that,' Mari whispered, not daring to look at Ethan in case she burst out laughing. 'Mr Chandler at his first Regatta dance. How old were you then? Fourteen?'

'Fourteen and a half and, boy, I had forgotten those hipster trousers! Maybe I thought sparkly was cool back then.' He pretended to shiver in horror.

'What about the matching skirts Mum made for Rosa and me? She was going through a phase of dressing us both up in identical outfits back then. Rosa hated it.'

Ethan chuckled. 'I remember. It caused chaos. Same clothes, same hair, same bag. It was like having double vision until you opened your mouth.'

His fingers played with the back of her hair, lifting strands above the collar of the hand-knit sweater she had borrowed from Rosa. 'I love what you've done with your hair. Elegant and stylish. It suits you.'

Mari felt her neck flush scarlet and pressed her lips together to stifle a giggle. 'Thank you.' Then she quickly changed the subject by pointing to a group photo. 'The high school science fair.' Mari shook her head. 'I had forgotten about that.'

'Your model was the San Andreas Fault system. Complete with a working friction model of the fault and photo displays.'

Mari turned around and stared, only too aware that her mouth had dropped slightly open in shock as Ethan continued, 'You had tectonic plates and ocean fissures, and could have been filmed for a TV documentary.'

'I can't believe that you remembered that,' Mari whispered, shaking her head. 'That has to be twelve years ago. It was the very last week at school before the summer holiday and Kit was so annoyed when you turned up with your parents while we were still trapped in the classroom.'

'I recall everything about that science fair. It changed my life.'

'What do you mean? Changed your life? You developed a passion for geological faults which made you turn to a life on the ocean wave?' Mari replied with a suppressed chuckle, suddenly concerned that this blast from the past was taking her to places she did not want to go after all. And it had nothing to do with models of geological fault systems.

Only Ethan didn't laugh, but focused on the photo in his hand.

'I looked at that model and the photo display, and then I looked around and saw you, just sitting at the back of the classroom with your head in a book. Oblivious to everyone else. All alone. Contained. And that's when I knew.'

He looked up at her and their eyes locked.

'Every other person in the class had done the minimum amount of work they'd needed to create a model to get the praise. The marks, the points, whatever. Not you. You didn't need me or Kit or Rosa or anyone else to validate you as a person. You spent the time making it perfect because that was who you were and the standards you set for yourself were so high—and so demanding that no boy was ever going to come up to those standards. I just wasn't good enough for you. Intellectually or as a person. It was a blow.'

Mari looked into his face and saw the kind of pain she had never seen before. No joking. This was real. 'I don't understand. All I can remember is that you teased me for days about how long I had spent working on it indoors, while I could have been outside at the beach with the rest of the family You were always making cutting remarks about me having my head in a book.'

'Don't you see? That was why I teased you. I was so attracted to you but I knew that you were so far out of my league that it was a joke. You weren't responsible for my massive inferiority complex. I was.'

'You liked me? I mean, you really liked me? I had no clue.'

Ethan chuckled and found something fascinating to look at in the hollow below Mari's ear. 'I made sure that you didn't. In fact, if it hadn't been for the big fight we had at your birthday, I probably would never had summoned up the courage to even try and kiss you. Until that moment I thought that you hated me. You'd closed down on me, and I didn't know how to reach you.'

Mari blew out. *Hard.*

'I didn't hate you, Ethan. I hated what Kit's death had done to my life and my family. They were destroyed. Nothing was ever going to be the same again. And when my dad didn't turn up on my birthday after I had waited all day? I was clever enough to know that the happy life I had known was finished. Over. For good.'

Mari swallowed down hard and blinked away tears before she gave Ethan a half smile. 'You came out to the beach and then followed me to the house. You were a convenient target. And I am so sorry for all of the horrible things that I said to you. I was so unfair. Can you forgive me?'

Ethan reached forward and gathered Mari into his arms, his chin pressed onto the top of her hair, and she sucked in deep breaths against his chest.

'There's nothing to forgive. I blamed myself for wanting to be with you and hold you even though I felt responsible for breaking up your wonderful family. I felt guilty that I kissed you and didn't know what to do about it the next day, so I left. Even though I knew in my heart that you would probably hate me for it.'

'Why? Why did you want me to hate you?'

Mari lifted her head so that she could look into Ethan's eyes.

'Oh, that's easy. I felt that I didn't deserve anything better. To see you cry, to hear your pain and suffering… that was so hard. I couldn't deal with it. I didn't know how.'

'Oh, Ethan. We were both grieving, I can see that, but why are you telling me this now?'

He shrugged. 'I thought you ought to know that I have never been more grateful that Kit chose me to be his friend and I had the privilege of knowing you and your family. That's all.'

She looked at him and then broke into a smile.

'You were a good team. No doubt about that. Kit loved the time he spent with you on the water.'

'We were the best. Nobody got close. Ethan Chandler and Kit Chance. How many times was that read out at the award ceremonies?'

'Damn right.'

Mari glanced up at him and realised that his eyes had never left her face. He wasn't looking at the photographs any more. *Just her.*

'I was looking for photos of Kit. We haven't really talked about him, have we?'

Her throat was suddenly dry and tight.

Ethan tilted his head. 'There's no need to. He's there in every conversation we ever had. Your family blamed me for his death, and I understand that completely and would probably feel the same in your shoes. I was in the boat, and I should have been able to save him. And I couldn't. There's not a week goes by, even now, when I don't see someone who reminds me of Kit. That never goes away.'

'No. It doesn't. We know that you tried to save him that day. But we're not fools. We all knew that Kit was so headstrong and so determined to beat you. He took too many risks and my dad…my dad let him do it. He was the parent and he was in the boat that day when you misjudged the wave and it caught the boat. And Kit…'

Ethan's reply was a long intake of breath, followed by a sharp nod.

'Kit went over and hit his head on the side of your dad's boat when it came alongside. And it killed him. You can say it, Mari. We both lost a wonderful friend that day. And your dad lost his son. And I'm sorry. I'm sorry that he died. More than I can say. Seeing you again also brought it home to me that I've not been very fair with my own parents. Kit was having fun that day, while I chose to put myself into the most dangerous waters on the planet. And that's not fair on them, or on anyone who cares about me. It's a hard life when you turn your back on those you love.'

Mari closed the covers of the photo album and pressed her fingers hard against the cover. 'You're right. You are selfish. But you know what you want and you go for it. And I respect that. But everything has changed, Ethan. You, Rosa and especially me. I'm not the sweet little daddy's girl I was back then. And Kit has gone and won't be coming back. I suppose there has to be a time when we decide to move forward, or stay trapped in the past.'

Her voice let her down, the burning tears she had held back pricking the back of her eyes.

'Then come to the Valentine dance with me tonight. As my date.'

Mari's head shot up and she blinked away tears of astonishment. 'You're asking me out on a date? You? Ethan Chandler, yachtsman extraordinaire?'

'How about Ethan, an old family friend? Does that make it easier to say yes? Because I would really like it if you did say yes. Please. Take a risk, Mari. Take a risk on enjoying yourself. What do you say? I thought that I didn't deserve a chance of happiness when Kit had his chances taken away from him. Maybe I was wrong about that. And I would like to find out more.'

And, without waiting for her answer, his hands came up to cup her chin and he pressed his full warm lips onto hers in a kiss so tender that she wanted it to go on for ever.

Her eyes were still closed when he slid his hands away. 'I'll pick you up at eight.' Then he gave her nose a gentle tap and, without waiting for her reply, he walked out of the door, leaving Mari sitting in silence, her heart thumping and a wide grin on her face. Only then did she dare to breathe.

* * *

It was two minutes before eight and Mari had been peeking out of the window every few minutes for the last half hour since Rosa left. *Just in case.*

So why was it that she was fluffing the sofa cushions to try and calm her nerves when she heard the gentle knock at the door? So that she practically stumbled in her haste to open it?

Ethan was wearing the smartest, sexiest dinner suit that she had ever seen.

He had shaved. His hair was swept back and styled. He was wearing shiny black shoes and a shirt so white she might need sunglasses if the fluorescent lights were working at the club.

All he needed now was a pair of sunglasses and he'd pass for a Hollywood movie star.

Ethan Chandler looked stunning, and her poor sensitive heart did a little flip. This was *her* date for the evening. *Oh, yes. Was that possible?*

Gulping away a sense that she was totally out of her depth here, Mari nodded slowly as she tried desperately to come up with a witty comment which would not betray her total wistful joy at seeing this man standing on her sister's doorstep.

'Um…I can see that your life as a fashion model was not entirely wasted. Looking good, Ethan.'

'Oh, this little old thing?' he joked and brushed an imaginary speck of dust from his jacket and then gave a low snort and his face instantly relaxed. 'I took myself off to Swanchester this afternoon and threw myself at the mercy of a menswear shop who specialise in formal wear. It was a new experience. But I like challenges. And these are for you.'

Ethan regally lifted up a small but perfect bouquet of

the most beautiful roses, freesias and tropical greenery and made a small bow before presenting her with the flowers.

'I have no idea what kind of flowers you like, but my mum loves these. Are they okay?' he asked through gritted teeth.

Mari took the bouquet with both of her hands and brought the flowers to her nose so that she could drink in the heavenly scent. 'Oh, that is so gorgeous. I adore freesias. It's like summer in one place. Yes, they are okay. In fact they are better than okay. Thank you.'

Ethan blew out one long breath of relief, then thrust his chin out and wriggled a forefinger down under his stiff white shirt collar.

'Comfy? Mari asked, chewing the inside of her cheek to fight down her laughter.

Ethan lifted his head and regally raked the fingers of his right hand back through his hair. Then relaxed and grinned at her.

'Not in the least. But my suffering is all in a good cause. This is our first date. I think it's traditional for the boy to be dressed by his mother for this rite of passage. I had to improvise.'

Mari stepped forward to straighten Ethan's black bow tie, making sure that, as she did so, their bodies were in contact from hips to chest. Her reward was the telltale increase in his breathing so that she could almost hear the beat of his heart under her hands.

'You look fine. Just. Fine.'

She dared to glance up and blushed from neck to toe at the look she saw in Ethan's eyes, which was positively indecent.

Sliding back down from tiptoe to the floor along the length of his body was no hardship at all.

'Every Valentine Fairy should have her prince. And I think you will do quite nicely.'

Mari caressed the front of Ethan's shirt, sensing the bands of muscle that lay beneath the fine fabrics. Gulping down something close to exuberance, she gave his chest one final pat, then stepped back.

'Don't I have the chance to see your dress for the evening?' he replied. 'Although your shoes are quite delightful.'

Mari looked down at her snow boots, which were sticking out from below her long padded winter coat, and waggled her toes.

'Ah. There's a reason for that. Think of it as a surprise. There's been a slight change of plan.' Mari sucked in a breath. 'Rosa had agreed to be the Valentine Fairy for the kids tonight at the party. Only with her arm out of action, she asked me to take her place.'

She pushed her lips together. 'I am so sorry about this, but the Valentine Fairy is quite a tradition in Swanhaven and I couldn't let the children down. The good news is that I only have to work for my supper for about half an hour, and then the rest of the evening is ours. Is that okay? Because Rosa has already gone ahead with all the props we need. And she says thank you for your understanding.'

Ethan smoothed back a wisp of hair which had fallen forward onto Mari's brow.

'Well, this is going to be a first in more ways than one. I've never had the pleasure of a date with a Valentine Fairy. It almost makes me feel special. Even if it does mean sharing my date with the good citizens of the town.'

'Then I shall have to make it up to you, won't I?' Mari said, fluttering her eyelashes at him. 'And the sooner we get the party started, the sooner we can really start our date.'

'I like the sound of that even more. Shall we go, my lady? Your carriage awaits.'

'One more minute.' Suddenly inspired, Mari reached into the bouquet of roses and freesias and selected a full pink rose and presented it to Ethan.

'Would you do the honours of completing my fairy crown, kind prince?'

'I would be honoured,' Ethan replied and pressed the stem of the rose into her hair behind her right ear, his fingers lingering on her cheek as he secured the blossom. Then they moved in slow circles across her temple into the wave of curls which had taken Rosa an hour to spray tight, and down into her neck.

'That's perfect. You are perfect.'

She could not resist it. She giggled. A proper girly giggle. Then stretched out both of her hands and gently clasped hold of Ethan's.

'Now look what you've done.' She laughed. 'Our first date and I am giggling already.'

And they just stood there, holding hands, smiling at one another like teenagers, as though nothing else mattered in the world.

It had taken Ethan five minutes to park his car in the snow, after dropping Mari at the entrance to the yacht club, and he opened the door just as a great round of cheering and applause went up from the other partygoers. He strode inside to see what all the excitement was about.

And instantly stopped in his tracks, scarcely believing what he was seeing.

Rosa and Mari Chance were skipping, arm in arm, into the clubhouse. But it was their choice of party-wear that was the main cause of the excitement.

Rosa and Mari were wearing identical pink ballet tutus and tight sparkly tops, waving tinsel wands with glitter stars at the ends. Plastic tiaras completed the ensemble, tied under the chin with a pink ribbon tied in a huge flower bow. Mari's crown was decorated with the pink rose and, apart from the strapping on Rosa's arm, they could have been twins.

And they were laughing like loons. Real laughter. The kind of laughter only sisters and close family could create in rare moments. He had missed that.

The magic fairy wands did not go unnoticed by the older members of the Chance extended family, who simply shook their heads and mumbled something about the crazy sisters and the dangers of alcohol at this time of year.

He thought they looked fabulous.

As for those legs? Those long, long legs? Well, it seemed that some things had improved over the years. Mari was about two inches taller than Rosa and he could look at her legs all night. She was wearing tiny ballet shoes with pink ribbons winding up each calf. Oh, boy.

At least they were a distraction from the tight tops. And he was not the only one to notice. Half the young and not-so-young single men in the room had abandoned their Valentine dates and made a beeline for the girls, who were obliging with twirls of their ballet skirts.

This was too good to miss, so Ethan resisted the temptation to reclaim his date and decided to watch for once and allow someone else to be the centre of attention.

The local police officer won a round of applause for pretending to arrest Rosa for causing a public disturbance, only Rosa stole his police hat while he was concentrating on writing down the details of the pink garter she was wearing, and he had to chase after her out of the door and onto the harbour, leaving Mari laughing her head off, calling out, 'Officer in hot pursuit.'

Where had this Mari come from?

He stared for a moment and listened to her laughter. Laughter so genuine and real that it eased its way into his heart like a great fire and stayed there, warming him through and through.

She really was quite remarkable.

And then she was swallowed up by the rest of her family, just as the Chairman of the Yacht Club came up to shake Ethan's hand. Did he have a few minutes to talk to him and Mrs Morris about how they would keep up Peter's sailing lessons? Apparently last night's accident had made Peter even keener to carry on. Ethan looked over one shoulder just in time to see Mari settling down with a cluster of exuberant, energetic ladies and decided that he could spare a couple of minutes. Just a couple.

By the time Ethan returned from supplying the entire yacht club with enough mulled wine to intoxicate a small army, he had somehow agreed to find Peter a place on one of his training ships and Mari was sitting on a bar chair, surrounded by a group of young girls listening intently to the story she was telling. She lowered the book just long enough to stare intently into the faces of each child in turn as she begged them to believe in fairies, who could give every girl and boy Valentine wishes and kisses.

A great chorus called out, 'We believe. We believe.'

Ah. Peter Pan and Tinkerbell. Nice one. The book snapped closed, the mothers clapped in applause and drifted away to eat burgers and hot dogs and chicken legs, each child taking a tiny tinsel star from Mari as they came for their hug.

Ethan casually strolled up and picked up a fallen star. 'Any hugs left, Tink?'

She looked up from refastening her thin-soled ballet shoes, seemingly unaware that she was displaying a healthy amount of leg in the process.

'You have to be under ten and female to qualify. And preferably less than six feet tall.'

'Ah! My faith has been restored. Ageist, sexist and heightist! All qualities to admire in the average Valentine's Day Fairy. Speaking of which—I thought *Peter Pan* was a Christmas story. You could be in great danger of confusing a lot of people here tonight.'

He casually returned her tinsel wand. 'Not that I'm complaining,' he added with a wink. 'Especially in that outfit! It truly is quite remarkable and I am officially a lucky man.'

Mari looked down at her pale pink pumps and wiggled her toes inside her pink tights. 'You can consider this a special performance. One night only. Never to be repeated.'

'Shame. So far, it is totally working. Where did Rosa find those costumes?'

'Apparently there are boxes of clothes up in her attic. My loving sister gave me two choices. It was either the Christmas Wish fairy or Mum's Dorothy costume. Complete with ruby slippers and a stuffed toy Toto that barks if you pull a string.'

Ethan nodded. 'No contest. I particularly like the tiara. It pulls the whole thing together.'

Mari reached up and touched the plastic rings with the crystal lampshade droplets.

'I think it suits me. Rosa looks weird. But on me? Cute. It's the rose that makes all the difference.'

She peeked out at him between her eyelashes and tried out a wide-eyed cheeky grin before asking, 'Do you think I look cute, Ethan?'

'You look very special, Miss Chance. Cute does not cover it.'

Mari curtseyed, holding out one side of her tutu, and then paused and waved her wand as a family passed by, then looked at him, hard, before going on, her eyes never leaving his face. 'There is another reason my lovely sister persuaded me to come dressed like this and make a fool of myself.' Mari sucked in a breath and the words gushed out. 'Now that Rosa is leaving Swanhaven to run a craft shop, this could be our last opportunity to be here as sisters. It's the end of an era, Ethan.'

Ethan looked out across the crowd and gestured towards Rosa as she chatted to friends and neighbours. 'Then good luck to her. That's a brave decision. Who knows? Maybe there will be two Chance sister entrepreneurs out in the world soon. That's a very scary thought.'

He gestured across to the barbecue with one thumb. 'So. Want a hot dog, Tink? Barbecue? You're going to need sustenance before I take you dancing!'

Mari shook her head in disbelief. 'The mulled wine is starting to kick in on an empty stomach. Because I thought you just asked me to dance. And you don't dance!'

Ethan smiled and planted his hands on his hips before nodding. 'Nothing gets past you, girl. I thought it was time to make an effort. Show you a few new moves I've picked up over the years.'

He reached out and meshed his fingers into hers. 'Come on. Take a risk, Mari. This could be your last chance.'

Mari sighed as Ethan stepped back, drawing her from the plastic chair, and was fluffing out her tutu one-handed to brave dancing in public with the most handsome man in the room when Rosa almost ran up to them.

'Come on, you two. The line dancing is just about to start and I've saved you a place in the front row. What are you waiting for? Get this show on the road. Let's rock this joint.'

Mari looked at Ethan. Ethan looked at Mari, then he stood ramrod straight, reached out, seized Mari's hand and whispered the magical words, 'I'll risk it if you will.'

CHAPTER TEN

'THIS has been quite some day!' Mari managed a faint smile as Ethan opened the passenger door of his car, and then shivered when the freezing-cold air hit her.

Without asking, Ethan slid off his sheepskin coat and wrapped it around her shoulders, before sliding one arm under her legs. 'Here. This coat suits you better than me. Keep it. And you'll never make it across the sludge in those magical slippers, Tinkerbell.'

Mari's arms instinctively wrapped around Ethan's neck as he swung her out of the seat, pushed the car door closed with his foot and strolled calmly down the path to Rosa's doorstep as though she weighed nothing and this was something he did every day of the week.

He didn't speak and she couldn't form the words. Her personal space expanded to include Ethan and it felt so amazing, so precious, that somehow words would only ruin the moment.

The movement of his steps ended only too soon, and he stood in the light of the porch. He simply looked down at her and her heart melted.

His arm moved slightly so that her legs slid gently to the sparkling frost of the stone step.

'Thank you,' she murmured. 'For the coat. Fo

night. And for being there today. I don't know if I could have got through it without you. And, most of all, thank you for tonight. I had a great time.'

Ethan's other arm freed itself from around her waist to press against her back as he opened his mouth to speak, then shook his head and lowered it so that his brow was pressed against her forehead. His breathing was hard and fast against her cheek as he opened his mouth to say something, then changed his mind and braved a small smile.

Whatever he wanted to say was probably not going to be good, but she knew she had to hear it before she changed her mind.

'Look at me,' she whispered. 'You can tell me. I may not like it, but after the day I've just had, I don't think anything could surprise me.'

Mari reached out and meshed her fingers with Ethan's as her eyes scanned his face. The blue of his eyes was iridescent in the reflection from the snow, from the streetlights and the warm glow from Rosa's cottage. His tan was a distant memory. His cheeks were burning red, and his lips were tinged with cold.

He looked absolutely gorgeous.

'Perhaps that gives me some hope that maybe, just maybe, you might let me into your life one of these fine days. And forgive me for surviving that accident when Kit died, because I'm not sure I can do it on my own.'

[illegible]han!' She had started to speak, desperate to tell [illegible]t he was the last person who needed to be for- [illegible]d the past was the past, but he gently pressed [illegible]rtip to her lips.

'Please let me finish. I need to say this now. Or not say it at all.'

She dropped her hand, but meshed her fingers even tighter into Ethan's, feeling him give reassuring pressure back.

'Let me introduce myself. I am Ethan Francis Chandler. The international yachtsman and, more recently, a new up-and-coming sailing instructor and charity worker. My name has been mentioned in magazines and on TV. My parents even have press cuttings, can you believe that? I can sail just about anything you throw at me from a raft to a super-yacht. I can cook. I can iron my own shirts. I have friends who actually like to go out with me to eat and drink. And enjoy themselves! In my company! And you…you are the most angry, most competitive, most challenging, most guarded and most stubborn woman I have ever met. What the hell is so wrong with you that you won't accept that I could care about you? And let yourself care about me right back?'

His voice was trembling now, the gaze in his eyes intense.

'I left Swanhaven to get away from you, and everything you made me feel, Mari Chance. The guilt about Kit and the pain of leaving your family like that has stayed with me every day of these last years. And seeing you here? Like this? Suddenly I'm seventeen again and just as confused and totally mesmerised by you as I was then. But some things are clear. I've been a fool, Mari. Ever since I met you at the jetty I knew that this was a second chance for us to finish what we started. We could make a future together. And that comes before anything else.'

Ethan broke eye contact to look around the snow-covered narrow streets that led down to the harbour and then back to Mari, who was staring intensely at his face, focusing on every word, every syllable coming out of his lips.

His breath was hot, fast. 'I have a wonderful job sharing my passion with kids like Peter. I have a lovely house and a great future ahead of me. And yet I still have that burning passion to sail away to some distant ocean to get away from my pain and my loss. After last night, and what has happened between us these past few days, I'm starting to realise that maybe, just maybe, I could stop running away and trying to live the life Kit never had. But I can't do that on my own.'

The pressure of his fingers increased until it was almost painful.

'But I don't want to live a life without you in it, Mari. Because I need you and I want to know if you feel the same way…' He could not speak any more.

His hand came up and cupped her chin, his thumb moving into her hair as his head tilted. Cold lips pressed into her cheek, the cold burning against the hot sweaty tears as she closed her eyes to revel in the sensation. Their fingers disengaged as Ethan's hand wound around her waist and drew her closer to his body.

His lips moved across one eyelid, gently, gently, then down to her upper lip. The pressure increased only for a second as she swallowed down a shivering breath.

His kiss was everything she had imagined it would be.

Warm and loving, so very loving.

The smell of his skin.

The sensation of his stubble on her face.

The thumping of his heart. Racing now as he drew her closer and moved his hand further into her hair.

'Come and live with me in Florida. I could help you rebuild your house here in Swanhaven and we could come back any time you like—but this has to be your choice. Your decision.'

His forehead pressed against hers, the hot breath steaming as they both panted open-mouthed in the freezing night air. Alive in the moment. 'You can work there. Make a career for yourself. Your company even has an office in my city.'

He leant back just enough so that she could focus on his smile.

'I believe in you. And I believe in your talent. You can do anything you want to in this world. You don't need to wait to create your own business. You can start it in Florida and I will be right there, helping you every step of the way.'

His thumb was moving across her chin as he stared into her face.

'I know you can find a way to make it happen. If you want it badly enough. So what do you say? Will you take the risk? Will you come back to Florida with me? We can do this if we work together.'

It was that final statement which broke the spell he had cast.

Mari inhaled the biting air and stepped back, desperate to regain some distance from this crazy intensity. She had not felt so scared for a long time.

'Oh, Ethan, I'm so confused. I was actually starting to think about how it would work, but this is too much for me to take in… I never imagined that…'

She looked into his shocked face and knew that it

was going to hurt, no matter how much she wanted to prevent his pain.

'You know more than anyone how hard it was for me when my dad left, and then you left with your family. And it broke my heart. It's taken me ten years to build up the barriers I need to protect myself from that kind of pain and loss. My life is finally coming together and I don't know if I'm ready to take that kind of risk.'

'What kind of life do you truly have, Mari? Because I know exactly how lonely my existence has become in sunny Florida. What does a great job and a sea view matter without the things that are important? It isn't enough. Not nearly enough.'

He stroked her cheek and smiled gently, sensing that he had just exposed a nerve.

'I want to make my home with the girl I'm still crazy about. Come on. You don't need to live in your old home on your own. I could help you make it a home again. A real home with a future.'

She closed her eyes and steadied herself before looking into Ethan's face. 'I'm scared.'

Shaking her head in disbelief at her own words, Mari pushed away from Ethan and started pacing, her hands pushed deep into the coat pockets to thaw out.

'Maybe the timing is all wrong, but suddenly I feel that my life is in total turmoil. I'm not sure about anything any more.'

Before she could speak another syllable, Ethan stepped forward, grabbed her around the waist with two strong hands and drew her towards him, chest to chest. So close she could smell the tang of his sweat on his shirt, the faint trace of his aftershave. The Ethan smell. The Ethan presence, which filled the moment to bursting.

'Chandler and Chance,' he whispered in a voice designed to send heat to the frozen tips of her ballet shoes. 'If we could work together we would be unstoppable. But you're right, this has been a long day. Will you think about what I've said? Please. Think about it.'

He held her face between his cupped hands as she nodded, then glanced down and smiled. 'Your poor feet. Crazy girl. Goodnight, Mari. I'll drop by to see you in the morning. Sleep well.'

He kissed her forehead once. Barely more than a brush of his lips across her skin. It felt like a branding iron, burning a mark that would never be erased. Then he turned around and walked slowly down the path to his four-wheel drive, one hand thrust into each pocket of his jeans, leaving her standing, stunned, shivering even inside the coat still around her shoulders, just watching him start up the car and drive away.

He didn't look back.

And she just stood there.

She had to.

Her moist ballet shoes had frozen to the ice on the doorstep.

The wind had picked up during the night and it buffeted Mari as she made her way along the top of the cliff path heading away from the centre of Swanhaven and out towards the headland. And the house where she used to live. The house which was going to become her new home.

She'd been so confident that this time she had a real chance of reconnecting with her old life when she had been so happy, safe and warm in a family who loved her and valued her. A family she could trust to do the right thing for her and never once complain that she was distant or that she had let them down by being 'emotionally unavailable,' as her old boyfriend has described her. Inside the warm embrace of her family, she had never felt the need to close down her heart.

It was daylight now but still too early in the morning for anyone else to be on the path. She could see a few dog-walkers playing with their dogs on the beach below and she envied them their carefree moments of fun and laughter. But right now she was grateful for the solitude and the familiar soundtrack of the sea crashing onto the rocks at the point, the call of seabirds and the sound of the wind in the trees on the other side of the fields and the crunch of her own footsteps on the cold stone chippings and frosty grass as she walked.

It had been a long night which she had got through in snatches of broken sleep and much tossing and turning before finally giving up and heading downstairs to the empty, cold kitchen and a hot drink before facing all that her first day as a homeowner in Swanhaven could bring.

Starting with seeing Ethan again.

His face and his soft voice had echoed through her dreams, filling her with a sense of belonging and warmth and familiar contentment which was so at odds with the turmoil seething though her that she had seized on to it like a life raft in those dark and lonely moments when everything that had happened over the week threatened to overwhelm her.

And that was so wrong. And unfair. *To both of them.*

Last night he had offered her his heart and she had been too terrified to accept it.

When had she lost the ability to trust and show her emotions? Was it when Kit died and their father left them? Or when she lashed out at Ethan on her sixteenth birthday? She had only dared to kiss him when the strength of her pent-up frustrations and anguish and grief had overcome the barriers she had created to protect herself.

Reliving their tender moments together when they kissed in the hospital, it had been her overwhelming sense of relief that he and Peter were safe and well that had broken down the flimsy barricades and allowed her the luxury of being able to show Ethan how she truly felt about him.

More than that, the power of those feelings had given her the freedom to believe that she could be attractive and worthy of being loved by a man like Ethan. If only for a few moments, she had enjoyed that remarkable sensation that she was ready to trust in another person and fall in love with him. And she was worthy of that love.

Spending these past few days with Ethan had made her feel things that she had never felt before. Oh, she had glimpsed what love could be like, but her ex-boyfriend was right that she had never been able to trust him enough to open her heart to love him. It was not an excuse for cheating on her! Far from it. But, the more she thought about it, the more she realised that perhaps she had chosen someone who she knew she would walk away from, in one way or another, before he got too serious.

Why not? When her self-esteem as a woman was so low.

Well, these past few days had opened her eyes about a lot of things.

Ethan had made her realise that she had to find her own way forward. Or face a lifetime of running away. Or, worse, running backwards.

A pair of herring gulls soared up from the edge of the chalk cliff on the wind, calling and squawking as they climbed higher and higher into the sky in front of Mari as she paused to watch them. They seemed to be mocking her and her weakness and lack of self-confidence.

Well, they were right about that, but she had made a start and there was a long way to go.

Head back, she closed her eyes and felt the wind blasting against the left side of her body, bringing with it the salty tang of sea and seaweed and all that she had grown up with and never once forgotten. She had walked this path at least once a day for the first sixteen years of her life and very little had changed.

Everything about this place and this moment was as different from her normal office life as anywhere in the world. But, as she stood there and listened to the sea and the bird calls and felt the wind and smelt the sea, she realised that in truth she had never left.

She had always carried this special place with her in her heart over these last ten years. It was the core of her sense of who she was and who she probably always would be. The self-confident girl who'd loved school and had a world of opportunity in front of her.

A smile crept onto Mari's face like a welcome friend. Strange. That idea had never even occurred to her until that moment. But it would explain why she felt so at peace here and why she felt compelled to go out on such a cold morning wearing the extra-long sheepskin coat that Ethan had given her when she could have stayed warm and snug in bed.

And of course there was one other reason why she had pulled on all of her winter clothing and borrowed Rosa's warm boots. She longed to see the house again so that she could start planning what improvements needed to be made.

Inhaling deeply, allowing the cold salty air to purge her lungs of the city smog, Mari finally opened her eyes and looked straight ahead of her.

She could just see the roof of the house, which was set back a few hundred feet away from the cliff path and, with renewed vigour and purpose, she set off walking towards it, covering the short distance in fast long strides, her eyes fixed on the red tiles.

She turned her back on the sea, swung open the garden gate and stood and stared at her old home. And her breath froze in her lungs. Transfixed by shock and amazement at what she was looking at.

The pretty flower beds and neat lawn where she had once played and held tea parties was a brown, barren wasteland of waist-high weeds and wild bushes that choked the evergreen shrubs which had been chosen with such loving care to flourish in the harsh sea breezes. Broken pieces of furniture, glass and plastic bottles and rubbish of all kinds spewed out from an open dustbin, which was jammed against what was left of the broken wooden fence which had once been white and fresh and welcoming.

But it was the house itself which was the greatest shock. The front picture windows were gone—covered over by pieces of timber which stared out like grey eyes, cold and lifeless. The window frames and the front door were rotten and splintered, uncared for and useless and the guttering was waving loose in the wind from a broken wooden fascia.

Tiles were missing from the roof. There was a crack in the main chimney and a wild thistle was growing in the drainpipe.

Tears of grief and the biting wind pricked Mari's eyes and she heaved in a breath.

This was where she had wanted her lovely sister to make a home! This was the house she had longed to come back to! This was the house she had just bought with all of her savings, a loan from Ethan and a lot more than she could afford.

What had she been expecting? The same house she'd last seen when her mother was alive and they had walked along the cliff path on a hot summer day arm in arm and made light of the fact that the elderly couple who lived there were lovely people but gardening was not their strength? How could the house have deteriorated so fast? She had seen it only a few years ago and it had been nothing like this. But of course she had only seen it at a distance from the beach. Any closer was too painful.

Rosa had tried to warn her, but nothing could have prepared her for this amount of neglect. It was going to take months of work and more money than she had to make the house fit to live in.

Oh, Ethan. You were so right. Where was her secure and loving home? This certainly was not it.

Taking a couple of deep breaths, Mari pushed her

way through the garden, being careful where she placed her feet, until she came to the kitchen door.

Once glance confirmed it. The door still had the original lock.

She glanced from side to side and immediately felt foolish because she had not seen anyone for the last ten minutes and she was the new owner on paper, then reached into her trouser pocket and pulled out a long brass key with an engraved handle.

Her father had made the keys and the lock by hand and given each of his family their own key. She had used this key once before, when she had sneaked in here with Ethan on the night of her sixteenth birthday, and she had kept it safe all of these years, waiting, just waiting, for this moment to use it again. *Time to see if it still fitted.*

Cautiously, she stretched out her hand, and then pulled it back again.

This was not her property yet! She couldn't simply go inside without asking permission. Could she?

The wind howled around her ankles and blew old leaves up in the air. She had come a long way to stand on this very special piece of earth. It was now or never.

Head up, Mari slowly and gently turned the key in the lock and felt the mechanism engage. The door itself had swollen in the winter rain and it took a little persuasion to open but, a few moments later, Mari Chance stepped inside the lobby and closed the door behind her.

She was back inside her home again.

This was the moment that had sustained her in the endless airport lounges and interminable meetings in boardrooms without windows. This should have been her great achievement.

She had come home. She was back.

And she felt sick at what she was looking at.

Her home was a shell of a building, dark, dank and gloomy and, in a moment of horror and barely suppressed claustrophobia, Mari stepped across the broken and filthy floor tiles they used to polish every Sunday evening to the window above the sink, and tugged hard at the plastic sheeting and cardboard which covered the window.

The flimsy sheets came away easily in her hands and pale February sunshine flooded into the dark kitchen, creating a spotlight around where she stood in the otherwise dark place. This window was north-facing and her mother had created stained glass panels in the top half of the window to add colour to the otherwise dull, flat light.

Mari blinked hard as the light flooded into the room through the large window that dominated the wall above the old ceramic sink.

Elsewhere in the stripped-out shell of a kitchen, there were dim shadows and corners of dark purple and grey above exposed electric wires and gas pipes, but Mari's attention was totally focused on the stained glass which, amazingly, wondrously, had survived intact and as bright and colourful as ever.

As she stepped closer, mesmerised, it was obvious that the glass in the window was not made from one continuous sheet of glass, but composed of separate smaller panels of varying thicknesses and slight colour differences which her mother had collected from old glass windows and painted by hand.

It was a garden with flowers and leaves of every colour in the spectrum.

Each piece was unique to itself but an essential component of the piece as they fitted together seamlessly to create the whole. Light hitting the thicker bevelled edges was deflected through multiple prisms to create rainbow spectra of colour which danced on the tiled floor at Mari's feet in a chaos of reds and pinks, pale violets and blues through to greens.

It was as though the light itself had taken on the colour of the glass, creating layers of different luminosity as it was diffracted and refracted and deflected through the uneven panels to produce a barrier between this space and the world outside.

Each panel was unique, creating a different illusion of the world beyond the glass.

On the other side of the glass, bare skeletons of trees bent towards the town in the howling wind from the sea, above the browns and russets of autumn colours. But here and there she could just make out the first signs of yellow daffodils and white snowdrops. Spring was on the way and in a few short weeks there would be new life and energy on the other side of the glass.

Mari sucked in a breath of cold, damp and dusty air, coughed and exhaled slowly as she glanced around this empty, echoing and frigid room.

Her life was in that window.

The past was captured in her reflection on the glass for a few fleeting seconds until she moved away and the moment was lost. On *this* side of the glass was the present, and a girl whose reflection was looking back at her. And on the other side of the glass? That was where the future lay. Still hazy but with the promise of sunny days ahead.

But not here. Not in this room and not in this building. There was nothing for her here any more.

Mari closed her eyes and let the tears finally fall down her cheeks unchecked as she mourned the loss of everything she'd thought that she wanted.

What a fool she had been.

She pushed the heel of her hand tight against her forehead.

This was not the home she remembered and it never could be. Her mother was gone, and Rosa was moving away to create a new life for herself.

Almost blinded by tears and with a burning throat, Mari forced herself to look around the bare walls and in an instant saw it for what it truly was. A shell of a house which had been cared for at one time when a family lived here, but that time was long gone.

Selfish, stupid girl. She had told herself that she wanted this house for Rosa, but that had been a pathetic delusion. This was all about what *she* wanted—for herself. Rosa was simply an excuse for justifying the years of hard work and sacrifice she had spent building up the finances to buy back this…what? This shell of a house filled with the echoes of ghosts and sadness? A tired and wrecked version of the home she had once known?

Mari leant back against the dirty painted kitchen wall, suddenly exhausted and bereft of ideas and energy.

She had to face the truth. It had never been the house she wanted. It had always been about the feeling of security and love. That was what she had hoped to bring back into her life through buying this building. As if a physical place could give her back her shattered self-confidence and make her open her heart to being loved.

Mari choked on the cold, dirty air she gulped into her lungs.

But there it was.

Ethan was right. She should be outside the window, looking at the new spring flowers, instead of inside her past, looking out in fear. But the idea was so hard to take.

Somehow she had to build up the strength to walk out of this room and this house, find Ethan and thank him again for loaning her the money and tell him it would not be needed after all.

It would be tough, embarrassing and humiliating, but that was what she had to do before she could move forward.

She had to accept the fact that she was not going to live here. The family who had wanted this house could buy it. And love it. And be happy here. This house needed a real family to transform it back into a loving home again, not a lonely single girl with delusions of bringing back the past.

Mari sniffled away the tears of grief at what she had lost and sacrificed, and she slid off her warm glove to dive into the pocket of Ethan's coat. Hopeful that he kept tissues somewhere down inside those extra-deep pockets.

Only instead of paper tissues her fingers closed around a package.

She pulled out a long oblong which had been gift-wrapped in bright red foil. A white adhesive label with Christmas holly leaves around the edges said: *A bit late for a Christmas present but I hope you like it. Thinking of you, Ethan.*

Mari swallowed down a lump in her throat the size of Dorset as she pressed her fingertip against the blue ink. She would have recognised his spidery-thin writing anywhere. Ethan had given her a present and not told her. Simply left it in his pocket for her to find.

She almost pushed it back into the pocket. She would be seeing him soon enough—he could present it to her properly then.

And yet... Her fingers smoothed the paper for a second before ripping open the tape to find a slim black photo album.

Should she open it? Now? Here? In this cold, echoing place, so remote from the cosy, sunny bedroom with the stunning sea view in the house Ethan had built with such love for his parents?

Maybe there was something in here which would take her back there to that calm and intimate space where she had almost felt relaxed and open enough to reveal her feelings, in spirit if not in body?

Mari slowly unzipped the case and looked at the first photograph.

It was a bright colour print of the teenage Ethan she remembered from his first summer in Swanhaven, his arm wrapped around the junior sailing regatta trophy while his parents stood on either side of him, their arms draped around his shoulders. His pretty English mother in a printed summer dress, and his American father, tall and stately in shorts and T-shirt which never had seemed right on him.

All three of them were so happy. Their laughter captured forever in that fraction of a second.

This was his family. This was what he wanted to create for himself.

But it was the second photograph which undid her. It was a perfect shot of Kit and Ethan messing about on Ethan's boat with her dad at the helm. And there she was, laughing and happy. Standing on the jetty watching the two boys and her dad having fun. The kind of event that was such a commonplace part of her life over those last few summer holidays that she had taken it for granted and not once even thought of capturing it with her camera. And now she was so grateful that someone had. Probably Ethan's mum.

The tears streamed down her face unchecked. There was no point trying to stop them; it was much too late for that. Because the next photograph, and the one after that, was of Mari and Kit standing next to Ethan with their arms wrapped around one another's shoulders at the Swanhaven sailing school prize-giving, just smiling at the camera with their whole bright future ahead of them. So happy and content and living in the moment, with not a care in the world.

Oh, Ethan. Thank you for giving me this photograph.

Mari dropped her head down and slowly pulled the paper cover back over the photograph, blinking away her tears as best she could. The other photographs were for later. When she was secure in her own room with the door locked. On her own. Where she could weep in private.

Mari looked around the room. And then looked again—only harder and through eyes that seemed to be seeing it for what it truly was, and not through rose-tinted glasses which only showed what it had been like so long ago.

She had never felt lonelier in her life.

What was she doing here? In this cold house that echoed with the footsteps of ghosts instead of real living people?

There was only one place she needed to be at that moment, and it wasn't here with the ghosts.

She couldn't build a secure future for herself here. It was time to reconnect with that earlier version of herself that she had just been looking at. The version that Ethan remembered and the version that somehow, amazingly, he still saw in her.

And that thought dazzled her.

Ethan had offered her a chance to build a home with him. *A real home.* The kind of home she'd dreamt of creating. And she had been too woolly headed to see the genuine love and affection in that offer.

Mari pressed the heel of her hand hard against her forehead a couple of times.

Idiot. She was the one who did not deserve him. And now she had probably lost him. Which made her the biggest fool in the universe.

All she had to do was run as fast as she could and tell him that she trusted him with her love and her heart and her future. That was all.

CHAPTER ELEVEN

MARI wiped her eyes and was just about to push away from the wall when the sound of a car engine echoed around the house.

Oh, no. Someone had come to the house. *Drat!* Mari hurriedly tucked the photo album down inside the coat pocket, wiped her eyes, anxious for a stranger not to see her tears, and strode over to the back door and opened it wide.

'Hey, darlin', I'm thinking of moving to California. Do you know if there's any work for retired sailors down there? Because you know what they say? All the nice girls love a sailor.'

Ethan Chandler stood outside on the stone step; he was smiling, but his body revealed the tension and anxiety he was trying to hide. His eyes flicked across her face, taking in the tears and trauma before he spoke again. 'Hi. Thought I might find you here.'

She couldn't speak.

He was here. Just when she needed him most. And he was here. *For her.*

So she did the most natural thing in the world. A gesture she had wanted to make a thousand times before.

She leant forward and gently, gently pressed her lips

onto his in thanks, before wrapping her arms around his neck and hugging him for all she was worth, pressing her body hard against the muscles of his chest so that she could feel his heart against hers. Holding him so tight in the hope that all of his strength and courage and trust in her could seep across the few layers of clothing that separated them and she could finally tell him how much he had come to mean to her.

Words were impossible, and his own response came in a husky whisper.

'Sorry I missed you at the house. I was too busy trying to come up with some cunning plan to entice you back to Florida with me. My parents have agreed to help me set up a trust fund for a sailing school where we can take the teenagers on longer sea voyages lasting a few months each summer. There will be experts on board to help with their problems. And I can show them what sailing really means.' He paused for a second, and then lowered his hands to cup her face before he went on. 'I want to call it the Kit Chance Sailing Trust. If that's okay with you.'

She looked into his eyes in shock. 'You want to teach sailing in memory of Kit? Oh, Ethan. Of course it's okay.'

Her eyes pricked with the sharp acid of fresh tears as his fingers wiped them away. He scanned her face. 'And now you've gone quiet on me again. What are you thinking?'

The words tumbled out on a breath. 'I was standing here feeling sorry for myself. Alone. And pathetic. And at the same time you were working on the best possible way I can think of for Kit to be remembered. Oh, Ethan, I have been such a fool. Thank you. Thank you for letting me go through with the biggest mistake of my life.'

She lifted her head and glanced around. 'I don't need this house to give me a false sense of security any longer. I've decided to take the initiative and accept redundancy from my company so I can make a fresh start. I'm not afraid of being rejected any longer. I can find work and trust myself to see it through. And I know I must sound totally crazy right now, but that's what I am going to do.'

Ethan eased back and took both of her hands in his, the gentleness and tenderness of his touch filling her heart with hope that he did not think her a complete idiot.

'No, it's not crazy. It's the most amazing thing I've ever heard in my life!'

Ethan pretended to glance around the room; only his thumbs were still stroking the back of her hands and, as he turned back to face her, he lifted her hands to his lips and kissed the knuckles. Kissed them as though they were the most precious things in the world to him, his eyes fixed on hers.

'Are you sure, Mari? Are you sure about giving up this house?'

All she could manage was a nod. 'You've shown me that it is possible to move on and make your own happiness. And that's what I want to do. Create my own future from what I want and need. And it's not this house. Another family can make it their home.'

Their eyes locked. She was hypnotised. Unable to break away.

'You're an amazing woman, Mari. I never thought you could surprise me any more, but you have done.

Any man would want to have you in his life. Want you in his bed. Make you the last thing he sees at night. The woman he wakes up with every morning.'

She knew he was smiling by the creases in the corners of both eyes.

'I was a boy who thought that he would never be good enough for someone as beautiful and clever as you. Will you give me a chance to prove that I have become a better man who is finally worthy of you? Because you were right. I have been running from my emotions for far too long. It's time I faced up to my feelings and told you that the only thing I need is you.'

Mari closed her eyes as his hands moved back to her waist and opened them just as he pressed his forehead onto hers. 'It broke my heart when you left, Ethan, and I blamed you for everything that had happened, but it wasn't ever about you. It was about me and how guilty I felt about wanting you to care about me. I was so angry and lonely. Rosa and our mother were relying on me to take care of things when our lives fell apart. I had lost my brother and then my father, and then you were gone. I had to protect myself from being rejected all over again. Do you see? I had to keep my feelings inside, just to get through each and every day.'

'Then let me show you that I'm back in your life and I am here to stay for as long as you want me to. I'm not just any man. I'm the man who wants to hold you in his arms and have you by my side every day. I want to spend the rest of my life showing you how much I need you. How much you mean to me. And how very, very beautiful you are. Can you trust me, Mari? Can you open your heart and let me love you?'

He swept both hands down from her forehead,

smoothing her hair down, over and over, building the strength to say the words, his eyes focused on hers, his voice broken and ragged with such intensity that it was impossible for her to reply. For once she had to listen.

'I love you, Marigold Chance. I've loved you since I was twelve years old. I walked into your mother's kitchen—this kitchen we're standing in now, a lonely boy in a new town who was trying so hard to find a place for himself in the world, and then you turned to me and smiled.'

Tears filled his eyes as he stroked her face.

'And I knew that everything was going to be okay. Because I had a friend who…'

His voice broke and he could only drop his hands to wrap around her back, pressing his body closer to hers, his head into her neck, where his breath came hot and fast from his heaving chest as he fought back fifteen years of suppressed desires and hopes.

She could feel the pressure of his lips on her skin, but everything was suddenly a blur. If only the fireworks would stop going off in her head, she might have a chance of making sense of those magical words. Except that rockets seemed to be exploding all around her in a glorious display of brilliant bursts of colour.

Ethan loved her. Ethan Chandler. Loved. Her.

With all of the strength she thought she had lost, Mari slid her hands from his waist up the front of his chest, resisting the temptation to rip his shirt off, and felt this man's heart thumping wildly under the cloth. His shirt was sweaty, and she could feel the moist hair on his chest under her fingers and, as she moved to his throat, the pulse rang out under her touch.

She forced her head back, away from his body, inches

away from this remarkable, precious man who had exposed his deepest dreams to her.

'I've looked everywhere for the missing parts, but nobody was able to mend it,' she whispered. 'And how could they, when it was right here all of the time? You were simply holding them safe for me. And…and I knew you were. I was just so scared that you would break my heart all over again. So scared.'

Her hand came up to stroke Ethan's face as he looked at her in silence, his chest heaving as he forced air into his lungs. 'Will you come and live with me, Mari? I can build you a house anywhere you like, but only you can make it a home, Mari. Only you. You can work from home, an office, a boat, anywhere you like, as long as we are together.'

His voice was full of excitement and energy, the desire burning in every word.

His eyes flicked across her face, trying to gauge her reaction.

'Will you be my partner, my lover, and the mother of my children? Can you do that? Can you take a chance at happiness with me?'

She gasped in a breath as the tears streamed down her face, knowing that he was saying the only words she had waited a lifetime to hear.

'Yes.'

He looked back at her and his mouth dropped open in shock. 'Yes?'

'Yes.' She laughed. 'Yes, yes, yes. Oh, Ethan, I love you so much.'

She had barely got the words out of her mouth before she was silenced by the pressure of his mouth, which would have knocked her backwards if not for the strong arms that pressed her body to his. Eyes closed, she revelled in the glorious sensation of his lips, tongue and body. Lights were going on in parts of her body where she had not known switches existed. She felt as if she was floating on air.

Her eyes flicked open to find that she *was* floating on air, as Ethan hoisted her up by the waist, twirling her around and around, two grown-up people hooting with joy, oblivious to the freezing cold, dank and dusty air. A kaleidoscope of happiness, colour and light.

Then she slid back down his body, her extended arms caressed lovingly by strong hands. And she wanted to be alone with this man and show him how she felt about him.

Marigold Chance was going to miss her flight. And take the first step on the greatest adventure of her life.

Mari looked into Ethan's smiling face, stunned by the joy she had brought to this precious man, and grinned.

'Don't you just love families? Let's go home, Ethan. Wherever you are in the world—that is my home and I don't want to spend another day away from you. Take me home, Ethan. Take me home.'

EPILOGUE

MARI CHANDLER looked up from the screen of her laptop just as Ethan helped one of his teenagers down from the rigging on the *Swanhaven Princess* and her foolish heart leapt and skipped just at the sight of the man she loved so very much.

Ethan was laughing, head back with such reckless delight at what his young sailor had achieved.

His passion for sailing was so infectious that he seemed to be able to break down any barrier. This boy had been afraid of heights only a few weeks ago when they left Swanhaven and now look at him! Ethan did amazing and wonderful work. She was so proud of what they had achieved.

Mari stretched her arms out above her head and arched her back like a cat to release her shoulders before sighing in sweet contentment. Warmth oozed back at her from the sun-baked cushion and polished wood and she sat back, eyes half-closed, just happy to enjoy the sensation of the warm light wind on her face as the wooden training ship ripped through the calm waters of the Aegean Sea.

It was hard to believe that a few months ago she had never known what it felt like to dive among corals and exotic striped fish she had only ever seen before in an aquarium. Now she spent her afternoons snorkelling with the teenagers and helping them learn to swim in the crystal-clear, warm shallow waters, safe in the knowledge that by her side was the only guide she could ever want. Ethan. *Her Ethan.*

There was a cheer from the cluster of teenagers around the helm and she opened her eyes and smiled for a second before reaching for her camera so she could capture this moment—for the boy who had just climbed to the top rigging, for his family and also for the online weblog which was already starting to create a huge internet following. The Kit Chance Sailing Trust was more than just an idea—it had become an international reality. This was her life and her job now.

And it was all down to the vision and passion of the man she was looking at now. The man who had half turned away from the group so that he could look at her. Simply look at her. And the love in those blue eyes the colour of the Greek sky was almost too much for her to take in.

Every day, just when she thought that she could not be more proud of Ethan or could love him more, he proved her wrong. He gave her so much. His love, his warmth and his total belief in her ability and talents. Sometimes it seemed like a happy dream, interrupted by the occasional teenage fight, or tantrums where the teenagers needed their mother on the other end of an internet telephone. The usual sort of thing which went on in any extended family.

And she adored it all.

The sun was starting to go down over the horizon in a blaze of incredible colour creating a miraculous sunset of orange flame, with shades of deep apricots over dark duck-egg-blues and greens. It felt as though the sky itself was celebrating the end of a perfect hot, sunny day in the Aegean.

But it was nothing compared to the warmth in Ethan's smile as he strolled over to the wooden table and sat down next to her, his arm around her bare shoulder. The feeling of his lips pressed against the side of her neck thrilled her with a delicious shiver of love and excitement, and the connection deep inside her tightened like a piece of taut rigging line, pulling her even closer to the man she had given her heart to.

'Do we really have to leave? I wish this could go on for ever,' she whispered and gently swept a loose curl of bleached blond hair back over one ear from his tanned forehead.

'It could—' he grinned and tilted his head '—but my dad has already booked himself onto the next sailing course around the Caribbean we promised them at the wedding. He can't wait for us to sail the *Princess* back to Swanhaven ready for the trip back to Florida. I can see a lot of sailing lessons on the horizon crossing the Atlantic. We have a lot of father-and-son time to catch up on.'

'It was a stroke of genius suggesting to your parents that they should take over the running of the sailing charity. Your mother is the most amazing fund-raiser and they both love working with the teenagers,' Mari replied with a chuckle. 'We're lucky to have them.'

'It was the best decision they ever made. Swanhaven or Florida. They love it. Speaking of which, have you heard from Rosa? We need T-shirts, sweaters, shorts—

everything. The kids go through clothing faster than I ever thought possible.'

Mari tapped Ethan once on the end of his nose. 'Relax—she e-mailed me this morning while you were working on the sails. It's all in hand. Rosa adores her new job, the new sailing-wear line has taken off and I have a feeling that the wedding dress she made me is not going to be her last. Perhaps you were right? Perhaps we might have two lady entrepreneurs in the family.' Mari stroked Ethan's face and watched his eyes flutter half-closed in pleasure and languorous delight. 'And that family includes you now, Mr Chandler.'

'Does it really, Mrs Chandler? Well, that could be a problem because the only family I want is right here on the deck wearing a very fetching bikini and a cheeky grin.' He shot a glance back at the teenage boys who were sniggering, winking at him or giving them a thumbs up. 'Or do you think that is being too selfish, seeing as we have an audience?'

'Selfish?' Mari pretended to consider the question before crossing her arms around Ethan's neck and pulling him closer. 'No, my love. Wherever you are is my home and my true family. Even if that home is in the galley of a wooden training ship surrounded by two dozen teenagers for a couple of months at a time. Thank heavens for modern technology and satellite communication systems.'

'Thank heavens,' he repeated, his nose nuzzling her throat for a second before getting back to his feet and drawing her up by his side. 'I did promise the kids that they could choose the music for our last night in the Aegean. And guess what? It looks like we'll be sailing into harbour to the tune of the latest trance tracks. Do you think the Greek islands are ready for that?'

Ethan moved to pull away but Mari stayed right where she was. 'Ready? Perhaps not. But this is our family. And families stick together.'

And her loving husband took a firmer grasp of her hand and they turned to face the cheering teenagers, ready for anything that life could throw at them. *Together.*

* * * * *